ALSO BY KAMI GARCIA

The Legion Series

Unbreakable

Unmarked

"Red Run": A Short Story

"Improbable Futures": A Short Story

The X-Files Origins: Agent of Chaos

Broken Battered Hearts

BY KAMI GARCIA AND MARGARET STOHL

Beautiful Creatures

Beautiful Darkness

Beautiful Chaos

Beautiful Redemption

Dangerous Creatures

Dangerous Deception

Dream Dark: A Beautiful Creatures Story

Dangerous Dream: A Beautiful Creatures Story

Beautiful Creatures: The Untold Stories

The Mortal Heart

The Seer's Spread

Before the Claiming

A Gatlin Wedding

KAMI GARCIA

The Lovely Reckless

{Imprint}
MAKE YOUR MARK

NEW YORK

SQUARE
FISH

An imprint of Macmillan Publishing Group, LLC
175 Fifth Avenue
New York, NY 10010
fiercereads.com

Our books may be purchased in bulk for promotional, educational, or business use.
Please contact your local bookseller or the Macmillan Corporate and Premium
Sales Department at (800) 221-7945 ext. 5442 or by e-mail at
MacmillanSpecialMarkets@macmillan.com.

Library of Congress Cataloging-in-Publication Data is available.

ISBN 978-1-250-12968-0 (paperback)   ISBN 978-1-250-07922-0 (ebook)

[Imprint]
MAKE YOUR MARK

@ImprintReads

Originally published in the United States by Imprint
First Square Fish Edition: 2017
Book designed by Liz Casal
Imprint logo designed by Amanda Spielman
Square Fish logo designed by Filomena Tuosto

1   3   5   7   9   10   8   6   4   2

LEXILE: HL650L

Whoever removes this book from the hands of its owner without permission,
or maliciously destroys it, will forever be plagued by speed traps, lost parking tickets,
and car trouble (of the expensive variety).

FOR ALEX, NICK, AND STELLA

Every word I write is for you—
and because of you.

Our heart is like an
unfinished puzzle—
that is why we search
for the perfect one
to complete it.

—UNKNOWN

CHAPTER 1

PIECES OF ME

A police officer shines a blinding light in my eyes. "Do you know why I pulled you over?"

To ruin what's left of my miserable life?

"Was I speeding?" I have no idea, but the swerving is probably the reason.

He knocks on the roof of the car. "I'm going to need you to step out of the car and show me your license and registration."

Red and blue lights flash in my rearview mirror, and the dull haze that kept me from falling apart earlier tonight begins to fade.

I don't want to feel anything. Most of all, I don't want to remember.

"Have you been drinking?" he asks when I get out.

I consider lying, but what's the point? There is nothing he can do to me that's worse than what I've already been through.

"Miss? I asked if you've been drinking," he repeats.

I look him in the eye. "Yes."

Riding in the back of a police car sobers me up fast, but not enough to pass a Breathalyzer test at the precinct.

"Your blood alcohol concentration is point one." Officer Tanner, the cop who pulled me over, writes it down on a form attached to his clipboard. "That's two points over the legal limit in the state of Maryland."

I stop listening and watch the second hand on the wall clock click past the numbers. It's 10:20 on a Tuesday night.

The old Frankie Devereux would be kissing her boyfriend good night in front of her house right now, or slaving over her Stanford University application. She didn't have the personal essay nailed down yet. But she wasn't worried. With a 4.0 grade point average, eight years of classical piano training, and two summers' worth of volunteer work at Children's Hospital, Stanford was well within her reach.

But the old Frankie died with Noah.

The girl I am now is sitting in a windowless interrogation room, staring at grayish-white walls the color of turkey lunch meat after it spoils. Not exactly how I thought the first day of senior year would end. Considering how badly it started, I should have known.

Of course Woodley Prep chose today to hold a memorial gathering in Noah's honor.

I begged Mom to let me stay home, but she was more concerned about her reputation than my sanity. "How will it *look* to people if you aren't there?" It only sounded like a question.

So after fifth period, our teacher marched us outside, where the rest of the senior class was already assembled in front of the English building.

Noah hated English.

They talked about Noah Wells. Captain of the lacrosse team. Blue eyes the color of the sky. The boy everyone loved, including me.

Dead at seventeen.

I watched students who barely knew Noah plant a stupid tree for my dead boyfriend—a guy who didn't even recycle.

With a Sour Patch Kids addiction like Noah's, he would have preferred a vending machine.

When the lopsided tree was finally in the ground, Noah's lacrosse coach said a few words and invited us all to his house that evening for another get-together in Noah's honor.

Noah died three months ago, and I still couldn't sleep at night. The wounds hadn't stopped bleeding, and my school was already tearing off the bandages.

It's almost over, I'd told myself. Or so I thought.

The poem was what sent me over the edge.

Student body president Katherine Calder had written it herself, and she read the poem in front of the entire senior class while her mother videotaped the performance. The little bitch finally had a meaningful personal experience to write about for the college Common App essay.

Everything went downhill from there.

After spending an hour at Coach's house, which included an encore of Katherine's *heartfelt* poem, I swiped a bottle of wine and drank it in the bathroom. By the time I left, the combination of anger, alcohol, and sleep deprivation had turned me into an emotional hand grenade with a set of car keys.

Mom won't see it that way. She'll be pissed. I actually feel sorry for the cop who got stuck calling her.

The doorknob turns, and I sit up straighter. Officer Tanner comes in and hands me a cup of burnt-smelling coffee. "Your mother is here."

This will be fun.

Mom is waiting in the lobby. Even at midnight, she looks perfectly pulled together, dressed in fitted black pants and a beige cashmere wrap. With only a hint of blush and her blond hair gathered in a low ponytail, she could pass for my older sister. When my parents were still married, her hair was the same shade of light brown that mine is now. I ditched the highlights months ago, along with any trace of the old Frankie.

Holding the white foam cup, I walk toward her. My eyes are swollen, and my face streaked with mascara. I don't care about getting in trouble. Listening to one of her guilt trips is a hundred times worse.

Mom storms past Officer Tanner without giving him so much as a look. Cops only interest her if the alarm system at our house goes off. "What were you thinking, Frankie? You could've killed someone—or yourself."

"I'd never want to hurt anyone else."

It's me I don't care about.

"Even if that's true, your behavior over the last few months proves you're out of control." Her voice rises with every word. "You've been on a downhill slide since Noah died, but this"— she gestures to our surroundings—"crosses the line."

I've never seen Mom this angry, and I know she's holding back. She hates making a scene in public. I stare down at my black Adidas Sambas, the beat-up pair of indoor-soccer shoes I salvaged from the basement. The old Frankie never would've been caught dead wearing them outside the gym. But I wear them everywhere.

"Mrs. Devereux?" Officer Tanner uses his cop tone.

Bad move.

"My last name is Rutherford, *not* Devereux." Mom closes her eyes and takes a deep breath, regaining her composure and trust-fund-baby charm. "I apologize, Officer . . . ?"

"Tanner," he finishes for her, even though his name is engraved on the pin above his pocket.

"The last few months have been difficult for all of us. Francesca suffers from PTSD—post-traumatic stress disorder," she explains, as if he isn't smart enough to recognize the acronym. "It's certainly no excuse, but she's never been in any trouble before. If you don't press charges—"

Officer Tanner holds up his hand. "Let me stop you right there, ma'am. I know this situation is upsetting, and I'd like to extend your husband a professional courtesy. But we're not talking about a speeding ticket."

Mom bristles when he refers to Dad as her husband, but she

doesn't correct him. "Francesca attends Woodley Prep, and if the headmaster finds out about this, she'll be expelled." Mom lowers her voice. "She's already been through so much. We still don't know what she saw that night."

Everything.

I saw everything.

I try not to think about it, but Mom's voice fades as other sounds cut in and out.

Don't panic. Breathe.

Isn't that what the last shrink told me to do? Or am I supposed to picture my safe place? I can't remember. A switch flips in my brain, and fragmented memories from the night Noah died hit me in rapid bursts—

Strobe lights flash.

A mass of bodies swells on the dance floor—arms raised. House music blaring and bass pumping.

My head pounds along with it.

Noah told me to wait inside while he got the car. But it's too loud.

Black velvet curtains part at the main entrance, and cool air hits me.

Dim streetlights glitter against the wet asphalt. I walk around the side of the building to the parking lot. Where did he park? I didn't pay attention. Noah always remembers.

The Sugar Factory's pink marquee glows above me.

Noah's voice, low and muffled. A glimpse of his baby-blue polo shirt. A guy standing in front of him, his face obscured by black shadows—as if it were erased.

But I see Noah clearly, and I can tell he sees me. He shakes his head slowly, the movements almost imperceptible. I recognize that look, and it sends pinpricks up my arms. I've seen it after lacrosse games when a player from the opposing team came up to Noah off the field, looking for a fight.

The look means: Don't come over here, Frankie. . . .

"Frankie?" Mom's voice scrambles the images, and Noah's face disappears.

I open my eyes and blink hard, battling double vision.

"Are you still drunk?" My mother doesn't recognize when I'm having a flashback, which only proves how wrong things are between us.

"I'm just tired." And completely screwed up.

The glass door to the precinct swings open, and Dad charges in like he owns the place. From his faded green Indian Motorcycles T-shirt and five-o'clock shadow to his scarred knuckles and crooked nose, he looks more like a middle-aged boxer or construction worker than an undercover cop. I guess that's the point.

He flashes his Maryland State Police badge at the county cop sitting behind the counter. Did Mom call him? Or one of the officers here?

It doesn't matter. He knows.

"Why don't you go sit down while I talk to your parents?" Officer Tanner nods at a row of red seats bolted to the wall. He doesn't have to tell me twice. He meets Dad in the middle of the hallway. "I'm sorry, Jimmy. I'd like to make this go away, but—"

Dad cuts him off. "You know I don't walk that line and I would never ask another cop to walk it, either."

7

I've heard my father talk about the line between right and wrong so many times. It defines every aspect of his life, and tonight I crossed it.

I slouch against the molded plastic seat and count the black rubber marks on the floor. My long hair falls over my shoulder and hides my face. I want to disappear, especially when the precinct door opens again.

"What the hell is going on?" King Richard, my pathetic excuse for a stepfather, bursts into the lobby.

"Why don't you take it down a notch, Richard? This isn't your office," Dad says. "Nobody here works for you."

"James." Only Mom calls my father by his given name. "You could at least try to be civil."

Dad crosses his arms. "I could do a lot of things. . . ."

Nobody pisses my mother off more than Dad. At least he gives her another target.

"That's enough, Elise." My stepfather shoots her a warning look.

Mom's heels click against the floor as she scurries over to her place beside King Richard. He rests his hand on the small of her back in case he needs to pull her invisible puppet strings.

Within seconds, they're arguing. It's nothing new, and I don't worry until the shouting dissolves into sharp whispers. Never a good sign.

Snippets of the conversation drift through the hallway, and I strain to listen.

"—ruined her chances of getting into Stanford." *Mom.*

"If she keeps this up—" *King Richard.*

"Ever since Noah died—" *Dad.*

"It's a shame she can't ID her boyfriend's killer." Officer Tanner doesn't bother whispering. "That son of a bitch should be locked up."

My stomach lurches like someone kicked me.

He's right, but it's not a shame.

It's pathetic.

My mind is damaged—shrink code for too weak to handle what I saw that night. Now I'm a hostage to the flashbacks that hit without warning and the insomnia that keeps me from sleeping more than three hours a night.

Mom and Dad walk toward me shoulder to shoulder. A united front. They divorced when I was three, and they get along about as well as two rabid dogs locked in a closet. If they managed to agree on anything, they must think I'm a few weeks away from hooking on a street corner.

For the first time tonight, I'm scared.

Mom looks at me like I'm a stranger. "I've tried to be understanding, Frankie. But you're out of control. Avoiding your friends, sneaking out of the house, drinking with the lifeguards from the club." Maybe she *has* been paying attention between tennis matches.

"That was *one* night," I argue. At least that she knows about.

"I hoped you would snap out of this and go back to being the girl you were before."

Before I watched someone beat my boyfriend to death in a beer-stained parking lot. Before I realized that doing all the right things doesn't matter. Noah was an honor student, a star

9

athlete with offer letters from three Ivy League universities, and a good person.

And he's still dead.

"I just want you to feel like yourself again, sweetheart," Mom says.

She doesn't realize that girl doesn't exist anymore.

"Your father and I think it's time for him to get more involved."

More involved?

Based on how involved he is now, that's a pretty low bar. I spend two weekends a month with Dad, if he isn't too busy working undercover in RATTF—Regional Auto Theft Task Force—a supercop unit. When I do see him, it's not exactly quality time. I usually end up eating leftover pizza until he gets home from pretending to be a car thief. On his days off, we practice what Dad calls Critical Life Skills—and what I call Ways to Dodge a Serial Killer. Fun stuff . . . like how to escape from the trunk of a car if it doesn't have an automatic-release handle inside.

"Maybe your father will be able to help you get back on track," Mom adds.

Doubtful.

"How is that supposed to work when we barely see each other?" I ask, ignoring my dad, even though he's standing right next to her.

Dad steps between us. "You're moving in with me."

CHAPTER 2

CLEAN SLATE

When I open my eyes, the first thing I see are sunny yellow walls—at least that's the way they looked to me as a kid. Now they make me feel like I'm trapped inside a stick of butter.

Reality hits me, like it has every morning for the last seven days.

I'm living with Dad.

And this butter stick is my bedroom.

I've spent the night here plenty of times, but this is different. I won't be standing by the window on Sunday afternoon waiting for Mom to pick me up. I'm staying here until at least the end of the school year.

For now, this is home.

I dig through a dresser drawer, searching for an outfit the old Frankie would hate. Frayed white button-down or black tee? Tough call, but I go with the button-down. The loose threads would drive the old Frankie crazy. I pull on a pair of skinny jeans, and my elbow whacks against the dresser.

This room is the size of my walk-in closet at Mom's house, and it's decorated like it belongs to a ten-year-old: a dresser and matching nightstand covered with hand-painted flowers and green vines, a twin bed with ruffled sheets—and let's not forget the yellow walls.

Unfortunately, I have bigger things to worry about today.

In the hall, Cujo, Dad's huge gray-black-and-white Akita, sits next to my door.

"Hey, buddy." I scratch the dog's big, square head, and he follows me. The apartment has a simple and borderline-claustrophobic layout—two bedrooms and bathrooms at one end of a narrow hallway lined with mismatched frames, and a living room–dining room combo and a galley kitchen at the other end.

In the kitchen, Dad surveys rows of cereal boxes in the pantry. There are at least a dozen different kinds.

"You're not making me a real breakfast?" I ask sarcastically, walking past him on my way to the fridge.

Dad swears under his breath. "Sorry. I'm not used to—"

"It was a joke." I scan the shelves stocked with Dad's staples: Diet Pepsi (Coke isn't sweet enough), whole milk (for his cereal), white bread and American cheese slices (in case he gets sick of cereal and switches to grilled cheese), and a gallon of 2 percent milk (store brand).

"I bought extra Diet Pepsi and the milk you like," he offers.

"I drink Diet Coke." And I stopped drinking 2 percent milk when I was ten, a fact I don't bother mentioning anymore.

My father memorizes dozens of car makes, models, and license plates so he can bust car thieves and the chop shops that sell stolen parts, but he can't remember what kind of milk I drink? Skim. I should make him a list of my food preferences and stop torturing us both.

"I've got cereal." He shakes a box of Froot Loops.

"No, thanks." I close the refrigerator empty-handed.

Cujo's ears perk up and he bounds for the front door.

"Did you hear something, partner?" Dad asks.

The dog barks, and a split second later, the doorbell rings.

"It's probably Lex." I give Cujo a quick scratch behind the ears and start unlocking the deadbolt.

"Frankie!" Dad shouts as if I'm a child about to run out into traffic.

I turn around, searching for a sign of danger. Nothing looks out of place. "What's wrong?"

Dad points at the front door with a fierce look in his eyes. "*Never* open a door without checking to see who is on the other side."

It's official. My father has crossed over from paranoid to crazy. "That's the reason you yelled at me like I was about to set off a bomb?"

"Depending on who is on the other side, you could've been."

I gesture at Cujo sitting next to me calmly, with his head cocked to the side. "Cujo isn't growling. He always growls if there's a stranger at the door." A retired K-9 handler trained

Cujo as a protection dog. He's the definition of an intruder's worst nightmare.

"You can't let anything lull you into a false sense of security. Letting your guard down one time is all it takes."

Does he think he's telling me something I don't know? I stifle a bitter laugh.

"This isn't funny, Frankie."

No, it's painful and pathetic, and I live with it every day.

Parents are supposed to understand their kids, or at least make an effort. Mine are clueless.

The doorbell rings again.

Crap. Lex is still standing in the hallway.

I make a dramatic show of peering through the eyehole and turn to Dad. "Happy?"

"These are critical life skills. As in, one day they might save your life," he says as I open the door.

Lex stands on the other side, smoothing a section of her choppy hair between her fingers. It's dyed a lighter shade than her usual honey blond, except for an inch of brown roots where her natural color is growing in. The inch is deliberate, like the smudged charcoal eye liner that looks slept in and makes her blue eyes pop against her coppery-brown skin.

Her eyes remind me of Noah's.

Thinking about him feels like standing in the ocean with my back to the waves. I never know when it's coming or how hard it will hit me.

"I was starting to wonder if you left without me." Lex breezes past me. "Ready for your first day in the public school

14

system, or, as my mom calls it, 'the place where every child is left behind'?"

We haven't seen each other since the beginning of the summer, but Lex makes it feel like it's only been days. I spent the last three months trying to leave the old Frankie behind, avoiding Lex and Abel, my closest friends, in the process.

"How's it going, Lex?" Dad asks.

"Pretty good." She yawns. "Please tell me you have coffee, Frankie. The line at Starbucks was insane."

"There's a pot in the kitchen," Dad offers.

"Thanks, Mr. Devereux." If she keeps acting this cheerful, Dad will think she's high. We've known each other forever, but when Lex developed a gross crush on my dad in seventh grade, it almost resulted in best friend excommunication.

"Don't thank him yet," I whisper. "His signature blend is burnt Maxwell House."

"I'd rather go without food for a week than caffeine for a day." Lex pours herself a cup of liquid coffee grounds.

Dad fishes a Velcro wallet out of his back pocket and lays two twenties on the table next to me. "Swing by the store after school and pick up some Diet Coke and anything else you want."

I leave the crumpled bills on the table. "I won't have time. Community service starts at three thirty, right after classes let out." Thanks to King Richard, I already have a probation officer and a community service assignment. He called in a favor at the district attorney's office, and my case was bumped to the top of the pile. "Lex is dropping me off at the rec center and picking me up when I'm done."

I told Dad all this last night.

"You don't mind?" he asks Lex. "You're already driving Frankie to school in the mornings. I would take her myself—"

"But you can't blow your cover. I totally get it." She takes a sip of her coffee and cringes, but Dad doesn't notice.

"You can't slip and make a comment like that at school." Dad gives us his serious cop look. "You both understand that, right?"

I ignore the question.

"Absolutely," Lex says. "I mean . . . I absolutely *won't* say anything."

"Good." Dad nods and looks over at me. "I would never send you to Monroe if I thought it would be an issue. The high school and the rec center are in the Third District—the nicer part of the Downs. It's nothing like the war zone where I work in the First District."

It's weird to hear him describe any part of the Downs as *nice*. I guess it seems that way if you compare the run-down projects, abandoned buildings, and streets lined with liquor stores in Dad's district with the neighborhoods near Monroe.

"People in one-D think I'm a car thief. If anyone finds out I'm a cop, I'll have to walk away from my open cases and transfer to a district outside the Downs."

Most people hear the word *undercover* and automatically think of DEA agents in movies—the ones who have to disappear without telling anyone where they're going and move into crappy apartments so they can infiltrate the mob or the Hells Angels. But that's not the way it works for regular undercover cops like Dad.

Obviously, he doesn't wear a T-shirt that says I'M A COP. But he also doesn't have to lie to the whole world about his job—just people who hang out in, or near, his district.

"Frankie? You understand, too, right?" He sounds irritated. That's what I get for ignoring his question the first time.

"I've never told anyone about your job except Lex, Abel, and Noah. Why would I start now? Maybe you should lecture Mom. She still bitches about it to all her friends."

Dad sighs. "I'm not trying to give you a hard time. I'm just reminding you to be careful what you say."

"Consider me reminded." I glare at him, and Dad turns to Lex.

"Your parents don't mind you driving Frankie to the rec center?"

"They're fine with it." They probably have no idea. Lex's parents are never around unless they need her to pose for press photos.

"Does your father still have family in the Downs?" Dad asks.

"Nope. The Senator moved everyone out as soon as he could afford it." Lex refuses to call her father Dad. Instead, she calls him the Senator because she says he cares more about being the first Puerto Rican–American senator in the United States than about being a father.

"I don't blame him," Dad says in his cop tone. "There's a lot of crime. It's a tough place for honest people to live. Make sure to keep the car doors locked while you're driving."

"We know, Dad."

He continues issuing instructions. "Remember to leave your

purse in the car when you get to the rec center. Just take your phone and some money. And I got you something." Dad opens the hall closet and fishes around in the pocket of his jacket. He returns with something pink in his hand. A flashlight? And two pieces of orange plastic?

Dad hands me the pink thing.

I take a closer look at the canister. "Pink pepper spray?"

"I think it's cute," Lex says.

"Then you can have it."

"It's pepper gel," Dad explains. "The spray can blow back at you, but this stuff shoots wherever you aim the nozzle. And the gel really sticks."

"I'm not carrying that around." I try to hand the canister back to him, but he won't take it. "What if I set it off accidentally? I'm sure there's a rule against bringing tear-inducing toxins to school."

"It has a safety, so it won't go off unless you want it to. Keep it in your bag." Dad points at the small black shoulder bag that already feels like the wrong choice.

I shove the pepper gel inside. Otherwise, he'll never leave me alone.

"And you both need one of these." Dad offers us each an orange piece of plastic.

Lex grabs one.

"It's a rape whistle," Dad says proudly.

I saw that coming.

She scrunches up her nose. "Umm . . . thanks."

I take mine and toss it in my army-green backpack.

He scratches his head as if he's forgetting something. "Wait inside the building until Lex gets there to pick you up."

And I won't take any candy from strangers.

"I'll be on time, even if I have to speed," Lex teases.

Dad misses the joke. "Do you have a clean driving record?"

"Except for a few parking tickets, but everyone has some of those, right?" She flashes him the perfect smile that you only end up with after four years of braces.

"I don't." Dad walks over to the sliding glass door that leads to the balcony, and he looks down at the parking lot. "Is your Fiat a stick shift?"

"Automatic," Lex says. "Frankie is the only person I know who can drive a stick."

Because my dad suffers from undercover-cop paranoia and he forced me to learn in case of emergency.

"One day you might need to drive a vehicle that isn't an automatic," he says.

I know exactly where this conversation is going. "Enough, Dad."

"What if you're alone and some lunatic grabs you off the street, and he drives a stick shift?" Dad asks, like it's a perfectly normal question. "If there's an opportunity to get away, you won't be able to take advantage of it."

Lex stares at my father, dumbfounded. She has heard me recount enough of these stories to know he's serious. Usually, he saves these questions for me.

"You should learn," Dad says. "If Frankie's license wasn't suspended, she could teach you."

My shoulders tense. I'm not letting him play his passive-aggressive games with me. "Is there something you want to say, Dad?"

"Just stating a fact." He stands his ground.

"Why? So I won't forget how badly I messed up my life?"

Dad sighs. "I'm trying to help you, Frankie." He isn't apologizing or admitting he's wrong.

"I don't want your help." I push Lex toward the apartment door. Before I follow her out, I turn back to look him in the eye. "I'm sorry you lost your perfect daughter. But I'm the one you're stuck with now."

CHAPTER 3

LOT B

Lex waves at Dad as she pulls out of the parking lot. "I know we're angry at your father, but can I just say that he is still off-the-charts gorgeous?"

"Are you serious right now?" I scrunch up my nose. "Because you're one comment away from making me throw up in your car."

"What are best friends for if they don't crush on your dad?"

"Actually, I think *your* dad is pretty—"

She pretends to gag. "Stop. New rule. Referring to the Senator as anything other than old and boring is a violation of BFC."

I'm surprised at how easily I fall back into my old routines with Lex. There's something about knowing a person for most of your life that makes it impossible to un-know them. "You can't pull Best Friend Code when you're the one who brought up hot dads."

"Hot *dad* . . . singular. As in *yours*." She flashes a mischievous smile. "Remind me again why your mom left him?"

"Who knows why my mother does anything?"

"I still can't believe she went through with it and made you move in with your dad. She's usually so full of crap."

Mom has always reigned supreme as the queen of empty threats . . . until now.

I prop my feet on the glove compartment and hug my knees. "She even carried my bags up to Dad's apartment. And Mom hates carrying things almost as much as she hates him." I packed my stuff in black trash bags instead of suitcases to make her feel guilty, or at least to force my mother to haul around what looked like garbage. But it didn't faze her. I'm not sure she noticed.

I leave out that part of the story, and the lull in the conversation lasts too long.

"Enough with the silence. I get plenty of that at home," Lex says. "Back to your mom. How did she pull this off so fast? It's only been a week since your DUI. Even the Senator would be impressed."

Fast is an understatement.

It's Wednesday morning. Seven days after I walked out of the police station with my parents and King Richard. The minute we got home, Mom told me to pack, like she couldn't wait to get rid of me, while my piece-of-crap stepfather hovered in the hallway.

Don't get me wrong—I was happy to go. The Heights reminds me of Noah and my screwed-up memory.

But Mom doesn't know I feel that way. That would require an actual conversation—something she left to the army of doctors, shrinks, and hypnotists she hired to bring back the old Frankie. Recovering my memories so I could identify Noah's killer and move on was never the real goal. Once I figured that out, I stopped talking to the shrinks. I'll find a way to remember without her help.

The next day, Mom drove me out of the Heights—our exclusive community in the Maryland suburbs outside Washington, DC—to Dad's two-bedroom apartment in Westridge, a neighborhood full of townhouses and garden apartments, less than six miles away. But six miles feels like a hundred when a five-minute car ride can mean the difference between living in the Heights or in Section 8 housing.

Mom left me on his doorstep with the garbage bags full of my stuff—like she had finally taken out the trash.

"Frankie?" Lex sounds worried.

I force a smile. "Sorry, I spaced. Dad is all over Project Reform Frankie, and it's stressing me out. If things had worked out the way he planned, I would've started school yesterday. But according to Dad, a Dolly Parton look-alike in the office at Monroe refused to call Woodley for my immunization records. She told him to drive over there and get them himself."

"That's Mrs. Lane. She doesn't take crap from anybody. Couldn't your dad get you out of community service?"

If hell froze over.

"In Dad's universe, rules don't bend. Everything is black or white. There is no gray."

Lex glances at my hands locked tight around my legs. "Nervous about your first day?"

Anything is better than going back to Woodley. Not that it was an option. Mom met with the headmaster and begged him not to expel me and ruin my chance at getting into Stanford. But she wasn't persuasive enough. Knowing Mom, she's probably devastated.

I'm relieved.

The Stanford dream belonged to the old Frankie—a girl who learned how to spin the straw she was given into the gold everyone else wanted.

The old Frankie played up her cute features with makeup tricks, hunted for jeans that made her boyish figure appear curvier, and adopted the style of her favorite fashion bloggers because she didn't trust her own. At parties, lots of fake giggling and bathroom trips to flush vodka shots down the toilet allowed her to act cool without doing anything that could jeopardize the Plan. A nothing-special-but-cute-enough girl who landed the captain of the lacrosse team because he'd had a crush on her since they were kids.

It's hard to believe I was ever that girl.

I lean against the headrest. "Monroe has to be an improvement."

"Was the first day at Woodley really that bad?"

"It was basically the seventh circle of hell. People taped notes and cards all over Noah's locker and left flowers and teddy bears on the floor in front of it."

"Woodley is full of attention whores. Getting kicked out of that place was a relief." Lex has been expelled from four private schools in two years, beginning with Woodley—not easy to pull off when you're the daughter of a senator. Lex takes pride in her academic rap sheet because every expulsion embarrasses her mother with her socialite friends.

She turns onto Bellflower Parkway, where the garden apartment complexes end and the nicest of the low-income developments in the Downs begin. Tan brick buildings with barred windows line the street, identical except for the collections of plastic high chairs, toys, and tricycles piled on the balconies.

Monroe High is only a few blocks away, in the good section of a bad neighborhood. But barred windows are barred windows.

Lex rakes her fingers through her hair, messing it up a little. "At least we're finally at the same school again."

A few months ago I would've loved the idea. But now I just want to start over. As much as I love Lex, that's harder to do with her around.

She glances at me, her lips pressed together.

Crap. That was my cue to act excited. I suck. "I know you have other friends at Monroe, Lex. I don't expect you to hang out with me all the time."

A hint of disappointment flickers across her face. "If you keep dressing like that, I won't. Your shirt looks like it came from the donation pile at the Salvation Army."

I used to waste hours shopping. Not anymore. "Think of it as my attempt to fit in."

She eyes my frayed white button-down and faded skinny

jeans. "With who? Meth heads? Are you trying to ruin my carefully crafted image at Monroe?"

Lex reinvents herself whenever she switches schools. Judging by her smudged eye liner and the combo of skinny jeans and kitten heels, she has rocker chic nailed.

"So what did you go with this time?" I ask. "Rich and Misunderstood Hottie? Or Unattainable New Girl Who Doesn't Give a Shit?"

She gives me a mischievous smile. "Scandalous Bad Girl with a Secret. A triple threat."

"I guess that makes me Screwed-Up Girl with Secrets She Can't Remember."

Her smile vanishes. "You can't change the past."

Not if you can't remember it.

Lex pulls into the parking lot. "A new school is a clean slate."

"I hope so."

Instead of tennis courts and a swimming pool, Monroe has DRUG-FREE ZONE signs posted every ten feet and temporary classrooms that look like orange shipping containers on the front lawn.

"Are you ready for this?" Lex asks.

"Ready is a relative term."

"You could get a private tutor instead," Lex teases. "It's not too late to guilt-trip your mom into letting you come home."

"Yes, it is."

It was too late the moment Noah's head hit the ground. Once the rumors spread through the Heights like bird flu, *too late* came and went.

The only thing left is now.

Here.

In Lot B, we drive past dozens of restored muscle cars and rusted-out Hondas. A vintage black pickup with yellow flames painted on the sides eases into a space in front of us, and Lex stops.

Outside my window, a group of guys stand huddled around a midnight-blue Mustang, checking out the engine. Noah and his friends from the lacrosse team used to form an almost identical huddle whenever one of them showed up with a new car. Except they were more interested in the upgrades inside than what was underneath the hood. Noah and his friends lived in lacrosse T-shirts or wrinkled button-downs with the sleeves rolled, and they all projected the same brand of confidence that comes from growing up with money.

In Lot B, there isn't a button-down in sight except mine. Instead, the guys wear low-slung jeans, have tattoos, and they are marked with the kind of confidence you earn.

The dark-haired guy standing closest to the Fiat leans over the side of the Mustang, looking under the hood. The black ink on his arm catches my eye. A pile of skulls begins at his wrist. Above them, more tattoos snake their way over his light brown skin—a tree twists up from the skulls and one of the branches transforms into the stem of a black rose. Tribal lines curve from its center and disappear under the sleeve of his dark gray T-shirt.

He looks over as if he senses me watching him. Dark eyes lock on mine. I stop breathing for a second. Guys at Woodley don't look like this—rough, inked, and muscular. His hair sticks up in the front like he started spiking it and lost interest halfway through the process.

He tilts his head, and a ghost of a smile crosses his lips.

The Fiat lurches forward and Lex swears under her breath. "Are you insane, Frankie? We're not in Kansas anymore. You can't stare at people from the Downs. They're not like the kids at Woodley."

I'm not naive. Washington Heights and Meadowbrook Downs didn't get their nicknames by accident. Money is the dividing line—the street you live on, the type of car you drive, and whether your family has a country club membership matter more than anything else.

Lex gestures at a Chevy with a spoiler that looks like it's worth more than the car. "I mean, who puts a spoiler on a piece of junk like that? You have to walk into this place like you *know* you're better than them, or they'll eat you alive."

"Are you listening to yourself right now? Because you sound like my mom, and that's scary. And hello? Your dad is from the Downs."

"That's the reason the Senator spends so much time trying to clean it up. If he knew I was driving you to the rec center, he would freak."

"But you and Abel went to some Monroe parties last year when I was out with Noah." I push away the memory of sitting in a movie theater with my head on Noah's shoulder, our hands bumping in the popcorn bucket.

Lex turns into Lot A and slips into an empty space between

28

an Audi and a Lexus. "Most of those parties were near your dad's apartment, and one of them was up the street from my house. We're not the only people from the Heights at Monroe. All the private-school rejects go here."

"I know how it works." Everyone does.

Parents in the Heights are always bitching about it. The county is divided up into zones based on income, and every public school has one wealthy neighborhood and one poor neighborhood that feed into it. The rest fall somewhere in between and make up the difference.

A zip code in the Heights means you end up at Monroe. Technically, we're only ten miles from the Heights, but it feels like ten thousand. That's why parents send their kids to private schools like Woodley Prep if they can afford it.

"So you've never been to a party in the Downs? Not even once?"

Lex glares at me. "You couldn't pay me to show up at one of those parties."

"Do you know elitist that sounds?"

She flips opens the visor and checks her makeup in the mirror. "I'm a realist, and you sound like a Peace Corps volunteer. Let's see how elitist you think I am by lunch."

I stare out the window, hoping to check out the other students . . . or the hot guy with the tattoos. Lot A doesn't look much different from the parking lot at the country club. Aside from a few Acuras, Honda SUVs, and Jeeps, it's packed with Audis, BMWs, Mercedes, and random sports cars like the Fiat. Judging from the jocks dressed like Abercrombie & Fitch models and the number of people holding Starbucks cups, no one from the Downs parks in this lot.

The cups are the real giveaway.

Dad's partner, Tyson, complains that the Downs is the only place on earth without a Starbucks.

"Is there assigned parking at Monroe?" I ask.

Lex gets out and adjusts the black studded leather bag on her shoulder. "No. Why?"

I look around. "It doesn't seem like anyone from the Downs parks here."

She locks the car. "They don't. By choice. They probably think we'll ding their custom paint jobs. Who knows?" She heads for the main building on the opposite side of the street. "Most Monroe students hang out with people from their own neighborhood. And don't give me that judgey look. I only transferred here last year. I'm not responsible for the social hierarchy."

"*Social hierarchy*? Wasn't that a vocab term from our SAT prep class?" I've missed teasing Lex.

"Whatever."

I follow her across the quad in front of a huge redbrick building, along with what seems like half the student body. Ahead of us, two girls dressed in Marc Jacobs drink Frappuccinos and text a few feet away from three guys wearing their jeans so low that I can read Tommy Hilfiger's name on their boxer briefs. To their credit, the guys hike up their jeans whenever they slide down past the halfway point on their asses. Give them belts and they're practically ready for cotillion.

30

Ass-riding jeans aside, Monroe isn't as bad as the private-school crowd thinks. I expected metal detectors and drug dealers handing out dime bags on the lawn.

This I can handle.

Before we make it to the sidewalk, the shouting starts.

CHAPTER 4

FIGHT CLUB

"Marco! I heard you were trying to get with my girl." A huge guy wearing a Baltimore Ravens jersey steps in front of a curvy redhead spilling out of her tank top—most likely the girlfriend in question. He stalks across the grass in our direction, looking big enough to *be* a linebacker for the Ravens.

Lex throws her head back and sighs. "Now we're going to be late for class. I don't know why these losers can't beat the crap out of each other off campus."

"Is it like this all the time?"

She rolls her eyes. "Only on slow days."

I catch a glimpse of his target . . . the linebacker called him Marco.

It's him.

It's the guy with the tattoos who smiled at me in Lot B, and up close he's jaw-droppingly gorgeous. I try not to stare at the black ink on his arm. I've seen tattoos before, but his are different—powerful and hypnotic.

He doesn't notice me.

A girl with a thick mane of black waves pulled into a high ponytail stands beside Marco. The combination of her delicate features and the way she's staring down the linebacker with her arms crossed gives her a pretty but tough vibe. Her white tank, dark jeans, and old-school gray-and-red Nike high-tops are borderline tomboy.

It's a look I wish I could pull off.

"Leone!" The linebacker points at Marco. "I'm talking to you."

The pretty girl with the ponytail grabs Marco's sleeve. "Walk away. He's a little bitch."

Marco's expression is calm and calculating, as if he knows something the rest of us don't. He crosses the lawn and stops in front of the linebacker, only a few feet away from Lex and me. "You really want to do this, Coop?"

The other guy's jaw twitches. "Nobody tries to take what's mine."

What's *his*? He's talking about the redhead like she's a personal possession—a jacket or a textbook he can toss into his locker.

Asshole.

"It's not my problem if you can't keep your girl happy," Marco says. "But don't worry. She's not my type."

"What's that supposed to mean?" The linebacker's hands curl into fists.

33

Marco cracks a cocky smile. "I'm not into girls who only look good from the neck down."

The guy in the Ravens jersey throws the first punch, and it catches Marco above the eye. Marco staggers, his feet criss-crossing.

Lex tries to yank me back, but there's a wall of people behind us now.

Marco regains his balance and charges. He jabs an uppercut into the linebacker's stomach, and the guy keels over, groaning and clutching his gut. Marco stands over him. "If you come at me like that again, you'll end up with more than a couple of scratches on your face."

As he turns to walk away, the linebacker pushes himself onto his knees. "I'd still look better than your sister."

The girl with Marco gasps and covers her mouth. I have no idea what the linebacker means, but everyone else seems to know. Whispers ripple through the crowd, and a few people call out.

"Aww, shit!"

"No, he didn't."

"Beat his ass, Marco."

Marco's cocky grin instantly vanishes. He charges and grabs the linebacker by the shoulders of his jersey. Marco jerks the linebacker down and simultaneously brings up his knee to meet the guy's nose. The linebacker's head snaps back violently on impact, and blood sprays across the grass.

I suck in a sharp breath, and the sky tilts.

Deep breath. Don't freak out.

A wave of dizziness crashes over me. My mind spins. I hear

the crowd urging Marco on, the crack of bone against bone, as my vision blurs. . . .

I'm in the parking lot next to the club.

Noah gives me the look—the signal that means, don't come over here. I drop to my knees and duck between two cars. The wet asphalt smells like beer and stale cigarettes, but I don't care. I have a clear view of Noah, and that's what matters.

The guy closes in on him. Why can't I see his face? He's talking to Noah.

No . . . yelling at him.

Heavy boots hit the asphalt. Cars speed by on the street behind me.

An arm swings. A fist hits Noah's jaw, and he staggers.

I can't see him anymore. Where is he now?

Something moves under the streetlights, and I see it—his baby-blue shirt. But it's not blue anymore. It's red.

Another fist rockets toward Noah's face. I don't hear the crack, but I swear I feel it.

One thought runs through my mind over and over. . . .

I can't let him hurt Noah again. I have to do something.

The guy has his back to me, and I lunge at him from behind, pulling and clawing his shirt.

"Frankie!" Lex yells.

The guy pivots in my direction without looking, and his elbow catches me in the stomach.

A jolt of pain hits, forcing the air out of my lungs, and I gasp.

Flashes of color, faces, the sky—it all spins by me in a split second—and I'm falling.

My back hits the grass. I hear Dad's voice in my head: *If*

someone gets you on the ground, roll into a ball and keep your face covered.

I shield my face, but my stomach cramps, and I can't pull up my knees.

Voices bombard me from every side.

"Someone help her!"

"Holy shit."

"Is she okay?"

"I didn't see her." A guy's voice. "I swear."

I open my eyes, expecting to see cars, streetlights, and the side of the club's marquee with *The Sugar Factory* lit up in neon pink. Instead, sunlight blinds me. It's not dark outside. A guy leans over me, blocking the sun . . . a guy I recognize. A redbrick building looms behind him. I'm not in the club parking lot.

Think. I try to clear my head. *I'm at Monroe. With Lex. Lot A. The fight. A hot guy with tattoos . . .*

"I thought you were one of his boys." His chest heaves like he's still out of breath from the fight. The hot guy . . . *Marco.*

My heart pounds, echoing in my ears.

"Are you okay?" Marco reaches for me, then pulls his hand back.

"Yeah." I nod in case he didn't hear me.

A trickle of blood runs down his cheek from a cut above his eye, but he doesn't wipe it off. The girl who was hanging out with Marco before the fight stands behind him, watching me. "Did she hit her head? She might have a concussion."

"Move!" Lex yells, shoving people aside. She puts herself between me and Marco. "Get away from her!"

Marco sits back on his heels, arms hanging at his sides as if he's waiting for her to punch him. He looks younger and less dangerous. "I didn't see her," he repeats.

"It was an accident." The girl with Marco rests her hand on his shoulder.

Lex drops down beside me. "Did that psycho hurt you?"

"I'm fine." A dull pain throbs in the pit of my stomach.

The guy in the Ravens jersey groans and rolls onto his side. Blood spatters cover the front of his shirt, and one of his eyes has swollen shut. Two of his friends drag him to the nearest tree and prop him up.

Without the bleeding linebacker next to us, I'm the main attraction. Just what I need on my first day at a new school. On the upside, getting knocked on my ass distracted the crowd. Hopefully, no one noticed me zoning out.

I stand up too fast and my legs turn into Jell-O. The ground slips out from under me, and Marco springs to his feet. He reaches for my elbow, but Lex beats him to it.

She slaps his hand away. "Don't touch her."

The pretty tomboy raises her eyebrows.

Marco steps back, his eyes locked on mine. The intensity of his gaze—the way he's staring directly at me—isn't helping my Jell-O legs situation.

"You okay, Angel?" Another question lingers in his eyes, but I don't know what he's asking.

"I'm—"

"Clear this area now!" a deep voice thunders across the quad. Within seconds, a man about Dad's age, with strong features and salt-and-pepper hair, crosses the lawn. Judging by his turtleneck and pressed jeans, he's a teacher.

He points at Marco. "Not you, Leone. Stay right where you are."

Marco raises his hands and clasps them behind his head like he's under arrest. "Whatever you say, Mr. S."

Mr. S takes one look at Lex shielding me from Marco and shoves him toward the sidewalk. Then he turns to me. "Are you all right?"

"I'm fine." How many times do I have to say it?

"Are you sure?" He has kind eyes and a soothing voice, now that he's not shouting.

"She's okay, really, Mr. Santiago." Lex hooks her arm through mine.

Mr. Santiago notices the guy in the bloody Ravens jersey near the sidewalk. "Why aren't I surprised to see you here, Mr. Cooper?" He snaps his fingers at the linebacker's friends. "Take him to the nurse. I want him out of my sight." Mr. Santiago zeroes in on Marco and points at the main building. "Start walking, Leone. You know the way."

With Marco safely on the sidewalk, Lex grabs my shoulders. "What were you thinking, Frankie?" She closes her eyes for a second. When she opens them again, I see it in her eyes. Pity. "Don't answer that. Come on. I'll drive you home."

Lex thinks I'm too fragile to hold it together, but she's wrong. I'm like a broken bone that wasn't set correctly. I might not heal perfectly, but I *will* heal.

I brush off my shirt and pick up my purse and backpack. "I'm not leaving."

"Do you always have to be so stubborn?"

I respond by crossing my arms.

Lex sighs. "I should've asked Mr. Santiago to write us a note. We're late for class."

"Is he the principal?"

"Security guard." Lex leads me across the quad, her arm looped through mine. "Welcome to Monroe."

CHAPTER 5
BEAUTIFUL BAD BOY

"Blue slip." My English teacher—Mrs. Hellstrom, according to my schedule—extends her hand without so much as a glance in my direction. Lex insisted on walking me to my first class, and now I'm standing in the front of the room while everyone stares.

"I don't have one. Just my schedule." I hold it out to her.

Mrs. Hellstrom doesn't look up from the book in front of her. She's a serious-looking woman with pasty skin and thin, penciled-in eyebrows. "You need to go to the office. I can't add you to the roster without a blue slip."

A few students take advantage of the distraction and whip out their cell phones. A guy in the back is asleep, with his head on his desk. The girl sitting next to him has violet-and-brown ombré hair, and she's painting her nails a matching

40

shade of purple. None of the girls at my old school would've had the guts to dye their hair like hers.

At Woodley, standing out wasn't a good thing, unless it involved scoring the "it" bag of the season or putting a unique spin on the currently accepted style. I always played it safe, choosing skinny jeans—from the dozens of almost identical pairs stacked in my closet—a simple top or tee under a fitted leather jacket, and cute flats or boots. I never cut my hair too short or grew it too long.

Pretty enough without stressing about it—that was my look.

At Monroe, the old sneakers and ratty button-down I'm wearing would fall into the category of not trying at all.

Mrs. Hellstrom notices everyone messing around and smacks her book shut. "People, this is *not* study hall. You can complete the questions on the required summer reading book in class now or in detention later. The choice is yours."

A chorus of groans travels through the room, followed by the sound of papers rustling. Two girls in the front row stare at my tiny purse and laugh.

Mrs. Hellstrom turns to me. "Front office. Blue slip."

I close the door and consider going back to Dad's apartment, but I don't have a car anymore, and I'm not busing it. I shove my stupid purse that probably screams the Heights into my backpack.

Finding the office isn't easy. Monroe is four times the size of my old school, and the hallways look identical—rows of powder-blue lockers, white cinder-block walls, and bulletin boards decorated with a tiny bearded leprechaun in a tailcoat, holding up his fists. Yeah, that's the mascot every high school wants.

I spot the office. A banner with the leprechaun in the corner hangs over the door: JAMES MONROE HIGH SCHOOL, HOME OF THE FIGHTING BARONS.

Behind a long counter inside, a lady with teased blond hair and an armload of brassy charm bracelets reads a magazine. Dad wasn't kidding. She looks exactly like Dolly Parton.

Dolly Parton notices me and tears herself away from the magazine that she pretends she's not reading. "Shouldn't you be in class? If you need the nurse, she's down the hall."

"It's my first day, and my English teacher, Mrs. Hellstrom, sent me here to get a blue slip."

She pushes her hot-pink reading glasses higher on the bridge of her nose and lets out a long breath. I'm clearly cutting into her reading time. "Take a seat. I'll be with you as soon as I finish this paperwork." I'm assuming that's code for *magazine*.

"Thanks." Hopefully, she won't finish until English class is over.

I choose a chair in the corner and close my eyes. This day feels like it will never end, and it's only first period.

Door hinges creak, and my eyes fly open.

A woman stuffed into a gray suit that's at least one size too small steps aside to let someone leave her office. "Don't go anywhere, Mr. Leone. We are not finished here."

Marco saunters out, hands in the pockets of his low-slung jeans, his black high-tops untied. My eyes are instantly drawn to the tribal lines inked on his arm, the intricate details beckoning me to come closer.

42

"Yes, ma'am." He flashes her a lopsided grin. There's no sign of the angry fighter I saw in the quad earlier. He taps on the counter as he passes Dolly Parton. "What's up, Mrs. Lane?"

Mrs. Lane scowls. "I'm tired of seeing you in here. Why don't you try behaving yourself for a week and see what happens?"

"I'd miss you too much." Marco grins at her, and turns away from the counter. He sees me and the dimple vanishes. His gaze darts between the empty chairs.

If there is a god, please don't let this guy sit next to me.

My mouth goes dry as he approaches. Marco drops into the vinyl chair across from mine, which is worse than if he sat next me, because now I have nowhere to look except at him.

Apparently, God is alive and well, and he has a sense of humor.

Marco rubs the back of his head, where the hair is cut closer to his scalp. It's longer in the front, and I like the way it sticks up all over the place. He seems nervous and clears his throat. "Are you—?"

Not again. "I'm fine."

"Yeah?"

I hold up three fingers in the shape of a W. "Girl Scout promise." I cringe. Those words did not just come out of my mouth.

He raises an eyebrow, and his cocky attitude returns. "Are you here to give your testimony?"

"What?"

"The fight. Did you get called in to tell the whole truth and nothing but the truth, Angel?"

Why does he keep calling me that? It must be an insult.

43

"No one called me in. I need a blue slip." Why am I explaining myself to him? Or talking to him in the first place?

Marco leans forward and props his elbows on his knees, clasping his hands between his long legs. "So are all the schools in the Heights full?"

"Excuse me?"

"Just wondering how you ended up at Monroe. Nobody from the Heights wants to transfer here."

How am I supposed to respond? Say something funny and risk offending him?

"I needed to start over," I blurt out.

"I can get you that blue slip now," Mrs. Lane waves me over, her brass bangles jingling.

I pick up my backpack and rush toward the counter. In a graceful move, I bump into Marco's leg and almost trip.

"Sorry," I mumble without turning around.

At the counter, I hand Mrs. Lane my schedule and watch as she writes each word. Anything to avoid looking at him. Marco's eyes burn into my back, and warmth spreads through my cheeks. Another minute and I'm out of here.

Mrs. Lane hands me the blue slip, and I snatch it out of her hand.

I'm halfway out the door when Marco calls after me. "See you around, Angel."

CHAPTER 6

PRACTICAL ARTS

After I leave the office, my morning gets progressively worse. My schedule sucks, a fact I didn't fully absorb until now.

In addition to Mrs. Hellstrom's English class, I have the first lunch period, which should be called breakfast based on how early it starts; chemistry, a subject my SAT scores proved I should avoid unless I want to fail a class; and no study hall.

I managed to dodge the music requirement thanks to the years I spent playing the piano—which seemed like a win. Until I realized that if an enthusiastic teacher reads my transcript and finds out that I have perfect pitch, I'll end up in a stupid musical to fulfill some public school requirement I don't know about.

But for reasons beyond explanation, my art history class from

Woodley doesn't fulfill the practical arts requirement here. So I end up in Monroe High's version of the arts—Auto Shop.

The Shop classroom is in the basement. I trudge down the steps, prepared to spend the semester memorizing the parts of an engine—or is it called a motor?

Whatever. I memorized hundreds of Renaissance paintings. How hard can this be?

The hallway at the bottom of the steps leads to a stainless-steel door covered with names, phone numbers, and personal details that qualify as TMI. Above the doorframe, graffiti-style letters spell out: WHAT HAPPENS IN SHOP STAYS IN SHOP.

When I crack the door and slip inside, I realize just how badly I misjudged this class. The proof sits raised on black rubber blocks in the middle of the room—a bright green Camaro, at least according to the chrome emblem. With two tires and the passenger-side door missing, it resembles a huge model car that no one ever finished. Next to the rubber blocks, toolboxes overflow with screwdrivers, hammers, and power tools I can't identify, confirming that I'm in over my head.

The girl with the ponytail who was outside with Marco this morning is the only other girl in class. Apparently, her name is Cruz, and she barely looks at me when our teacher—a weather-beaten old guy everyone calls Chief—seats me at the workstation next to hers. The lesson requires using a socket wrench. The tool turns out to be more complicated than the actual assignment, which I never start.

After Shop class, I hunt down my locker because my *Automotive Basics* textbook weighs more than an encyclopedia. Cars are way more complicated than I thought.

My locker is down the hall from the vending machine.

Noah would've loved this.

I find the number that matches the one on my schedule and try to open the dented metal door. It won't budge.

Perfect.

I drop my backpack on the floor and fiddle with the rusty latch.

Come on. Open already.

The stupid thing isn't even locked.

"Shit." I slam my hand against the metal, and flecks of powder-blue paint flutter to the floor. If I'm lucky, maybe I'll get lead poisoning.

"Rough day?" asks a familiar voice.

I spin around and Abel grins at me, his face framed by a short cloud of dark brown twists.

"What are you doing here?" I ask. "Did you blow off class?"

"Nope." Abel gives me the sexy smile that drives other girls crazy—including the two staring at him from across the hallway. Abel and I have been friends since sixth grade, and he's more like a brother to me, but I get it.

His lean build, boyish good looks, and the gorgeous contrast between his St. Lucian mother's light green eyes and his Jamaican father's deep brown skin never fails to send girls into a feeding frenzy. That's not the only thing Abel inherited from his father. Dressed in skinny jeans, a vintage Alice in Chains T-shirt, and his dad's beat-up Doc Martens, he bears a creepy resemblance to his dad, Tommy Ryder—the front man for the band Dirty Rotten Devils and a rock legend who overdosed when Abel was eleven.

He waves at the girls, and I roll my eyes. "Are you ever *not* flirting?"

Abel clutches his chest like he's wounded. "You know my heart only belongs to one girl."

Lex. The two of them have been crazy about each other forever, a fact that hasn't brought them any closer to dating. For years, Lex wouldn't even admit she had feelings for him.

Noah was the one who finally coaxed the truth out of her. He had a way of making people feel comfortable enough to tell him anything. Thinking about Noah triggers the hollow ache in my chest.

"So did you come to check up on me?" I force a smile.

Abel holds up a thick white form that looks suspiciously similar to my class schedule. "Technically, I transferred yesterday, but I had to pick up a copy of my immunization records this morning."

My mouth falls open. "You left Woodley?"

"Yep. I'm officially a member of the masses." He slings his arm over my shoulder. "Like I'd let you spend senior year without me. You'd never survive the withdrawal."

More like he can't survive being away from Lex, and now he has an excuse to transfer.

"Your mom is okay with this?"

He laughs. "Now, let's not get crazy. But there's nothing she can do about it. I'm eighteen."

"Look who finally showed." Lex strolls up behind him. "It took you long enough."

"You knew?" Of course she did.

Lex hands Abel her books. "I know everything before it happens, kind of like the pope."

"I think you mean God," Abel says.

She leans closer to him. "I'm flattered, but you can call me Lex."

A fresh wave of students floods the hallway, and Abel starts attracting serious attention. Some girls stop walking altogether, while others backtrack and cluster near the lockers, whispering and trying to make eye contact. Half of them are staring because he's gorgeous, and the other half probably recognize him from the random tabloid photos of Abel and his mom doing boring things like grocery shopping.

Lex glares at his groupies. "You've only been here five minutes, and your fan club is already forming."

Abel winks at her. "It's a gift."

"Move along." Lex shoos away the girls with a flick of her wrist. A curvy brunette bats her over-mascaraed lashes at Abel and blows him a kiss as she leaves.

He tugs on the sleeve of my shirt. "Forget to do your laundry?"

"I'm flying under the radar."

He peels opens a pack of SweeTarts and pops a few into his mouth. "How's that working for you?"

"Shitty. But if I can open my locker—which, by the way, isn't even locked—I'll upgrade it to 'slightly shitty.'"

"Step aside. I've got this." Abel bends down and inspects the handle, rattling the latch. "It's probably rusted shut."

"Perfect."

"Let me see your schedule, Romeo." Lex plucks it out of his back pocket and unfolds it, running her finger down the page. "Someone forgot to turn on the charm in the office. Your schedule sucks almost as much as Frankie's. At least you have second lunch."

"With study hall right after," Abel says. "It doesn't get better than that."

"Lex has the same lunch period," I offer. "You can sit together in the cafeteria."

"Not with me." Lex tucks Abel's schedule in his shirt pocket. "I don't eat in District 12."

I lean against the locker next to mine and listen while the two of them argue about whether Abel can talk Mrs. Lane into changing his schedule by the end of the day. It turns into a challenge, like everything else between the two of them. The stakes are just getting interesting when a tattooed arm reaches over my shoulder.

Marco bangs the side of his fist against my locker, and it springs open.

Mr. Santiago is right behind him. "Keep moving, Leone. You're out of here."

"It's your world, Mr. S. I'm just living in it." Marco pushes his way through the double doors that lead outside. Before I have a chance to thank him, he's gone.

50

"Who was that?" Abel asks, examining the lock to see what he missed.

Lex waits until the doors slam behind them. "You don't want to know."

CHAPTER 7

DREAMS DIE IN THE DOWNS

Lex parks in front of the rec center between a shiny black Cadillac and a Volkswagen Jetta with a zoo of stuffed animals lined up in the rear window.

"Have I mentioned that I think this is a terrible idea?" she asks.

"Only about twenty times." I hate relying on Lex for rides. Hanging out with her makes it harder to forget about my old life and start a new one at Monroe. So many of my memories with Lex and Abel include Noah.

But I feel like a bitch for not wanting her around.

Unfortunately, my transportation options are severely limited without a car (repo'd by Mom), a driver's license (currently suspended), or a bus route to the Downs that doesn't include drunks, perverts, and pickpockets (according to Dad).

A group of shirtless guys wearing basketball shorts lean against the wall of the building and watch us. One of them grabs his crotch and blows Lex a kiss. She throws the car into reverse. "We are out of here."

I grab the wheel. "I can't leave. I'm on probation."

Lex puts the Fiat back into park and studies the gray building. Something catches her attention, and she leans over the steering wheel, squinting. "What does it say above the door?"

Graffiti covers the original inscription, and now it reads DREAMS DIE IN THE DOWNS.

It takes Lex a minute to decipher the letters. "You actually expect me to leave you here?" Her gaze darts between the graffiti and the basketball players, who have moved on to more *creative* gestures.

"You're overreacting." Hopefully. I dig through my purse, shove a credit card and a twenty in the pocket of my jeans, and sling my green canvas backpack over my shoulder. "I'm leaving my purse."

"I'll be back at seven to pick you up. If anything happens, text me."

"Nothing is going to happen." I get out and walk up the steps to the building where I'll spend my afternoons for the next four months.

"Hey, princess! Get tired of those bitch-ass rich boys in the Heights?" One of the guys leaning against the wall calls out and grabs his crotch again. "Looking for some of this?"

Nice.

"Think I'll pass." I fake a confident smile.

A mangy cat prowls across the sidewalk in front of them. It hears me and turns, its spine arched and the hair on its back standing on end. It's missing an eye—the empty cavity covered in a layer of gnarled skin. Bald patches all over the cat's body reveal more battle scars.

The mutant cat hisses, ears flattened against its skull.

Shit.

I skid to a stop, hoping it will take off. But this animal is a fighter, and right now I'm the enemy. Images of rabid animals from a video we watched in seventh-grade science flicker through my mind, and I back away slowly. The cat matches me step for step, lowering its head and advancing like a tiger ready to spring.

A dog barks, and the one-eyed cat's head jerks toward the parking lot. Some kind of husky mix darts between the cars and up the hill beside the steps where I'm standing.

The cat has no chance.

The husky reaches the sidewalk, and the one-eyed cat lunges, hissing and clawing. The dog trips over its paws as it changes direction and retreats down the hill, with the cat tearing across the asphalt behind it.

I suck in a sharp breath, and the basketball players laugh. They haven't moved from the wall. I hope they get rabies.

The glass door swings open, and a woman about my mom's age with an Afro of soft spirals strolls out of the rec center. "I see you met Cyclops."

"Is that your cat?" I wipe my sweaty palms on my jeans.

"He's nobody's cat. The kids here gave him that name. Not

54

that he lets any of them get within ten feet of him. He doesn't like people."

"I picked up on that, thanks."

She raises an eyebrow, a warning to watch my attitude. "Is there something I can help you with?" It's clear from her tone that helping me is the last thing she wants to do.

"My name is Frankie Devereux. I'm supposed to check in with Mrs. Johnson."

She sizes me up from beneath expertly shaped eyebrows. "Francesca Devereux?"

"Yes, ma'am."

"Follow me." She opens the heavy glass door and heads for the check-in desk. She scribbles something on a clipboard, and her expression hardens. "I don't know how they do things in the Heights, and I don't care. But the kids in my after-school program come here to stay *out* of trouble."

"Yes, ma'am."

She points the clipboard at me. "I expect you to use better judgment than you did when you decided to get behind the wheel of a car drunk."

For some reason, I want to tell her that it happened after my dead boyfriend's tree-planting ceremony and that it was the only time I've ever driven with a drop of alcohol in my system. But I have a feeling it wouldn't matter to Mrs. Johnson.

"I will."

Mrs. Johnson gives me a slow nod. "Then we understand each other."

"Yes, m—"

"Stop calling me ma'am. Everyone here calls me Miss Lorraine."

I follow Miss Lorraine past a mural of a sunny garden that doesn't resemble anything I've seen in the Downs. The happy-faced flowers cover the whole wall, but the cinder blocks are still visible underneath.

"You'll be working with the middle school group. Thirteen-year-olds." Miss Lorraine spots a boy nuzzling a girl's neck near the weight room. She steps between them and pushes the boy out of her way, giving him an icy stare—all without breaking stride.

I like this lady already.

"Help the kids with their homework and keep an eye on them until they get picked up," she says. "And don't let any of the boys go to the bathroom at the same time as the girls."

"Why not?"

She looks at me like I'm an idiot. "Because when they go at the same time, they're probably not using the bathroom."

"Oh." The idea of thirteen-year-old middle school students making out in a public restroom reminds me how different things are in the Downs. Not that middle school kids from the Heights don't make out. They just do it behind the pro shop at the country club or at the parties they throw when their parents are out of town.

Miss Lorraine leads me to the back of the building. At the end of the hall, a muscular guy wearing dark jeans and a baseball cap under the hood of his sweatshirt stands in the doorway of the emergency exit. He's probably close to my age, and he's whispering in the ear of a girl who looks way too young for him.

"Deacon Kelley!" Miss Lorraine yells.

The guy looks up and twirls the toothpick tucked in the corner of his mouth, studying Miss Lorraine with ice-blue eyes. A web of raised pink-and-white scars creates a jagged path down the side of his neck and disappears under his shirt. "How's it going, Miss Lorraine?"

She points at the exit door held open by a cinder block. "You've got one minute to get out of my rec center before I call the police."

Deacon Kelley whispers something to the girl, and she rushes past Miss Lorraine with her head down. After she's gone, he flashes Miss Lorraine the kind of smile that says *Don't push me*. "You're forgetting something."

"What would that be, Deacon?"

He backs through the door and kicks away the cinder block. "It was *my* rec center first."

The metal door slams, and Miss Lorraine's shoulders relax. She walks toward the room closest to the exit. "Your group meets in there."

Seven middle school kids hang out on the other side of a long window next to the door—gossiping, listening to music, and dancing. Only one girl has a book open, but it's not clear if she's actually reading or just using it to hide behind while she checks out the boy sitting across from her.

When Miss Lorraine opens the door, the kids scramble, rushing to their seats and digging through their backpacks for the homework they should've been doing.

"It's nice to see how hard everyone works when I'm not in here." She walks over to the girl's desk and flips her book around so it's right side up.

"We were just taking a break." A boy with long eyelashes and a mop of dark brown curls grins at Miss Lorraine. In soccer shorts, an Italian World Cup jersey, and black sweatbands around both wrists, he looks like a thirteen-year-old professional soccer player.

"Your break is over. This is Frankie." She waves a hand in my direction. The kids' expressions range from completely bored and mildly curious to *Lord of the Flies* territory. "She'll be in charge in the afternoons."

Several kids groan.

A girl wearing bright red lipstick and a gold nameplate necklace that reads DIVA rolls her eyes. "Whatever."

Miss Lorraine walks over to her desk. "I don't remember asking your opinion, Kumiko."

Kumiko stares me down from behind her shiny black bangs. "Need some community service for your college applications? That's the only reason girls like you come around."

Everyone waits for me to respond. This is a test, and I can't afford to fail. Not if I'm stuck with these kids for the next four months.

I smile at Kumiko. "Nope. It was this or jail."

She raises an eyebrow, and the corner of Miss Lorraine's mouth twitches as if she's fighting a smile.

"All right, then." Miss Lorraine raps on the desk closest to the door. "Homework before house parties. And Frankie's rules are my rules, so don't try selling her any sob stories or you'll end up with the elementary school kids. Do we understand each other?"

"Yep."

"Got it."

The moment Miss Lorraine disappears down the hall, the kids start talking again. At least now they have their books out. Maybe I should do that teacher thing and go around the room and make them tell me their names. Kumiko gives me the once-over and whispers to the girl next to her. Maybe not.

As the minutes tick by, it's clear no one wants my help with homework. It gives me a chance to catch up on mine.

I'm studying an engine diagram in my gigantic Shop textbook when the future World Cup soccer player notices. He points at the page in front of me. "You're taking Shop?"

"Unfortunately." I pause. "Sorry . . . I don't know your name."

"Daniel Pontafonesco."

"Why do you tell everyone your last name all the time?" asks a lanky boy with a black buzz cut and ear gauges who is lounging in the seat next to him. "You want people to think you're related to one of those famous mob guys like Tony Soprano, don't you?"

I dig my nails into my palms, praying I won't have to break up a fight.

Daniel wads up a piece of paper and chucks it at the other boy. "I keep telling people because none of you can pronounce it. And not all Italians are in the mob, Carlos."

The paper hits Carlos, and he falls back in his chair like he's wounded. They're just joking around. Instantly, I relax.

Kumiko yawns. "Tony Soprano isn't a real person. He's from a TV show, genius."

Carlos turns around in his chair and glares at her. "I'm not the one failing government after only a week of school."

"It was *one* quiz," she snaps.

Time to change the subject. "So do you know a lot about cars, Daniel?"

He laughs, along with some of the other kids.

"Everyone in the Downs knows about cars," Carlos says.

"Except you." Daniel smirks at Carlos, who responds by throwing a fake jab.

He grins. "But I know how to box."

The cute girl with the book takes a break from staring at Daniel and moves two seats closer to me. She has long brown hair that's so dark it almost looks black and thick lashes fluttering against her light brown skin.

She gestures at my textbook. "It's easier to remember the parts if you know how they work. There's a cool app that lets you take the engine apart and put it back together again. Want me to find it for you?"

I key the passcode into my cell phone and hand it to her. "Thanks . . . ?"

"Sofia." She scrolls through the list of apps. "Got it." She turns in her chair so I can see the screen, too. Raised pink-and-white slash marks—scars from some kind of cuts—cover the left side of the beautiful thirteen-year-old's face, as if she survived an animal attack.

I try not to stare.

"Car accident," Sofia says, as if she's used to explaining.

"I'm sorry. I didn't mean—"

She shrugs. "No big deal. It could've been worse."

I point at the diagram, ashamed of myself for staring at this brave girl's scars. "So tell me how it works."

"The rectangular thing in the middle is called the block. . . ."

Thirty minutes later, I can identify the block, pistons, camshaft, and flywheel, thanks to Sofia.

"Tomorrow, we'll go over the pistons, piston rings, connecting rods and bearings," she says proudly.

It's like listening to someone speaking a foreign language. "Thanks. I need the help, and you're a great teacher."

"My brother taught me. He knows everything about cars, and he's really patient."

Daniel leans over his desk and checks out my book again. "Are you gonna start racing now, Frankie?"

"I'm not exactly Danica Patrick. I just want to pass Shop." I laugh, hoping to impress them by mentioning the female NASCAR driver. I'm not about to tell them that I read about her in a fashion magazine.

The other kids smirk and trade glances. I'm definitely missing something.

"He's talking about street racing," Sofia whispers, filling in the blanks.

Ugh . . . how did I miss that? I've heard about the illegal street races in the Downs, but I've never given them much thought. Nobody I know has ever been to one. My friends from the Heights avoid the Downs like it's a nuclear waste site. "Is that a big thing around here?"

Sofia leans toward me, and her dark waves fall over one

shoulder, covering her scars. "For lots of people, it's the *only* thing."

By seven o'clock, Sofia is the only kid left in the room.

"My brother should be here any minute. He comes straight from work." She watches the door. "I'm not allowed to walk home alone. He's super strict."

"I don't mind waiting. Does he keep an eye on you after you leave the rec center?"

She shoves her books inside her backpack. "And the rest of the time. My mom died of cancer when I was nine, and my dad's not around . . ." She pauses. "Much."

"I'm sorry."

Sofia smiles, and it lights up her whole face. "At least I have my brother."

Someone knocks on the window, and the door opens.

Marco Leone walks in and my heart slams against my chest. *What's he doing here?*

"Hey, Sopaipilla, how was school?" His gentle tone sounds unrecognizable—it's not the one that belonged to the fierce fighter in the quad or the cocky guy in the school office. He lifts Sofia's backpack off her shoulder.

"It was good," she says. "And this afternoon, I taught Frankie about engine blocks."

The side of his mouth tips up. "Who's Frankie? A boy at school?"

I bite my lip, and my throat turns to sandpaper.

Sofia laughs and wheels her brother around. "No, silly."

Our eyes meet, and his go wide. It's the third time I've seen Marco up close—at least when I wasn't terrified—and he gets better-looking every time.

I give him a tiny wave. "Hi."

Sofia seems to sense the awkwardness between us. "Do you know each other?" She frowns and puts a hand on her hip. "Marco, you didn't . . ."

"No, it's nothing like that." He rubs his hands over his face.

My cheeks heat up when I realize she thinks we hooked up . . . or something.

Sofia turns to me. "But you guys do know each other, right?"

"No," I say at the same time Marco says, "Yes."

I shrug. "Sort of."

"Are you *positive* you didn't mess around with her?" Sofia whispers to her brother a little too loudly.

Now my cheeks are on fire.

Marco flashes me a dangerous smile. "I'm pretty sure I'd remember."

CHAPTER 8

HIGHWAY RUNNERS

When I get home, there's a note from Dad and a pizza box on the kitchen counter. He's investigating a "big case" with his partner, Tyson. He's really sorry.

Whatever.

I have no idea what makes a case big or small, unless it's related to the value of the stolen car. What I *do* know is that the investigation requires him to work lots of nights, a fact that makes me so happy I almost feel guilty.

Almost.

Cujo sits next to the table staring at the pizza box. I'm actually hungry, so I flip it open. Spinach and mushrooms. This has to be a joke. I hold up a slice. Vegetables do not belong on pizza. Dad knows this. Cujo tracks the slice as I drop it back into the box.

The dog follows me around the apartment like a furry bodyguard. He's probably the only reason Dad didn't hire a babysitter to stay with me at night. If Cujo wants spinach-and-mushroom pizza, I'll give it to him. I put a slice in his food bowl, and he scarfs it down.

My cell rings and Mom's face pops up on the screen. I haven't spoken to her since she dropped me off at Dad's, and today isn't going to be the day I do. I let the phone ring, and seconds after it stops, I get a text.

> Are you ignoring my calls? I have
> something important to tell you.

Maybe she wants to apologize.

> > what?

> I would prefer to tell you on the
> phone.

Mom can text her apology. I'm still hurt—about the way she dumped me here like she didn't care, the disappointed looks she has given me for months now, and the fact that she cares more about the girl I was than the one I am now. But I'm not ready to tell her any of that.

> > i'm studying. u want me to do
> > well right?

> Richard has a meeting with one of
> the deans at Stanford.
> Can you believe it?!

> > no.

The words sting. She's not sorry.

I wonder how much that cost King Richard.

> He explained your condition and the
> extenuating circumstances.

My *condition*? Is that what they're calling my PTSD now?

> **dog is barking. have 2 go.**

I pocket my phone without waiting for a response. I'm not wasting money on a school I don't care about anymore, even if the money happens to be my mother's.

At least my first afternoon at the rec center wasn't a complete disaster. The kids liked me for the most part, and with Sofia's help, I might have a shot at passing Shop. Thinking about Sofia leads directly to Marco.

Who is this guy?

During the fight, he went from cocky to out of control in seconds, and it scared the crap out of me. But the look on his face after he plowed into me was pure panic. Not exactly how he acted in the office. I'll take panicked and *real* over smart-ass bad boy any day, unless Option C is affectionate brother who carries his little sister's backpack.

Everyone in high school fakes it on some level—in the Heights and in the Downs. Offering a bunch of strangers a window into your soul guarantees four years of total misery. Maybe Marco just fakes it better than the rest of us do.

Remembering the way he stared at me in the parking lot makes my stomach flutter.

What's wrong with me?

Marco is not my problem, and after witnessing his cage match on the quad this morning and the personal escort from Mr. Santiago, I probably won't see much of him.

Except when he picks up his sister every day.

After trashing the rest of the pizza, I find a lone box of mac and cheese behind the cereal. I'm shaking orange powder onto the noodles when my cell phone rings. It's Lex.

"Is your dad home?" she asks the second I pick up.

"No. Why?"

"Abel is in some serious shit. I'm on my way to pick you up."

"What happened?" This isn't the first time I've gotten a call like this from Lex.

"He's in the Downs. He bet on a street race, and now he owes some lowlife asshole money. The guy won't let Abel leave until he pays him."

"How did he end up at a street race?"

Lex falls silent. "A lot of stuff happened over the summer with Abel. He's been doing crazy things."

"Can you be more specific?" I jam my feet into my sneakers and grab my house key.

"Acting secretive, checking his phone every ten seconds, gambling, disappearing for days. But he never mentioned street races before."

I lean against the wall and close my eyes.

I didn't know.

One of my best friends was disappearing for days, and I had no clue.

Lex's car horn blares at the other end of the line. "Move your ass or get out of the fast lane!" she shouts at another driver.

"How long until you get here?" I ask.

"Two minutes."

I rush to my room and open the top drawer of my ugly dresser. I unfold a pair of fuzzy pink socks shoved in the corner and pocket the bills hidden inside. Two hundred dollars. It's all I have now that Mom isn't transferring money into my checking account every week.

Cujo barks as I head out the front door. "I wish I could bring you with us." I would feel a lot safer.

Jogging down the steps outside, I try not to think about what Dad will do if he finds out I left the house. Odds are he'll never know. Working undercover keeps him out of the precinct and on the street. He won't risk someone overhearing a personal conversation, so he never calls. Instead, he relies on cryptic and excessive texts.

A flash of red tears around the corner, tires squealing.

I hop into the Fiat, hoping that no one sees me. "Next time, why don't you take out an ad and let everyone in the neighborhood know I'm sneaking out?"

She peels away from the curb. "Please. It's not like your dad is a social butterfly. He probably doesn't even know his neighbors." True.

"What else did Abel say?"

Lex weaves between lanes and swallows hard. "Just that he bet on a race and lost, and he needs us to bring him five hundred bucks, or they're going to beat the shit out of him."

"We can't take that much out of an ATM, but I've got two hundred on me."

"Relax. I've got it covered." She flips over her purse and dumps the contents onto the console between us. Makeup and loose change fall into my lap and onto the floor—along with a wad of bills. "The ATM machine in the Senator's sock drawer doesn't have a daily limit."

I collect the bills and count them—five hundred dollars. I roll up the money and clench it in my fist. "I still don't understand why Abel went to a street race. Usually, he screws up closer to home, and there are plenty of places to gamble in the Heights."

Rich guys from Woodley and the other private schools in the Heights will bet on anything.

"We're talking about Abel, and he's been even more unpredictable than usual." Lex flies across three lanes of traffic to catch the V Street exit.

"What set him off? His mom?"

Lex doesn't respond. Instead, she stares down the dark street. There's something she's not telling me, but pressing her for answers never works.

"He said to turn on Second Street," she says finally.

"We just passed it."

She flips a U-turn and loops back. Three tough-looking men sit on the porch of a boarded-up house, smoking. "I can't believe he came here."

The street runs parallel to a set of train tracks rusting on the other side of a chain-link fence. Trains stopped coming through the Downs a decade ago.

"Headlights." I point at glowing halos in the distance. "Park under a streetlight."

"I'm not walking all the way over there."

"If the cars racing here look anything like the ones in Lot B, the Fiat won't exactly blend in."

"Fine." Lex parks next to the curb. "But if it gets stolen, Abel is buying me a new one."

I hope that's the least of our problems.

Lex follows me toward the lights. "He said to look for a black car with white racing stripes. I can't remember what he called it."

We reach the edge of the crowd and spot the main attraction—dozens of classic muscle cars, like the Camaro in Shop class, and sports cars with flashy paint jobs, lined up a row. Hoods are popped and doors hang open while music pulses from sound systems loud enough to rival the ones in most clubs. Girls dressed in everything from fitted shorts and heels to boyfriend jeans and metallic high-tops mill around between the cars or check out the engines with the guys like they're at a car show, while the owners lounge in the driver's seats.

At the end of the row of cars, people are standing along an empty stretch of road.

"Who's ready to race?" a girl with straight jet-black hair that reaches past her waist shouts from the middle of the street. The combination of knee-high lace-up boots, black tank, shiny black pants, and deep red lipstick against her alabaster skin makes her look like a character from a video game.

People whistle and shout, and the atmosphere instantly changes from street party to casino floor. Bookies rush to collect bets as a midnight-blue Mustang and an iridescent-white Acura line up side by side in front of Video Game Girl. Engines rev, and a surge of energy buzzes through the crowd like an electric current.

Video Game Girl raises her arms.

The moment they drop, tires squeal and clouds of exhaust billow into the air. The whole place smells like burnt rubber and rotten eggs.

I scan the sea of unfamiliar faces, searching for Abel or a car like the one Lex described.

Off to the side of the racing strip, three guys are drinking in front of a black car parked on the grass—a car with white stripes running down the middle. A guy wearing a hooded leather jacket bends down and grabs a huge beer can. I catch a glimpse of another leather jacket—the worn black one that belonged to Abel's dad.

"I see him." I'm not about to point at anybody here.

"Where?" Lex pushes up on her toes as people weave in front of us and block her view.

"To my left, by the car. He's standing between the guy who just grabbed a beer and the one with the writing tattooed on his neck." I nudge her with my elbow when she stares too long. "Be subtle. They don't look friendly."

Lex stops walking, and a girl behind us bumps into me.

"Excuse you!" she snaps.

"Sorry." I grab Lex's arm and pull her away from the crowd. "Are you trying to get our asses kicked?"

Lex stares back at me, chin trembling. "What if your dad

wasn't working tonight and you couldn't get out of the house? I'd be here alone right now."

"Bullshit. I never would've let you come by yourself."

"But Abel *did*." Her eyes well. "He should've told me to bring someone. He wasn't even worried about me."

I take her by the shoulders. "You don't know that for sure."

"Yes, I do." She swallows hard. "Because I'm *here*."

"He knew you'd bring me," I try to reassure her.

The sound of roaring engines fills the silence, and people yell and whistle near the starting line. The race must be over.

"Let's pay these guys and get Abel. Then we'll figure out what's going on with him. Okay?"

Lex nods and wipes her face, even though she didn't let a single tear fall. In elementary school, she cried all the time. Her parents traveled constantly, leaving Lex at home with a rotating team of nannies. I got used to her tears, and then one day they stopped. *Crying doesn't make you feel better*, Lex told me. *It's just a different kind of miserable.*

I never understood what she meant until after Noah died. I sobbed for weeks, but it didn't dull the pain. I carry it with me. I'm not strong enough to watch anyone else I care about get hurt.

Abel hasn't moved from his spot between the two guys, who are still hammering down beers. Not good. Assholes and alcohol don't mix. Abel crosses and uncrosses his arms, the way he does whenever he's nervous.

This situation could go bad really fast. People engaging in illegal activities aren't generally fans of new faces, and I've suffered through enough of Dad's what-if scenarios to recognize a potentially dangerous situation.

The guy with the black letters tattooed around his neck falls into that category. He leans casually against the driver's-side door of the car. The curved fenders remind me of the Batmobile, but the guy with the neck ink looks more like a prison inmate than a superhero.

Abel notices us walking toward them and says something to him. The guy tips his chin at us. Even in this light, I notice how flushed his face is from drinking.

Shit.

He punches Abel in the arm. "Check it out, Rock Star. Your groupies came to bail out your sorry ass." His friend laughs as he looks Lex and me up and down.

"Race is starting, Turk." A third loser climbs out of the passenger seat. He's taller than his friends, and he smiles at me with a mouthful of crooked teeth.

"We brought the money," I shout over the engines and the music.

"After the race. I've got two fifty riding on this one." Turk waves us off and angles his body toward the street, offering me a clearer view of the writing wrapped around his throat like a dog collar. It's hard to read, but I make out two of the words: PLAY HARD.

Abel clears his throat in an obvious move to get our attention. He gives Lex and me a pleading look and mouths, *Sorry.*

Puppy dog eyes and an apology won't cut it. This isn't like the time he called us from the police station after streaking through the mall in his underwear on a dare. Or when he needed a ride home from a club after the two girls he was dating at the same time ran into each other, and one of them left with his car.

A yellow Nissan and a silver Honda hatchback pull up for the next race. Video Game Girl walks between the cars and talks to the drivers. When she returns to her spot on the white starting line, the drivers gun the engines louder, and the crowd snaps to attention.

Conversations stop, and spectators climb onto the roofs of the crappier cars for a better view.

Video Game Girl raises her arms above her head.

When they drop, tires screech and the stench of burnt rubber fills the air again. The cars rocket down the street faster than I've ever seen any vehicle move in real life. Their taillights grow smaller and smaller until both cars vanish into the darkness.

"What are you doing here?" I ask Abel, ignoring the guy in the hooded leather jacket next to him.

He shrugs. "I met a girl in class. She told me people were racing tonight."

Lex's eyes drill into him. "Why doesn't that surprise me?"

Abel stares at the ground. "People started taking bets, and one thing led to another."

"I've heard that before," Lex says.

I jab a finger against his chest. "Save your bullshit for someone who believes it. When we get out of here, you're going to tell me how long you've been doing this." If I'm risking my dad's wrath, I want to know why.

Abel's prison guard smirks.

Headlights blink in the distance, and a wave of excitement ripples through the crowd. The two cars emerge from the darkness neck and neck. At the last possible second, the yellow Nissan pulls ahead and crosses the line first.

"That's what I'm talking about!" Turk snaps his fingers and points at the tall guy with the crooked teeth. "Shawn? Pass me another forty."

"Heads up." Shawn tosses Turk a huge beer can.

He catches it, pops the tab, and chugs the beer, giving me a clear view of his tattoo. The uneven block letters read PLAY HARD. DRIVE HARD.

Turk finishes the beer and gestures at the money rolled up in my hand. "Let's see what you got."

I move toward him, holding up the bills between my fingers to avoid touching him. Up close, his eyes are glassy, and his face looks even redder.

"Sung, count it," Turk says to the guy in the leather jacket.

The bills slide effortlessly between Sung's fingers as he counts them like a blackjack dealer. He finishes and slaps the money in Turk's hand. "They're short three hundred."

"I thought he owes you five hundred dollars." I make eye contact with Turk.

"I do." Abel's eyes dart between us.

Turk laughs. "You forgot about interest."

CHAPTER 9

JEKYLL AND HYDE

A dangerous situation is like dog crap: You don't always see it until you're standing in it. Or, like Lex, Abel, and me, until you are knee-deep.

Nobody knows we came to V Street tonight, and it's the last place anyone would look for us. Why didn't I leave Dad a note? Nothing too specific, or he'd send his cop buddies to find me the minute he realized I'd snuck out. Just a trail of bread crumbs to follow in case something went wrong.

Now Turk holds all the cards.

"This is bullshit." Abel's jaw twitches. "I only owe you five hundred bucks. You can't hustle me just because you know I've got money."

"I can do whatever I want because this"—Turk opens his arms wide—"is *my* house. That means you play by *my* rules."

"Fine. Take me to an ATM, and I'll get the rest," Abel says.

"You aren't real smart, are you, Rich Boy? 'Cause we covered this after the race. Do I look like a taxi service?" Turk's neck muscles bulge, distorting the words on his neck.

Even if I throw in my two hundred, Abel will still be short a hundred dollars. I don't see Turk giving him a discount.

Calm down and think.

Dad started teaching me his this-might-save-your-life-one-day skills when I was in kindergarten, but none of them helped the night Noah died.

That's because you didn't do anything.

I mentally scroll through the list, searching for a way out of this mess. *If you're outnumbered, act crazy,* Dad told me at least a dozen times. *Start pacing and talking to yourself about crap like aliens and conspiracy theories. No one wants to screw with a crazy person. Unstable equals unpredictable.*

Dad demonstrated while I lectured him about the harsh realities of mental illness. His world and mine were so different, and until three months ago, I had never witnessed the kind of violence he faced every day.

Even if I could pull off conspiracy theory–level crazy, the window for convincing Turk I'm unstable has already closed. Dog psychology—*Act dominant to establish the alpha position*—is also out. Turk looks like the kind of guy who would love to get aggressive.

What he cares about is money. . . .

"I have two hundred dollars on me." I pull out the cash I brought and gesture at Lex. "What if we go and get the rest of the money instead? Give us thirty minutes, and we'll bring you two hundred more." Maybe the extra hundred will satisfy him.

Turk whips around, invading my personal space. "Nobody's leaving. You think I'm stupid?" *Yes.* The suffocating combination of sweat and cheap cologne clings to his body, which is way too close to mine.

"Turk, this is between you and me." Abel tries to take a step, but Sung throws his arm up in front of Abel, blocking his path.

"Send one of your friends with us if you don't trust me." The thought of being in the same car with either of them makes my skin crawl. "If we don't go, you only get the seven hundred we have on us."

"Frankie?" Lex sounds like a little girl calling for her mom in the dark. She's losing it.

I give her a death glare and focus on Turk. "Will that work?" *Come on. . . . Say yes already.*

He nods. "But your friends stay here. Both of them. You're the only one who goes."

"Get your ass out of my way," a girl snaps.

Cruz, the girl from my Shop class, shoves Shawn and heads in our direction. She's wearing tight jeans, like most of the other girls here tonight. But with her high ponytail, black Lycra tank, and turquoise-silver-and-black Nike basketball high-tops, she comes off as confident and tough.

Abel points at her. "That's the girl I met in class."

Cruz looks at Abel like he's an idiot and stops beside me. Not that she acknowledges my existence. It's a replay of Shop class.

"Is this a private party, Turk?" She toys with the silver chain around her neck.

"Not without you, baby." He stares at her chest without bothering to hide it. "Just handling some business."

"When did you start doing business with the Royals?" She throws a disgusted look at Abel, Lex, and me.

"I don't discriminate when it comes to money." Turk rolls his shoulders in an obvious check-out-my-muscles move.

She smiles at him. "Then get your money and send them back to the Heights so we can have a beer."

"I need some time. They're short, but Sung's gonna take care of it." Turk's cell rings, and he checks the display. "I gotta take this," he tells Cruz, stepping away. "It's business."

"You owe him money and you don't have it?" Cruz hisses under her breath. "Are you crazy?"

Turk's rejects notice her talking to me, but they seem amused by the dirty looks Cruz keeps throwing my way. I'm not sure if she wants to help me or hurt me.

"My friend Abel owes him money. We brought it down here for him, but Turk changed the amount."

"Shit."

Turk pockets his cell and points at Sung with his beer can. "Go get my money."

"On it." Sung shoves Abel against the car and heads in my direction. He's bigger than I thought, and his huge thighs make him bowlegged. As he walks by, his hand clamps around the top of my arm.

"I can walk by myself." I try to pull away, but he jerks me forward.

Lex watches, frozen in place. I catch a glimpse of something behind her—two silhouettes moving toward us. One is closer and picks up speed.

"Cruz?" a guy calls out.

"Over here!" she shouts.

Deacon Kelley—the guy Miss Lorraine kicked out of the rec center—charges in our direction. He's wearing a sleeveless black T-shirt, and the lights illuminate his pale skin. And his scars. The gnarled web runs halfway down his arm, twisting through a black tattoo as if it was designed around the scars. On his forearm, a withered hand reaches for a girl trapped in a birdcage inked on his shoulder. The hand strains against the scars wrapped around it like ropes.

Deacon stops short, his ice-blue eyes darting past me to where Cruz is standing. "What's going on?" Without waiting for a response, he turns on Sung. "Are you assholes messing with my girl?"

Cruz rolls her eyes. "I'm not your girl anymore, Deacon. It's been *two* years."

Deacon takes off his baseball cap and chucks it at the ground, scowling. He paces in a circle, rubbing his hand over the inch of white-blond hair covering his scalp. It blends into his skin perfectly, and at first glance he looks bald.

Cruz's comment clearly bothered him.

"Stop it, Deacon. Not now," she says. "Get your shit together."

Deacon nods, then picks up his cap and puts it back on. Okay, he's officially crazy—and if his expression is any indication, seriously pissed off. He slides a toothpick into the corner of his mouth and turns his attention back to Sung. "You going somewhere?"

"Why do you care?"

Deacon's mouth curls into a deranged smile. "I don't. I've just never seen you with a girl before. Did you dose her drink?"

"What did you say just to me?"

The second figure emerges from the glow of the headlights behind Lex.

Marco.

He stops and stares at the spot where Sung's fingers are pressed against my skin. "Take your hand off her now, or I'll rip your arm out of its socket."

Shit.

"I don't want anyone fighting because of me," I say. "I'm fine."

Deacon frowns and hikes up the jeans falling off his hips. "I think we're working off a different definition of *fine*."

I need to get away from Sung fast. "Let go before this gets worse," I whisper to him.

"Leone!" Turk calls out.

Marco doesn't look up.

Turk jogs over, holding a beer. Cruz follows, dragging a dazed Lex by the hand, and Abel trails behind them with Shawn.

"What's the problem?" Turk storms past us and heads for Marco and Deacon.

Marco keeps his eyes trained on Sung. "If he doesn't let go of her in the next thirty seconds, I'm going to take him apart."

Turk points at me. "Her boy owes me money. Sung is riding with her to get it. There's no problem here. Don't start shit we'll all have to finish."

"Twenty seconds."

Turk and Shawn flank Sung and me like soldiers in a firing line.

Deacon turns his baseball cap around backward. It's like watching Clark Kent change into Superman . . . if Superman was a bloodthirsty lunatic. He pounds on his chest. "Who's up first? 'Cause I haven't sent anybody to the hospital in a long-ass time."

Lex gasps, and Cruz rushes toward Deacon like she's trying to prevent a bomb from detonating.

"Eight seconds." Marco sounds too calm—the kind of calm that comes from not caring what happens to you. "Seven. Six."

Why is he doing this?

"I don't need your help, Marco. Just leave."

Cruz wedges herself between Deacon and his targets.

"Five." Marco keeps counting.

"Shit." Turk crushes his beer can and chucks it against the ground. "Turn her loose, Sung."

"Four."

The grip on my arm releases, and Sung backs away, holding up his hands so Marco will see that he isn't touching me.

Is it over?

Deacon flips his baseball cap back around and points at Shawn. "You and me . . . we'll dance another time."

"Enough." Cruz shoves Deacon's chest with both hands, but he doesn't budge.

"I love it when you crack the whip." He swings his arms around her petite frame and traps her in a bear hug.

I want to get farther away from Sung and his asshole friends, but my legs feel like rubber. Lex stumbles toward me like she read my mind.

"Rich Boy still owes me money," Turk tells Marco. "You know how this works. You lose, you pay. No one walks away without paying."

Marco's eyes meet mine for a second, then his gaze drifts down to my arm. His hands curl into fists. "Quarter mile. You pick the driver."

Deacon cocks his head to the side.

Marco gestures at the row of cars lined up near the racing strip. "Anyone from your crew. When I win, you let the rich boy go back to the Heights with his friends."

All eyes are on Turk. "And if you lose?"

The corner of Marco's mouth turns up for the first time. "I won't lose."

CHAPTER 10

QUARTER MILE

Turk studies Marco for a minute before responding. "If you win, Rich Boy pays me the five hundred he lost on the race and he walks. But if you lose, I take your cut of whatever you make off your next race."

His cut? Who takes the rest of the money?

Marco stiffens.

"You in or out?" Turk asks.

"In."

"You're lucky I'm in a good mood tonight," Turk says. "I made some money when Cruz smoked that Accord in the last race."

The Honda and the yellow Nissan . . . Cruz was driving the Nissan.

"You're up, Sung." Turk gestures at the street. "Smoke his ass."

"I've got this. He can't beat me in that piece-of-shit Fastback."
Sung taps his fist against Turk's and heads for a silver car with
a spoiler.

Marco stops walking when he notices Turk isn't behind
him. "You coming to watch your boy lose or what?"

"Why are you getting in the middle of this shit, Leone?"
Turk asks.

Good question. Since I never asked for his help.

Marco looks right at me, and my stomach does a somersault
even though I'm angry.

"Is this some kind of macho pissing contest?" Lex whispers,
sounding like herself again.

Shawn laughs. "Leone's doing a Royal."

My cheeks burn.

Turk leers in our direction, then grins at Marco. "I feel you,
bro. She's a hot piece of ass. I wouldn't mind getting in those
jeans."

"That's *never* happening," I shoot back.

The muscles in Marco's arms tense, and he lowers his voice,
stepping closer to Turk. "If you even look at her while I'm driving, you'll be in a wheelchair tomorrow. Do we understand
each other?"

My heart jumps, but I ignore it. "Don't talk about me like
I'm not here."

Marco heads for the cars. He slows down as he passes me,
dipping his head close to my ear. "I'm trying to protect you."

"Maybe I don't need protecting."

He jerks his head up and stares directly into my eyes. "Just

85

don't move until I get back." The intensity of his gaze sends pinpricks up my arms, and I swallow hard, watching him walk away.

"Holy shit," Lex whispers.

Deacon and Cruz stick close to Marco as he slides behind the wheel of his Mustang. It's the car from the race that started right after Lex and I arrived tonight.

Marco drives to the line, where Sung is waiting.

"Keep your eye on them," Turk tells Shawn.

"What the hell just happened?" Abel whispers.

"I have no idea." It's true.

"Then why did Marco Leone threaten to disable a guy if he looked at you?" Lex put a hand on her hip, the first Lex-like thing she's done since we got here.

"Maybe he has an issue with these guys and he wanted to pick a fight?" The possibility makes me sick . . . and angry. "But he's not using me as an excuse to do it."

Lex watches me. "I think it's more than that."

"There's no *more*. I work with his younger sister in the after-school program. He probably doesn't want her to lose her tutor."

More like I don't want to lose mine.

"Nice try," she says.

"Actually, I'm secretly dating the most dangerous guy at Monroe after exactly one day there." I lay on the sarcasm, but I'm also annoyed. "Sorry I didn't tell you sooner."

Abel grins. "He must *really* love his sister."

I glare at him. "Don't say a word unless you have a better

explanation for why you came down here than 'I met a girl in class.'"

Video Game Girl stands in front of the cars and raises her arms, and I wait for them to drop.

One.

Two.

Three.

Tires squeal and exhaust fills the air. Lex grabs my hand, and I squeeze hers. Pissed off or not, I still want Marco to win. His Mustang is on the left. Within seconds, his taillights appear smaller than the ones on Sung's car. Or were they always smaller? Why didn't I pay closer attention?

"Come on. Stay ahead of him . . ." Abel whispers.

"Shit!" Turk shouts from the line.

Is it over?

From Turk's tight-lipped expression, I'm guessing the answer is yes.

Abel lets out a long breath. "I think your friend won."

"We're not friends. I barely know him."

Marco stalks toward us with Cruz ahead of him. Deacon isn't with them anymore. Marco stops in front of Shawn and holds out his hand. "Keys."

The tall guy fishes Abel's keys out of his pocket and tosses them to Marco, who catches them in the air.

Marco slaps the keys against Abel's palm. "Get out of here before Turk changes his mind." He gestures at Lex and me. "Take them with you."

"We came in my car," Lex says. "I can't leave it here."

Marco shakes his head and looks at me. "Let's go."

"Thanks," I snap. "But I don't need help figuring out when it's time to move."

He frowns and opens his mouth to say something, then stops. Lex rushes ahead with Cruz as if she can't get away from this place fast enough.

Marco points at Abel. "I told you to get out of here."

"Right." Abel jogs off in the opposite direction.

As we follow Lex and Cruz, the crowd parts for Marco, and people compliment him on his driving. He's polite but never stops moving, like I'm a live grenade and he can't wait to get rid of me.

"Where did you park?" he asks.

"Over there by the streetlight," I say.

The Fiat comes into view, and Lex exhales.

"Where are your keys?" Cruz asks her.

Lex searches through her bag. Dad would freak if I walked up to my car at night without the keys in my hand, ready to unlock the door. "Found them." She holds up her Tiffany key chain.

"Come on." Cruz walks ahead of Lex like a bodyguard.

Marco clears his throat. "Can we talk for a second?"

"Fine." I hang back and watch as Lex gets in the car. Cruz leans against the passenger side.

Marco steps in front of me so I have no choice but to look at him. "I think you're pissed at the wrong guy. Your boyfriend is an asshole for asking you to come down here and bail him out."

My *what*?

"Abel? He's not my boyfriend. I've known him forever. And

no one asked you to get involved and start World War III. I had it worked out."

"Which part? Sung dragging you around, or what could've happened if you got into a car alone with him?" My hands start shaking, and I jam them in my pockets so he won't notice. "Things could've ended differently tonight. The guys who hang out at the races aren't good guys."

"You hang out here," I say.

"Exactly."

Is he trying to scare me?

Marco rubs the back of his neck. "I grew up in the Downs, so I know how to take care of myself. But a girl like you shouldn't come here. Ever."

A girl like you. There it is.

A rich girl from the Heights? A girl who doesn't do anything when someone beats her boyfriend to death? A girl who can't even remember who did it?

Anger twists me into knots. Anger at Abel for getting himself into this mess. Anger at myself for coming here alone with Lex. Anger at Marco for acting like I can't take care of myself.

"A girl like what? A stupid girl? Is that what you were going to say?" I walk away. I've taken enough crap for one night.

"Hold up a second. If I thought you were stupid, I'd say so."

I whip around. "Then what did you mean by 'a girl like you'? What kind of girl am I, Marco?"

"I'm not sure yet." His voice sounds the way it did when he spoke to Sofia—gentle and sincere. But it doesn't matter. It feels like I'm standing on a ledge with the wind blowing, and all it would take is a tiny push to make me fall. Marco could be that push.

This time, I look him in the eye. "Let me know if you figure it out."

Turning my back on him, I walk to the Fiat, even though what I really want to do is run. Before I close the door I sneak one last glance at him.

He's staring right at me.

Lex doesn't say a word until we hit the beltway. "What just happened?"

"Which part?" I'm still trying to figure it out myself.

"I don't know . . . how about why Marco Leone put his ass on the line for us? Or why he was staring at you like something was going on, and threatening anyone who came near you?" She taps on her temple. "Pick one." The edge in her voice feels like an accusation.

"Why do you sound pissed off?"

She pulls at the choppy ends of her hair. "So is there something going on between you two? Because he's a total lunatic, in case you didn't pick up on that after this morning and tonight."

"Nothing is going on. I don't know why Marco did any of that stuff. I talked to him for two minutes when he picked up his sister from the rec center." It's all true, and pointing out how much I can't explain just makes it more confusing.

Lex's cell phone chirps for the tenth time, signaling an incoming text. She ignores it. A second later, my phone vibrates.

> i screwed up. i'm sorry.
> ???
> u there?

I hold up my phone so she can see the text. "It's Abel."

Lex tightens her grip on the wheel and speeds up. "I don't care."

"Will you tell me what's going on with him?"

"After we finish talking about you and Marco."

"There's no me and Marco. Why are you acting so bitchy? Do you think I'm lying? What could possibly have happened since this morning?"

Her phone chirps again, and she tosses it on the dash without looking at the message. "Marco Leone is trouble. Ask anyone at Monroe. He gets in fights constantly, and a he's total manwhore."

"You did not just say *manwhore*."

She glares at me. "He has hooked up or slept with at least half the girls at Monroe, maybe more. Please stay away from him, Frankie. The way he was looking at you . . ."

"What?"

"He's interested." Lex passes a car that's driving too slowly in the left lane.

The idea of Marco hooking up with lots of girls bothers me more than it should. The only girl I've seen him with is Cruz.

I never went through the bad-boy phase like most of my

friends. Clean-cut was my type—ink-free jocks who spent their nights at lacrosse or ice hockey practice, not driving in illegal street races. Bad boys equaled risk, and the old Frankie didn't take chances. Then again, there weren't a lot of gorgeous, tattooed bad boys hanging around the Heights.

Lex glances over at me. "Whatever you're thinking . . . you should think about something else, or someone else. Anyone but Marco. You don't need any more trouble."

Something snaps inside me, setting off a chain reaction of emotions. Frustration, anger, sadness, and shame—they fall one by one like dominoes.

"You sound like my dad." I'm sick of everyone telling me what to do and who I should be. I'm not a rebellious kid screwing up to get attention.

"I don't want to see you get hurt, Frankie." Lex takes a deep breath. "I really missed you this summer. You would've known what to do about Abel."

"When did he start gambling?"

"I'm not sure. I didn't figure it out right away. At least I don't think I did." Lex talks fast, the way she always does when she's nervous or upset. "I found sixty or seventy scratch-off lotto tickets crammed in the pockets of his jeans one night when I stayed over. Who buys sixty scratch-off tickets in one day?"

"Back up. Why were you sleeping over? And where did you find his jeans?"

"Hold on." She turns into Dad's complex. "Which one is it again? They all look the same at night."

From the outside, the garden apartments are identical—

two-story brown buildings, with balconies that offer sweeping views of the parking lot. "Last building on the right. If he's home from work, I'm dead."

I forget about Lex, Abel, and Marco and hold my breath.

Dad's Chevy Tahoe isn't in the parking lot. Am I really this lucky?

"He's still at work."

Lex doesn't bother to park. "Go. Before he gets home."

"We'll finish talking about Abel later." I jump out of the Fiat, praying Dad doesn't show up before I make it inside.

Cujo barks when I open the door and follows me to my room. "You won't tell him what time I came home, will you, buddy?"

I change into sweats and curl up on my bed so Dad will think I've been in here studying. It's quiet now, and I finally have time to think. I replay the last few hours in my mind, but it feels surreal.

Marco's swoop-in-and-save-the-girl rescue mission annoyed the hell out of me, but he didn't have to help us. So why did he do it? His reaction when he saw Sung holding my arm was even stranger.

Was it really about me?

I can't stop picturing the way Marco stared into my eyes without a hint of self-consciousness.

Fearless and unapologetic.

Who did he see?

The rich girl with a perfect life . . . or the broken girl who replaced her?

CHAPTER 11

RICH GIRL

When I finally haul myself out of bed in the morning, the apartment smells like burnt toast and cheap instant coffee. I'm halfway down the hall when I hear Dad talking on his cell phone. "We're not dealing with a couple of kids stealing cars with dent pullers and screwdrivers, Tyson. They're driving these cars straight into shipping containers."

Great. Undercover-cop talk at seven o'clock, the only thing worse than Dad's coffee.

"Already ran him through the system," Dad says. "He lives with his father, and he has a record."

Boring.

In the kitchen, Dad stands in front of the toaster oven with his back to me. He finishes the call and drops his cell on the counter. "I wasn't sure how you like your eggs these days, so I scrambled them," he says without turning around. Sneaking up on a cop is impossible.

"I don't eat eggs. Or breakfast."

"Why not?" He sounds offended, as if he invented the concept of breakfast.

"Why? Is this a quiz?" It feels weird explaining basic stuff about myself to my father. When I only visited for a few days at a time, I never bothered.

"Listen, I know you've been through a lot. You experienced the kind of trauma most people only see on TV, and you don't have any closure. But the police are still investigating Noah's death. No one is giving up."

Now he's a shrink?

I laugh, without caring how bitter it sounds. "The police have no leads. They won't be able to find Noah's killer until I remember what he looks like."

"The guys in homicide are good. They'll find the bastard." Dad opens the toaster oven and jabs at a charred slice of bread with his finger. He winces and yanks his hand back.

"You okay?"

"It's nothing." He shakes his wrist a few times, then scoops a pile of eggs onto a plate. "The toaster is new. I haven't figured out the timing yet." He puts the plate on the counter in front of me.

What part of "I don't eat breakfast" is he confused about?

I push it aside, and he pours himself a cup of sludge. "So how did things go at the rec center?"

"Fine. I'm working with middle school kids, helping them

with their homework and keeping an eye on them. Miss Lorraine, the woman in charge, is hard-core. I'm surprised she didn't have my mug shot hanging on the wall."

Dad's back goes rigid. "That's not funny, Frankie. You're in serious trouble. I thought you understood that."

Is he starting this again?

"I know *exactly* how much trouble I'm in, but thanks for reminding me. Getting kicked out of school and doing community service every day *never* would've tipped me off."

"Did anyone there give you a hard time?"

"The kids are thirteen." I don't mention the basketball players hanging around out front.

"I meant in general. There's a lot of crime in the Downs— and the criminals and junkies who go along with it."

"Not everyone in the Downs is a criminal or a drug addict. Lex's father grew up there, and now he's a senator. All it took was hard work and a bigger bank account." It's a fact people forget all the time. Nobody around here cares where you came from once you have money.

"Things have changed a lot since then."

"You're the one who said Monroe and the rec center are in the nicer parts of the Downs." I throw his words back at him.

Dad paces. "*Nicer* than my district—where people get knifed in broad daylight and kids can't play in the park because the ground is covered with dirty needles and burnt aluminum foil instead of grass."

"I'm not naive."

"More kids are getting into serious trouble." Dad shakes his head, still pacing. "More than I realized. Some of the students at your school already have police records."

"And some of the kids at Monroe are from the Heights," I shoot back.

"Not the ones at the rec center." He bangs his fist against the wall. "That's the last place I wanted you doing community service."

Is he serious?

"If it bothered you so much, why didn't you do something about it? I don't know . . . like ask them to move me? You're a cop. I'm sure you know someone in the probation office."

"The probation office doesn't take requests, and I won't ask anyone for special treatment."

"Whatever." I sling my backpack over my shoulder and head for the front door.

"Just be careful about who you hang out with. That's all I'm saying. You don't need any more problems."

I stop walking and turn around to face him. "Wow. One stupid decision and I'm a total screwup? It's good to know where I stand."

He rubs his temples like I'm giving him a headache. "Drinking and driving is more than a stupid decision. Someone could've died."

The words twist like a screwdriver inside me. "I know."

"And you weren't exactly on the straight and narrow before the DUI. Your mom told me that you quit playing piano and volunteering at the hospital and started sneaking out and drinking instead. By my count, that's more than one bad decision."

My extracurricular activities aren't *me*. They're things I *do*, not who I *am*.

Mom will never see it that way, but I hoped Dad might understand.

Guess not.

A car horn honks outside. "This was fun, Dad, but I've had enough bonding for one morning. I'm going to be late for school."

"Frankie, wait," Dad calls after me.

The apartment door bangs shut as I run down the steps to the parking lot.

I'm done waiting.

Lex doesn't say much in the car on the way to school. The most I get out of her is that she gave in and talked to Abel last night, and they ended up fighting. After what my dad said this morning, I'm fine with silence.

At school, I take out my frustration on my locker when it won't open. I bang the side of my fist against it the way Marco did yesterday.

Nothing.

Today officially sucks.

I spot Marco coming down the hall.

"Hey," I call out. He looks up, a hint of a smile playing on his lips. "Want to show a rich girl how to open her locker? It seems like you're the only person around here who knows how to get into it."

Marco walks toward me. "I never called you that."

But he probably thought it.

"Right. I should've said 'a Royal'."

He slouches a little. "I never called you that, either." The scent of leather and citrus envelops me when he reaches my locker. "Just so I'm clear, you're asking for my help, right?"

I cock my head to the side and throw him some attitude. "Weren't you suspended?"

"Just for the day. The teachers miss me if I'm not around." He leans his shoulder against the locker next to mine and stares down at me. "And you never answered my question. Are you asking for my help?"

"Are you going to show me or not? Otherwise, I'll just go to the office and tell Mrs. Lane I need another one."

It's almost time for first period, and other students filter into the hallway. Marco's presence at my locker doesn't go unnoticed. Girls stare, and a couple of them give me dirty looks.

"He'd never be into *her*," one of them whispers.

Because I'm not his type? Or because I'm from the Heights?

I fiddle with the latch on my locker, hoping Marco didn't hear. I'm used to people talking about me. Watching your boyfriend get beaten to death outside the hottest new club in the Heights guarantees a certain amount of gossip. But it feels different with Marco standing next to me.

Marco touches my arm. His fingertips linger longer than necessary, and my skin tingles. "So there's a trick to opening

99

it." He points at the number on top of the door: 231. "You have to hit the two."

"That's all?"

He steps aside. "Try it."

Curling my hand, I hit the side of my fist against the number two. The locker springs open, and I break into a smile. I can't help it.

"It worked." I close it and try again. The rusty blue door swings open a second time.

Marco watches me.

My cheeks heat up, and I change the subject. "How did you figure out the trick?"

He gives me a sheepish smile. "This was my friend Deacon's locker. The guy who was with me last night. He rigged it so no one could break in."

None of Turk's friends wanted to mess with the scarred blond any more than Miss Lorraine wanted him in the rec center. And Marco is his friend. Not a good sign.

"Did he graduate?" More people around us are beginning to stare.

"Not before he got expelled." Either Marco doesn't notice we're attracting attention or he doesn't care.

Why should he? Gossip never hurts guys like Marco.

The bell rings, and I slip past him. "Thanks for the help." I force my legs to move, my skin still buzzing from his touch.

"Hey, Frankie?" he calls out.

I glance back at him, ignoring the eyes on us. "Yeah?"

"You should smile more often."

A hint of one tugs at the corner of my mouth. "I'll think about it."

I turn around and start walking, careful to keep my head down so that no one sees the moment when the huge smile I was fighting finally breaks free. It takes every ounce of self-control not to look back and see if he's watching.

CHAPTER 12

ROCK STARS, POETS, AND SINNERS

I make it to English class moments before the bell. Most of the seats are taken except the ones in the front. The firing zone.

No, thanks.

An empty desk in the back corner offers a glimmer of hope—and a familiar face. Cruz lounges in the next seat over. After last night, I'm not sure what to expect.

Mrs. Hellstrom taps a stack of papers against her desk. "Put away your cell phones, ladies and gentlemen. Today we are discussing the requirements for the long-term assignment that will account for forty percent of your English grade this semester. So if I were you, I would pay attention."

Cruz gives me a nod. Coming from her, it feels like an invitation. I take the empty seat and dig through my backpack. Where's my pen?

She reaches in front of me and puts a pencil on my desk.

"Thanks," I whisper.

Cruz points at the front of the room with her pen. "Take notes. Mrs. Hellstrom is a hardass."

In Shop class, Cruz barely acknowledged my existence. Then last night she tried to help me, and now she's lending me a pencil and giving me advice?

The drama at the street races proved that I'm completely out of my element—and that one of my best friends has zero common sense. I'm sure that didn't impress anyone.

So what did I miss?

Mrs. Hellstrom scrawls a series of names on the board in illegible serial killer handwriting. "Sylvia Plath. Ralph Waldo Emerson. Virginia Woolf. F. Scott Fitzgerald. Alice Walker." She stretches her arm across the whiteboard and draws a line under the names. "What do these writers have in common?"

The guy who looked like he was asleep in the back of the room yesterday raises his hand.

"Jamal?" Mrs. Hellstrom watches him expectantly.

"They're all novelists or poets."

"Jamal is correct, but they have something else in common." When no one volunteers an answer, Mrs. Hellstrom perches on the front of her desk, half sitting and half standing in one of those I'm-a-cool-teacher poses. "All these authors kept journals."

"So they wrote in diaries?" asks a girl in the second row.

Mrs. Hellstrom starts pacing, as if whatever she's about to tell us is so exciting she can't sit still any longer. "Their journals weren't accounts of their day-to-day lives, like traditional diaries. They were far less structured."

She retrieves a stack of handouts from her desk and gives some to the first person in each row to pass back. "These packets include samples from the journals of the authors whose names are on the board, in addition to some other artists you might recognize."

I flip through the photocopied pages. Sylvia Plath. Henry David Thoreau. Anne Frank. Frida Kahlo. Kurt Cobain. Pages of poetry, song lyrics, doodles, lists, and anecdotes mixed in with longer entries.

Abel once told me that his dad used to make lists of words and phrases whenever he worked on a new song.

"These are kinda personal," Cruz says.

"You're right," Mrs. Hellstrom says. "These excerpts contain everything from observations and ideas for stories, songs, and poems to the thoughts and dreams of the journal writers." She's borderline euphoric now. "Their hopes and fears . . . they're all here in different forms. This semester, each of you will create a journal that reflects who you are as a writer."

Is this woman insane? I don't like discussing my fears with my friends. There's no way I'm sharing them with her—in writing.

And my hopes?

I hope I can sleep for more than three hours a night. I hope the flashbacks of Noah's head hitting the ground will stop and I'll remember the faces of his attacker instead. I hope my dad gets off my back. I hope Mrs. Hellstrom quits tomorrow and takes this nightmarish assignment with her.

Mrs. Hellstrom flips through the packet, reading Kurt Cobain lyrics that never made it into his songs, and passages from what she calls a coming-of-age art journal.

I sigh and drop my head on my desk.

"She assigns crazy-ass stuff like this every year," Cruz whispers. She stops talking every time Mrs. Hellstrom glances up from the packet.

"Okay," I manage.

Cruz raises her hand.

"Isabella? Do you have a question?" our insane teacher asks.

"So you want us to tell you our secrets?"

"I'm not asking you to share anything you're uncomfortable with, Isabella. The journals are a place to experiment, so you can find *your* voices as writers. They can be full of short stories or poetry if you don't want to write about yourself directly. But I think you'll find that even journals composed of narrative entries are a reflection of the writer."

"Isabella?" I whisper when Mrs. Hellstrom turns to answer another question.

She rolls her eyes. "Isabella Vera Cruz. But nobody calls me that except annoying teachers like her."

"Trust me, I get it." I point at myself. "Francesca Devereux."

She laughs, and Mrs. Hellstrom glares at us.

Eventually, we get paired up to answer boring questions about the entries from the dead and famous.

"So are you okay after everything that went down last night?" Cruz asks me.

"Yeah." The realization hits me all at once. I'm not just saying it because she is the one asking.

For the first time in months, it's true.

I am okay.

Last night I held it together when Sung grabbed me, and this morning I stood my ground with Dad—something the old Frankie never would've done. It feels like I'm finally waking up after being asleep for years.

"When I mentioned the street races to your friend Abel, I didn't think he'd really come. Or that it would start such a shit storm." Cruz shakes her head. At least that part of Abel's story was true. "But I couldn't believe you showed up."

"Why?" Now that I asked, I'm not sure I want to know the answer.

"Girls from the Heights don't usually come to the street races."

"Abel is one of my best friends, and he was in trouble. It's not like I had a choice." A second too late, I realize the way it sounds. "Not that there's anything wrong with where you race."

"You had a choice. Most people won't have your back if it means putting their own ass on the line. Trust me."

"I don't have many real friends." The words tumble out. Perfect. She probably thinks I sit alone at a huge table in the cafeteria every day.

"Me neither."

The bell rings, and Mrs. Hellstrom issues last-minute instructions as chair legs scrape and students bolt out the door. I close the photocopied packet of other people's private thoughts and stuff it in my backpack.

Cruz tucks her pen in the pocket of the painted-on jeans that manage to look cool on her, instead of like she's trying too hard.

I follow her out of the classroom, expecting her to ditch me. Instead, she falls into step beside me. "So what's the deal between you and Marco?"

Is it that obvious?

"There's no deal."

"He doesn't stick his neck out for just anyone."

"His sister is in my group at the rec center. He probably wanted to make sure her tutor didn't get kidnapped." It's pretty much the same answer I gave Lex, and from the look on Cruz's face, she isn't buying it, either.

Cruz owns the hallway. Guys stare and girls move aside. A jock wearing a Monroe Soccer T-shirt and a Tag Heuer watch that's worth at least nine hundred dollars checks out Cruz instead of paying attention to the cheerleader batting her lashes at him.

The jock grins at Cruz, and she gives him the finger. "Guys from the Heights are assholes."

All of a sudden, it feels like I'm standing on the wrong side of enemy lines. But the truth is, lots of guys from the Heights are arrogant, selfish, and entitled. Noah was an exception. "You're right. Most of them are."

"You don't have to agree with me to avoid an awkward moment. I can deal with awkward. It's bullshit I can't handle."

"I'm not that nice anymore."

She sizes me up and watches the activity in the hallway at the same time. She would make a good cop. "Now that we've established this is a bullshit-free zone, there's really nothing going on with you and Marco?"

"He's not my type, and I'm probably not his, either." I sound like my six-year-old cousin when he can't have something and he says, *Then I don't want it anyway.* "I'm not going to jump in bed with him just because he's hot."

"Most girls do." It sounds like she's stating a fact. "But you think he's hot?"

"That's not what I meant." Especially now that I know Lex wasn't exaggerating about his reputation.

"It's what you said."

"I'm not going to be Marco Leone's flavor of the week, and I don't want a relationship with anyone."

She flashes a smug smile when I say the word *relationship*.

"Not that I think Marco is relationship material."

Cruz's smile fades. "You would be surprised."

CHAPTER 13
ONE-EYED CAT

When Lex drops me off at the rec center after school, the three shirtless basketball players are already standing against the wall. They're wearing different nylon basketball shorts and leather high-tops, but otherwise they look exactly the same.

"Hey, princess. You're back."

"Come on over here and say hi."

One of them flicks his tongue at me. "We missed you."

Gross.

They blow me kisses and I ignore them, taking the steps two at a time.

Inside, Sofia sits perched on Miss Lorraine's chair behind the counter. Miss Lorraine is busy lecturing a boy about how low his jeans are riding.

Sofia notices me watching Miss Lorraine. "She's really nice

when you get to know her. I stay at her house when Marco works late. She's just sad. Her daughter, Kira, died five years ago, and they were really close."

I think of Miss Lorraine as the tough woman in charge of the rec center and my unofficial probation officer (aside from my *actual* probation officer, who I have to meet with every six weeks)—someone watching and waiting for me to screw up. I never imagined the kind of life she had when she left the rec center.

"How did her daughter die?" I whisper.

Sofia twists, and the seat moves from side to side. "A drive-by. The guy who lived next door to them sold meth. He cheated some bad guys. They were trying to kill him, but they got the address wrong."

"I remember the story. It was all over the news when I was in middle school."

"Miss Lorraine says we're all her kids now." Sofia hops down from the chair, and we walk toward the room where my group meets. "So how did you do in Shop?"

"Better. I actually know the difference between the engine block and the cylinders, I think. Now Chief has moved on to five-speed transmissions."

She sits next to Daniel, and he kicks his backpack under the chair to make space for hers on the floor between them. He runs his hands over the curls sticking up around his face, like he's worried about impressing her. I don't blame him.

Sofia is beautiful, inside and out. Two clips hold back her curly hair, exposing the brutal scars on her face and neck. The fearless way Sofia allows the world to see what most people would hide makes me uncomfortable. I'd never willingly reveal the scars from my past to anyone. My own mind won't even let me remember them.

Today everyone settles down easily, but there's less chatter and more whispering.

When most of the kids in my after-school group filter out around six thirty, the whispers increase. Kumiko moves her book closer to my table—and Sofia, Daniel, and Carlos.

"Frankie, can I ask you something?" Kumiko shifts in her seat.

"Sure." *Please don't let it be about birth control.*

"We heard some stuff at school and want to know if it's true."

"What kind of *stuff*?" I ask, dreading the answer.

Kumiko squirms a little more. "The guy from the Heights who got killed last June . . . he was your boyfriend, right?"

I'm never prepared when people ask about Noah's death. Usually, I see the question coming, which gives me time to deflect it. But Kumiko caught me off guard. Worse, there's nowhere to run. And what does it say about me if I dodge their questions?

Sofia watches me from across the table. If she's brave enough to let the world see her scars, I can answer their questions about Noah.

"Yeah. He was." I fight to keep my voice steady.

The kids exchange glances, and Daniel clears his throat. I guess he's up next. "Is it true you were there but you can't remember what happened?"

"I remember some things, but not others." Like the face of the guy who killed my boyfriend.

"At least you don't have amnesia." Kumiko tosses her glossy black hair over her shoulder and turns her attention back to her homework.

"That's true." I force a weak smile.

In the days that followed Noah's death, I would have given anything to forget. Now all I want to do is remember. I owe it to Noah.

We grew up together, and our friendship always mattered more to me than dating him. It's hard to admit now that he's gone. People expect me to pretend Noah and I were soul mates, destined to walk down the aisle five minutes after college graduation. But we didn't have a forever, I-can't-live-without-you kind of love. It was more like the I'll-never-forget-you kind.

The kind of love you have for a boy who said you were beautiful before it was actually true. A boy who knew you couldn't ride a bike until seventh grade but never told anyone. It's a love born from knowing someone for so long that most of your memories include him.

Admitting that Noah was anything less than my dream guy makes me feel like an awful person. But I'm determined to do something more than idealize our relationship.

I'm going to figure out who killed him—one memory at a time.

Sofia and I are the only ones in the room again when Marco shows up to get her.

"Hey." He smiles at me, and my stomach flips a little.

"Hi." I dig through my backpack to avoid looking at him. Why does he have to be so gorgeous?

Sofia gathers her stuff. "Marco? Do you have any money for the vending machine?"

He takes a worn leather wallet out of his back pocket and hands her a five. "Don't buy too much junk."

"Deal." Sofia ducks under his arm and bounds down the hall. "Bye, Frankie."

"Bye." I wave, but she's already gone.

Marco lingers by the door for a moment. "I'll see you around, Angel."

"Why do you keep calling me that?"

"Does it bother you?" He cracks a half smile, and a dimple presses into his cheek. My eyes drift to his lips—full and wide.

Look somewhere else.

"That's not the point." I stuff the chemistry textbook in my backpack. Anything to keep from staring at his mouth. "I have a name."

"I know." Marco holds my gaze a second too long, and my cheeks warm.

Does he ever blink?

When he closes the door and disappears down the hall, I switch off the lights and finally let myself exhale. Pretending Marco doesn't affect me is harder than I expected.

A minute later Marco passes the window. He's carrying a plastic milk bottle from the vending machine, and he leaves through the emergency exit. Where is he going? There's nothing behind the building except a bunch of run-down playground equipment that Miss Lorraine won't let the kids near.

It's a borderline stalker move, but I follow him.

I crack the door and peek outside. Streetlights illuminate a rotted play structure and the sidewalk at the end of the parking lot, leaving the back of the building, where I'm standing, in darkness.

A flash of brown and white darts through a pale circle of light. Cyclops, the one-eyed cat, slinks toward a yellow slide attached to the play structure.

"Hey, Cyclops. Brought you dinner." Marco stands near the perimeter of the playground and sets a red plastic ashtray on the ground.

The cat runs toward him. It arches its back and circles Marco. Is he crazy? Any second it will hiss and foam at the mouth.

Marco pours the milk in the ashtray. Cyclops circles again, closer this time, and the cat's back relaxes. The animal that won't let anyone come near it sits at Marco's feet, lapping up the milk.

My cell vibrates. Lex is here. Before I go inside, I take one last look at the broken animal and the guy feeding it.

Cyclops trusts Marco.

I can't help but wonder if that cat knows something I don't.

I hardly sleep at night—another delightful side effect of PTSD. Filling those extra hours isn't easy. I've already reorganized the contents of my drawers and Dad's cereal cupboard, watched hours of mind-numbing reality shows, and I'm still wide awake. Insomnia isn't the even worst part.

It's the not remembering and then remembering—that's the only way to describe it. I can't recall certain details from the night Noah died, but when the flashbacks hit out of nowhere, I'm back there again watching him die. I can't stop the flashbacks or turn them off. I relive the worst ten minutes of my life over and over and over, except for the one part I want to remember.

I reach for a magazine on the nightstand, and my fingers brush a metal coil.

Crap.

My English journal—the one I'm supposed to turn in on Friday. Does Mrs. Hellstrom honestly expect us to tell her about our true selves? What if we don't know who that person is—or we don't want to find out?

One of the psychiatrists who treated me suggested I keep a journal. She said writing about a tragic experience helps the mind process it and heal. I don't believe for a second that writing in a stupid notebook will take away the pain. But something else she said seems possible: *A journal might help you remember.*

If that's true, I owe it to Noah to try.

I lean against the wall behind my bed and search through my backpack for a pen. I settle for a pencil with bite marks along the side, turn to the first page, and start writing.

I met Noah when I was eleven and he was twelve.
He had dirty-blond hair the color of buttered toast and

eyes the color of a September blue sky. We played truth or dare a hundred times that summer, and I only picked dare once. Noah dared me to ride a bike down the biggest hill in the Heights. When I admitted that I never learned how, Noah let me ride down on his bike with him.

When Noah turned thirteen, he nicknamed me Chicken Legs for a whole year. But at fourteen, he beat up Bobby McIntyre for calling me the same thing.

At fifteen, Noah told me I shouldn't trust a boy if he said he loved me (because high school boys only wanted one thing).

But the night of his sixteenth birthday, he was the boy who said it.

Noah was beautiful, athletic, funny, and smart.

Everyone said it would never last.

They were right.

Noah died at seventeen, a week before his eighteenth birthday.

My eyes skim the words. They don't capture the boy I remember, but they bring him closer. They remind me of the Noah I knew, not the one I lost. But nothing I wrote relates to the night he died.

How do I get from what's on the page to there?

Across from my bed, six silver frames are lined up on top of the flowered dresser. Images of Lex, Abel, and me stare back from behind the glass, along with my favorite photo of Lex and me from the eighth-grade dance. Our braces and overly glossed lips, glittery dresses, and kitten heels we couldn't walk in make us look like refugees from an outdated music video. Other frames lay scattered around them, facedown. I walk over and touch one.

Even with the frame flipped over, I know exactly which photo is on the other side.

First row, third frame from the left—Noah and me standing next to his Mongoose after our epic ride down the big hill. We jumped the curb at the bottom and crashed in the grass. We are a little banged up in the photo Noah took with his phone, but we're both smiling.

The memory creates a familiar hollow ache in my chest, and I force the pain deeper, where it belongs. I'm not ready to turn the frame over . . . not yet.

Maybe never.

I cram the journal in my backpack, even though I'd rather stab myself in the eye with a fork than show it to Mrs. Hellstrom. I've become an expert at avoiding things that could hurt me—which means I will figure out how to stay away from Marco Leone.

CHAPTER 14

BITE POINT

Lex is too quiet when she picks me up on Friday morning. Her smudged eye liner looks darker today because of the shadows under her eyes. Maybe she's still fighting with Abel.

Or he's buying a hundred scratch-off lottery tickets.

It's hard to put any distance between us when Lex drives me around every day. All this time together makes me realize how much I've missed her. But hanging out with Lex and Abel also reminds me of the girl I want to leave behind and the boy who is already gone. The four of us did so many things together, even before I started dating Noah. Separating all those memories—searching for the ones that don't include Noah or pretending he wasn't part of them—feels impossible.

Maintaining that distance is what keeps me from asking her what's wrong right away. I could check my e-mail and delete some from Mom, or bitch about Dad until we get to school. But it's hard to ignore Lex when I know she's hurting. She is still my best friend.

Lex stops at an intersection and glances to the right. Her beautiful blue eyes will always remind me of Noah's.

"Want to tell me what's wrong?" I finally ask.

She props her elbow on the lip above the door panel and rests her head in her hand. "It would take less time to tell you what's *right*."

"Does it have anything to do with Abel? You never finished telling me what happened over the summer or how you ended up sleeping at his house." Lex and Abel have been crazy about each other since eighth grade. But she was the one who didn't want to cross the line.

"I crashed over there a lot. You weren't around, and his mom is always out of town sharing her insights about Tommy Ryder and his Golden Fingers, so it was just Abel and me." She makes it sound like I was on a trip instead of avoiding them. "We got closer."

I turn toward her. "How *much* closer?"

Lex turns into the parking lot, and I fight the urge to look for Marco in Lot B. She shrugs.

"Did you two get together?" Aside from the occasional drunken kiss, nothing has ever happened between them. Lex says it's not worth risking their friendship. Abel says she's just scared. Did things go a little further this time?

As we cross over into Lot A, I take a quick look in the side mirror.

No sign of Marco.

I focus on Lex again. "Well?"

"Yes. And it was obviously a mistake." The moment she says it, I spot Abel's Land Cruiser.

Lex pulls into a parking space and practically jumps out of the car. "I don't want to talk to him."

I do.

Abel jogs toward the Fiat as I get out. He cuts her off before she makes it very far. "Come on, Lex. How long are you going to stay mad?"

She glares at him. "I don't know. How long are you going to keep lying and gambling?"

He facepalms his forehead. "It was one night. I haven't been back to V Street since . . ."

"The other night when you dragged me and Frankie down there to get manhandled?" She tries to circle around Abel, and he reaches for her arm. She jerks away. "Don't!"

Lex makes a beeline for the quad, leaving me with Abel.

"You'd better tell me what you've been doing." I jab his chest. "Because I've never seen her like this."

Abel crosses and uncrosses his arms. "I made a few bets over the summer. Horse races and a couple of boxing matches—nothing big. But it freaked Lex out, and I promised to stop."

"And you didn't."

He nods.

"Horse racing and boxing? Nothing else?" It's the kind of question Dad asks me when he already knows the answer—a test to see if I'll tell him the truth.

"That's all, except for the race I bet on the other night." He scratches the back of his neck, a textbook sign of lying. "Will you talk to her for me?"

"No." I push past him and speed-walk toward the admin building.

Abel keeps up. "Frankie—"

I stop at the edge of the sidewalk. "Did you forget about the sixty scratch-offs, or whatever ridiculous number it was?"

"I thought you meant placing bets."

"Come talk to me when you're done lying." I leave him standing there.

As I walk up the steps, I see Marco on the quad. He's leaning against a tree not far from where Abel and I were talking. He sees me watching him, and our eyes meet for a second before I get caught in the current of students pouring into the building.

Cruz isn't in English, so it's more boring than usual, and I don't have a pen until halfway through the period. When the bell rings, Mrs. Hellstrom collects our journals. I'm one of the first people out the door after I mumble something about leaving mine at home.

In the hall, I turn the corner and spot Cruz standing against the wall.

She falls in step next to me. "How was class?"

"Boring. Did you ditch?" It doesn't seem like the kind of question that will offend her.

"No, I had to take my little sister Teresa to urgent care before school. She has asthma."

"Is she okay?"

"She just needed a new inhaler. So are you ready for Shop?"

I shrug. "There are too many different screwdrivers or whatever you call them."

She laughs. "Socket wrenches. And you're gonna need to learn the names of the tools and how to use them if you want to pass. Chief takes cars seriously." Like Cruz does—a girl who can hold her own, both in Shop and behind the wheel.

How would it feel to be that confident?

"Why does everyone call him Chief?"

"He was a crew chief on the NASCAR circuit for twenty years. One day, he just left. Walked away and came back here."

"What happened? Did he get hurt?"

"No. Someone else did," Cruz stares straight ahead, distracted. She notices me watching her and snaps out of it. "I mean, nobody knows. Just rumors."

The conversation about Chief is clearly over. Not that I blame her. I hate the thought of people talking about him.

Cruz stops at a locker near the stairs and grabs her books.

Two girls across the hall are looking at us.

"Next to Cruz," a pasty redhead across the hall whispers. She's wearing the kind of glittery eye shadow that most girls only wear at night. "Her boyfriend was that guy who got killed in the parking lot of the Sugar Factory in the Heights."

"The chick who got booted from the rich-bitch private school?" her friend asks.

The redhead nods. "I heard she's mental and takes a ton of meds."

"That's bullshit," I say softly, my fingers digging into the strap of my backpack.

Cruz watches the girls, tapping her foot like a sprinter itching to run. "Screw this." She drops her books and they smack against the floor. The sound echoes through the hallway, and people turn around to see what's happening.

"You talk too much, Christine." Cruz walks up to the redhead, who is wearing foundation that makes her skin look orange.

Christine shrinks back against the lockers. "I was just repeating what I heard. I didn't mean anything by it."

"You should be more careful what you say in the future." Cruz smiles, and it carries an unspoken threat. "You never know who's listening."

Cruz picks up her books. Within seconds, the sounds of locker doors slamming and people talking resume as if nothing happened. People give me curious looks, like they're wondering why Cruz defended me. I'd love to know, too.

Am I supposed to thank her? That won't be embarrassing or anything.

We turn the corner and Cruz stops me by the stairs. "Don't let people talk shit about you, Frankie. Ignoring it is the same as giving them permission. Never give anyone permission to disrespect you."

I almost say, *It doesn't matter.*

But the words catch in my throat.

I follow Cruz down the steps to the basement.

Inside, we walk past the green Camaro and take our seats. Chief stands at the whiteboard, drawing a stick-figure diagram of a car halfway up a steep hill. He's the only teacher I've ever had who wears jeans and a baseball cap in class. Then again, he also wears short-sleeve button-downs and tucks them into his jeans.

I like him. He reminds me of my dad's father—if Granddad worked on cars instead of motorcycles and wore hats with motor oil logos on them.

I also like Shop. It's a class I never would've taken at Woodley, not that the school offered it. Kids in the Heights pay other people to fix their cars, and when the new-leather smell wears off or they crash them—whichever comes first—their parents buy them the newer model.

Nobody at Woodley would waste time restoring an old muscle car. Why bother if you can buy a brand-new one?

Chief finishes the diagram and turns to the class. "You're driving a car with manual transmission and you get stuck on a hill in traffic. What happens if you let up on the clutch too fast when everyone starts moving again?"

"Easy," a guy calls out from the back. "The car stalls."

"Good to know I wasn't talking to myself last year." Chief pushes his Valvoline cap farther back on his head. "Anybody know *why*?"

Cruz opens her textbook and slides it across the table between us. She taps on a subtitle toward the bottom: *Manual Transmission*. It's the kind of thing a friend would do.

I'm not interested in sharing my secrets or baring my soul to anyone. But Cruz doesn't strike me as the soul-baring type.

Scanning the text between us, I search for the answer to the question. "The bite point," I call out.

Chief cracks a smile and nods. "That's right, Frankie. Go on."

Clearly, he expects me to explain the relationship between the bite point and stalling—something I couldn't do if my life depended on it.

"I don't really know what it means," I admit.

"That's all right. We're here to learn," Chief says. "Anyone who has ever raced a car should know what the bite point is. Cruz, why don't you explain it to Frankie?"

The guys in class go crazy. "Damn, Cruz. Chief called you out."

Cruz shakes her head. "The bite point is the sweet spot when you let up on the clutch and give the car some gas, and the clutch engages."

The cute guy who sits at the table next to ours and has been staring at Cruz for most of the class drops down on one knee next to her, his hand over his heart. "It's like falling in love. You know it when you feel it."

She pushes him with her foot. "Shut it, Ortiz."

"Mr. Ortiz is right about one thing." Chief taps his dry-erase marker on the diagram. "You know it when you feel it. But it's easy to miss the bite point when the car is on a slope and you're worried about easing off the clutch into first without rolling backward or stalling."

"Chief, are you trying to teach my boys how to get to first?

'Cause the ladies will tell you I've got that covered." Ortiz grins, and the other guys start laughing again.

"You'd better keep it covered, Ortiz," Cruz says. "Or you'll end up being some girl's baby daddy."

Chief crosses his arms and tucks his hands under his armpits, shaking his head. The old guy is either embarrassed or trying not to laugh.

"Ortiz is a fool, but he throws a hell of a party." Cruz keeps her voice low. "He's having one tonight. You should come. Bring your friends. The one Turk hustled is cute. Unless he's yours . . ."

"Abel? Definitely not mine. He's like my brother, and he needs to get in a little less trouble."

She scribbles an address in her notebook, tears off a corner of the page, and hands it to me. "Then come by yourself. We'll hang out."

Chief looks up, grinning. "Let me put it another way for those of you with cleaner imaginations than Mr. Ortiz. When you start to let up on the clutch, you'll feel it engage. That's your signal to move your other foot from the brake to the gas pedal." Chief toys with his cap again. "If you know when to make that move, you won't stall and you won't crash. You'll fly."

Before Noah died, I never took risks. I was too afraid of disappointing someone or screwing up the Plan. Now I've disappointed everyone.

There's no Plan and no Noah, and I'm still afraid.

Just once, I wish I knew what it felt like to fly.

CHAPTER 15

—

NIGHT TRAIN

I'm not brave enough to take public transit to the party, so I end up in a cab. It would have been cheaper to leave from the rec center instead of the gas station near Dad's apartment. But that would've required calling Lex and explaining why I didn't need a ride home, and I couldn't come up with a decent excuse.

The driver turns into a run-down town house complex, and I get out a block away from the address Cruz gave me. It isn't hard to find. Bass thumps from inside the town house, and the party spills onto the sidewalk out front. The last time I went to a real party, Noah was still alive.

Over the summer, I sat around drinking with lifeguards and caddies from the club. We even went to a so-called party on the golf course, but it was just a bunch of people standing around in the wet grass.

Three guys hang out on the steps, holding red plastic Solo cups and checking out girls as they walk by.

I'm up next.

"You need a drink, baby?" one asks.

I keep moving. "I'm good."

He raises the plastic cup in a mock toast. "If you change your mind . . ."

Inside, music vibrates through the drywall. A deejay stands behind a table made out of a sheet of plywood and plastic milk crates, spinning the dials on a massive stereo system. Hips grind and hands wave to the beat.

The kitchen is crammed with people lined up at the keg. I scan the room for Cruz and squeeze through the wall of bodies. A kid who looks like he's still in middle school hands me a cup.

"She nailed it again," someone calls out.

"Drink up, boys, and cough up your money." Cruz stands and holds out her hand. Her competitors hand over their cash. She spots me and waves me over to the table, where they're playing quarters, and judging by how drunk the guys are compared with Cruz, she's kicking their asses.

She shoves the guy sitting next to her. "Frankie needs a seat, and you look like you're gonna puke. Move it."

"Only if you promise to find me later," he slurs, and stands.

"Not if the fate of mankind depended on it." Cruz positions a shot glass in the center of the table and then pats the empty seat. "I wasn't sure you'd show."

I maneuver between the people watching and sit down. "Why not?"

Cruz flicks the quarter between her fingers. It hits the table once and bounces into the cup. "This neighborhood isn't exactly the Heights."

"I don't live in the Heights anymore. I moved in with my dad, in Westridge."

She nods her approval. Maybe I went up a notch. "Wanna play and help me prove to these boys that women are superior?"

I've played quarters before. Twice. My performance didn't rank in the superior range. I pick up a quarter anyway. My days of playing it safe are over.

"I'm in."

"Bring it." A wasted guy sitting across from Cruz slams his cup down.

She puts one elbow on the table, holding her arm straight up, with the quarter between her forefinger and her thumb. She squints and lets the quarter roll off her thumb. It bounces on the table and lands in the shot glass.

"Aw."

"Damn."

A chorus of groans travels around the table, but approving nods show the guys are impressed. Cruz pours syrupy red liquor from the bottle in front of her. Night Train Express. It smells like cherry cough syrup.

The guys slam their shots, wincing or shaking their heads like wet puppies.

"You're up, Frankie." Cruz slides a quarter in front of me. "Show 'em what you've got."

Nothing. That's what I've got.

I focus on the shot glass. *Don't overthink it.* I snap the quarter, and it bounces off the table and lands next to the cup.

"You know what that means." A guy across from us pours a shot, and everyone points at me. "Drink."

I chug the liquid, and it burns its way down my throat. It's the worst thing I've ever tasted. I cough, and the burning sensation moves into my nasal passages. "What's in that stuff?"

Cruz smiles. "You don't wanna know."

She nails her target, round after round, banking the quarter into the shot glass so many times I stop counting. I'm on a roll, too. The kind that ends with me drinking what I'm 99 percent sure is lighter fluid on every other turn.

"How are you holding up, Frankie?" Cruz nudges my shoulder, and it throws me off balance. She catches my arm and laughs. "I think you've had enough."

"Yeah. I'm done." I get up and squeeze past Cruz as gracefully as possible. Okay. I'm not exactly graceful, but I don't trip.

"Where are you going?" Cruz asks.

"I'll be in there." I point toward the front room with the deejay.

She nods. "Give me twenty minutes, and I'll catch up with you. These guys still have some money left in their pockets."

"Come on, don't go," another guy says. "You were starting to get the hang of it."

Cruz waves her hand over the table. "All right, all right. Settle down. She'll be back. And I'm not going anywhere yet, losers."

I squeeze past the crowd at the keg and the couples making

out against the wall. The inside of my mouth tastes like cherry cough syrup. A wave of dizziness hits before I make it to the living room.

I need some air.

Outside, smokers gather in a pack on the sidewalk. Someone whistles at me, but I keep moving.

My head is fuzzy in a good way, but I can't say the same about my stomach. The Night Train shots live up to their name. It feels like a train wreck in there.

A hunk of metal with no tires and a missing window is parked next to Cruz's car. Judging by the white-and-blue primer covering the car and the missing parts, it looks like it's either abandoned or getting an overhaul. When my head goes from fuzzy to woozy, the hood of the junker seems like the perfect place to sit.

Cool air settles my stomach enough to keep me from throwing up.

Even if I do, I'm glad I came tonight. I wasn't calculating my every move or feeling guilty about the choices I made—or didn't make. Maybe I *can* start over.

My stomach rumbles, and I take a deep breath.

Don't puke in the street at your first Monroe party. Definitely not cool.

The stars are out tonight. I close my eyes and pretend the last three months never happened.

Where would I be right now?

Who would I be?

A stressed-out senior at Woodley, playing a piano I don't

miss and torturing myself over college essays to get into a school I can't even remember if I liked? Instead of a sleep-deprived senior at Monroe, hanging out with a girl who street races and drinking shots of Night Train?

If Noah were still alive, I can't think of a single scenario that would end with me at a party in the Downs.

"Frankie?"

I know that voice. . . .

Marco.

My eyes fly open. He's standing on the sidewalk in front of the fender, less than two feet away from me. His black shirt clings to his arms and chest, outlining his muscles. He really is gorgeous.

"What are you doing here?" He asks the question as if I don't belong at the party, which immediately annoys me.

"I was *invited*." I press my hands against the hood of the car to brace myself.

"Are you alone?" He looks around. "Where are your friends?"

"Cruz is inside." I point at the house and realize too late that my aim is way off, and I'm pointing at the street. So much for acting cool.

A smile tugs at the corners of my lips, and I burst out laughing. I can't help it. Trying to act cool in front of a hot guy while I'm wearing ratty jeans and my eighth-grade soccer sneakers is ridiculous.

"You came with Cruz?" Marco cusses under his breath.

"I met up with her at the party." Now he's pissing me off. "What's your problem?"

132

"You're drunk and she let you come outside alone." His jaw twitches.

"Ugh . . ." I fall back against the hood for a second. "She doesn't even know I'm out here." I push myself back up, my legs dangling over the front bumper. "And I'm not drunk. I only had a few shots." I hold up two fingers in the shape of a V. "Girl Scout promise, or two-thirds of it, anyway."

Marco steps closer, and we're practically nose-to-nose. "Can you be more specific? Because you look pretty wasted, Angel." He closes his hand over my fingers and lowers my arm. My skin burns beneath his touch, and when my palm grazes the hood of the car, the nerve endings tingle.

How many shots did I drink? I lost count. "Five or six. And stop calling me that."

"Why?"

I push the hair out of my face and tuck it roughly behind my ear. He knows what happened. Everyone does. "I'm sure you heard that I got kicked out of my old school. I'm about as far away from being an angel as you can get."

"So you made some mistakes." Marco jams his hands in the pockets of his low-riding jeans, his eyes trained on the ground. "Compared to the crap I've done, you're a saint."

The pain and regret in his voice tug at my heart. He's hurting, and I want to make the pain go away.

For both of us.

"I don't believe that," I say softly.

Marco's eyes widen, and I stare back at him. Big mistake. Heat radiates from his body—a body insanely close to mine—and suddenly I feel exposed. I cover my face with my hands and take a deep breath.

Why did I drink so much?

"What's wrong? Did something happen in there?" He sounds worried.

"No," I say from behind my hands.

"If nothing happened, why won't you look at me?"

Because you'll know exactly what I'm feeling.

He touches my wrists and curls his fingers around them, moving my hands away from my face. Marco's eyes drill into me, and my heart crashes against my ribs.

"I'm just . . . uncomfortable." I motion between us. "I'm not used to *this*."

Marco looks confused for a second and steps back. "You mean me. I make you uncomfortable. Is that it? I'm a thug from the Downs. We're all alone and it's dark. I get it."

"I'm not scared of you."

"Yeah, I can tell." He sounds hurt.

"I'm not." I start to slide off the hood, but Marco leans over and boxes me in with his arms. Our lips are inches apart.

If I lean forward the tiniest bit . . .

His eyes drift down to my lips and then my neck. "So this doesn't bother you?"

It does. But not for the reason he thinks.

I've never wanted to kiss anyone as much I want to kiss Marco right now. I want to know what it feels like to have his arms wrapped around me.

Forcing myself to look into his dark eyes, I call his bluff. "Nope."

Marco doesn't move. He's sizing me up, deciding whether or not he believes my lie. If my heart beats any louder, he'll know.

"Prove it." A slow smile spreads across his lips. "Kiss me."

I wait for him to laugh. When he doesn't, I lay on the sarcasm. "After all the girls you've hooked up with, I wouldn't want to be a disappointment."

He doesn't break eye contact, and with just inches between us, the intensity is nerve-racking. "There's nothing disappointing about you, Frankie."

Marco's voice is full of need and desire—the same things I'm feeling. I try to memorize the way each word sounded so I can remember them later when I'm alone, when he isn't staring at me like kissing me is more important than breathing.

The possibility hangs between us.

I want to know what his lips feel like against mine.

Just once.

Would the kiss be fast and hungry or slow and deliberate?

The old Frankie never acted on her feelings. She never kissed a guy first. Instead, she waited for him to make the first move.

But I'm not the old Frankie, and I'm tired of waiting.

I lean forward and press my mouth against Marco's. The moment our lips touch, heat sears through my veins. He hooks his arm around my back and pulls me toward him.

My hands find his chest, fists clutching at his shirt. I can't get close enough.

Marco slides his tongue in my mouth, and there's nothing but hunger right now. Him and me. I swear, nothing has ever felt this good. He trails his fingers up my neck and into my hair.

My breath hitches, and his iron grip tightens around my back. I tug on his bottom lip, and he moans. "Frankie."

The moment my name leaves his lips, I come apart.

This is more than a kiss—too much more. I need to stop.

I break away first, and Marco stares at me glassy-eyed, his fingers still tangled in my hair.

This can't happen. Not with a guy who takes me apart with a kiss. I don't want to get attached to anybody now that I know how quickly someone can be taken away. I haven't even recovered my memories from the night Noah died. I need to be stronger, not more vulnerable. But I'm not admitting that to Marco.

I catch my breath and erase any hint of emotion from my voice, as if the kiss had no effect on me. "Was that enough proof?"

Marco smiles like he thinks I'm teasing him. It takes every ounce of strength I have not to smile back. When he realizes I'm serious, confusion flickers in his eyes. His shoulders tense, and he becomes all hard edges and sharp corners again. "So did I measure up?" he asks.

"What are you talking about?"

"Rich girls like you only kiss guys like me because you're curious. You want to see how a tattooed thug compares to a rich boy from Heights. I'm the guy you hook up with when you're pissed off at Daddy or you want to make your rich private-school boyfriend jealous." The second he says it, Marco cringes.

But the words punch holes in me like bullets. I put both

hands on his chest and shove him away. "Then you have nothing to worry about, because *my* rich boyfriend is dead."

Marco drags his hands over his face and stares at the ground. "I wasn't thinking, Frankie. I'm an asshole."

"You're right." I slide off the hood and walk away without looking back.

CHAPTER 16

CRITICAL LIFE SKILLS

After the party and my conversation with Marco, I can't sleep.

I shouldn't want him, but I do.

Worse . . . I want *him* to want *me*.

I need to stop thinking about him—and the kiss. And his expression when I pretended it didn't mean anything. He looked hurt, but it was probably shock. I injured his pride, that's all.

Marco wouldn't let a girl from the Heights have the upper hand.

By now everyone in the Downs probably knows I kissed him. That will make afternoons at the rec center fun. Listening to thirteen-year-olds gossip about me ranks right below attending another tree-planting ceremony.

If I know the kiss didn't mean anything, and I'll probably pay for every second of it at school on Monday, why am I still thinking about it?

When our lips touched, my fears fell away, and I felt safe for the first time since Noah died.

Noah.

My first kiss.

My first everything.

Why didn't my body melt into Noah's like that when he touched me? Why wasn't it more intense? Maybe I'm so emotionally screwed up that I can't tell the difference. It's easier to tell myself that than feel guilty about the truth.

Noah was so many things . . . a kick-ass lacrosse player and a terrible speller, a guy who would never turn his back on a friend or pass up seconds at Thanksgiving, the kind of guy who seemed so perfect that you wanted to hate him until he admitted all his flaws. He should've been the guy who melted me with a kiss. Not Marco.

Intensity isn't what I need.

Guys like Marco want girls they can get into bed. I'm not that girl. So why does his kiss still haunt me?

When it comes to Noah—the real ghost in my life—I find myself turning to the journal I started for Mrs. Hellstrom's class. Maybe writing Noah's story gives me a place to put all the fears and emotions I can't express out loud.

And maybe it will help me remember.

I pull the notebook out of my backpack and turn to a blank page.

Noah died in a parking lot in the Heights, seven days before his eighteenth birthday.

    Most people know that part of the story.

The son of a wealthy Washington, DC, entrepreneur being beaten to death on the pavement outside a club sent the local media into overdrive.

Every detail related to the crime became public knowledge.

Noah's time of death.

His blood alcohol concentration.

When the reporters ran out of relevant information and I refused to talk to them, they settled for whatever they could dig up. Interviews with Noah's teachers as they clutched tissues and chronicled his years of academic success. Photos of him wearing his lacrosse uniform or standing next to his father in the suits Noah hated wearing. His favorite food (Hawaiian pizza) and his favorite subject (history, according to his mom—but in reality, study hall).

The only parts of the story the press never figured out were the ones that actually mattered.

Who killed him.

And why.

Abel texts me way too early on Sunday morning, to ask if he can come by and talk. I'm still angry with him, but he never gets up early unless he has to, and Abel doesn't do serious talks. Those are two red flags.

I meet Abel in front of Dad's building. He sits slouched in

the driver's seat of his Land Cruiser, staring blankly at a plastic tricycle on the grass. I knock on the passenger-side window, and it takes him a moment to react.

He hits the unlock button, and I climb in next to him.

"Sorry. Rough night." Abel runs a hand over his face. He looks like crap. The shadows under his eyes are dark enough to pass for bruises, and there's no sign of his easy smile.

"What happened?"

Abel tightens his grip on the steering wheel. "Lex told me she doesn't want to see me anymore. I've never been dumped by someone who refuses to be my girlfriend."

"You lied to her more than once. What did you expect?"

"I screwed up. I get it. But this is about more than that. She's been looking for an excuse to bolt." Abel picks at a hole in his T-shirt. "After everything that happened this summer, I thought things would finally work out with us."

"What do you mean by 'everything that happened this summer'?"

He shakes his head. "I figured Lex told you. I guess it didn't mean anything to her."

"*What?* You have to give me more than that."

"We hooked up . . . more than hooked up." He hesitates, like he wants to get the next part just right. "We were together, like a real couple. Even if we never talked about it. But the closer we got, the more it scared her. She used the gambling as an excuse to walk away."

Together, like a real couple.

They slept together. That's what he means.

It's the part Lex keeps leaving out. My best friend lost her virginity with our other best friend, and she didn't tell me.

Why am I surprised? I spent the whole summer avoiding them both. But Lex kept calling and e-mailing. She never gave up. She even picked me up on the first day of school and acted like nothing had happened.

Abel rests his forehead against the steering wheel. "Who ends a relationship before it even starts?"

His question plays on repeat in my mind, daring me to answer.

It's after midnight, and I'm in the kitchen getting a drink when I hear the apartment door close and the sound of keys hitting the counter. Dad is home.

I'm not in the mood for an argument.

I'll just ignore him.

When I see my father, I stop short.

His perpetual five-o'clock shadow resembles the beginning of a patchy beard, and the long hair around his face that he normally slicks back hangs in his eyes. He looks like the kind of guy I would cross the street to avoid walking past. Dad slouches deeper into the dark hoodie he's wearing over a pair of baggy jeans and boots.

"Sorry about this." He gestures at his clothes. "I always changed out of my work clothes before I picked you up at your mother's. But if you want to catch criminals, you have to look like one of them."

"It's fine." I shrug.

"How about a truce? Maybe we can talk like a regular father and daughter." He's offering me an olive branch. Dad kicks off his boots and puts them in the hall closet.

"You said not to put shoes in there."

"I said not to put *your* shoes in there. That's where I keep my work clothes."

Now I'm curious.

When I was young, the hall closet was off-limits because that's where Dad kept the lockbox for his gun. I've peeked in the closet a few times since then, usually around Christmastime when I was searching for my presents. But it's always the same old stuff—ugly jackets and what I assumed were Goodwill donation boxes.

I take a closer look.

The ugly coats hang crammed together on the rod—canvas construction coats, hoodies, and a tacky leather jacket. The boxes are still there, too. One is full of shirts and thermals, and the other holds shoes and belts. The only new additions are the stack of jeans and a black knit hat on the shelf above the rod.

"Why do you keep all this ugly stuff in here?"

Dad turns on the kitchen faucet and digs his nails into a bar of green soap he keeps next to the sink. "I can't wear my regular clothes when I'm on the street."

I understand why he needs a different car when he's working, but different clothes?

"If RATTF raids a chop shop or we make a home arrest, undercover troopers like me wear ski masks. But criminals pay attention to details, especially if they can't see your face. A jacket with a patch or a rip in a specific spot, a discontinued pair of sneakers—that's how they ID us. A trooper on the Homicide Team had his cover blown because a suspect recognized his high-tops."

I sit down at the table. "Were they an unusual color?"

"Nope. Just red and white. But one of the sides was worn down from the way the guy walked. Combined with the color, that was all the suspect needed." He dries his hands and grabs a Diet Pepsi.

"Why haven't you told me about anything like that before?" I know the basics.

My father is a Maryland State Police trooper on a task force that targets auto theft rings and chop shops. On the street, people think he and his partner, Tyson, are car thieves. But I had no idea that Dad has two separate wardrobes or that he wears a ski mask during busts.

He shrugs. "You never asked."

It's true.

"Your mom wasn't a big fan of talking about my job. I just assumed you wouldn't be, either." Dad finishes off his Diet Pepsi and grabs another can. "There aren't a lot of happy endings. We bust a lot of crews, but it's hard to nail the brokers who make the deals to sell the stolen cars and parts. Unless we catch them and break the chain, a new crew will crop up, and it starts all over. You don't want to hear about depressing stuff like that."

"Wait. You quiz me about things like how to track the route

a kidnapper drives if I'm blindfolded and the fastest way to get out of handcuffs before he kills me, but you think your work stories are depressing?"

"Those are—"

"Critical life skills," I finish for him. "I know. But practicing serial killer evasion isn't exactly a mood booster."

"I worry, that's all. I wanted to be home more while you were getting settled, but we're in the middle of an investigation." He rubs the back of his neck. "I don't usually work this many nights. I never asked if you were uncomfortable staying alone."

"I'm not alone. Cujo is here."

"Your mother called to check on you, and she wasn't thrilled when I mentioned it."

"Since when do you take orders from Mom?" It's an obvious move on my part, but it usually works. "If something happened, Cujo would protect me, right?"

The Akita barks when he hears his name.

Dad nods. "He won't let anyone come through the door unless you let them in."

"Then everything is fine."

"Would you tell me if it wasn't?" He leans against the counter, watching me.

It's a cop thing. He's looking for a gesture or an expression that will reveal what I'm feeling. But what Dad knows about me is surface-level stuff. That's how well he knew the old Frankie. When it comes to the new Frankie, he doesn't have a clue.

CHAPTER 17

PROXY

Lex pulls into Lot B on Monday morning, and I look for Marco's Mustang. I spot the sloped back end right away. But today he isn't standing next to his car with the hood popped.

The lightness I felt on the ride over instantly vanishes, replaced by the familiar weight that I'm tired of carrying. After a weekend of thinking about Marco—or trying not to—I wanted to see him. I'm still angry about what happened between us at the party, and I didn't plan to talk to him. But I won't lie. The way he kissed me . . . it felt like more than a hookup.

I don't see Cruz, either, or her yellow Nissan.

English will suck more than usual.

Lex picks through the receipts and gum wrappers on her console. "Do you see a folded piece of loose leaf paper anywhere? It's my calculus homework."

"Hold on." I push around the empty soda cans on the floor with my foot. "If you cleaned out this car once in a while, you wouldn't lose things every five minutes."

"Thanks for the tip, Mom." She leans between our seats and digs through a mountain of clothes.

Across the street, students pile out of a yellow school bus parked in front of the admin building. As it pulls away, I catch a glimpse of Cruz on the sidewalk, her long ponytail swinging behind her. She's walking next to Marco, cradling her arm.

Is she wearing a cast?

They enter the building through the side door near the stairs to the basement.

"It's not up here, Lex." I grab my backpack and get out. "I'm going inside. I need to get something out of my locker before English."

"Okay." She gives me a strange look. Last year I would've waited for her.

"See you later." I close the car door and rush across the street. I didn't talk to her about Abel. I'll bring it up later.

When I get inside, I jog down the steps to Shop. The metal door is cracked open, like someone forgot to pull it shut.

"Why didn't you call me?" Marco's voice drifts into the hallway.

"Because you would've done something stupid." Cruz sniffles.

I peek through the crack. They're standing in front of the Camaro with Chief.

"She's right," Chief takes his cap off and scratches his head. "And the cops are who you should be calling."

147

Cruz doesn't seem like the kind of girl who cries easily, and if Chief wants the police involved, then whatever happened must be serious.

"No *cops*." She spits out the word like it is cigarette ash in her mouth. She turns her back on Chief, offering me a clear view of the white first-aid sling supporting her arm.

I burst into the room, not caring if I'm intruding. "What happened?"

Cruz swipes at her eyes with the back of her uninjured hand. "My dad went after my little sister Teresa and"—she raises her arm in the sling—"I got in the way."

"He hit you?" I've seen plenty of movies with abusive fathers—drunks stumbling around in dingy white tank tops, the ones the kids at the rec center call wifebeaters. But none of my friends' fathers had ever laid a hand on them.

"More like he grabbed it and twisted." She closes her eyes. "It's not the first time."

"It's the *last* time, or he'll end up in the ground." Marco shoves his hands in the pockets of his jeans and stares at the floor like he's trying to drill a hole in it.

The last time I saw him we were kissing . . . and yelling. My lips tingle just thinking about it. Why is that kiss so hard to forget?

Marco looks up. I try to turn away and avoid an awkward moment, but I'm not quick enough. His eyes soften, and I feel the kiss all over again.

I turn my attention back to Cruz, where it belongs. "What are you going to do about your dad?"

She bites her nails. "I've got bigger problems right now."

Bigger than her dad practically breaking her arm?

"Maybe Chief is right about calling the police," I say gently.

"Whose story do you think my mom will back up? His or mine?" Cruz swallows hard. "I'll get thrown out of the house."

Chief drops down into the passenger seat of the doorless Camaro, stone-faced. "Or the police believe you and lock him up."

Cruz shakes her head. "Until Child Services gets the police report, declares my mom an unfit parent, and sends my sisters to foster care."

Marco slides his cell out of his back pocket and reads a text. His expression darkens. "Shit."

"What's wrong?" Cruz asks.

"Deacon knows." Marco bolts for the door.

"I'm coming with you," she says.

He stops. "No, you're not. If Deacon sees you in that sling, he'll kill your dad. Stay here."

Her bottom lip trembles as Marco tears up the stairs. I walk over and loop my arm through her uninjured one, the way Lex does whenever I'm upset.

Cruz looks over at Chief. "If Deacon finds my dad before Marco gets to him . . ."

"He won't really kill your father, will he?" I ask.

"I don't think so, but with Deacon . . . you never know. He's unpredictable. It's the reason we broke up. That and his temper."

"Did he hurt you?" After hearing what Cruz's father did to her, I'm afraid to hear the answer.

"Cruz is probably the only person he'd never hurt." Chief

takes his cap off again, then puts it back on a second later. "I failed with Deacon. Got to him too late. A kid can only take so many beatings until the good gets beaten out of him, too. It's a damn shame. The only person I've seen in years who drove a car better than Deacon or Marco is you."

The color drains from Cruz's face, and she covers her mouth. "I'm supposed to race on Thursday, and I'm right-handed." She can't shift.

Chief climbs out of the Camaro and points an angry finger at her. "You shouldn't be racing at all, unless it's on a track. You and Marco are going to get yourselves killed. What will happen to your sisters then?"

Her hand shakes. "I don't have a choice. Someone has to pay the rent, buy food—"

"I've heard this song before." Chief dismisses her argument with a wave. "When Deacon got expelled. When Marco dropped out of all his AP classes. When you and Marco started racing. I'm ready to hear a new one."

Marco was in AP classes? Why would he drop out?

The bell rings.

"Get to class." Chief takes a seat in his chair. "Unless you're ditching, too."

Cruz's shoulders sag as she heads for the stairs.

I wait until we reach the top before I steer her toward the stairwell. "Can you postpone the race until your arm heals?"

Trying to talk her out of racing is a waste of time. She can't snap her fingers and change her situation just because I ask.

Right after Noah died, mom begged me to pull myself

together—to hang out with my friends at Woodley and pick up where I left off like Noah's death had never happened.

Can't we move on? she asked me a hundred times.

Can't you forget? That's what she really meant.

I can't rewrite history any more than Cruz can find a job that pays a seventeen-year-old enough to cover rent—or trade a father who hurts her for one who takes care of her.

"It doesn't work that way." She wipes underneath her eyes with the hem of her shirt, and the mascara smudges disappear. "The race is Thursday night. If my car isn't in it, it's an automatic loss." She inhales. "I won't be able to make rent, and I'll owe money I don't have."

"How much?" I still have two hundred dollars.

"Twelve hundred."

I could swallow my pride and ask Mom for the money. But Cruz probably wouldn't take it, and the offer might offend her. I have another idea. "You said your car has to be in the race. Does that mean someone else can drive it?"

"Yeah, but—"

"What about Marco?"

"Nobody would ever be stupid enough to agree to let Marco drive proxy. He's too good."

Think.

"What about someone nobody knows? Someone who has never raced before?"

She shrugs. "I guess. But if the person doesn't know anything about racing, they'd have no chance of winning."

"I will if you teach me."

Cruz stares at me like I'm crazy. "You would do that?"

I can't tell if she's asking because she likes the idea or hates it. "If you think I have a chance at winning."

"We'd have to start practicing tonight." She rubs her arm through the sling and winces.

"Are you okay?" I hate seeing her in pain, and I hate her father for doing this to her.

She squeezes her eyes shut and takes a deep breath before opening them again. "I'm good. What time are you free?"

"I finish working at the rec center at seven." I'm really doing this.

"I'll meet you in the parking lot. My other sister Ava is a sophomore. She can drive us in my car."

There's no way I can get out of riding with Lex, not without an airtight story. "Actually, that won't work. Can you meet me near my dad's apartment in Westridge instead?"

"You name the place. Just text me the address. I'm not showing up to class with mascara all over my face and my arm in a sling. Put your number in here for me." She hands me her cell.

I add my number and return the phone. "I'll see you tonight."

"This is more than a favor, Frankie. If you do this, I'll owe you." She's serious. I hear it in her voice.

"You don't owe me anything. That's not why I'm doing it." I want to help Cruz. I think of her as a friend, and she wasn't racing for fun.

She shakes her head and smiles to herself. "It makes sense."

"What does?" I ask.

"Why Marco is crazy about you." She takes off down the hall, leaving me speechless.

Did Marco actually say that to her? Or anything remotely close to it?

I climb the stairs to the second floor and walk to the end of the hallway, where a window overlooks the quad. The side door opens and Cruz slips out, leaving the same way she came in. Time to face Mrs. Hellstrom alone.

I'm about to head to English when I notice someone else crossing the quad toward the parking lot.

Where the hell is he going?

If Abel wants to sneak around, he needs to stop wearing a dead rock star's leather jacket.

Lex drives faster than usual on the way to the rec center.

Does she know Abel left school before first period? Did they have another fight?

Lex weaves between lanes, and I feel seasick.

"I need to talk to you about Abel. I saw him ditching this morning before first period."

She pulls at the ends of her hair. "Why do you care? You have new friends now."

Her comment hits a nerve. "I'm going to ignore that."

"What about Abel?" I try again. "Do you know why he left?"

She pulls into the rec center parking lot. "No. And I don't care." The pain in her voice says otherwise.

"Yes, you do."

"But I wish I didn't," she says softly.

Cruz chose a parking garage for our first lesson, which seemed like a strange place to practice street racing. But she insisted it was perfect. Her cousin worked the evening shift, so he could play lookout.

When we arrive at the garage later that night, Cruz's cousin raises the electric arm and waves us through. Ava grinds the gears, and Cruz cringes. "Easy. You're going to wear out the transmission."

Ava glares at her. "Guess you should've given me driving lessons when I asked last year."

"Just stop on the second level and let Frankie take over before you give me a heart attack."

Ava hops out on level 2 and sits on the trunk of a stranger's Lincoln Town Car with her legs crossed. "I'll watch from here. I value my life."

Not encouraging. "So what's the plan? How do you race in a parking garage?"

Cruz laughs. "You don't. I'm teaching you how to get off the line when the flagger gives the signal. If you can't do that, there's no race." She points at the ramp. "Stop halfway up."

"I'll never get the car out of first gear fast enough without stalling or rolling backward."

"Are you saying you can't drive stick?" she asks.

"It's been a while. Am I racing uphill?"

"Getting off the line fast is all about the bite point. If you can't tell when the clutch engages, you'll stall on the line and the rest won't matter." She points at the ramp. "Let's do this."

I drive halfway up and stop.

Cruz runs her hand along the dash and takes a deep breath. "Try to go easy on her. Technically, she isn't mine. If we screw anything up, I have to fix it or cough up the money to pay someone else to do it. And if we total the car, I have to replace it. A Nissan GT-R in this condition isn't easy to find."

Great. No pressure.

"Who owns the car?"

"A guy named Kong. He owns King Kong Bodyworks. He lends us his cars, and he gets a cut of whatever we win racing. It's like a lease."

"Does he own Marco's car, too?"

"Yep. Mine, Marco's, Deacon's, and a few others. It works out for everyone. We're the only people on V Street with top-of-the-line cars who aren't dealers. Everyone else buys a piece of shit and puts their money under the hood." Cruz's expression turns serious. "This stays between us, right? Kong is a good guy, but the cops won't see it that way."

"Yeah. Of course."

"Are you ready to do this?"

"I think so." I have no idea.

I press the clutch to the floor and shift into first gear. I let up on the clutch and give the Nissan some gas, trying to synchronize the two movements. The engine revs along with my pulse, and the car starts rolling backward.

"Brake!" Cruz shouts. "Don't hit the wall!"

I slam my foot against the brake pedal, and the Nissan jerks to a stop.

"Don't worry. I'll get it."

"If my clutch survives." Cruz rubs her temples and exhales slowly. "Straighten out the wheel and try again."

After thirty minutes of stalling and sliding backward, I'm ready to give up.

"Stop overthinking it, Frankie. Trust your instincts."

In theory, it sounds easy. But after all the wrong turns I've taken—the choices I let other people make for me and the bad ones I made on my own—trusting myself feels impossible.

With the clutch pinned to the floor, I shift into first again.

I can do this.

One foot is on the clutch, the other on the brake. I picture the pedals on a piano, the way my feet controlled them as my fingers danced across the keys. Playing the piano requires a firm but delicate touch . . . and timing. Getting up this ramp can't be harder than playing Mozart's Concerto no. 19 in F Major.

I release the clutch, balancing the weight between the pedals, easing up on the brake and pressing down on the gas. The car starts rolling backward, and my first instinct is to hit the brake again. But I feel the clutch catch.

A little more gas . . .

The car springs forward, and the engine revs higher than it should. I shift into second gear, and the GT-R launches up the ramp.

Cruz smiles. "See. Piece of cake. Now let's do it a couple more times."

"Okay." I don't move. "This is just a ramp, Cruz. I'm guessing a race will be a lot harder. Maybe we need to come up with a plan B?"

"You *are* plan B."

CHAPTER 18
PERFECT PITCH

It's only eight o'clock in the morning, and I need a nap. Practicing on the ramp last night was nerve-racking. I lean against my locker and zone out. I don't see Marco until he reaches over my shoulder and puts his hand on the door above me. He angles his body, caging me in on the other side, and looks down at me.

My mind flashes back to the kiss, the way his lips felt against mine. Without thinking, I touch my mouth. Marco sucks in a sharp breath.

He's so close. The scent of leather and citrus envelops me.

The only interaction we've had since the kiss and the disaster that followed was with Cruz before school yesterday, and it didn't involve talking to each other.

"I have to go."

"Don't leave," he whispers, warm breath tickling my neck. "I was waiting for you."

"Why?" I pretend he isn't inches from nuzzling my neck.

"To say I'm sorry." For yelling at me or kissing me? Marco shifts, and his chest brushes my shoulder.

Why does the slightest physical contact with him send my pulse into overdrive?

Because you made out with him on the hood of a car, and it was the most amazing kiss you've ever had.

"Don't worry about it."

"Does that mean you accept my apology?" he asks. "Only an asshole would make a comment like that after what happened to your boyfriend. I wasn't thinking."

"It's fine." I try to maneuver around him, but Marco steps in front of me and I plow into him.

He catches me by the shoulders. "It's not fine—not what I said or what happened to him."

The hallway is packed. Footsteps echo. Locker doors slam. Voices become muffled and distorted. I can't have a flashback now—not in the hallway in front of everyone. Not in front of Marco.

"I don't want to talk about it." It's a plea.

Marco nods and lets his hands slide down my arms, his brown eyes locked on mine. "Why did you kiss me, Frankie?"

It's the last question I expected him to ask, and I don't have an answer—not one I'm willing to say out loud. The bell rings, and students rush down the hallway like the building is on fire.

"Because you were drunk, right?" he asks.

Say yes and he'll leave you alone.

"It doesn't matter." I step around Marco and walk into the crowd, but I hear him call out behind me.

"What if it matters to me?"

"What's going on between you and Marco Leone?" Lex asks the minute we pull out of Lot A. "And don't say nothing, because everyone is talking about you two."

Perfect.

Lex tightens her grip on the wheel. "If you don't want to tell me, then just say so. But don't lie to me."

I pull at the loose threads on my shoelaces. "I'm not sure."

"But *something* is going on?"

I lean back against the headrest. "We kissed. Once."

And I've thought about it a hundred times since then.

Lex chews on her bottom lip. "Were you going to tell me at all?"

"Were you going to tell me you slept with Abel?"

"Fine. We're even." Her shoulders sag. "But you don't want to get involved with Marco. You'll be the one who gets hurt."

"We're not involved. We kissed one time." Knowing how Lex feels about Marco, I'm uncomfortable talking about him with her. We ride the rest of the way in silence, something Lex used to hate.

"How's your hand-eye coordination?" Cruz asks later that night. We're on a dead-end street behind an old recycling plant for more street-racing prep. The whole place reeks of wet newspaper.

"Why? Are we playing tennis?" I'm in a rotten mood. At school today, I overheard Abel on his cell talking about bidding on something.

Cruz gives me a strange look. "My racket is in the shop."

"Stupid joke."

"You think?" Cruz angles her body toward me. "Back to the original question. Do you have good hand-eye coordination or what?"

"I can play treble and bass clef scales on the piano simultaneously, which, musically speaking, is pretty badass."

Cruz taps on the gearshift. She's all business tonight. "Then it's time to teach you the hard part."

"Wait. I thought the ramp was the hard part."

"Getting off the line will make or break you in a race. But even if you don't stall, you've still gotta shift from first gear to sixth as fast as possible." She taps on the plastic in front of the speedometer and gas gauge. "The tachometer will let you know when it's time to shift into the next gear."

Don't stall on the line. Watch the street and the tachometer. Get to sixth gear fast. That's not complicated or anything.

"Frankie? You ready?" Cruz watches me expectantly.

Will she kill me if I say no? "Yeah."

"I'm gonna count to three."

I position my feet on the pedals and shift into first. A little gas, and the six-cylinder engine roars to life.

"One."

The tachometer reads five thousand RPMs. Exactly where I want it.

"Two."

"Three."

I dump the clutch too fast, and the car jerks to a stop. "Shit."

Cruz taps on the dashboard. "Back up and try again."

I stall two more times before I start listening—not to Cruz but to the engine.

On my fourth attempt, I hold the GT-R at five thousand RPMs as Cruz counts down.

The engine revs. . . .

I hear it and my feet synchronize. I hit the gas, let off the clutch, and with tires squealing, the car flies off the line.

My eyes dart between the street and the tachometer. The arrow shoots up. When it hits a little over nine thousand, I feel the pull that tells me to shift to the next gear. I repeat the process, trying to watch the tachometer and the road at the same time, until I hit fourth gear and realize I don't need to check the RPMs anymore.

When the engine reaches the magic number, it revs at exactly the same pitch and intensity. All I have to do is listen.

"Check your tach!" Cruz barks from the passenger seat. "If you push her too hard, the engine will blow."

Tuning out Cruz's voice, I listen for the ramping sound that means the car has hit nine thousand. Relying on my ears instead of my eyes makes sliding into fifth and sixth gears faster and smoother.

The GT-R crosses the mock finish line, and I circle around to where we started. "How was it? Don't sugarcoat it."

"Slow." Cruz doesn't sound annoyed. "You have to check the tach. If you lose the race, it's one thing. Frying my engine is something else. I'd owe Kong more than a cut of my winnings."

"I don't need to look at the gauge. Listening to the engine is easier. I figured it out when I hit fourth gear."

Cruz shakes her head like she's trying to wrap her mind around what I told her. "Hold on. Are you saying you can already hear when it's time to shift?"

"Yeah. The engine makes this whirring noise like it's winding up, and the pitch spikes."

"Uh-huh." She stares at me like I just told her I could read minds. "Do it again."

It takes three more runs before Cruz believes me. Who knew perfect pitch was good for more than singing and playing an instrument?

I fall into bed that night with my shoulders aching, proof that every minute was real. Another feeling eclipses the pain pounding my body.

Pride.

The old Frankie finally brought something valuable to the table.

CHAPTER 19
BFFS

I make it to English just before the bell the next morning. Cruz is already sitting in the back of the classroom, her silver-studded black-leather high-tops propped on the chair in front of her. I take a seat next to her.

"So what's going on between you and Marco?" she asks the moment I sit down.

"I don't know what you're talking about."

"Marco doesn't stand in the hall and stare at girls or beg them to talk to him."

As usual, I search through my backpack for a pen. "There was no begging involved."

"That's not what I heard from my sources in Lot B this morning."

"Please take out your journals." Mrs. Hellstrom waves a

composition notebook in the air. "Hopefully, everyone spent some time writing, because your first assignment is due today. Of course, I would never ask my students to engage in an activity without doing it myself. So I'll start by reading from my journal."

We're screwed. She's one of those teachers who thinks we'll be inspired if she participates in this experiment along with us. Mrs. Hellstrom dives into a painful selection about what a loser she was in high school, pausing at the more dramatic moments.

Cruz kicks my chair and holds out her hands in a *what the hell?* gesture.

I tear off a piece of paper and scribble the words across it. I'm not about to risk someone overhearing me say them out loud.

We kissed.

Folding the scrap in half, I pass it to her.

"No shit?" Cruz blurts out when she reads it.

"Miss Vera Cruz," Mrs. Hellstrom snaps, her arm extended with the open journal balanced on her palm. "You may not use that kind of language in my class."

"Sorry," Cruz says. "Your writing is just so . . . deep. You know?"

A few people turn around and look at Cruz like she's crazy. Not Mrs. Hellstrom. She raises her chin proudly. "Thank you, Miss Vera Cruz. Please watch your language in the future."

When Mrs. Hellstrom finishes, she closes the notebook and waits as if she expects applause. "Who else would like to read?

Don't be shy." No one volunteers. "A show of hands. How many of you completed the journal assignment?"

Two hands go up.

A guy in the back fake-coughs. "Liars."

I'm not the only person who doesn't want to bare my soul.

Instead of admitting defeat, Mrs. Hellstrom gives us the rest of the class period to catch up. The minute she turns away, Cruz kicks my chair again.

"Let's get back to Marco kissing you."

I'm not sure if telling her was a good idea, but it's too late.

I lean closer. "Actually, *I* kissed *him*. He basically dared me to do it."

Cruz raises her eyebrows. "Uh-huh."

"I'm serious."

"So you just kissed him?" The hint of a smile plays on her lips. "At least that explains why he was following you in the hallway like a puppy."

"You're exaggerating."

Mrs. Hellstrom looks up.

Cruz waits until she returns to her book, then whispers. "I've known Marco since elementary school. He doesn't follow girls around."

Mrs. Hellstrom snaps her book shut and we all jump. "Ladies. We are working, not talking."

"Sorry, Mrs. Hellstrom. I'm still having trouble writing with my left hand. Frankie was giving me tips."

Was Cruz serious about Marco?

Did he really act differently around me? If he did, why me?

People *were* staring at us in the hallway. Then again, Marco always attracts attention at Monroe, on V Street . . . probably everywhere he goes.

Cruz chews on the end of her pen between pages. She came up with a genius solution to the journal problem early on. She's making hers up. Technically, the writers of her grandmother's favorite telenovela are doing all the work. The hopes, secrets, and fears in Cruz's journal belong to Anna Maria Cortez, daughter of a powerful cartel leader.

I flip through the pages of my journal. Did I really write this much?

The old Frankie never wrote anything creative or risky. Essay topics were chosen based on how many similar papers popped up in an online search. If less than a few dozen hits showed up, she picked another subject. At Woodley, safe kept you out of the headmaster's office and in the teachers' good graces.

I take a deep breath and clear my head.

Noah and I argued the night he died.

I didn't want to stand in line at the Sugar Factory, the current "it" club with a bouncer that accepted twenties as stand-ins for IDs. I didn't want to get dressed up and eat sushi for the third time that week. I didn't want to ride in his father's new Lexus SUV, with a backseat big enough to guarantee another "will we or won't we" sex conversation.

But I gave in, maintaining the status quo like the perfect girlfriend Noah wanted, programmed to say and do all the right things. Maybe if I had been a little less Barbie Dream Girl, Noah would still be alive.

That was the thing about Noah—he wasn't a selfish jerk. He cared about me. Anything I gave up—or every time I gave in—it was my choice. I know that now. Making everyone else happy always mattered more than making myself happy.

The Sugar Factory lived up to its name—white walls, mirrored ceilings, chandeliers, and a blond selling Ecstasy in the ladies' room.

"It's like one of those LA clubs I was telling you about," Noah said as he dragged me between the dance floor and the leather sofas. At least we weren't in the back of the SUV.

We danced, my arms hooked around Noah's neck, and everything felt perfect.

Perfect club.

Perfect boyfriend.

Perfect life.

The song changed, from can't-catch-your-breath fast to let's-do-it-right-here-on-the-dance-floor slow.

When my head started pounding from the music, Noah decided it was time to leave.

He told me to wait inside. I didn't.

I wish it made a difference.

I wish I could remember that bastard's face.

The bell rings, and I jump.

"Hand in your journals on the way out." Mrs. Hellstrom takes a seat behind her desk.

I tuck mine in my backpack. I haven't figured out how to avoid turning it in without failing English in the process. But I'll have to find a way if I want to graduate.

Cruz finishes writing a sentence. "Let's see what Mrs. Hellstrom thinks about Anna Maria Cortez hooking up with her sister's boyfriend."

"You did not write that." Her soap opera makes my journal seem a little less dramatic.

She waves her notebook in the air. "This is good stuff. I'm gonna get an A. Watch."

As we walk down the center aisle between the desks, I panic. "I can't give her my notebook, Cruz."

"Why not?"

I tighten my grip on the strap of my backpack. "I just can't."

One by one, my classmates drop their notebooks on Mrs. Hellstrom's desk as she watches. We're at the end of the line, with only two people ahead of us.

"Thank you, Mr. Navarro. Miss Denning." Mrs. Hellstrom nods her approval. Cruz adds hers to the pile. "Miss Vera Cruz."

Our teacher watches me expectantly. "Where is your journal, Miss Devereux? I noticed you writing in it just before the bell rang."

My mouth goes dry. "I can't turn it in yet."

She frowns. "Why not?"

"Umm . . ."

Cruz cuts in, rolling her eyes. "Frankie wants it to be perfect before you read it. Isn't that crazy?" she asks, as if the two of them are best friends swapping secrets.

Mrs. Hellstrom gives me a reassuring smile. "Nothing we write is ever perfect."

"See?" Cruz nudges me and turns back to our teacher. "That's exactly what I told her, but she won't listen. It's probably a writer thing. You must know what it's like, Mrs. Hellstrom. I mean, you're a writer. Does this ever happen to you?"

Mrs. Hellstrom sits straighter. "Of course. It happens to *all* writers."

"Maybe Frankie could have a little more time?" Cruz asks.

"I'm not here to judge, Frankie. That's not the purpose of the assignment, but I do need to know you're working."

"Oh, she's definitely working." Cruz opens my backpack and grabs my notebook. I lunge for it, but she pivots away from me. She tucks it under her chin and flips through the pages with her good hand. "Look at all this."

Mrs. Hellstrom is too far away to read the words, but I snatch the notebook from Cruz anyway and clutch it against my chest.

"How much time do you think you need, Frankie?" Mrs. Hellstrom asks.

"I'm not sure. I'm still trying to figure out where it's going."

She nods and straightens a stack of papers on her desk. "Why don't you check in with me on Friday?"

Not the response I was expecting. "That would be great."

Cruz grabs my sleeve and drags me out. "Gotta go or we'll be late for Shop."

"Did that really just happen?" I ask Cruz as soon as we're in the hallway and out of earshot.

170

She glances at my sneakers. "You can bet your sad-looking Adidas it did."

"Seriously, Cruz, I owe you."

"Technically, you owe my grandmother. She says people can learn everything they need to know about life from a good telenovela. And you can't owe me, since I already owe you."

Today when we walk down the hall, I only attract a few stares.

"Thanks." I need to hold on to the journal, and not just to keep my English teacher from reading my private thoughts. Ever since I started writing in it, I've remembered more and more about the night Noah died.

It might be a coincidence. But what if it isn't?

Cruz throws me a sideways look. "You don't have to thank me. We're friends. That's the kind of stuff BFFs do for each other, right?"

"Yeah." Lex would do anything for me—not that I deserve it after the way I've treated her. "But Lex has never pulled off a performance like that to save my ass with a teacher. That's probably normal best friend stuff at Monroe."

"I wouldn't know." Cruz stares straight ahead, owning the hallway as usual. "I've never had a best friend before."

CHAPTER 20

TITANIUM

When Lex drops me off at the rec center, I bypass the front steps—and the raunchy basketball rejects who never seem to play any basketball—and walk behind the building. I slip a furry mouse-shaped toy out of my pocket and look around for Cyclops. I bought it last night at the grocery store when Cruz decided we had to celebrate my triumph over the ramp with powdered donuts.

There's no sign of Cyclops, but he'll end up back here sooner or later if Marco keeps bringing him milk from the vending machine. I leave the fur mouse next to the rotted playground structure where I saw Marco feed him.

As I circle back around to the front, I catch a glimpse of a Dodge Charger parked near the Section 8 apartments across the street—Dad's undercover car. The matte-black paint job and cage of metal bars protecting the bumper and front end make his car unmistakable. Dad's partner, Tyson, lights a cigarette and slouches against his vintage Crown Vic. Dad hassles him about driving the car model favored by police departments all over the country, but Tyson says that's why he chose it. A car thief who drives a Crown Vic isn't afraid of anyone.

I don't see Dad, but he must be nearby.

Tyson watches the apartment building next to him, his ebony skin and pretty-boy bone structure partially hidden by the folds of his navy hoodie.

What are they doing here?

Dad said they never work in this part of the Downs. It feels strange, as if the two different worlds I live in suddenly intersected without my permission, and I make a quick dash for the glass doors.

Inside, the kids in my group are listening to music, dancing, and playing games on their cell phones instead of studying. The moment I walk through the door, Daniel calls out, "Hey, Frankie. We thought you ditched us."

I drop my backpack next to my usual seat. "You're not that lucky. Why isn't anyone working?"

"We had an assembly today," Daniel explains.

Sofia smiles. "Which means no homework."

Carlos turns up the music playing on his phone. "That's right."

"Don't you have any long-term projects?" I ask. *Like a private journal your English teacher expects you to turn in?*

Kumiko and her friends dance in a circle. "It's only the first month of school."

I flip open my chemistry book and take out a piece of paper. "Just don't get me in trouble with Miss Lorraine."

"Deal." Kumiko swings her hips to the beat of a pop song the radio stations play a hundred times a day.

For the next three hours, the kids dance, talk, and text while chemistry kicks my ass. It's almost six thirty when I finally give up. The song changes, and the second I hear the melody, my blood turns to ice.

"Titanium"—the song that was playing at the Sugar Factory right before I went outside.

The room heats up, and a wave of dizziness rolls over me.

Noah's baby-blue polo shirt—

"Frankie? Are you okay?" Sofia asks.

"She doesn't look so good." Daniel.

A guy with a blurred face—

I want to tell the kids I'm okay, but I can't get the words out. . . .

Noah shakes his head at me—

"She needs help." Kumiko's voice is the last thing I hear.

I drop to my knees and duck between two cars just as the first hit catches Noah in the jaw. His head snaps back, then falls forward. An uppercut meets Noah's chin and slams his head back again.

Threads of blood and saliva splatter across his shirt.

My body convulses, and I cover my mouth to keep from gagging.

Another hit from the side. Noah sways and falls. His back slams against the asphalt with a sickening thud. The guy with the blurred face grabs Noah's collar and pulls him up so he can hit him again and again and again.

Blood. Everywhere.

The pink glow from the club marquee and the stench of stale beer and copper pennies.

The bastard's arm cocking back over and over and sounds I will never forget—the crunch of bone against bone, the back of Noah's head cracking against the shiny black asphalt.

The guy with the blurred face stands, his hands coated with blood so dark it looks black. He wipes Noah's blood on the front of his hoodie.

Noah isn't moving. He's lying on the ground, bleeding and broken, arms splayed out at his sides.

The bastard laughs and says something to Noah.

Why can't I hear him?

I want to close my eyes—to stop seeing.

"Frankie?" Someone calls my name.

"I think she's gonna pass out, bro."

"Move!" Another voice.

The room tilts, and I force my eyes open.

Black splotches . . . white cardboard ceiling tiles. I feel myself being lifted, or maybe I'm falling.

"Hang on, Frankie." A guy's voice.

The sound of metal scraping against concrete, followed by a blast of cool air on my skin. I suck in a long breath, and the dizziness settles into ripples instead of waves.

I'm leaning against someone's chest, and the familiar mix of leather and citrus clings to his skin. Marco. His heartbeat races, his chest rising and falling beneath my cheek.

"I'm okay," I mumble.

"Bullshit." It's definitely Marco.

"Frankie, I need you to look at me." Miss Lorraine.

My eyelids flutter.

It's dusk, and darkness spreads across the blue-black sky like spilled paint. Miss Lorraine and Sofia kneel next to Marco, whose arms stay clamped around me.

Miss Lorraine brushes the hair away from my face. "I'm going to call your father."

"No." I bolt upright, almost smacking my head into Marco's chin. "My dad's at work, and he's already worried about me."

Miss Lorraine touches Sofia's shoulder. "Go inside, sweetheart. She's okay."

Sofia nods and walks toward the emergency exit. When she's inside, Miss Lorraine presses her fingers against her temples. "You need to see a doctor. You almost passed out."

If I don't explain what happened, she'll call my dad. But if I do, Marco will find out how screwed up I am.

"Please don't call." I rub my hands over my face.

Miss Lorraine's expression darkens. "Did you take something? Pills or—"

"I don't do drugs." I'm out of options. "I have PTSD."

Marco smooths my hair, and I realize how much he saw. He carried me outside and had a front-row seat to the Frankie Devereux Show.

"I have flashbacks from the night—" I don't want to say this in front of him.

She rests her hand on top of mine. "I know what happened. You don't have to talk about it unless you want to."

176

I never want to talk about it again unless I can identify Noah's killer. My eyes burn, but I won't let myself cry. "When the flashbacks hit, I get dizzy. I've seen tons of doctors, and they all say it's normal."

Normal if you're broken and glue isn't strong enough to hold you together.

"Are you being straight with me, Frankie?" Miss Lorraine's eyes drill into me.

"I swear."

"I'm trusting you. Don't make me regret my decision." When Miss Lorraine reaches the exit door, she points at me. "And I want to see you before you leave tonight."

My cell vibrates in my pocket, and I slide off Marco's lap and sit in the dirt next to him. It's a text from Lex.

running late. senator's fault.

Great. Now I get to stay here and answer questions. I chuck the phone, and it lands in a patch of dirt in front of me.

Marco touches my shoulder.

I shove his hand away. "You can go inside. I don't need a babysitter."

"I'm not leaving you alone." Marco hesitates. "That's what happened the first day we met, when I got into the fight in the quad. You had a flashback?"

Just hearing the word makes me cringe and reminds me that I can't leave the old Frankie behind. The flashbacks are proof, and now Marco knows they happen all the time.

He knows what a mess I am.

I jump to my feet, desperate to put space between us. "Why do you care if I'm alone or if I have flashbacks? I'm not your problem."

He stands, too. "What if I want you to be?"

It hits me, and I realize what's going on. "Why? So you can add me to the list of girls you've slept with at Monroe? I hear it's a long list."

"Who told you that?"

"Are you saying it's not true?" I ask as Marco walks toward me. "Or was the Frankie Devereux freak show a turnoff? At least you can tell your friends why the new girl lost her appeal. I don't want to ruin your track record."

He looks me in the eyes. "I won't tell anyone what happened, Frankie."

"Eventually, you will."

I imagine walking through the halls, hearing the whispers and feeling the stares. Knowing what a basket case I am is hard enough. How will it feel when the whole school finds out?

Marco closes the distance between us. He touches my face, tracing a path across my jawline and over my bottom lip. "You don't know me as well as you think. If you give me a chance, I might surprise you."

CHAPTER 21

NOTHING TO LOSE

"Guess what my mother springs on me last night? Jonathan Strathmore," Lex says as we drive back from the rec center on Thursday night. It's seven thirty, and I'm racing for Cruz in less than two hours.

"The idiot from Saint John's?"

She nods. "The one who wears pastel V-neck sweaters all the time. He looks like he raided the wardrobe of an eighty-year-old golfer. My mom wants me to go to the gala with him."

"What did you tell her?"

"I said no." Lex leans over the steering wheel and frowns as she pulls up to Dad's building. "Isn't that your mom's car?"

Mom's Lexus is parked next to Dad's Tahoe.

This is not good.

I didn't expect Dad to be home, let alone both my parents, who can't stand being together in the same room.

"Do you want me to come in with you?" Lex pulls into the space on the other side of the Tahoe. "Your mom won't make a scene if I'm there."

"Yeah, okay."

When we get to the door, I hold a finger up to my lips, signaling her to be quiet. My parents' voices are muffled, but they're talking.

My original plan for tonight was to hop in a cab as soon as Lex dropped me off, but that's clearly not going to happen now.

I open the door. Mom is perched on the edge of the sofa, and Dad is standing across the room. They both look relieved they aren't alone anymore.

Mom stands and rushes toward us. "Frankie. It's so good to see you, sweetheart." She leans in to hug me, but I pretend not to notice and slip past her. She doesn't even flinch and turns to Lex. "It's nice to see you, too, Lex."

"Thanks, Mrs. Rutherford."

"What's going on, Mom?" We both know she wouldn't show up here without a reason.

"I've been trying to reach you, but I keep getting your voice mail. So I decided to stop by and give you the good news myself."

Dad rubs the back of his neck.

"Richard met with the dean of admissions at Stanford, and he is willing to interview you. Isn't that fantastic? They rarely grant interviews, but Richard talked him into it."

How much did that cost him?

"I never wanted to go to Stanford, Mom. It's a great school, but I didn't feel comfortable there when we visited." She opens her mouth to respond, but I'm not finished. "It wasn't the right place for *me*."

Mom presses her lips together. "It's the right place for anyone lucky enough to get in." She looks at my father. "Did you turn her against the idea of going to Stanford?"

Dad raises his eyebrows and laughs. "It looks like you did that all on your own, Elise."

"It has nothing to do with Dad. I'm not going to the interview."

Mom's posture turns rigid. "People don't turn down interviews at Standard, and you won't, either. Are you determined to sabotage your future?"

"Maybe your mother is right, Frankie." Dad says. "You don't have as many options as you did before."

"I'm tired of everyone bringing up my mistakes."

Mom crosses her arms. "Then you should stop making so many."

"I'm sorry my mistakes are limiting your opportunities to live vicariously through me." I storm back toward the apartment door, and Lex scrambles to keep up. I'm done talking to my mother. "Dad, I'm going to study at Lex's. I'll text you when I get there."

"Frankie! Don't you dare leave while we're having a conversation." Mom's composure cracks.

I turn around and face my mother. "A conversation requires two people, which means we haven't had one in a long time."

Lex follows me out and catches up with me at the bottom of the stairs. "I feel bad leaving your dad in there. Your mom looked like someone just told her that she's carrying a fake Chanel bag."

I don't have time to enjoy the moment. The race starts in an hour and a half. Mom's surprise visit gave me an excuse to get out of the apartment without making Dad suspicious, but it won't matter if I'm late.

I wait until Lex pulls out of Dad's complex before I ask her to drop me off.

"Why would I leave you at the gas station?" she asks.

"I need to catch a cab." I avoid giving her too many details.

"Where are you going? I thought you said you were coming to my house."

"There's something I have to do first."

"We shouldn't be here." Lex studies the crowd on V Street.

"Cruz promised no one will hassle us." I should say *me* because Cruz has no idea I'm bringing Lex.

"And you believe her because . . . ?"

After arguing with my parents, I'm not in the mood to fight with Lex. "I told you I'd take a cab."

"Right. Then I'll turn on the news tomorrow and find out that Hannibal Lecter is making a coat out of you." Lex weaves around couples hooking up against car bumpers and people checking out the gleaming engines under popped hoods. "I just don't get it."

"I'll explain later. I promise."

And then you'll freak out.

"I don't put as much stock in promises these days." Under normal circumstances, Lex wouldn't let me get away with a cop-out answer like that, but she's too busy worrying to notice.

I spot Cruz standing with Ava next to the GT-R. "Come on."

Even in my tightest pair of black jeans and a T-shirt that is clingier than the ones I normally wear, my Sambas and unfussy waves don't exactly blend in.

Lex sees Cruz and rolls her eyes. "Your new best friend is over there. What's with the sling? Did she get injured assaulting someone?"

"Her father jerked it out of the socket. Does that count?"

Lex bites her lip and trains her eyes on the ground. "Is she okay?"

"No. Cruz was supposed to race tonight. She needs the money to pay her family's rent."

"What's she going to do?" Lex sounds genuinely concerned.

This is the part where I tell her the reason we're here and she kills me. I keep walking. "If someone else races Cruz's car and wins, she still gets the money."

"She should get Marco to race for her," Lex says. "Aren't they super close? And he can drive his ass off."

Here goes. "That's the problem . . . he's *too* good. And the guy Cruz is supposed to race has to agree on her proxy."

Lex squishes her eyebrows together.

"The person racing for her." I have roughly thirty seconds

before Lex figures out why we're really here. The universe decides to throw in some extra drama—Cruz sees me.

She walks toward us, slipping through the crowd like a pro. "You made it. And you brought your friend."

"Yeah. You remember Lex, right?"

Cruz leads us to the curb across from the row of cars, where it's less crowded. She tips her chin at Lex. "How's it going? Did you come to cheer Frankie on?"

Shit.

"Cheer her on?" Understanding flashes in Lex's eyes and she turns to me. "She doesn't mean—"

"It's no big deal. The whole thing takes less than a minute." I try to sound reassuring.

"Are you completely insane?" Lex drags her hands through her hair. "Did you forget what happened when Abel screwed with the wrong people here?"

"It won't go down like that tonight." Cruz rushes to cover for me. "Frankie is just driving. If she loses, I'm the one who is on the hook for the money. Not her."

Lex ignores her and stares at me. "I would tell you not to do this, but I'll save us both some time and skip to the part where you won't listen."

"It's going to be fine. I swear."

Lex covers her ears. "Stop. Ever since Noah died, I've watched you take bigger risks, walking closer and closer to the edge. I won't watch you jump. I'll be in the car when you're done."

Cruz stares at Lex as she walks away. "Sorry. I figured she knew."

"It's not your fault." I should've told Lex before we got here.

"I won't give you any shit if you're having second thoughts."

"I'm not."

Cruz lets out a sigh of relief. "Then I've got good news. Pryor agreed to race to the halfway mark, so you won't have to turn around and come back to the starting line. And he's gonna give you a car length." I must look clueless, because she adds, "It means you get to start the race a car length ahead of him. Plus he's racing an RX-7 he bought a week ago. He hasn't lowered it yet, or put on the airdam or the rear wing. He hasn't even replaced the shocks or tuned the engine yet! It will be slow as hell."

"Why would he give me an advantage?"

"He isn't thinking about it that way. You're a rich girl from the Heights who has never raced before. He doesn't think you have a chance."

Rich girl from the Heights—will that label ever stop defining me? In Mom's world, it's an asset. Here, it's a liability.

"Do you think I have a chance?"

"I'm letting you drive my car, aren't I? Besides, winning is easier when you've got nothing to lose."

Hearing the words out loud shocks me into silence. I've been telling myself that, but is that really who I am now?

A girl with nothing to lose?

I used to worry about every aspect of my life—the way I looked and the clothes I wore, my GPA, practicing the piano or *not* practicing the piano, every word that came out of my mouth and the way other people interpreted them. The list was end-less. Everyone else's opinion mattered more than mine.

I'm done carrying the weight of the old Frankie's fears and other people's expectations. The day Noah died, he had no idea that it would be his last.

My future could end tomorrow, and if it does, I want to remember racing Cruz's car.

And winning.

CHAPTER 22

RACER GIRL

A lanky guy with pockmarked skin stands next to an RX-7 painted an obnoxious shade of neon green that gives me a headache. He tips his chin at Cruz. "You ready or what?"

She leans against her car, hip cocked to the side. "Just waiting on you, Pryor."

Pryor gives me a slow once-over, his eyes lingering everywhere they shouldn't. He licks his lips and leers at Cruz. "You don't have to wait on me. I'm ready whenever you need some love."

"Which will be the same day they pass out fur coats in hell," Cruz says under her breath. She opens the passenger-side door and gestures at the driver's side. "Get in. I'll ride with you to the line."

As we drive past the crowd, people tap on the roof of Cruz's

187

car. Some even wish me luck. Others give me dirty looks. Pryor waits at the starting line, and I drive past the RX-7 until Cruz tells me to stop.

"Remember not to hit the gas until *after* her arms drop, and don't let off the clutch too fast—" She stops talking, and her expression darkens. "Shit."

A figure walks up to the passenger side. I catch a glimpse of Deacon's baseball cap and streaks of angry scars in my peripheral vision. Cruz angles her body toward the window and props her good arm on the ledge. She's trying to hide her sling.

Deacon bends down to her eye level and studies me behind the wheel. "When did you start teaching driver's ed, Cruz?"

"Don't be a jerk, Deacon. Frankie's a good driver, and she wants to race."

I sit up straighter and raise my chin, hoping I'm worthy of the compliment.

"Marco is gonna lose his shit when he hears about this." Deacon laughs. "But you knew that, didn't you?"

Cruz looks away.

Why would Marco care if I race Cruz's car?

Deacon tucks a toothpick into the corner of his mouth, studying Cruz. "You're the reason Chief asked Marco to help him work on his piece of shit Chevy tonight. I didn't know you were such a good liar. Was Chief in on it, too?"

"Of course not. He hates street racing."

Deacon's pale blue eyes darken, and he leans closer. "At least I'm not the only person you lied to."

Cruz's breath catches. "Deacon—"

"Let me see your arm." He yanks open the door.

Cruz flies out of the car. "Did you do something stupid?"

"Your asshole of a father won't hit you again."

I tighten my grip on the steering wheel to keep my hands from shaking.

"Are we racing or what?" Pryor calls out.

Deacon turns around, the veins in his neck bulging. "Keep talking and you won't be able to race."

Pryor shrinks back against the seat. "Sorry, man."

Cruz grabs Deacon's arm. "Tell me what you did."

"Less than I should've. But Teresa was home, and I didn't want to scare her." Is he serious? I wasn't even there and I'm scared. Deacon shrugs. "I broke his wrist . . . maybe his arm, too. I don't know. But I dislocated his shoulder for sure."

Cruz doesn't even flinch as she texts faster with one hand than I can with two. "What if he calls the cops?"

"What's your dad gonna tell them? That he got his ass beat for pushing his daughter around?" Deacon tries to read over her shoulder and she shoves him.

After a moment she relaxes. "He didn't call the cops. At least, Teresa doesn't think so. She says he's in his room, and Mom keeps sending her to the kitchen to get bags of frozen vegetables."

Deacon brushes Cruz's ponytail over her shoulder. "See? Everything's all good." He gestures at me. "Until Marco finds out that you let her race."

"I'll deal with Marco." She taps the roof of her car and pokes her head through the window. "Are you ready?"

189

"Yeah."

Cruz walks over to where Video Game Girl stands on the curb, twirling her hair like she's bored.

"You look good in the driver's seat," Deacon says before he jogs away and joins Cruz on the curb.

I'm not sure if he's making fun of me, but I feel powerful behind the wheel of Cruz's car. I wish my mom could see me right now. Would an Ivy League girl be sitting in the driver's seat of a modified GT-R, getting ready to haul ass in an illegal street race?

The RX-7 roars, and headlights blind me in the rearview mirror.

I block out the sounds around me—people shouting, music pumping, engines revving. It's a skill I perfected to survive a summer of country club condolences. The distance is a quarter mile, although technically less, with the lead my rich-girl-from-the-Heights status earned me.

After practicing for hours on the garage ramp and the dead-end street, I understand the delicate balance between letting off the clutch and giving the car enough gas. And thanks to years of piano practice, I know when to shift gears just by listening to the subtle differences in the sound of the engine, without looking down at the tachometer.

Video Game Girl takes her place in front of us, her waist-length black hair arranged in two high braids like pigtails.

I press the clutch to the floor and shift into first gear. Then I give the car just enough gas to keep it at five thousand RPMs, walking the tightrope between moving and staying still.

Video Game Girl raises her arms. Exhaust burns my nasal passages. Headlights blink behind me as Pryor signals that he's ready. I follow his lead and flick my headlights on and off the way Cruz taught me.

The floorboards vibrate against my feet, but I hold them in place.

Any second now . . .

Her arms drop, and my foot slams on the gas pedal.

I shift into second, and Cruz's car lurches forward as I slide the gearshift from second gear to third, fourth, fifth, and up to sixth in rapid succession.

Adrenaline shoots through my veins, and my pulse rages.

The rush is insane. That's the only way to describe the speed—a rush of adrenaline and energy, rubber and metal.

The steering wheel shakes like the Nissan is fighting for control. I hear Cruz's voice in my head: *Keep your eyes on the finish line and the pedal on the floor. Don't worry about the other car.*

Up ahead, the finish line is only a few car lengths away, and the RX-7 hasn't pulled in front of me. I steal a glance in the driver's-side mirror and watch the splash of neon green grow smaller and smaller.

Wait? Why isn't Pryor's car moving?

The Nissan streaks across the finish line and I brake, but I don't know if I actually won the race.

Why would he stop?

Did I jump the line? If I did, it's an automatic loss, and he wouldn't have bothered to keep going.

I flip a U-turn and drive back to the starting line and the

crowd at a normal speed. If I screwed up, I don't want to know yet. For a few more seconds, I want to enjoy the rush.

Cruz runs toward the car, waving and smiling. I stop just shy of the starting line. She opens the door and pulls me out with her good arm. "I can't believe it. You smoked his ass."

"Does that mean I won?" I ask.

Cruz laughs. "Hell yeah."

I won.

A smile stretches across my face. "I had a head start."

"And his engine flooded, but this isn't NASCAR. We don't give trophies for second place. You won." Cruz leads me through packs of spectators, and I can't stop smiling. Strangers pat me on the back and congratulate me.

My heartbeat still hasn't returned to normal when an arm latches on to my wrist and pulls me through the crowd, away from everyone—bands of black ink wrapping around beautiful tan skin. My legs are numb from the vibrating floorboards, and I stumble.

Marco whips me around and stares back at me, our faces only inches apart.

"How long have you and Cruz been planning this bullshit behind my back?" Anger rages in his eyes, and a frown line cuts between his brows.

"I don't know. A few days?"

People walk around us, giving Marco a wide berth.

"You need to calm down, Marco," Cruz says evenly. She's beside me again, but she sounded more confident when she was dealing with Deacon.

"Don't say anything right now, Cruz. You lied to me." He shakes his head, his chest heaving like he's about to explode. Deacon warned her that Marco wouldn't be happy about me racing. Apparently, it was the understatement of the year.

"The whole thing was my idea," she says.

"No, it wasn't." I'm not letting her take the fall for me. "I offered."

"You offered?" Marco's brown eyes drill into me. He gave me the same look after I kissed him at the party—a mixture of shock and confusion. "Of course you did."

Marco turns his back on me and stalks toward the grass.

"What's that supposed to mean?" I ask, following him.

"Frankie, wait," Cruz calls after me.

"Hey!" I'm right behind Marco. "You can't say something like that and walk away."

He makes it to the grass, then turns around so fast that we almost collide. "What the hell were you thinking?"

"Umm . . . I don't know," I say sarcastically. "How about Cruz needed someone to drive her car so she could pay the rent?"

"That's not your problem."

"She's my friend."

Marco presses the heels of his hands against his forehead. "Your *friend*? You hardly know her."

"You're pissed off because I'm friends with Cruz?" It hurts coming from Marco, but I won't give him the satisfaction of letting him know.

"Hold on. That's why you think I'm angry?" He shakes his head as if my response doesn't make any sense.

"If that's not it, then what's your problem?" Because I don't have a clue.

"Street racing is dangerous. You could've been killed. Or arrested." Marco hesitates as if he wants to say more but he's holding back. "Is that what you want, Frankie? Because every time I turn around, you're doing something reckless. Jumping into fights. Showing up here with Lex and a wad of cash. Getting wasted at a party with people you barely know. And now you're racing Cruz's car. What's next? Skydiving without a parachute?"

The last time we talked, I was in flashback freak-out mode. He probably thinks I'm crazy.

"Unless you're suddenly perfect and I missed the memo, you don't get to judge me," I yell, even though anger isn't what I'm feeling. I'm scared—of Marco and how easily he sees the truth about me. Of myself and how much I can't see.

"Say whatever you want about me, Frankie. Odds are if it's bad, it's probably true." Marco rubs the back of his neck, dark clouds churning in his eyes. "I'm a screwup. But you aren't. Promise me you won't do anything that stupid again."

Why does he care?

My eyes burn, but I won't cry in front of him. "I just want everyone to leave me alone."

Marco reaches out and touches my cheek. "You sure about that?"

I stare at my sneakers.

His expression softens. "Every once in a while, the universe gives us what we ask for, so just make sure you're asking for the right things."

"What do you ask for?"

Marco looks stunned, as if no one has ever bothered to ask him a question like that before. We aren't as different as he thinks. Part of me wants to tell him that—to take some of the sadness out of those brown eyes—but I've already let myself get too close.

"I want Sofia to graduate," he says finally. "To go to college and get out of the Downs. I want Cruz's dad to stop beating the crap out of her."

"None of that is for you."

He keeps his gaze focused on me. "There's no room in my life for what I want."

"But if there was?"

"I still couldn't have it." Marco stares at the ground between us, hands shoved in his pockets. "Some things aren't meant for guys like me."

CHAPTER 23

UNSOLVABLE EQUATIONS

The ride back from V Street consisted of lots of apologies from me and icy stares from Lex. I avoided the subject of my risky, ledge-walking behavior, and she didn't bring it up, either. Instead, Lex tortured me with the street-racing statistics she looked up online while I was racing—fun stuff like the number of annual deaths and arrests.

Lex is still angry with me the next day, and she barely talks to me on the way to school in the morning. We're halfway to the rec center in the afternoon when I try to break the ice.

"I'm sorry I didn't tell you about the race."

"Why would you?" She shrugs. "You don't tell me anything."

"That's not true."

She looks over at me. "Are you serious right now? Before you started at Monroe, we hardly talked at all. When Noah died, you shut me out. I called and texted you all summer, and you almost never responded. And if I tried to make plans or come over, you gave me a bullshit excuse. I thought things would change when you transferred to Monroe, but now instead of ignoring everyone, you only ignore me. If you didn't need me to drive you to school and the rec center, I'd probably never hear from you."

She's right, and it kills me.

"I'm sorry."

Lex pulls into the parking lot and cuts the engine. "Don't be. You have new friends, and if you don't want to hang out any- more, just say so. Because I'm tired of being the only person in this friendship."

The thought of not talking to Lex at all makes me realize how important she is to me. "I screwed up, Lex. It's just . . ."

I'm the shittiest best friend in the history of shitty best friends.

"What?"

"It was you and me and Abel and Noah for such a long time. And it's hard to think about him."

Her expression softens. "That's what this is about? I thought you were trying to replace me."

"I just wanted to forget."

Lex throws her arms around me. "As long as you don't forget about me, too."

I hug her back, and my eyes flicker to the front of the building.

The three shirtless basketball players are watching us. Two of them flick their tongues at us, and the third guy has added a new crude gesture to his repertoire.

"Look."

Lex glances at them. "They really are assholes."

"Agreed."

She gestures at the door. "Now get out of here before you end up with more community service. I'll pick you up at seven."

I watch her drive away as I walk up the hill.

Dirt clings to my sneakers, and I realize it's everywhere. I never paid much attention before, but there's almost no grass around the rec center—not even under the abandoned playground structures behind the building.

Dad said there is no grass on the playgrounds in 1-D. At least the ground here isn't littered with dirty needles and burnt aluminum foil. In a strange way the rec center feels like an island all its own—a place safe from the world around it.

It's not the Heights. The air here smells like rubber and damp soil, salt 'n' vinegar potato chips, and the perfume aisle in a department store, but that's okay.

The air smells like something else, too.

Asphalt.

The scent gets stronger, and I hear Noah laughing. . . .

"You're such a liar." I'm barefoot, in cutoffs and a tank top.

"I'm not lying." Noah shrugs, wearing board shorts and his X Games T-shirt. "It's my favorite smell after cotton candy."

I roll my eyes. "Then you're the only person in the universe whose second-favorite smell is asphalt."

He circles around me on his Mongoose and does a crazy trick. "Want to know why?"

I put my hands on my hips. "Not even a little bit."

198

Noah flips a 360 on the back wheel. "It reminds me of riding my bike in the summer. That's when they fill the potholes and my wheels get the best spin."

"Whatever. I hate bikes."

Noah grins at me. "That's because you don't know how to ride one."

"I never should've told you!" I storm down the sidewalk, my long hair swishing behind me.

The real world starts to seep in from the corners, the way a sheet of paper burns if you hold a match at the bottom.

The rec center's glass doors . . .

Dirt on the ground where there should be grass . . .

The images fade, taking young Frankie and young Noah with them.

"Hey, Frankie?" Noah calls out. "If you want to learn how to ride, I'll teach you."

I put my hands on my knees and take a deep breath. But I'm not shaking or dizzy, and my heart isn't racing. The flashbacks are changing. This one wasn't even about the night Noah died.

Why now?

Why this memory instead of the one I need?

I don't want to remember random moments from our childhoods. I want to remember a *specific* moment from the night at the Sugar Factory.

I'm still trying to make sense of it when I walk into the room where my group meets. The kids are hanging out. I tell them it's time to start working, and I take out my chemistry book.

Daniel points at my book. "Need any help?"

I flip it around so he can see the cover. "Are you any good at chemistry?"

Carlos laughs. "Daniel can't even add."

Daniel punches him in the arm, clearly embarrassed. "Shut your mouth, or I'll do it for you."

"All right. Let's get to work," I say. "Or Miss Lorraine will kick your butts, and mine."

While the kids pretend they're doing homework, I tackle my own. Without my overpriced science tutor to interpret the foreign language in my textbook, just copying the equations correctly feels like a win. Unfortunately, I doubt my chemistry teacher will agree.

Mom would hire me a tutor if I asked. But I'm not calling her. She's still texting and leaving messages about the Stanford interview.

Three hours later, Sofia and I are alone, as usual. She pulls her chair next to mine, and we wrestle with our homework side by side. What I remember from eighth-grade algebra would fit on an index card, but I do my best to help her.

I'm not as lucky. After four failed attempts at solving the same chemistry equation, I shove the textbook over the edge of the desk, and it smacks against the floor. "I officially give up."

"Shouldn't you give an impressionable young mind a more positive example?" Marco stands in the doorway grinning, his muscular arms crossed over a chest I've imagined shirtless more than once. He's the perfect combination of strong and cut without being overdeveloped—the kind of body most guys spend all day in the weight room to achieve. Marco probably doesn't even work out.

But I'm still not happy about the way he acted after the race, even if he did say something that might mean he has feelings for me.

"Don't give Frankie a hard time," Sofia says as she puts away her homework. "Her science class seems really awful."

Marco strolls over and picks up the book. "Chemistry, huh? Want some help?"

Is he joking?

Sofia slings her backpack over her shoulder. "He's good at science." She turns to Marco. "Can I hang out in the gym until you're done? There's a basketball game."

He nods. "Don't go anywhere else."

"Got it," she says and takes off down the hall.

Marco holds up my chemistry textbook. "Want me to take a look?"

"You're serious?"

He puts the book on my desk and places a hand over his heart. "You doubt me? There's a lot more to this package than a killer smile."

Marco comes around to my side and glances at the top of my paper. Then he flips to the page that has been taunting me all afternoon. He skims it quickly, his brows furrowed in concentration. "This isn't that bad." He sits in the empty seat next to me and reaches for my pencil. He holds out his hand. "Paper?"

Handing him the paper, I rack my brain for a smart-ass comment—until he starts writing.

"It's not as complicated as it looks. You're just balancing equations." He points at the directions at the top of the page.

"You need to end up with the same number of atoms on both sides."

I stare at him, my mouth hanging open. "How do you know all that?"

Marco copies the first problem, which I had solved incorrectly. "I took AP Chemistry last year." He stops writing and studies me. "Let me guess—you assumed I was stupid because I'm from the Downs?"

"I didn't expect you to be in AP classes because you got suspended the first day we met." I don't want him to know that Chief mentioned anything to me.

Marco seems satisfied with my response and works through the first three problems with me. Sofia is right; he's a good teacher. He frowns a little when he concentrates, and I'm having a hard time keeping my mind on chemistry.

"Are you in any other AP classes?" I want him to tell me why he dropped them.

Marco clenches his jaw and draws triangles in the margin of the scratch paper we're using. "Not since last year."

"Why not?" It's none of my business, but the more I learn about Marco, the more I want to know.

He pushes his chair back and leans forward, hands clasped between his knees. He keeps his eyes trained on the floor. "My life got screwed up, and last year it all caught up to me."

The raw emotion in his voice makes it seems like the wounds are still fresh.

Without thinking, I touch his shoulder. Marco's pain feels familiar, like we're haunted by similar ghosts. He flinches

202

beneath my fingers, and I start to pull my hand away. He catches my wrist and lets his thumb drift to my palm, tracing tiny circles on my skin.

"If I asked what happened, would you tell me?"

Marco pulls my hand in front of him along with his and slides his fingers between mine. My skin tingles.

I'm afraid to move. We're holding hands. What if it was an accident? But he closes his other hand on top like he's worried I'll let go.

I won't.

He takes a deep breath. "My mom died of cancer when I was thirteen."

"I'm sorry." I squeeze his hand.

"It happened fast, which is good, I guess, because she didn't suffer long. But my old man was already screwed up, and her death threw him over the edge."

"What do you mean by 'screwed up'?" I'm praying he doesn't tell me his father is a drug addict or an alcoholic who beat his kids.

"My dad used to street race in high school. Someone on the NASCAR circuit heard about him, and my dad ended up racing for real. But his career didn't last long, and he came back here and married my mom. He always drank, but when she died, he started racing again—on the street, at the track. Anywhere he could lose money."

"Is that who taught you to race?"

Marco clings to my hand. "Yeah. But only because it's easier to con people into racing a fourteen-year-old."

What kind of father pimps his son out to race for him? My mom always chose Richard over me, Lex's parents have no idea where she is 90 percent of the time, and Abel's mom drinks her way through life one glass of wine after another. But none of them have ever used us to make money.

"I'm sorry."

Marco's frown deepens, and he runs his fingers over our joined hands. He raises his eyes and looks at me for the first time since he started talking about his father. "You know what sucks? That's the happiest part of the story."

I know how it feels to carry a story inside you—one that you want to share with someone, but you can't find the words. "If you don't want to talk about this anymore, I understand."

"This might not make any sense, but I want to say it out loud. Deacon, Cruz, people in my neighborhood—they know what happened. But I've never told anyone else."

And he chose me.

Marco clears his throat. "Racing didn't satisfy my dad for long. He wanted more money and the respect he lost when his NASCAR career ended, so he upped his game. He stopped racing cars and started stealing them."

His father is a car thief—the kind of criminal my dad spends every day trying to catch.

"That's what he was doing the night of Sofia's accident. The asshole was delivering a stolen car. It was Sofia's birthday. He promised to take her out for ice cream after they dropped it off. But the cops caught up with him first." Marco lets my hand slip out of his and folds his arms over his head, shielding himself.

"He crashed the car. All those NASCAR races he won . . . and he crashed the car. Maybe if the cops weren't chasing him, he wouldn't have crashed." His breathing grows heavy, and he shoves the desk in front of him. The metal legs screech across the floor.

"Is that how she got the scars?" I ask softly.

He nods. "It was a vintage car, so the windows weren't made of safety glass. The windshield sliced Sofia up when it shattered, and she was trapped inside." Marco jumps out of the chair and paces, as if it's physically painful for him to stay still.

"What about your dad? Was he all right?"

He slumps against the whiteboard behind him. "The asshole walked away with a few bruises. Actually, he *ran* away." Marco takes a deep breath. "He left her, Frankie. And the cops didn't know Sofia was in the car. Her head didn't reach the top of the seat, and by the time the cops caught up to the car, my dad was already running."

Without thinking, I'm out of my chair and across the room. I pull him against me and wrap my arms around him. His heart pounds against my cheek.

"The car flipped, and it was crushed. She couldn't get out." Marco buries his face in my neck and leans against me, his breathing ragged. The weight he's carrying bears down on me, heavier than my own.

"Did the police figure out she was in the car?"

"No. Deacon lived up the street from where they crashed. His dad used to beat the crap out of him, and they got into it that night. Deacon was walking it off, and he saw the accident.

He had to climb through what was left of the windshield to get her out."

The scars on Deacon's neck and arms—the ones that look like someone slashed him with a knife.

"I wasn't there," he says softly. "I should've been there."

"It's not your fault. Sofia is okay. More than okay. She's smart and funny and beautiful. She's fine."

Marco pulls back and looks at me. "You think she's beautiful?"

"Don't you?"

"Of course I do. But not everyone sees past her scars. What happens when some guy won't go out with her because of them?"

"Sofia can handle it. Sometimes scars make people stronger."

Before I realize what he's doing, Marco presses his lips against mine.

My mouth tingles, and the sensation travels all the way down to my toes. The Night Train must have dulled my senses the first time we kissed, because as incredible as that kiss was— this one sets every nerve in my body on fire. My hands move to his chest, and his heart pounds beneath them.

Marco responds by drawing me closer. His tongue finds mine, exploring and teasing. He tugs on my lip with his teeth, and I fall apart.

Our bodies melt like they belong together.

Like *we* belong together.

But I can't belong to anyone again.

I pull back and turn to lean against the whiteboard next to

him, breathless. "This isn't a good idea . . . whatever we're doing." Making out?

Kissing Marco feels like more.

He pivots in front of me and cages me against the white-board with his arms. "Why does it feel like you're always running away from me?"

Because I am.

If I was braver, I'd tell him the truth—that I'm scared to feel anything or need anyone.

He runs his hand along my cheek, and I close my eyes. I'm feeling too much again, and all I want to feel is nothing. "I can't do this."

"Why not?"

Because if I let myself feel one thing, I'll feel everything. Because if my walls come down, the dam inside me will break, and I'll drown. Because I can't risk losing someone else I care about.

I stare at the ground, hiding behind the long waves falling over my shoulder.

Marco tucks my hair behind my ears and raises my chin. "I don't want to stay away from you, Frankie. I'm not even sure I can. But I'll try if that's what you want."

The thought of not seeing Marco—of not touching him—rips at the seams holding me together. I suck in a trembling breath. "It's not."

He pulls me against his chest and kisses his way up my neck until he reaches my ear. "What are you so afraid of?"

"Everything," I whisper.

"Me too."

CHAPTER 24

THE SAME SKY

I don't want to stay away from you, Frankie. I'm not even sure I can.

I replayed my conversation with Marco over and over last night instead of sleeping, and those are the words that make me smile into my pillow. With his arms wrapped around me and his breath against my skin, he seemed so vulnerable.

Burrowing deeper under the covers, I close my eyes and remember kissing him. Our hands aren't the only parts of our bodies that fit perfectly. When we kissed, it felt like we were made for each other.

My cell phone rings, and it takes a few seconds to untangle myself from the covers. It's probably Lex. "Hello?"

"Frankie?" I hear Marco's voice at the other end of the line, and I sit up with a jerk. He asked for my number last night, but

I didn't think he would call. Not right away, on Saturday morning, while I'm daydreaming about him.

A rush of warmth spreads through me.

"If it's too early, I can call back later."

"Don't call back," I blurt out. "I mean, it's not too early."

"You sound like you just woke up."

And he sounds amazing.

"How can you tell?" I ask, suddenly self-conscious.

"Your voice is even sexier than usual."

Sexy? I've been called cute and pretty and, once in a while, even beautiful. But not sexy.

I laugh. "I think you might need a hearing aid."

"There's nothing wrong with my hearing. You have the kind of voice that keeps guys up at night."

I'm speechless.

"So . . . I wanted to ask you something." He hesitates. "Were you serious last night about not wanting me to stay away from you?"

I wind a section of my long hair around my finger. "Were you?"

"I wouldn't be calling at ten in the morning if I wasn't."

"I was serious."

"Are you ever going to ask her?" Sofia whisper-shouts in the background.

Scratchy muffled sounds come through from Marco's end, like he's covering the speaker. I hear him say, "Close the door." Marco returns to the line. "Sorry."

"He wants you to come over tonight," Sofia yells louder this time. "For dinner." She squeals, and a door slams.

"I guess you heard all that," he says sheepishly. "Any chance you want to come over later? I'll make dinner."

Dinner at his house . . . he's asking me out. "You're going to cook?"

"Yeah. I have to feed Sofia. I hope you don't mind hanging out here."

"That's fine, especially if I'm getting dinner out of it," I tease. "Let me check with my dad. What time?"

"Six? Whatever works. I just want to see you."

"I'll text you after I talk to him, but I'm sure it's fine."

Or I'll make *it fine.*

After we hang up, I sit on my bed and stare at the phone, trying to wrap my mind around what just happened. Marco called me at ten in the morning, told me my voice was sexy, and invited me to his house for dinner. In any universe, that sounds like a date. Right?

I change three times before settling on dark jeans and a violet top that skims my small curves. I try on a pair of black flats, but my sneakers have become part of my look. I twist my long hair into a messy bun and I'm ready.

Except I'm not . . . because I'm going to Marco's house. Where he sleeps.

Marco knows I don't drive (unless, I'm in an illegal street race). He offered to pick me up, but I'm pretty sure Dad wouldn't be okay with me dating anyone right now, and I don't want to put a street racer on his radar. Dad thinks I'm going to Lex's, so I make a quick exit when he holes up in his room on a call with Tyson. I cut through the back of the apartment complex to catch the bus and take it three stops to where Marco is waiting.

I get in the Fastback, and the scent of leather and citrus hits me. The whole car smells like I'm pressed against his chest.

"Hi."

Marco stares at me, lips parted and eyes dark. "I've never seen your hair up before."

"Is that good or bad?"

"Everything about you is good." He reaches out and touches the back of my neck. The contact sends a tiny shiver down my spine. I bite my lip as Marco's eyes move to my mouth. "If you keep doing that, I'm won't be able to stop myself from kissing you."

I want him to kiss me . . . a lot.

As he drives, I steal glances at him. His gorgeous profile, the way the muscles in his arm flex when he shifts gears, and how the ink of his tattoos seems to move. I catch him looking at me, too. He touches my neck again at a stoplight.

"Do you miss your old school?" he asks as we pass Monroe.

"No."

He grins. "I don't miss you being there, either."

Marco parks in front of an old three-story apartment building. The windows are barred, but the freshly painted white brick and the houseplants on the balconies make the building feel welcoming.

Marco walks around to my side of the car. When I get out,

he's standing so close that my body almost touches his. He takes my hand and leads me up the steps to the second floor.

He hesitates at the apartment door. "It's nothing fancy."

"I'm not into fancy. I prefer real." His hand is over mine, and I brush my knuckles against his palm. "And I'm not judging."

Marco squeezes my hand. "Sofia might act a little weird. I've never brought a girl home before, except Cruz."

Is he serious? I want to ask, but I'm not sure how to do it without giving away my feelings.

"And she's not really a girl," he adds.

I nudge him in the ribs. "Cruz would kick your ass for saying that."

He grins. "You really do know her."

The minute Marco unlocks the door, Sofia comes running. She hugs me and pulls me inside. "I'm so glad you're here."

"Me too."

The apartment is warm and cozy—white walls with framed family photos and faded children's artwork, a round oak kitchen table with four chairs. The cushions on the brown sofa in the living room are sunken in from use, and two bed pillows are stacked at one end.

White Christmas lights outline the inside of the door, and a drinking glass with pink and yellow flowers sits on the coffee table.

I touch the lights. "Your apartment is so pretty," I tell Sofia, who stands expectantly in front of a hallway.

"Thanks." She smiles, bouncing on her heels, then turns to her brother. "Marco, I think the chicken is done."

"Thanks, Sopaipilla. Why don't you show Frankie your room?"

Sofia beams and drags me by the hand down the hallway. We pass the photos on the wall. Most of them are ripped down one side, where someone was torn out of the picture—Marco's dad, I'm guessing. Then each photo was returned to its frame, minus one family member.

"Here it is." Sofia opens the door proudly. Her lavender walls are covered with posters of boy bands and concept cars. She has two photos on her nightstand—one of a beautiful woman who must be her mom, with the same tan skin and mass of black curls as Sofia, and the other of Marco standing outside the rec center with Sofia.

"I love it in here," I tell her. "Did you decorate it yourself?"

"My mom painted the walls before she got sick, but I picked out everything else."

I let her walk me through and point out all the details. Marco appears in the doorway and watches us, his strong arms folded across his chest. "Are you two ready to eat? The chicken is done."

"We're coming," Sofia says.

Marco walks ahead of us to the kitchen. I pause at the door across from Sofia's. "Is that your brother's room?"

"No." Sofia lowers her voice. "It was my parents' room, and then after my mom died, just my dad's. Marco hates our dad, so he won't take it, and he wouldn't let me switch with him. He still sleeps on the sofa, like he always has."

I nod, but I hate the thought of Marco not having a bedroom because of his father. How much can one person take from you? On my way back through the living room, I look closer. Car magazines are piled on the floor. An alarm clock and a picture of a little boy in overalls holding a woman's hand sit on the end table next to the sofa. Marco and his mom.

Dinner is amazing. Marco made arroz con pollo, a garlicky chicken with rice. I never would have pictured him cooking. We eat and laugh, and afterward we play board games with Sofia. She's a real-estate tycoon when it comes to Monopoly, and she beats us in half the time it normally takes to finish the game. Once she's settled on the sofa with a movie, Marco walks me out to a small balcony at the far end of the living room.

He drops down into a big plastic chair and pats the seat between his legs. "Come here."

I sit in the empty space, and he pulls me back against his chest.

"Thanks for coming. I haven't seen Sofia that happy in a long time." His breath tickles my bare neck, and I have to fight to stay focused. "She really likes you."

I snuggle against him. "I like her, too."

A question lingers in my mind, but I'm not sure how to ask him without making a fool of myself.

Stop overthinking it.

I take a deep breath. "You said you've never brought a girl home before . . . so why me?"

In a fluid movement, Marco hooks his arms under my leg and flips me around so I'm facing him and my legs are hanging over the sides. The position is intimate—the way our bodies are pressed together and I feel parts of him against me that make my whole body buzz, the way his hand rests on my hip and our faces are so close that I have to lean back a little to keep from seeing double.

Marco's other hand moves to my neck, and his fingers drift across my skin, teasing. "When I saw you in the parking lot on your first day at Monroe, I couldn't stop staring because you were so damn gorgeous. I figured you were just another rich girl from the Heights. When you jumped into the fight on the quad, I knew you were different. Then you showed up at the races to help your friend. Most girls wouldn't do that, Frankie. Most guys wouldn't."

It feels like he's talking about someone else.

He frowns. "When I saw Sung with his hands on you, and I thought about what could have happened if Deacon and I weren't there . . . that's when I knew I felt something. And I couldn't make it go away."

"Did you want to make it go away?"

His lips brush mine. "Yes and no. I wanted you, but it seemed like I always said the wrong thing. And I didn't want to fall for anyone."

My breath hitches. "Is that what's happening?"

He tugs on the knot in my hair, and it spills over my shoulders. "It already happened."

"We're not as different as you think, Marco." He tightens his hold on me when I say his name. "We both have things in our pasts that we would rather forget, and we've both made mistakes. We look at the same stars and see the same sky."

"I wish that was true. But the stars don't look the same in the Downs. It's tough to see past the projects to notice the sky."

I take his face in my hands. "You just have to look harder."

CHAPTER 25

___

CRIMINAL INTENT

I've been in my bedroom since I got back from Marco's, replaying every detail of the night—especially the part that involved his hands and lips touching me. The apartment door slams. Cujo raises his head, mildly interested.

Dad walks into my room without knocking, his jaw clenched and nostrils flaring.

Something is wrong.

He tosses a stack of papers on the bed next to me. Not papers. Photographs.

Glossy black-and-white images of Marco and Deacon—in the parking lot at the rec center, on the steps of an apartment building in the Downs, behind the wheels of their cars on V Street. I fan out the photos. . . . There must be at least twenty.

One catches my eye. A picture of me folded in Marco's arms behind the rec center from the day I had the flashback.

"Are you spying on me?" I stand, holding the photo between us.

"Cops aren't allowed to use department resources to spy on their daughters."

"Then how do you explain these?" I gesture at the pile.

"They're surveillance photos from an ongoing investigation. Tyson pulled out the ones you're in before anyone else saw them."

An investigation that involves the boy I'm falling for.

A boy Dad won't want me to see, now that he knows Marco races. I know it's illegal, but there are worse things.

"When did RATTF start investigating street racers?" Does he know I was racing?

He gives me a strange look. "When they started stealing cars."

"What?" The world around me stops.

Dad snatches the picture out of my hand. "He's a car thief. Do you want to explain what the hell you're doing with him?"

It's a mistake.

"Marco doesn't steal cars."

"A month ago high-end cars started disappearing—the kind you can't resell on the street. Somebody was brokering stolen cars and selling them overseas. So Tyson and I started watching all the major crews to figure out who was actually stealing the cars. We weren't looking for a high school kid and a dropout. Not until a witness remembered seeing a kid with scars on his neck hanging around before one of the cars disappeared."

"That doesn't mean Marco had anything to do with it."

He holds up the photo in his hand. "Are you involved with this boy, Frankie?" Dad eyes flicker to the image of Marco holding me, and his jaw twitches. "Is he your boyfriend? I hope you don't hang all over your friends like this."

My mind races, and I'm only half listening.

Dad takes my silence as a yes and crushes the photo in his hand, crumpling it into a ball. "Have you been listening to me? We're building a case against Marco Leone and Deacon Kelley, and whoever the two of them are working for."

"You're wrong about Marco."

"No. *You're* wrong about him. Did you know Marco's father is serving ten years in Jessup for grand theft? He liked to steal cars, too. Maybe they'll let him share a cell with his son." Dad turns his back on me and hangs his head, gripping the sides of my dresser.

"You're judging him because of his father? Marco is a good person. His mom died, and he takes care of his younger sister. If something happens to him, she has nobody." I'm panicking, but I don't know what to do. Not with surveillance photos scattered all over my bed and Dad talking about Marco going to prison.

My father raises his head and looks at my reflection in the mirror above the dresser. "He should've thought about that before he broke the law."

"Do you have any real proof? Things aren't always black and white. Sometimes they're gray."

He turns and faces me, his eyes full of rage. "*Gray* is what happens when people aren't strong enough or honest enough to do the right thing. *Gray* is the list of bullshit excuses criminals give me when they're cuffed in the backseat of my car. And *you*"—he points at me—"have no idea how the world works, or you would realize that hanging out with a bunch of kids at a rec center in the Downs doesn't mean you understand what it's like to live there or how dangerous it is for the people who do. Monroe and that rec center might as well be Disneyland, compared to the rougher neighborhoods."

"I know that."

"I'm not so sure." He scrubs a hand over his face. "Innocent people in the Downs get hurt every day. They can't walk to work or take a bus without worrying about getting mugged or worse. Crime is completely out of control, and there aren't enough of us on the street to make a dent."

Us.

Dad means cops—the good guys. Which makes Marco one of the bad guys.

I know Dad is wrong about Marco, but I'm supposed to . . . what? Pretend he's right? Act like an obedient daughter and do what I'm told?

He grabs the photos off the bed and shakes them in front of me. "These boys are *criminals*. Is that black and white enough for you?"

"Actually, it's not." I retrieve the photo Dad wadded up of Marco hugging me and unfold it. "These boys don't have anyone to take care of them. They're just trying to survive. And I'm not 'hanging all over' Marco in this picture. He's helping me through one of my flashbacks, a really bad one."

I pluck another photo out of Dad's hand. "I don't really know Deacon. But I do know that he crawled through a shattered windshield to pull Marco's sister out of a car wreck. He even has the scars to prove it. That sounds pretty black and white to me."

"Do you know what else your friend Deacon Kelley has to go along with those scars? A record. His most recent arrest was for robbing a 7-Eleven."

Shit.

So much for my brilliant argument. "I just told you that I hardly know Deacon, and Marco is nothing like him."

"But he's friends with Kelley, isn't he? 'As close as brothers,' some of their old teachers said. Honest kids don't hang out with convicted felons. What does that tell you about Marco?"

Nothing. But it tells my father everything. "It tells me Deacon saved his sister's life," I say, but I know it's useless.

Dad lives by a code. It's the foundation of everything he believes, the way he has survived working on the streets for the last eighteen years. Asking him to believe it's possible for somebody to hang out with a criminal without being one themselves is asking him to take a sledgehammer to that foundation.

He points at me. "You are not seeing Marco Leone again. Are we clear?"

Something inside me snaps.

I'm falling for Marco . . . maybe I've already fallen. I can't pretend he doesn't matter anymore.

I only have two choices now—deny the way I feel or admit it.

Run away again or fight.

The old Frankie wasn't a fighter, but I'm not that girl anymore. Marco matters to me.

We matter.

I won't let my dad take him away from me. I've already lost too much. I'm done losing.

"You can't order me around like a child."

"I am your *father*," he roars, the anger boiling over. "And *you* are *my* child. So you'll do what I tell you."

"You should've spent more time with me if you wanted to pull the dad card," I fire back.

Dad stares at me, looking defeated. "Dammit, Frankie. I know I haven't been the best parent, but you can't just clock out when you work undercover. And you've always had your mom."

"Bullshit. The only person who has Mom is Richard." I've never cussed at my father before—or told him how I felt about anything. But I'm not letting him off easy. Not when he's tearing my life apart.

Dad leans against the dresser. "I get it. I'm a shitty father, and you want to punish me."

"Excuse me?"

He sighs. "I spend every day trying to bust guys who steal cars, so you decide to go out with one of them?"

Them.

Dad says it like he's talking about serial killers or mass murderers. Not a seventeen-year-old former AP student trying to hold together what's left of his family. Dad must not have any real proof that Marco steals cars, or he would've arrested him or thrown the information in my face by now. But he's already decided Marco is guilty.

"If you want to punish me, I can live with that," Dad says. "But don't punish yourself by dating a piece of trash like Marco Leone. Haven't you hurt yourself enough?"

Knowing how my dad feels about Marco makes me wonder what he really thinks of me.

"You're right about one thing, Dad. I have hurt myself, and I've made plenty of mistakes, like driving drunk—which on your 'everything is black or white, right or wrong' scale definitely falls into the black category."

Jimmy Devereux the cop knows I'm going somewhere with this, but when his shoulders sag, I know James Devereux the father won out. "Frankie, you've always been a good kid. But you're going down the wrong road, and hanging out with criminals won't help you get back on the right one."

"Is it even possible for me to get back on the right road? If we're working from your definition, I'm a criminal. Not 'strong enough or honest enough to do the right thing.'" I do a bad impression of his voice. "Isn't that what you said?"

The color drains from his face. "That's not what I meant."

I look him in the eye. "I don't believe you."

CHAPTER 26

NO GOING BACK

I con Lex into driving me to school early on Monday, and I head straight for Lot B, where Marco hangs out with Cruz and the other street racers who idolize them.

I'm all raw emotions and exposed nerves, playing a torturous game of *what if* with myself. What if Dad and Tyson are wrong about Marco, but there's no way to prove it? What if Marco thinks I gave them information, and he never wants to speak to me again?

This situation must be some kind of mix-up, a case of being in the wrong place at the wrong time—or, if you're Marco, having the wrong best friend. But I need Marco to tell me that himself.

I need to hear him say he's not a thief.

Pretending I don't have feelings for him isn't an option

anymore, because Marco made me care. Now every feeling is that much bigger, stronger, and more dangerous.

I spot him standing next to his Mustang, and my legs stop moving. One of the guys hanging out with him and Cruz says something, and Marco laughs. All I see is the boy who gave up everything for his sister, who held me when the flashback hit, who feeds a one-eyed stray cat . . . the boy who is afraid to want anything for himself.

He's not a criminal.

He can't be.

Marco notices me, and his face lights up.

What if it's true and I have to walk away? Will I be able to forget that smile?

Cruz waves, but I haven't moved. I'm not even breathing. Marco's smile fades, and he jogs toward me.

"What's wrong?" He reaches for me and I step back.

"Wait." I hold up my hand so he'll stop talking. My mind cycles through variations of the same question, searching for one that doesn't sound like an accusation.

"Frankie?"

"Do you steal cars?" The moment the words leave my lips, I want to hit rewind and take them back.

Marco steers me away from the parking lot. "Is this a joke?"

"That's not an answer."

A familiar numbness wraps itself around me. It feels like I'm watching the situation from the outside, the way it did when a band of idiots planted a tree for my dead boyfriend, or my mom dumped me at Dad's like a bag of garbage, or the flashbacks swallowed me whole without showing me the one piece of the story I need to see.

Marco leads me behind the gym, across from Lot B, where no one will overhear us. "Who told you that? Somebody at the rec center?"

He's not denying it.

The truth etches itself into every line on his beautiful face.

"Is it true?" I already know the answer, but I don't want to believe it.

"Shit." Marco knots his fingers in his hair like he wants to rip it out of his scalp.

Everything I thought I knew about him—everything he said to me—was it all lies? "Were you ever going to tell me?"

Marco moves closer, but he doesn't touch me. "I wanted to, Frankie. I swear. But I didn't know how to explain."

"There's nothing to explain. You're a *thief*. Do you know how I found out? My dad dumped a pile of surveillance photos on my bed—of you and Deacon. And me!"

He shrinks back. "What are you talking about?"

Anger explodes inside me. "My dad is a cop!"

My heart pounds, and I can't catch my breath.

I told him. The one thing Dad asked me to keep secret.

I crossed a line that I can't uncross.

"You can't tell anyone, Marco." I lower my voice to almost a whisper. "Please. He works undercover, and no one can know."

"I won't say anything, I swear." Marco stares at the ground.

"I'm trusting you."

"I don't know why." Marco looks dazed. He turns toward

the wall behind him and leans his forehead against the brick, his palms on the wall. "I screwed everything up. My life. Sofia's. Yours . . ."

"Tell me why. I deserve that much." I shouldn't drag this out, but I can't force myself to walk away yet.

"When my father went to prison, I inherited his debt."

"Who does he owe? The bank? Credit card companies?"

"I wish." Marco turns around slowly, but he won't look at me. "The car he crashed—the one Sofia almost died in—it was worth sixty grand, and my old man never delivered it. So the guy he worked for came looking for me. He gave me a choice. Work off the money my dad owed him, or watch Sofia grow up in a foster home. He threatened to report us to Child Services. It would take a social worker about ten minutes to figure out that our legal guardian doesn't live with us."

"Who is your guardian?"

"My aunt. But she had no idea until my dad was arrested and the court contacted her." Marco shakes his head, eyes still trained on the ground. "I guess my parents just wrote down her name."

"If she knows, why isn't she living with you?"

"She manages an estate for a big shot on Capitol Hill and his family. My aunt is in charge of everyone who works there, and she loves it. But it's a live-in position. What could she do? Ask her boss to let her niece and nephew move in?"

Or quit and take care of them.

Marco takes a deep breath. "I know it sounds like an excuse, but I didn't have any options."

"So you started stealing cars?" I try to imagine the kind

of choice he's describing, but I can't. Dad was right about one thing. Working at the rec center in the Downs isn't the same as living there.

"At first I tried to pay off the debt with the money I made working at Kong's, but the guy my dad owed kept tacking on interest. So I started stripping cars, but it still wasn't enough to cover the debt." Marco's shoulders shake. "I didn't want to do it. But I couldn't let them take Sofia."

At my old school, none of my friends had trouble paying their bills. They bought whatever they wanted. Nobody at Woodley had a parent in prison. Their lives were easy—and until Noah died, mine was, too.

Marco didn't start stealing cars because he wanted extra money to burn. He was trying to protect his sister, the person he loves more than anyone. I don't have any siblings, but if I had to choose between stealing and watching Lex or Abel get hurt, I would steal almost anything.

Unless . . .

"Is there anyone in the cars when you take them?"

Marco's head snaps up. "I'm not a carjacker, if that's what you're asking. I would never hurt anyone." The shame in his eyes makes me feel guilty for asking, but I needed to know.

There's a difference between stealing *things* and hurting *people*. It's the line I wouldn't cross, and Marco hasn't crossed it.

Eight steps.

That's how many it takes to reach him.

I slip my arms around Marco's waist and rest my cheek against his chest. He freezes, muscles tense beneath his T-shirt.

"It's not your fault. I'm not saying that what you're doing is right, but I understand why you started doing it."

He wraps his arms around me. "I know I don't deserve you, but I just found you. I don't want to lose you."

My heart stalls. "I don't want to get lost."

He traces a path along the side of my face and tucks my hair behind my ear. "The way I feel about you, Frankie . . . there's no going back."

CHAPTER 27

THE CHEMISTRY OF TRUST

It's been six days since Dad showed me the surveillance photos, and we still aren't speaking. Though he makes an exception every morning to remind me that I'm grounded indefinitely. I don't say a word.

I'm not interested in talking to my father—not even to tell him things are over between Marco and me. Instead, I left him a note on the kitchen counter.

It won't stop Dad and Tyson from watching Marco, but if they thought we were still seeing each other, Dad would have S.W.A.T. camped out in Lot B.

Now spending time with Marco requires a covert operation. Sneaking out isn't an option. I'm sure Dad has someone keeping an eye on the apartment to make sure I don't leave at night—the neighbor who offered to babysit me.

Inside the school is the only place safe from police surveillance, but after Marco's confession Monday, I need to talk to him one-on-one.

I walk into the kitchen, and the smell of burnt coffee lingers in the air. Dad sits at the dining room table, reading the *Washington Post* and tossing Cujo sugarcoated pieces of Trix cereal. He's drinking his coffee from a mug with #1 DAD scrawled across the side in messy kid handwriting. I made it for him in first grade as a Father's Day gift.

That mug will mysteriously disappear by tomorrow.

"Come straight home from the rec center." He doesn't look up from the newspaper.

"I'm having trouble in chemistry, and Lex offered to help me at her house after she picks me up." The chemistry part is true. A lie is more convincing if it's rooted in the truth. Dad taught me that.

He puts down the paper. "Lex takes chemistry?"

"Yeah, and she's good at it. Why?" I crack open a can of double-shot espresso from my stash in the fridge.

"She doesn't look like a science whiz."

I can't believe he just used those words.

"What do science whizzes look like? Nerds with glasses and pocket protectors? If you're going to judge people by the way they look, you need a more reliable scale than outdated stereotypes." I slam the can against the counter for emphasis. If I start acting pleasant out of nowhere, he'll know I'm up to something.

"Tell Lex to come over here." He's calling my bluff. Nicely played.

"No, thanks. I don't want her to end up in the photo album you and Tyson have going."

Dad's jaw muscles jump under his skin. Did I go too far?

He carries his annoying mug to the sink. "We only spy on criminals."

"I'm a criminal, remember?"

Dad leans against the counter, watching me, but he doesn't take the bait. "I'm sure your mother would get you a tutor."

I couldn't ask for a better setup. "I don't want anything from her or King Richard."

The corner of his mouth twitches as he fights a smile. He's the only person who hates my stepfather as much as I do. "Leave me Lex's home number and text me when you get to her house. I want to talk to her mom. If her mom won't be there, you aren't going. Are we clear?"

"Fine." I storm out of the apartment and down the steps. I don't let myself smile until I'm at the bottom and Lex pulls up in front of the building.

"I got you out of the apartment, and it wasn't easy," Lex says. We're at her house later that night. "My mom doesn't like talking to strangers unless they're donating money to one of her charities. And you're lucky she doesn't pay any attention to me, or she would know that I'm not taking chemistry. So what's the big favor?" She holds up her hand. "Wait. Let me guess. Your dad is home, and you need me to cover while you race cars or meet up with your new boyfriend?"

I'm not lying to her anymore. She's my best friend and I owe her the truth, whether she ends up helping me or not. "It's so much worse."

She finally looks at me, her blue eyes rimmed with smudged black eyeliner. "How much worse?"

"My dad and Tyson have been investigating a crew, and Marco is involved."

We're sitting across from each other on her king-size bed, the way we've done since we were sharing secrets about the boys we had crushes on in elementary school.

Lex crosses her legs. "Marco knows who is doing it, doesn't he?"

My eyes sting and my throat burns. "It's him, Lex. He's stealing cars. Marco's dad is in jail, and he owed some lowlife money. Marco has to work off his father's debt, or his sister will end up in foster care."

Lex blinks, like she's still processing what I said. "Did you tell your dad about Marco's father and the guy threatening Marco and his sister?"

"I can't betray Marco's trust, and Dad won't believe me anyway. In his eyes, Marco is a thief. Dad will never be able to see him as a victim."

"Don't hate me for asking, but are you sure Marco is telling the truth? What if he made up the whole story?"

"He's not lying, Lex. You have to trust me."

Worry lines form between her eyebrows. "I think you have feelings for this guy, and it's affecting your judgment."

"I need to see him, and I can't take the chance of doing it at the rec center."

232

Lex jumps off the bed and circles the room. "You want me to let him come *here*? Are you crazy?"

Probably.

I'm crazy about Marco and desperate to help him. It's impossible to explain, but I know he's telling the truth. I feel it in every kiss. Every touch. It's in Marco's eyes when he looks at me and in his voice when he says my name.

Marco said there was no going back when it came to his feelings for me. There's no going back for me, either.

"I'm not asking you to trust him or like him. I'm not even asking you to help him. I'm asking you to help *me*."

Lex stares at me like I'm standing on that ledge and she's afraid I'll jump. "Are you're falling for him?"

"He makes me feel safe. For the first time in months, I care about the future."

Marco makes the future feel possible, a place worth imagining. As long as he's in it.

Lex walks over to her desk and picks up a crystal-studded frame with a picture of the two of us at the eighth-grade dance.

I love that picture, almost as much as I love Lex. I can't leave her or Abel behind, even if Lex's blue eyes will always remind me of Noah's, and so many of my memories of Abel and Lex include him. Even if I have to carry some part of the old Frankie with me so I can carry them, too.

Lex touches the spot where our faces smile from behind the glass. "Sometimes I wish we could go back. You and me and Abel—best friends—eating candy from the broken vending machine at the club and cannonballing into the pool until the old ladies complained. Things are so complicated now."

I don't think she's talking about the two of us anymore. "Do you know what's going on with Abel? I haven't had a chance to call him."

"No, but right now, we're talking about you." She sets the frame back on her desk. "I don't want you to get hurt. You've lost so much."

"That's why I can't lose Marco, too." Saying the words—the thought of never feeling his arms around me again—threatens to break me. "Will you help me?"

"Haven't I always been there when you needed me?"

I don't hesitate. "Yes."

"There's your answer. You can talk to him in the pool house. My parents won't go down there unless the house is on fire. Maybe not even then." Lex forces a tiny smile that looks sadder than tears.

I jump off the bed and throw my arms around her. "Thank you."

She squeezes me tighter. "Just don't get hurt."

I almost say I won't, but the situation between Marco and me has hurt written all over it.

I'm okay with hurt.

It's losing I can't handle.

CHAPTER 28

DIFFERENT PERFECT

The pool house in Lex's backyard is bigger than Marco's entire apartment. Her mom spared no expense outfitting it with an L-shaped sofa and a flat-screen TV, a pool table and air hockey, and a stocked kitchen and full-size bathroom.

In middle school, Lex and I spent hours planning the parties we'd throw here and which boys we'd kiss when we played Spin the Bottle. We only ended up playing once, with Abel and his cousin who was visiting for the summer. After a six-pack of beer and a dozen do-overs, Lex's spin landed on Abel, and she freaked out and puked in the bathroom before she kissed him.

Right now, I'm the one who feels like puking. I don't know if Marco will go for my plan.

Perched on the window seat, I hug my knees in the dark, watching for signs of movement near the driveway. The rain plays tricks on my eyes. It feels like forever before I spot Marco's familiar gait. Strong and lean, hands shoved in his pockets as if nothing can touch him.

I crack the door open, and he speeds up when he sees me. God, he's beautiful—even with a T-shirt plastered to his chest and rain running down his face.

He stops at the door, and the hunger in his eyes makes my knees weak. I grab his wet shirt and pull him inside. "You're soaked. How far away did you park?"

"Far enough to keep Lex from getting in trouble." Marco touches my hips and tugs me toward him, careful to leave just enough distance between us to keep me dry. His fingers graze the skin above the waistband of my jeans, sending shivers up my spine. He shakes his head and squeezes his eyes shut, as if he's in physical pain.

I push the wet hair away from his eyes and press my hand against his cheek. "Are you all right? Did something happen?" I search his face for bruises or signs of a fight.

"I didn't think you'd call."

"I told you how I felt about you." My hand slides behind his neck.

"I know. But I figured after you had some time to let it all sink in, you'd change your mind." He raises his head, and our eyes lock. "You deserve a lot better than a car thief, Frankie."

I hook both arms around his neck and press closer. The water from his wet shirt and jeans seeps into mine. "That isn't who you are."

Marco's eyes flicker to my mouth, and he leans closer. I lick my lips and he watches, his breath coming faster. His lips crush mine, and our mouths fall into perfect rhythm. He wraps an arm around my waist and picks me up. I lean against the wall behind me and drag his hips closer.

Marco moans against my lips. "What are you doing to me, Angel?"

The sound of his voice ignites a need in me that I never knew existed. With our bodies pressed together like this, it's impossible not to feel Marco's need, too. His lips brush mine and he pulls back, leaving his arms draped over my shoulders.

I search his face for a clue that will tell me why he stopped.

"What's wrong?"

"Would it sound crazy if I said this was *too right*?" His voice is raw and deep.

"Yes."

He goes silent for what feels like minutes when he's looking me in the eye like this. "Kissing you isn't like kissing other girls." I cringe, and he curses under his breath. "That came out wrong. I meant it's different with you."

Not helping. "Different *good* or different *bad*?"

He moves one of his hands away from the wall and traces a line with his fingertip from the bridge of my nose down the center of my lips to the hollow at the bottom of my throat. "Different *perfect*. The kind of perfect that tells me I'll never be able to forget kissing you."

No one has ever said anything like that to me. I repeat the words in my head so I can remember exactly the way Marco said them.

"Do you want to forget?"

"Your dad is investigating me, Frankie. And he's *not* wrong." He shivers, and I touch his arm. He's freezing.

"I have an idea. But you need to get out of these wet clothes." I tug on the hem of his shirt.

He smiles—that sexy-sweet bad-boy smile I think about way too often. "Are you asking me to strip?"

"Go in the bathroom and find something dry." I give him a little shove. "There's a changing room."

"I bet." Marco looks around for the first time. He's probably comparing it to his modest apartment, and I'm embarrassed by the excess. He kicks off his high-tops and crosses the dark room.

When Marco returns, he's shirtless and barefoot, still wearing his wet jeans.

"You didn't change." Not that I'm complaining. The moonlight skims every gorgeous muscle from his shoulders to his abs.

He tosses the towel into the bathroom. "Whoever wears all those checkered golf shorts in there isn't exactly my size. This is as close to dry as I could get." Marco sits next to me on the sofa.

I've never seen his tattoos all at once, and I can't look away.

Black bands encircle one arm, and the sleeve of tattoos covers the outside of the other. I touch the pile of skulls that curves around his wrist and trace the tree growing up from the center, along the outside of his arm. The tree branches out, curving into what looks like a cliff at Marco's elbow. But it's another skull, less detailed than the ones near his wrist. I drag my finger over the branch that moves up his arm and morphs into the stem of a black rose. The petals open over Marco's bicep.

What comes next takes my breath away.

The bottom of a lion's mane curves up from the center of the rose and spreads over Marco's shoulder. It's drawn in a tribal style that's different from the rest of the tattoo.

"So what's your idea?" he asks.

"My dad and his partner aren't really interested in you. They want the person at the top of the food chain—whoever is selling the cars. Catching the people who steal the cars is just a way to follow the chain."

Marco frowns and clasps his hands together. "Okay . . . ?"

"Is the guy your father owes at the top?"

"As far as I know. He's the one who moves the cars and has them delivered to the clients. We just drop them at the docks." Marco frowns. "Wait. I don't like where this is going."

"Hear me out." I touch his knee, and he covers my hand with his.

"If you tell my dad who he is, you can make a deal. The guy who is blackmailing you will go to prison, where he belongs."

Marco bolts off the sofa and stands across from me, his bare chest heaving like he just ran a mile. "I'm not talking to the cops, Frankie."

"I'll talk to my dad ahead of time and make sure you won't get in any trouble." The conversation isn't going the way I hoped. "Trust me, please."

He rakes his hands through his damp hair. "I'll find another way out of this."

"If you had another option, we wouldn't be having this conversation."

Marco folds his arms across his chest. "The answer is still no."

"Why?" A knot forms in my throat.

He moves toward me, arms open. "Come here."

I want nothing more than to fall into his arms and ignore my fears and forget the pain. But I can't ignore things anymore. I spent the summer trying, and it didn't change anything.

I stand and hold out my hand, signaling him to stop. "No. I want an answer. Why won't you talk to my dad if he guarantees there won't be any fallout for you and Sofia?"

"What about Deacon? Will your father let him walk away, too? He's in deeper than me, Frankie. When he was expelled, stealing cars became his full-time job. If we're under investigation, your dad and his partner have probably figured that out by now." Marco's eyes plead for understanding. "I can't give your dad the kind of information he'll want without selling out Deacon. And I won't do that."

"Is the guy you work for threatening Deacon, too?"

He shakes his head. "No. Deacon wanted in."

"Then he belongs in jail. Are you willing to throw away your future for him?"

Marco moves toward me again, but I turn my back on him. I sense it the moment he's behind me, even before he touches me. My body is so aware of him now. He brushes the hair over my shoulder, his fingers grazing my neck.

"Don't."

He steps closer, and his breath tickles the back of my neck. Strong arms reach over my shoulders and hug my back against his bare skin. "I can't help it," he murmurs against my neck. "Every time I see you, I want to hold you."

"You won't be able to if you're in jail."

Marco kisses my neck and slides around so he's in front of me. "Look at me."

If I do, I'll break.

I keep my lashes down. "I can't."

He cups my face in his hands and gently raises my chin. "Before you kissed me at the party, I imagined what it would feel like. How it would feel to hold you. But I never thought . . ." He releases me and presses the heels of his hands against his forehead. I hate the confusion and pain in Marco's eyes. I hate that I'm causing any part of it.

My fingers find his again, tethering us. "You never thought what?"

"I'd get the chance."

I'm not brave enough to tell him how often he crossed my mind. "I doubt you have trouble finding girls who want to kiss you." I nudge him with my shoulder, trying to sound playful instead of jealous.

"You're the only girl I want to kiss." Marco raises our intertwined hands and holds them against his heart. Our hands fit together perfectly. Not all hands fit. Or all people. "I plan on doing a lot more of it if you'll let me. But I can't turn on Deacon. We're brothers, whether we share the same blood or not. He saved Sofia's life, and he's had my back whenever I needed him."

The jagged scars on Deacon's neck flash through my mind—proof of the sacrifice he made. Even if I'm not crazy about Deacon, he must have some good inside.

"My dad and his partner are really good at their jobs. It's only a matter of time before someone screws up or they find the evidence they need to make an arrest." And it scares me to death.

Marco rubs his nose against mine. Mom used to do the same thing, back when she was still my mom and not King Richard's robotic queen.

"I don't have the right to ask, but if you stick with me, all this will be over soon. Except the part about your dad hating my guts." He nuzzles my neck, sending waves of heat through every inch of my body. "If you don't want to decide now, I'll give you space." His fingers tighten around mine, his heart beating fast beneath our joined hands.

With my free hand I trace a path from the hollow of his neck and down his chest until I reach his waistband. I freeze, my hand on his stomach. "I don't want space. I want . . ."

If you say it out loud, it's real.

"What?" The anticipation in his voice makes me bold.

"I want you." I untangle my fingers from his and loop my arms around his neck, my damp T-shirt pressing against his warm skin.

Marco stares at me, his eyes searching mine. "There's something I need to tell you. But I'm scared it will come out wrong."

I swallow hard. I'm afraid to ask, but I'm just as afraid *not* to ask. "Tell me anyway."

He pulls me closer. "I love you, Frankie. And it's the always kind."

He loves me.

I forget to breathe. Or maybe I can't.

I've never felt like this about anyone. I love Marco's strength and his kindness, the way he protects the people he loves and makes me feel safe.

I love him.

But I didn't think he could feel that way about me.

Marco's lips brush across mine slowly . . . so slow that it creates sensations I've never experienced before. I bite my bottom lip, fighting the urge to press my mouth against his. Whatever he's doing—the slow and deliberate contact—creates a sweet push and pull inside me.

When the tension feels unbearable, I kiss my way up his neck, and he moans. "You're killing me." His hands slide under my shirt, pulling it up as they reach the edge of my lacy bra. I sigh, and it unleashes the hunger between us like a dam breaking.

Marco picks me up, and I hook my legs around him. He carries me to the sofa like I weigh nothing. When my back hits the soft cushions, I tug on his bottom lip because it drives him crazy. He lowers himself over me, somehow managing to press his body against mine without crushing me with his weight.

Marco pushes my shirt up again, and I love the way his skin feels against my stomach. "Can I take this off? I want to look at you."

I try to slip my arms out, but the damp cotton clings to me.

Marco does a sweeping move with his hand, gathering the hem and slipping it up my arms and over my head.

He sits back on his heels and stares at me. The room doesn't seem half as dark now that a gorgeous guy is checking me out in my bra. Thank you, pushy old lady in the lingerie department, for talking me into buying a decent-looking bra—one that makes what little I have appear bigger.

I cross my arms over my chest, which is one small piece of lace away from being completely exposed.

"Don't do that." He runs his index finger down the center of my neck, gently nudging my arms away from my chest as he continues the path to my belly button. "You're beautiful."

"Stop." I try to pull him down. When he won't budge, I prop myself up on my elbows.

He stares into my eyes with an intensity that makes me feel naked. "I want to remember this."

Tiny flashes of light catch in my peripheral vision.

A cell phone hovering above me.

"Ready?" Noah asks. "I'll take the picture on three. I want to remember this."

Another flash and the memory disappears in a split second.

"Frankie?" Marco touches my cheek. "What happened?"

"I just want to remember, too."

CHAPTER 29

FRACTURED MEMORIES

Rain pelts my skin like bullets as I stand in front of the pool house and watch Marco leave. He's walking backward, smiling at me, clothes soaked and hair plastered against his skin. I love his smile. And him.

He blows me a kiss just before he's out of sight.

Not knowing when we'll have a chance to be alone again—to kiss, share secrets, and all the other things you do with someone at the beginning of a relationship—leaves me feeling lost. Worrying about whether my dad will arrest the guy I've fallen for makes it even worse.

The odds are against Marco, and us. We agreed to meet in the basement by the Shop classroom before school in the mornings so we can see each other.

I go back to the main house, where Lex puts my clothes in

the dryer while I copy the chemistry homework Marco completed into my own handwriting. It's the first thing Dad will ask to see when I get home.

Lex drives, and I stare out the window, listening to the thump of the windshield wipers.

"Did you guys figure things out?" she asks eventually, without taking her eyes off the road.

Did we? I don't even know.

"Some of it. But the situation is so complicated. I'm not sure if we can figure it all out." I tilt my head to the side and lean against the passenger-side window.

"But he makes you happy?"

I look over at Lex and nod. "Happier than anyone or anything has ever made me. What about Abel?"

"Over the summer, things between us felt *right*. Like magic. And I let myself care . . . so much more than I ever have before." Lex takes a deep breath. "He promised not to hurt me. Instead, he's hurting himself. He doesn't understand that it's the same thing."

"He's lost. I know how that feels, Lex. He just has to find his way back."

"What if he can't?"

I take her hand. "Then we'll find him ourselves."

"Are you in love with Marco?"

I don't hesitate. "Yes."

"Does he know that?" Lex never lets me off easy.

"Does Abel know you're in love with him?"

"I can't afford to take that kind of chance with him. He'll break my heart." She sounds so sad and scared.

I tuck one of my legs underneath me. "Abel has been in love with you forever, Lex. He would never hurt you."

"Not intentionally," she says. "But people hurt each other all the time without meaning to. It doesn't make it any easier when you're the one who gets hurt."

"You can't hide from pain. I've tried."

She turns onto the street that leads into Dad's development. "At least it buys me some time."

Dad's Tahoe is parked out front.

Lex kills the engine, and rain bangs against the roof of the car. She leans over and hugs me. "Just take care of yourself, Frankie. I need my best friend."

"Me too."

I pull up the hood of my borrowed sweatshirt. The living room light glows in the apartment, and the drapes in front of the balcony doors slide open. I can't see Dad through the rain, but I sense him watching me. "Wish me luck."

"Luck," Lex says as I jump out and run through the downpour.

By the time I make it to the stairs, I'm drenched. The second my key slides into the lock, Dad opens the door. I slip past him without a word and peel off the wet hoodie that weighs a ton now, along with my sneakers and socks.

"How did chemistry go?" he asks.

"Fine." That's all he's getting from me.

"Can I see what you worked on?"

He's so predictable.

"Why? Don't you trust me, Dad?" I ask sarcastically.

He holds out his hand and I drop the binder on the table in front of him.

"I'll be in my room. Just leave it on the kitchen table when you're done."

"Can you take a break from hating me for a few minutes? I'd like to talk." He gestures at the chair across from him.

I take a seat. If he wants to talk, he can go first. He raps on the table a few times, then runs his hands over the stubble along his jawline. This is the Dad I'm used to—awkward and nervous around the daughter he barely knows.

"This isn't how I wanted things to go between us." He sighs. "I wasn't happy about the reason you moved in, but I wanted you here. It felt like our chance to get to know each other and make up for lost time."

"It's called lost time for a reason. You can't get it back once it's gone. You want to get to know the old Frankie, not me."

"You're wrong. I know death affects people, and I warned your mom that Noah's would change you. But your mother hears what she wants."

I tried to tell her I wasn't the same person, too. But Mom chalked it up to a temporary case of PTSD.

Dad watches me the way he always does—measuring my responses, noting my body language, judging. "I don't care if you play the piano or go to Stanford. I want you to be yourself— the fearless little girl who drew on my bathroom walls with lipstick and wanted to help me catch bad guys. As you got older, that girl disappeared."

The red lipstick smudges are still there. "Every kid likes to play cops and robbers. It had nothing to do with being fearless."

He tries to make eye contact. "I disagree. I think it's the reason you're interested in a kid from the Downs. He takes chances, something you never used to do."

I'm not with Marco because of some subconscious need to rebel. He hates the risks I take, just as much as my dad would if he knew about them.

"Is this what you wanted to talk about?" I ask. "It's pretty pointless, since I'm not seeing him anymore."

Dad leans back in his chair and crosses his arms. Not the reaction he was hoping for, I guess. "I'm trying to protect you. Marco probably seems like a nice guy, and maybe he is. But he's also a felon."

"You don't know that for sure." I push my chair away from the table and stand. "I'm going to my room."

"Someday you'll realize I'm doing this because I love you," Dad calls after me.

I'm raw—my frayed emotions ripped to shreds and tied back together in ugly knots. "Don't use love as an excuse to hurt me. Find something else to call it. If you loved me, you'd never treat me like this."

"That's not true." Dad stares at me, looking shell-shocked.

"Lots of things aren't true, but it doesn't stop people from believing them."

I'm in my bedroom, thinking about Marco when my cell vibrates. I can't stop myself from smiling when I read the text.

> miss you angel

I run my fingers over the words, and my chest aches.

> me 2

A bubble of tiny dots appears as he writes back.

> feels like i'm still holding you. is
> that crazy?

> i wish

The bubble appears, and I wait for Marco's text. When it doesn't come through after a few minutes, I text again.

> you still there?

> yeah

My hand shakes as I type the next message. Now that I know how dangerous Marco's life really is, it's easy to imagine dozens of scenarios that would prevent him from responding.

> what's wrong?

His response comes more quickly this time.

> feels too good to be real. like i'll
> wake up tomorrow & you'll be gone

How can I tell him I feel the same way without making it worse?

> i won't. promise

> till tomorrow

> nite

I want to read the words over and over so I take a screenshot and e-mail it to myself before I delete the messages and the photo from my phone. Erasing Marco's messages feels like I'm letting my father chip away at something precious that belongs to me. But Dad is more than just a nosy parent. He's a cop.

A cop with the power to destroy Marco's life.

The thought terrifies me, and I'm sick of being afraid.

I yank my journal out of my backpack. Writing makes me feel strong. It helps me dig through the rubble in my head—bits and pieces of memories that don't fit together yet. I want to be strong enough to stand up to my dad and prove him wrong.

Strong enough to face the past and remember.

For Noah and me, one moment changed everything. It took his life and altered mine. Broke his body and my memory.

I've asked myself a thousand times if Noah would still be alive if either of us had done just one thing differently.

If we had left the house a half hour earlier or later.

If we had picked a different club or danced to one more song.

If I had gone out to the parking lot with him.

Playing *what if* will drive you crazy, but I can't help it.

Abel still plays it when he thinks about the night his dad OD'd. What if his father hadn't been alone? What if someone had called an ambulance when it happened? Would Tommy Ryder still be alive?

Those questions won't bring back the people we loved.

But figuring out who killed Noah might bring *me* back. The answer is somewhere inside me.

I just need a way to drag it out.

An old episode of VH1'S *Behind the Music* flashes through

my mind—the one about Tommy Ryder. Abel made me watch it with him a dozen times.

An interviewer with teased hair sits across from a leather-clad Tommy and asks the rock legend about his writing process. Tommy talks about the lists of words and phrases he makes, free association, and unlocking his subconscious. "The ideas are already in there, man. I've just gotta listen."

Maybe I just have to listen, too?

It's worth a try.

I open my journal and flip to a clean page, picturing the inside of the club just before I went out to the parking lot.

White mist from the smoke machine smells like strawberries and burnt matches.

The deejay in a room with a big window above the dance floor.

A bottle breaking.

Couples making out.

"Titanium" starts playing.

The soles of my wedges stick to the floor.

I have a headache and I want to leave.

The velvety texture of the black fabric in front of the door leading outside and static electricity in my hair.

Cars. Streetlights. The parking lot.

Cool air and the stench of stale beer.

More sticky stuff on the ground. My soles make a suction cup noise every time I take a step.

Where is he?

Noah's baby-blue polo shirt.

A figure. Slim but muscular, average height, wearing untied work boots and dark jeans.

Noah sees me and subtly shakes his head.

A fist to Noah's face, and my pulse races.

I duck between two cars and peer around the back. Liquid seeps through the knees of my jeans.

A voice that doesn't belong to Noah. "We can do this the easy way, the hard way, or my way."

"Screw you," Noah says.

The next thing I see is a fist.

Noah's head snaps back.

Blood—thick and viscous, like red maple syrup.

Noah's body falling . . .

I hear his killer's voice in the fuzzy way you hear things when there's water in your ears or a pillow over your head.

We can do this the easy way, the hard way, or my way.

My hand shakes and I drop the pen.

During the last flashback, I didn't remember the conversation between Noah and his attacker. Am I imagining it?

No. . . . What the killer said was too specific, and I've never heard anyone say that before.

Realization settles over me, and my next thought seems impossible. After all this time—all the pain, the guilt, and the what-ifs—*I remembered something.*

CHAPTER 30

DEAD-END DREAMS

Mornings are the hardest. I fall asleep and Marco takes over my dreams. The first moments after I wake up—when my lids are still heavy—those dreams feel real. Dad isn't investigating Marco, and he isn't stealing cars. Spending time with Marco doesn't require sneaking around, and no one is watching our every move.

Then reality sets in, and I have another day of lying and hiding ahead of me.

Thanks to Lex, the next week takes on a predictable pattern. She picks me up early to help me with chemistry before school—at least that's the story we tell Dad. Marco meets me in the basement near the Shop classroom, and we steal some time alone before Chief shows up. Then we spend another twenty minutes in the Shop room, where chemistry tutoring takes place, along with hand holding under the worktable.

Chief isn't stupid. He knows Marco and I are together. He seems almost hopeful every time Marco shows me how to balance an equation, as if he thinks Marco is a step away from getting back on the AP track.

Being so close to Marco makes me desperate for a repeat performance of our make-out session in Lex's pool house. I want to run my hands over his skin and feel his hands on mine.

It's Friday, one week since Marco told me he loved me, and I finally remembered an important detail from the night Noah died. My heart and my mind are getting stronger. That's the reason I haven't shared my breakthrough with anyone yet. I need to see the killer's face, and I'm close.

The steps creak above me, and my heart leaps. But instead of the sound of high-tops pounding the steps, these footfalls belong to someone moving more slowly. Chief rounds the corner of the landing a moment later. This morning he's wearing a Pennzoil cap and a NASCAR jacket over his short-sleeved button-down. He spots me and adjusts his cap.

"Where's your other half?" He walks past me and unlocks the door.

"He's not here yet." I fail at hiding my disappointment.

Chief puts a travel mug on his desk and thumbs through a stack of papers. I settle into my usual seat—the same place I sit during Shop class—and check my text messages.

Nothing.

Without Marco, my chemistry homework reads like a secret code. I draw circles in the margin of my paper. I hate the way we have to sneak around to spend time together. But the fact that he steals cars bothers me even more. I understand why he's doing it, but I still think Marco should tell the police what he knows. If he's so determined to save Deacon, they could go in together.

"Something bothering you?" Chief leans back in his chair and tugs on the bill of his hat. "You haven't done much writing."

I rub my forehead. "I know."

"Does it have anything to do with the boy who sits right there every morning?" He points to Marco's seat. "And stares at you like the sun rises and sets because of you."

Heat creeps up my neck. "He does not."

Chief laughs. "I've known Marco a long time, and I've never seen him look at a girl the way he looks at you. That boy deserves some happiness."

It's easy to see why Marco respects Chief so much. He cares about Marco.

"Can I ask you a question?"

Chief pushes up the bill of his cap. "Is it about chemistry? Because I didn't do so well when I took it in school, and that was a long time ago. They even renamed some planets since then."

"It's not about chemistry."

"All right. Then shoot."

"Do you think it's okay to do the wrong thing for the right reason?" I ask.

Chief adjusts his hat, and for a moment he's quiet. "It depends on what the right reason and wrong thing are. But I figure it's better than doing the wrong thing for the wrong reason."

I tilt my head and smile. "That's obvious."

"Not always. Fear makes the wrong thing seem right sometimes."

I walk over to the table in front of his desk and sit on the top. "What do you mean?"

"Fear is like a ten-cent magician. If you watch the trick a couple of times, you see the flaws and you know how the magician is doing it. But the first time, that same trick looks good. When we're scared, we don't always think things through. We react. It's human nature. Fear can make the wrong decision feel right." He runs his fingers over the patches on his NASCAR jacket. "By then, it's too late."

I point at the NASCAR patch toward the top. "Why did you leave?" I immediately regret asking. The question is too personal. "I'm sorry. That's none of my business."

He holds up his hand, indicating that it's okay. "I gave up too easy. Remember when we talked about shifting gears when a car's on a hill?"

I nod.

"I guess you could say I slid backward and crashed."

"How?"

He takes off his hat and shapes the bill. "Lost a driver. The best one I ever crewed for."

"He died?" I swallow hard.

Chief shakes his head. "No. But he killed his career, and it was my fault."

"What happened?"

"That boy could drive a stock car like nobody I'd ever

seen. But he was young and hotheaded. He wasn't ready for NASCAR, not up here anyway." He taps his head. "I hadn't crewed for anyone that good in a long time. I pushed him too hard and threw him into races with seasoned pros before he was ready. I loved that boy like a son, and I should've been thinking about what was best for him."

Chief frowns and tugs his hat on again. "My driver had a bad race, a real big loss. He blamed it on another driver—one who put his car into the wall and cost him the race. He threatened to tamper with the other guy's car. It was just talk, but in organized racing, that's as good as a death threat."

This story is headed somewhere bad. "What happened?"

"The NASCAR commission banned him from racing. I tried to tell him there were other kinds of racing. I even offered to go with him. But he didn't see the doors open to him, only the one that was shut. He went back to where I found him racing as a teenager, and I followed him. Decided I was done teaching kids how to race, and I started teaching them how cars work instead."

Chief pauses and looks at me. "I've only seen one driver with as much natural talent behind the wheel. His son."

My mind spins, and the pieces click into place. "Wait? You're not talking about Marco, are you?"

"Wish I wasn't. Marco's life would've turned out a lot different if I hadn't made so many mistakes with his father. I failed Marco's dad the same way I failed Deacon. And myself. Like I said, I gave up too easy. In life, a person has to fight for the things that matter to them—and that includes yourself."

"Why are you telling me this?"

"Marco will fight for his sister, for his friends, and I'm willing to bet he'd fight to the ends of the earth for you. But he won't fight for himself. He only sees one door, Frankie. He needs someone to show him the other ones."

The conversation with Chief leaves me reeling. Marco's dad wasn't just a monster who taught his son to street race so he could make money betting on Marco's races. His father raced professionally—at the highest level. Why didn't he teach Marco how to race on a track, or ask Chief to teach him?

Marco loves cars and he's smart. He could've followed in his father's footsteps and raced legally. Instead, he's street racing and stealing cars.

With the exception of a few people rifling through their lockers or sitting on the floor doing homework, the hallways are still empty. I push through the double doors and cross the quad.

I feel around inside my backpack for my cell phone and walk toward Lot B. Marco is usually here by now.

Deacon's hunter-green Firebird sits at the far end, parked diagonally across two spaces. Typical. I've never seen him on campus before, and I'm not thrilled to see his car. I turn around, still watching the Firebird, and I smack right into someone.

Hard blue eyes settle on me. From this angle, Deacon's scars look straight, like one smooth slash instead of lots of jagged cuts. He rolls the toothpick in his mouth with his teeth.

"Have you seen Marco?" I keep my tone light.

He tips his chin toward the opposite end of Lot B. "Something wrong?"

"No. I just wanted to talk to him before first period."

Deacon watches me, slow and lazy like a tiger before it pounces on an antelope and tears it apart. His neck muscles twitch down to his shoulders.

"I'm thinking it's better if you don't." He studies me from under the curved bill of his baseball cap. "Talk to him, I mean."

"What?" I laugh, pretending that I think he's joking.

Deacon turns the toothpick. Wearing a ribbed white tank without his hoodie, he looks bigger than he did the night of the street races. "You've been doing too much talking, and now you've got my boy's head all screwed up." He winds his finger in a circular motion next to his temple.

"I don't know what you're talking about."

He reaches out and lifts a few strands of my hair and rubs them between his fingers. "A smart girl like you from the Heights . . ." He drops my hair. "I bet you can figure it out."

I shrink back and hate myself for letting a guy like Deacon Kelley intimidate me. I know he helped Sofia, but I still think he's scum. But he's dangerous scum, so I play along. "You don't like Marco dating a girl from the Heights. Is that it?"

Deacon raises an eyebrow and gives me his poor imitation of a smile. "Dating? Is that what you think you two are doing?"

Why did I use that word in front of him?

"I don't give a shit who Marco screws." Deacon lowers his

voice. "You're not the first girl he hooked up with from the Heights. He's always had a thing for rich chicks."

He is trying to upset me. I meet his gaze. "I guess you just don't like girls like me."

Deacon shifts his weight. "Hey, come on now. I never said I didn't like you, *Angel*." The word sounds toxic coming from him. "This isn't personal. You're a distraction, and me and Marco have shit to take care of."

"What kind of shit?"

Deacon's ice-blue eyes turn dark. "With all the talking you two have been doing, I bet you know." He doesn't blink. He's analyzing my reaction, the same way Dad does. "Don't you, Frankie?"

"Is this some kind of test? Because I'm not interested." Lying to Deacon can't be any harder than lying to my father.

A Mazda honks, and Deacon's head snaps in its direction. The kid behind the wheel turns pale. "Sorry, Deacon. I didn't know it was you."

Deacon brings his fist down on the hood of the car, and it leaves a dent. "Pay attention, or something might happen to this piece of shit you're driving."

The kid nods, his hands glued to the wheel.

A line of cars forms behind the Mazda. I step out of the way, and Deacon follows. If I don't act normal, he'll figure out I know more than I'm telling him.

"I gotta take off, Frankie. I'm glad we had time to talk." He walks toward the Firebird. "I don't want you to get the wrong idea. I'm just looking out for you. This thing with you and Marco

261

will get old, and he'll move on." He pauses, and his expression hardens. "I'd hate to see a pretty girl like you get hurt."

Marco pulls in just minutes after Deacon leaves. After my conversation with his so-called best friend, my knees still feel like rubber. I must look rattled, because Marco rushes over the moment he sees me.

He slides his arm around my waist, and I lean against him. Usually, I keep my distance until we're inside the school, just in case Dad has someone watching me. Right now I don't care. As soon as he touches me, I feel safe.

"Are you okay?"

"I was worried," I manage.

He brings his lips to my ear. "Me too. I texted you three times."

I'm two seconds away from spilling every word Deacon said when a gut feeling stops me. Deacon isn't as stupid as people think. He's playing a chess game, and I'm just one of the pieces. But I haven't figured out his strategy yet.

I take a deep breath and run my fingers along the side of Marco's face. "Did you think someone kidnapped me?"

Marco stiffens and looks at me. "Not funny."

I push out my bottom lip and give him my best pout. "Come on . . . it's a little funny."

"If you keep looking at me like that, I'll kidnap you myself."

"Promise?"

Marco smiles and grabs my hand, pulling me through the doors of the main building. "What were you doing in the parking lot, anyway?"

"Looking for you."

Inside, he walks me to my locker. I bang the side of my fist against the number two on the door, and it pops open. Most days, the instant gratification puts a smile on my face, but remembering that I'm using Deacon's old locker makes me hate it all over again. I'll ask Mrs. Lane to assign me a new one as soon as I have time. If she won't let me switch, I will carry my books around for the rest of the year.

My cell vibrates.

> We are leaving for Richard's
> college reunion at Yale. Hope all is
> well. We'll bring you a sweatshirt.
> I'll see you at the gala. xo Mom

Only my mother texts in complete sentences and ignores the fact that we aren't speaking.

Marco rubs the back of my neck with his thumb. "I'd give kidnapping some thought if it was the only way to be alone with you."

"Don't plan any kidnappings yet. I think I just figured out a way for us to get some alone time."

He grins. "How?"

The bell rings, and Cruz turns the corner like clockwork. She snaps her fingers and points in the direction of our classroom. "Let's go. We've got poetry to destroy and a teacher to shock."

"I'll tell you later." I shut my locker and let go of Marco's hand at the last possible moment, rushing to catch up with Cruz.

I grab her arm just before we enter the classroom. "How well do you really know Deacon?"

"Too well. Why?"

"Will you tell me about him?" If Deacon is already playing a game, I need to catch up.

She gives me a strange look. "What do you want to know?"

"Everything."

CHAPTER 31

THE ALWAYS KIND

When I slide my key into the lock and the door opens, I'm surprised it still works. The strange landscaping along the driveway and the newly painted green door made me wonder if I had walked up to the wrong house. Disney World–esque sculpted trees have replaced the cherry blossoms all the neighbors envied.

Mom loves taking a chain saw to the past and starting over. The house has been redecorated so many times that I can look at the wallpaper in a photo and pinpoint the year it was taken. But this is another level. Even Lex looked shocked when she dropped me off in front of the fawn-shaped bushes.

Lex agreed to lie for me again—well, technically her mom was doing the lying, but Lex had to physically hand her mom the phone to make it happen.

I walk across the marble entryway, relieved that Mom hasn't changed anything inside. As far as I can see, anyway. She probably converted my bedroom into a gift-wrapping room or something equally pretentious.

The front of the house faces the driveway. I sit on the bottom step of the main staircase and wait.

Within minutes, my cell vibrates. It's him. He's walking up the driveway. I catch a glimpse of myself in the gilded mirror Mom shipped home from Venice a few summers ago. Moonlight from the skylights streaks the glass, giving my skin a pale glow. I shake out my dark waves.

Two light knocks on the door, and my stomach flutters. I open the door and Marco slips inside, pushing it closed with one hand and sliding the other around my waist. "Hey."

The desire in his eyes is only a fraction of the tension building inside me. "Hey."

"I missed you." He brushes the hair over my shoulders and away from my face. His thumb grazes the sensitive skin along my collarbone, and the tension coils tighter.

"You saw me a few hours ago," I say, as if I didn't miss him just as much.

Marco tugs on the belt loops of my jeans, pulling me against him. "Four and a half, if we're counting." He licks his lips, staring down at me. "Which I am."

"Me too." I rest my hands on his hips, wishing it were raining outside so I'd have an excuse to make him take off his shirt again.

"You're sure you won't get in trouble?" he asks. "What if Lex's mom figures out you aren't there?"

"That would require her mom to pay attention. If that happens, we should prepare for Armageddon."

"How much time do we have?" He tunnels his hand through my hair.

Not enough. "Two hours."

A week ago, that would've felt like plenty of time. Now it seems like seconds. It's crazy how much your life can change so fast. How someone you like can become the person you can't live without.

Tugging on Marco's shirt, I walk backward to the marble staircase. "Come on."

He looks up at the massive crystal chandelier hanging above our heads. "I'm not arguing." He takes my hand, and I lead him up the steps and down the hallway toward my bedroom. Marco takes in the surroundings—colorful oil paintings, Impressionist landscapes, and a charcoal Miró sketch; stained red cherry floors; and Turkish rugs worth more than his car. I walk faster, embarrassed by the extravagance.

Marco has never seen this part of my life. I can't help but wonder if it will change what he thinks of me.

I stop at my bedroom door, hand on the knob and my heart beating wildly in my chest. I've never had a boy in my room before—except Abel, and he doesn't count, because we were never more than friends. Noah and I had to hang out in the living room or the basement—rooms without a bed.

"What's wrong?" Marco senses my hesitation. "You don't have to take me in your bedroom." He wraps his arms around my waist from where he stands behind me.

"I want to." I turn the knob and press the pad that switches on the crystal chandelier on the ceiling, sending dots of light dancing across the pale blue walls. Blue and silver. Velvet and silk. Mom wanted my room to look like the inside of a Tiffany's little blue box.

Marco walks over to my dresser and picks up one of the silver frames I left behind. It's a shot of me playing the piano at a showcase concert last year. "I didn't know you played the piano."

"I don't anymore."

He reaches for one of the frames lying facedown.

"Not that one." I rush to stop him.

"Is that him?" He keeps his hand on the frame but doesn't pick it up.

"Yeah. I haven't turned it over since . . ." I look down and study the pattern on the rug. It's hard to distinguish between the blues and greens in the dim light.

Marco lifts my chin with his finger. "If you need more time because . . . you're not over him." He rubs the back of his neck. "I'm an idiot. Of course you aren't over him. Maybe you're still in love with him?"

"Stop." I touch his lips with my finger. "I miss him, but it's not what you think. We grew up together, and Noah was one of my best friends. But he feels so far away." I feel guilty admitting it.

And you're my right now.

The corner of his mouth turns up. "I like your room."

It looks like a page out of a trendy magazine. "No, you don't."

He takes my hand and leads me to the end of the bed. We sit on the edge and he smiles sheepishly, planting a quick kiss on my lips. "Okay. I don't. It doesn't feel like you in here."

"I know." Mom decorated every inch, and except for a few framed photos, there's nothing personal in this room.

"Sofia would love it."

I try to imagine how it looks from his point of view.

"What's going on in your head?" Marco asks.

"My bedroom—this house—it must make me look like a spoiled rich girl from the Heights. But I'm not that girl anymore."

"I know who you are, Frankie." He reaches out and traces a line down the center of my lips, and my breath catches. "You're so beautiful it hurts to look at you. And you're even more beautiful on the inside."

I touch his chest and feel his heart pounding. He's the beautiful one. I tug on his T-shirt, needing him closer. "Come here."

He watches me from beneath long lashes, drinking me in. I clutch his shirt tighter and press my forehead against his. Marco's response is immediate—his fingers slip under the hem of my T-shirt and press against my sides.

"I'm scared." Finally, I say something true.

"Me too," he whispers. "Whenever you're one minute late, I think you aren't going to show. That you finally figured out I'm not good enough for you. I used to be different. Maybe if you'd met me back then . . . before my mom died and my dad got locked up. But after the accident, things changed, and I can't go back."

Every word feels like it could have come from my lips. I'm not the same person I was before Noah died. If anyone understands how one experience can change your entire life, it's me. "I used to be different, too. Noah's death changed me. I'm broken, Marco." A knot forms in my throat, and I can't choke it down. "And there's no way to fix me."

His lips graze mine, and he pauses to suck my lower lip. The ice inside me melts, and a sigh escapes my lips. "I don't want to fix you, Angel. I just want *you*."

He kisses me again. Suddenly, anything seems possible. I feel it every time we're together now—possibility.

When we come up for air and he grabs the waistband of my jeans to tug me closer, every part of me is on fire. I never imagined feeling the way I do right now—like nothing matters more than the boy in my arms. Like no one has ever understood me the way he does.

Marco runs his hand across my stomach and presses his fingers against my back, urging me closer. I drag my fingers over his side, feeling goose bumps spring up beneath my touch. Our legs twist together and Marco rolls onto his back, taking me with him. I feel waves of heat, and a tingling sensation that starts in my belly travels down to my toes, dragging me to the edge and then releasing me again just before I break.

"Marco." The need in my voice when I say his name creates an unbearable tension.

"Frankie . . ." My name sounds like a moan, and I feel how much he wants me as I press against him.

"Maybe we should slow down. I—" *What? Want you more than I've ever wanted anyone, and it scares the crap out of me? And I'm feeling things I've never felt—sensations I never realized my body could feel—and I'm terrified to lose control?*

I can't tell him the truth.

Marco freezes, his fingers touching the silky strip of fabric underneath the zipper of my jeans. His chest heaves against mine, and without his hands and lips to distract me, I realize how fast my heart is beating. He has probably slept with dozens of girls. Maybe more. He's not the kind of guy who takes things slow.

He slides his hand up to the curve of my waist, just above the waistband of my jeans, and pulls back so he can look at me. His dark eyes lock with mine. "Have you ever done this before?"

I know what he's asking, but I don't want to answer. I bite my lip and turn my head away.

"Don't do that, Frankie. Look at me." His voice is low and raw from kissing me. It's crazy how much I love the way Marco says my name. He moves his hand away from my waist and brings it up to my face, tracing a path along my jawline. He turns my face toward him gently. "Look at me."

I force myself to meet his gaze. Marco's brows pull together, worry branded on his beautiful features.

Please don't ask. Just kiss me.

I repeat the words over and over in my head, hoping I'll develop telepathic abilities in the next ten seconds.

He takes a breath, and I know the question is coming. "Are you a virgin?"

271

I bite my lip and cover my face with my hands. I nod—the tiniest movement imaginable. I want to evaporate into the air.

"Shit." He eases off me and pulls me up against his chest, and his cheek brushes mine as he brings his lips to my ear. "Don't hide from me. You don't have to be embarrassed. I'm the jerk." He rests his forehead on my shoulder. "We can take things as slow as you want. I'll never ask you to do anything you aren't ready for. Just don't go anywhere, okay?"

I uncover my face and slide my arms around Marco's neck.

He notices the time illuminated on my alarm clock. "Lex will be here in a few minutes to pick you up."

"It's not enough time." I press my face against his chest,

He strokes my hair. "I know. Having you in my arms like this is all I want."

"Will you text me tonight and tell me that ten more times? Or twenty?"

Marco grins. "I'll tell you a hundred times." He bites his lip. "But I want you to be sure. All this sneaking around . . . if it's too hard—"

"It doesn't matter how hard it is." I take his face in my hands. "Because I'm in love with you."

I fell for him the first night I kissed him, but falling in love didn't happen because of one mind-blowing event. It happened during dozens of everyday moments—watching him carry his sister's backpack, listening to him talk about his mom, hearing the sound of my name on his lips. Now it feels like I've loved him forever.

Marco stares at me with a dazed look, like I just told him I was a mermaid. "Don't feel like you have to say it just because I did."

"I love you, Marco Leone. And it's the always kind."

CHAPTER 32

—

HANDCUFFS AND HEARTBREAK

The streetlight in front of the apartment building blinks, on the verge of burning out. Lex parks in the spot in front of the balcony, and Cujo stands on his hind legs, paws up against the window ledge, as if he senses I'm out here.

Colored lights flicker behind his pointy ears. Dad leaves the TV on for Cujo if he'll be gone for a long time—a crime show channel, because he thinks our dog likes reruns of *Law & Order* and *Cold Case*.

Our dog.

I stare at the two-story garden apartment building with the shitty outdoor staircase that sucks even more if it's raining, the identical balconies with the parking-lot views, and the sliding glass doors that offer zero privacy.

This place is home, and that's okay.

The fact that I can't stand to look at Dad doesn't matter. I feel like myself here—or at least like I'm getting closer to figuring out who I am now.

"Do you believe everything happens for a reason?" Lex looks straight ahead, her expression impossible to read. We used to sit outside behind my house for hours, lying on our backs and staring at the stars in silence. A person really understands you if you don't have to say a word to hear each other. "Frankie?"

"I'm not sure. That would mean Noah's death happened for a reason, and I can't think of one that makes sense. Maybe some things do and others don't."

Lex props her elbow against the window. "It feels so arbitrary."

"I know." I get out, but I don't close the car door. "I'm worried about him, Lex."

She knows I'm talking about Marco. "Worrying won't change anything. It's just a way to fool yourself into believing things will turn out differently."

I'm not sure what she means. As she drives away, a heaviness settles in my stomach. Marco isn't the only person I'm worried about.

The note on the kitchen table is barely legible.

Working late. There's pizza in the freezer.
Don't forget to lock the door. Dad

At least he won't be here all night spying on me. I crumple the message and toss it in the trash.

After an hour of bad TV, my cell phone rings.

"Frankie? It's Cruz," she says before I say hello. "Are you there? Frankie?"

"Did she pick up?" Ava asks in the background.

"What's wrong?" I hear it in her voice. Something bad happened.

"Marco was arrested."

The world stops, and there's nothing but panic and a loud echoing sound, like a big seashell is pressed against my ear. But instead of ocean waves, wind rips through my head. It's like I'm in a flashback with no images. Picturing Marco in jail . . . I can't do it. Or I won't let myself.

"Frankie?"

"I'm here." The words sound far away. "Did he get caught racing?"

She's silent for a second at the other end of the line. "Marco told me that you know about his . . . *situation*. He wasn't racing. The cops busted him in a stolen car."

He stole another car.

What did I expect? Marco never told me he'd stop.

But I hoped he would.

Why? Because he loves me? Or because I told him I loved him tonight? Love doesn't pay the bills.

Cruz starts talking again. "Marco couldn't say much. But it sounded like someone set him up. The cops were waiting. State troopers. They busted him right after he got in the car."

"Who could've set him up?" I ask.

"Maybe someone overheard a conversation. I'm on my way to the police station now."

The cops won't let her see Marco. Only a lawyer or a legal guardian will get past Dad and Tyson—and I know they're involved. They call the shots in RATTF, which means my father arrested the guy I love, or he knew about it.

"Come get me." I grab my backpack and head for the front door.

"Text me your address. But you shouldn't go down there, Frankie. There's nothing you can do."

If only that were true.

Ava parks next to a fleet of Crown Vics and SUVs at the state police barracks. Cruz bites her nails as she eyes the uniformed state troopers walking in and out. I'm not ready to tell Cruz that my dad is one of them, especially not with her sister sitting next to her. If she comes inside, it won't take her long to figure it out.

"Maybe I should go in alone." It takes every ounce of strength to keep my tone casual. The thought of Marco in handcuffs or inside a cell tears me up.

Cruz gives me a strange look. "Why?"

Here goes. Either she'll buy it or she won't. "Marco is a minor. The only people who can see him are his lawyers or legal guardians. It's in every cop movie."

She rubs her eyes. "You're right."

"Then why would you go in?" Ava asks. Smart girl.

"We're closer to the Heights than the Downs. Maybe they'll give a nice rich girl from the Heights some information."

Cruz shrugs. "It's worth a try." It kills me how easily she accepts the idea that they might treat me differently. I get out of the car and walk toward the barracks—that's what the state police call their precincts.

Dad can walk into any one of them and use the facilities, but the undercover task forces don't have regular offices in police buildings. They rent commercial office space above law firms and interior-design studios.

This is one of the older barracks, tan brick with a brown shingled roof. It looks like it belongs in a documentary from the nineties. The Maryland state flag flying out front is the only thing that isn't outdated.

Dad won't be happy if I walk in there, but I'm doing it for Marco.

I push through the door and walk straight to the counter. An officer wearing a brown-and-tan uniform eyes me suspiciously. "Can I help you, young lady?"

"Yes, sir. I think my dad is here. Jimmy Devereux? He's with the Regional Auto Theft Task Force." I say each word with confidence, as if I drop by to visit my dad all the time.

The trooper peers over the counter. "You're Jimmy's daughter? Frances, right?"

"Frankie."

"I was close. Jimmy talks about you whenever he comes in."

He smiles. I'm a cop's daughter, which makes me one of their own. He points at the door to my left. "Come on back, and I'll see if I can track him down."

He reaches for the phone receiver in front of him.

"I wanted to surprise him," I say quickly.

"All right."

He buzzes the door open for me. On the other side, desks are arranged in rows.

The officer who buzzed me in talks to a few cops in street clothes wearing shoulder holsters over their T-shirts.

"Your dad is sitting in on an interrogation," he says when he comes back. "When he takes a break, we'll call him out."

"Thanks."

"You can wait over there." He points at a bank of white plastic chairs that look like the red ones in the lobby where I sat on the night of my DUI.

The room smells like old sneakers and hamburgers.

A cop barrels his way through, followed by another officer and a pissed-off guy in handcuffs. The guy jerks against the cop's hold, and I shrink back.

"Get your hands off me, or I'll sue your asses for police brutality." The guy's nose bleeds onto his lips, and he spits on the floor. "I know my rights. You can't bust into somebody's house."

Watching the guy walk away in cuffs makes me think of Marco. Is he handcuffed right now? I spot my father across the room. He rushes toward me, his expression shifting from concerned to suspicious.

"How did you know I was here?" He already knows the answer, and his expression darkens. "You came because of *him*." I'm betraying my dad—that's the message.

I push myself out of the sticky plastic seat, knees shaking. "Dad—"

"Not here." He clenches his jaw and takes my elbow, leading me toward the offices in the back. I smile at the cops who say hi as we pass. I'm not trying to humiliate my father. I'm trying to save the boy I love.

Dad opens one of the doors and pushes me inside. Tyson stands by an open window holding a cigarette and a portable travel fan. "Hey, Frankie."

"I told you to stop smoking in here." Dad points at the cigarette.

Tyson holds up his blue fan. "I've got the fan on, Jimmy. Relax."

"We need some privacy. Father-daughter talk." Dad's tone is icy.

Tyson stubs out the cigarette on the bottom of his work boot and shuts the door as he leaves.

I've never seen Dad so angry. He turns on me the second Tyson closes the door. "I told you not to see Marco Leone again, didn't I? Or did you think that was a request?"

"I'm sorry, Dad. But you can't charge him. Please." My voice shakes.

"Do you think I brought him here for a tour? We busted him sitting behind the wheel of a *stolen* car." Dad stands and presses his palms against the table in front of him. "Let me repeat that part in case you missed it the first time. He was sitting in a *stolen* car with the key in the ignition."

"You don't know the whole story. Marco's dad stole cars for someone else before he was arrested. After his father went to jail, the guy he worked for came after Marco. The guy told Marco that he had to pay off his father's debt." I'm talking too fast, but if I slow down, Dad might cut me off before I finish. "He knew Marco and his sister were living alone, and he threatened to report them to Child Services if Marco didn't pay him."

"Marco should've gone to the police."

I'm not getting through to my dad. "He couldn't, not without losing his sister. Marco didn't want to steal cars. His dad's boss forced—"

"Forced him to do it?" Dad shouts over me. "Is that what you want me to believe? When Tyson and I followed him, Marco drove straight from the Heights to that car. No one was forcing him. I could've waited until he drove it to the dockyard and arrested him for felony theft."

My head spins, caught on something Dad said.

When Tyson and I followed him, he drove straight from the Heights . . .

I jump out of the chair. It tips over and falls backward, crashing against the floor.

"You *used* me!" I shout.

Dad leans toward me, his hands still planted on the desk. "No. You *lied* to me, and I found out."

"I'm in love with him, and there's nothing you can do about

it." My voice cracks, and I can't hold back the tears. "I'll be eighteen in four months."

"He'll be in jail by then."

"They have visiting hours." I swipe at my face, brushing away the tears. "So do whatever you want, Dad. You can't stop me from loving him. It's the one thing you can't control."

His expression is unreadable. "Are you really in love with this boy, Frankie? Do you even know what that means?"

"Of course I do."

"What are you willing to do to protect him?" Dad asks.

"Anything." I look my father in the eye.

He nods slowly and paces the length of the room. "I'll make you a deal. Give me your word that you'll end things with Marco, and I'll let him walk."

"What?" I must have misunderstood. Dad would never bend the rules—let alone the law. Not even for me.

"You heard me."

I shake my head in disbelief. "You'd never let someone break the law and walk."

"I would if it helps me catch his boss. If you're right and Marco is stealing these cars for someone else, that person is the one we want."

"Marco probably won't tell you." Not after the way he reacted when I suggested it.

"Maybe he won't have to. Let me worry about how to do my job." Dad crosses his arms. "No games this time. If you start seeing Marco Leone again, we'll charge him for his felony stunt tonight and let a court decide if he's guilty and I will make it my personal mission to dig up every bit of dirt under that boy's fingernails. And if he steals another car or commits a crime of any kind, the deal is off."

"Why are you doing this?" I stare at my father, the man who is supposed to protect me. The man hurting me more than anyone ever has.

"I'm saving you from ruining the rest of your life."

"I don't need anyone to save me!" I yell so loud that my throat feels raw.

Dad doesn't flinch. "So what's it going to be, Frankie? Do you love this boy enough to give him up?"

CHAPTER 33

THE SPEED OF SORROW

I don't remember leaving the barracks. Everything feels like a blur after Dad's *deal*—that's what he's calling the choice he gave me. *Destroying your daughter's life* doesn't have quite the same ring to it.

Outside, I stumble down the steps and miss the last one, cracking my knee on the sidewalk. The odors of gasoline, stale cigarette smoke, and vending-machine coffee mingle in the air. Cruz gets out of the car the moment she sees me.

What do I tell her?

"Frankie?" She frowns.

Around me, sirens wail and red and blue lights flash as police cars fly out of the parking lot. It reminds me of the night Noah died.

"What happened in there? You look like someone beat the crap out of you."

Someone did.

We're only a few parking spaces away from Cruz's car. Ava watches us from the driver's-side window.

"Wait." I stop walking. "I need to tell you something, but not in front of your sister. Can we drop her off?"

"Yeah, but we can't hang out at my house. My dad doesn't let us have anyone over."

"We'll drop Ava off and go somewhere else."

"I still can't drive." Cruz lifts her sling away from her chest.

"I can."

"Your license is suspended."

"Ask me if I care." My voice cracks, and I close my eyes.

"Now you're freaking me out." She grabs my arm and drags me to the car.

As Ava drives, I stare out the window from the backseat. Cruz turns around to check on me, but she doesn't ask any questions. The ride isn't long enough, and I still haven't figured out how to tell her that my dad is the cop who arrested Marco.

But I am going to tell her.

Cruz trusted me with the truth about her abusive father—a secret that could land Cruz and her sisters in foster care if the wrong person found out.

We drop Ava off, and I slide into the driver's seat. I hit the gas, the GT-R flies backward out of the parking space. A quick jerk on the wheel, and the car fishtails and ends up facing in the direction I want to go.

Away from here.

Cruz puts her hand on the dashboard for support. "Are you crazy? Or do you want to end up in jail, too?"

The gearshift slides from fourth to fifth gear, and we pass the recycling plant where Cruz coached me before the race.

"Where are you going?" she asks. When I don't respond, she smacks her hand against the dash. "Frankie? Answer me or pull over."

"To V Street." I wasn't sure until now.

"For what? Did you hear something at the police station?"

"I need to drive." Fast and hard—if I want to outrun the feelings that will break my heart when they catch up with me.

"Pull over." Cruz isn't screwing around, but I can't stop.

My hands tighten on the wheel. "If I keep moving, nothing will change. Everything will be okay."

"Why isn't everything okay?" Cruz sounds calmer, as if she sees the hurricane churning around me.

Headlights flicker in the distance.

"Because my dad is a cop."

Cruz falls back against the seat, her eyes wide. "You're bullshitting me, right?"

The gas pedal vibrates under my foot. The rest of my body is numb. "He works undercover on an auto theft task force. He's the one who busted Marco." My voice cracks. "And he used me to do it. Marco met me at my mom's house, and my dad followed him after he left."

Up ahead, a row of cars form a path to the strip of asphalt the street racers use as a track. I downshift, and the car slows to a normal speed.

"Does Marco know?" Cruz asks. Her voice sounds cold.

"Yes."

She nods and stares straight ahead. "Did you set Marco up?"

Music pulses outside, but with the windows rolled up, we remain insulated—in a cocoon that's unraveling around us.

"I would *never* do anything like that to Marco. I'm in love with him."

Cruz sighs. "I had to ask." She turns in her seat, and I feel her eyes drilling into me. "Your dad's job was a big secret to keep from me. I thought we were friends."

"We are," I say.

"Friends are supposed to trust each other."

"I do trust you, or I wouldn't have told you. If anyone finds out he's a cop—"

"I won't tell anyone, if that's what you're worried about." Cruz ignores the people waving at her as we drive past the parked cars. "Sofia has nowhere to go if Marco ends up in jail."

"Where is Sofia now? Is she alone?"

Cruz shakes her head. "Don't worry. She's at Miss Lorraine's. She stays there on nights Marco races or . . . you know. Miss Lorraine thinks he's working at the body shop after hours. What if he gets locked up, Frankie?"

"He won't." I pull over, my eyes trained on Video Game Girl as her arms drop and two cars launch down the street. "My dad isn't charging Marco. He's letting him go." Darkness swallows the two cars, and I want to disappear, too.

"Why would he do that?" she asks.

"We made a deal. I stop seeing Marco and my dad lets him

walk, as long as he doesn't get into any more trouble." I roll down the window.

The smell of burnt rubber and exhaust reminds me of the night I raced Cruz's car. With my feet on the pedals and my hand on the gearshift, the outside world didn't exist. I want that feeling again—the rush of driving over a hundred miles an hour. The distraction of vibrating floorboards and an engine revving in subtle ways that only I can hear.

"Marco will never go for it," Cruz says finally.

"He will if I don't tell him." The next thought makes my throat burn, and I can't hold back the tears. "I'm going to end it."

Cruz sucks in a breath. "Without telling him why?"

The street racers return to the starting line.

"It's the only way to protect him . . . and Sofia." Saying the words steals whatever false hope I have left. I'll never kiss Marco again or feel his arms around me.

"I want to race your car." I curl my fingers around the wheel. Losing myself—blocking out the pain—it's the only way I'll survive giving him up.

"You're bawling, and you want to race?"

I wipe my eyes on the bottom of my shirt. "Yes."

"This is a bad idea. You're losing your shit right now, and you aren't thinking straight. The race against Pryor wasn't the way things normally go. He gave you a car length, and he was driving an unmodified car." She points at the racing strip. "You won't get those odds twice."

"I don't care."

Cruz shakes her head. "You can't just race for fun. You've gotta put up money or a car—and if you think I'm letting you bet a car that doesn't even belong to me—"

"I've got money." I pull a wad of bills out of my bag.

"Do you always carry around that much cash?"

"I brought it in case we needed it for bail."

Cruz holds out her hand. "How much?"

I give her the money, and the bills unfold into a crumpled mess in her palm. "Two hundred."

"You've obviously never bailed anyone out of jail before, because this wouldn't cover it."

"He won't need it now," I say softly.

"This is still a lot of money. Are you sure you want to throw it away on a race?"

"Unless you'll take it. You could use it for part of the rent next month."

Cruz laughs. "Thanks. But I'll be out of this sling in a week. I like to pay my own way."

"Then I want to race." I'll do anything to take this pain away, even for a minute. But there's another reason. I need to say good-bye.

Good-bye to the girl who fell in love with a street racer—a girl who raced one crazy night and won. I'm still that girl, but part of her belongs to Marco.

"Wait here. I'll see what I can do." Cruz heads into the crowd, blending in with the other girls from the Downs. I'll never be one of them, but I don't feel like I'm from the Heights anymore, either. I'm caught in the middle.

I'm not sure how long Cruz is gone. Eventually, I see her silhouette and long ponytail swaying behind her. She opens the door and slides into the passenger seat. "I scored you a race, but it wasn't easy. Most people want to race for more than two hundred bucks." She gestures at the starting line. "Let's go."

I focus on Video Game Girl leaning through the window of a black muscle car.

When I pull up next to the car, Cruz gets out and Video Game Girl snaps to attention. As she steps away from the car, I see the driver.

Ortiz from Shop class grins at me. "You sure about this, Frankie? I don't wanna take your money."

"I'm sure."

"You don't have to tell me twice." He pats the dashboard. "My girl needs a racing clutch."

Cruz steps away from the car and joins the crowd. Video Game Girl follows the same sequence she did when I raced before—she checks in with the drivers, issues instructions, and stands in her designated spot.

We flash our headlights to signal we're ready.

My movements feel more natural this time as my feet exert the ideal amount of pressure on the pedals to hold the GT-R at five thousand RPMs. I keep my hand on the gearshift, eyes on the road, and ears tuned to the engine. I focus on the gold bangles on Video Game Girl's wrists, waiting for her arms to drop.

The second they do, I let out the clutch and hit the gas. The engine guns, and when I hear the RPMs reach the magic number, I shift.

Second gear . . .

Third . . .

Ortiz pulls ahead, and his engine roars.

Fourth . . .

Fifth . . .

Sixth . . .

His taillights fly ahead of me, as if Cruz's car is moving in slow motion and Ortiz is driving at warp speed.

I don't care.

Adrenaline races through my veins, and my bones thrum from the speed. In this moment, no one else controls me or my future. No one decides who I love or hate.

Ortiz crosses the finish line as I'm circling back. The headlights from the rows of cars on V Street fade, and there's nothing but darkness—the kind I want to lose myself in.

When I make it back, Cruz runs up to the car and hops in, her forehead creased with worry. "You okay?"

"No." My voice is a whisper.

Ortiz jogs up to Cruz's car and taps on the roof. "Nice job, Frankie." He winks at Cruz. "I get a warm and fuzzy feeling inside knowing that my future wife is a good teacher."

She rolls her eyes and holds out the cash. "You'd think a guy with an imagination like yours would get better grades."

"I feel bad taking your money, Frankie." Ortiz stares at the bills in Cruz's hand.

"But let me guess?" she asks. "You'll still take it?"

"Damn straight." He stuffs it into the pocket of his jeans and jogs toward a group of girls shouting his name. "Duty calls."

"Did racing make you feel any better?" Cruz asks when he's gone.

"I'm not ready to lose him." My voice trembles.

Cruz bites her lip. "He won't get over this, Frankie."

"Neither will I."

CHAPTER 34

THIS IS HOW WE BREAK

I leave the house the next morning in time to watch an angry sunrise—a yellow sky streaked with red. Dad came home after two o'clock in the morning and cracked my bedroom door to see if I was still awake. I kept my face buried in the damp pillow under my cheek and pretended to be asleep.

I texted Marco right away.

r u up?

After a few minutes the bubbles appeared on the screen.

yeah. i need to talk to you.

We agreed to meet just after sunrise—early enough that Dad would still be asleep, but late enough that I wasn't sneaking out in the middle of the night. I left a note on the kitchen table.

Keeping my end of the deal.
Be back.

No *Love, Frankie*. Dad and I were way past that.

I took the bus and walked under the last red streaks in the sky, and now I'm sitting on the curb in Lot B, waiting for Marco. The first time I saw him was in this parking lot. It wasn't that long ago, but it feels like forever now that it's about to end.

Across the street, kids in pajamas push their way out of the 7-Eleven, their parents carrying white paper bags and coffee cups. As a kid, I loved Saturday mornings. I spent most of the day in my pajamas, too.

After today I'll hate Saturdays and angry sunrises, the sight of 7-Eleven and Lot B.

Marco pulls in a few spaces away from where I'm sitting, but he doesn't rush over and scoop me up in his arms. He approaches me slowly, the dark circles around his eyes proof that he didn't sleep last night, either.

My heart skips.

How am I going to break his heart and mine—and walk away?

Because you love him, you have to protect him.

Marco stops in front of me, shoulders hunched. "Did you tell your dad I was meeting you at Lex's?"

"How can you ask me that?" The words hit me like a slap.

He drags his hands over his head and sits next to me. "I need you to answer me."

"Of course not." A bitter laugh escapes my lips. "I told you I love you, and you're asking me if I sold you out to my father? It's nice to know what you really think of me." I turn and head toward the sidewalk.

He doesn't trust me. Maybe he doesn't love me, either.

My chest tightens.

"Frankie!"

Keep moving. One foot in front of the other.

Sneakers pound the street, and Marco circles around me, blocking my path. "I'm sorry. I don't know what I was thinking."

I stop. "Sure you do."

"You're right. I'm thinking I am a jerk for asking you something like that. You warned me that your dad was good at his job. I guess I didn't realize how good." He dips his head, trying to get me to look at him. "I'm sorry. Forgive me?"

I nod and sit on the curb.

Marco sits next to me and takes my hand, turning it over in his. "What did your father say?"

"That I can't see you anymore."

He squeezes my hand. "I figured that much. We should probably stick to hanging out before school for a while. I don't want him to catch you lying about being at Lex's."

This is it. Say it.

Marco touches my face, and I shatter inside. "What's wrong? Are you still pissed at me?"

Lex pushed me into her pool once when the heater was broken. She didn't know, and it was April, only a month after it had stopped snowing. When I hit the water, it knocked the air out of my lungs, and my legs felt like they weighed hundreds of pounds. For the first few seconds, the cold stabbed at my skin like bee stings. Then my skin went numb. I still couldn't catch my breath, but I didn't feel cold.

I feel the same way now.

"We can't see each other anymore." I can't look at him.

"You mean outside of school, until things settle down with your dad? Right?"

"I mean at all." My vision blurs, and tears threaten to spill over. "My dad is a *cop*, and you are a *car thief*. This will never work out."

Marco slides around and kneels in front of me, cradling my face in his hands. His dark eyes find mine, the weight of what's happening bearing down on him.

My mind flashes to the night I knelt in a different parking lot with my heart breaking. This time I'm not the one kneeling, but my heart is breaking all over again.

"You don't mean that, Frankie. You're scared. I get it. But you love me, right?" The pain in his voice pulls the loose thread holding me together, and I can't stop the tears.

Inside, I'm coming apart. "It doesn't matter if I love you."

"Bullshit." He wipes my tears with his thumbs, but they keep falling. "It's the only thing that matters." He presses his lips against mine, and my heart doesn't shatter—it explodes like a bomb inside me, destroying every shred of happiness.

I pull back and scramble to my feet. "I can't do this. I won't let my dad use me to bust you. And I can't let my dad lose his job. He's still my father. It's better if we end things now, or it will only hurt even more when it doesn't work out later."

Marco stands, his eyes trained on me. "How could it hurt more than this?"

"I'm—" I choke back a sob. "I'm not trying to hurt you. This isn't easy for me, either."

Tears pool in his eyes. "Then don't do it." It's a whisper. "I can't lose you. Don't give up on us. I'm begging you."

When Lex pushed me into the pool, my limbs went numb, but they kept thrashing. My body never gave up. Lex pulled me out before it got to that point.

This time there's no one to pull me out, and the numbness spreads like an infection.

"I'm sorry." My voice sounds hoarse. "I have to go."

"Don't do this, Angel."

I turn away and head across the parking lot before I fall apart.

If I make it to the bus stop, I'll be okay.

"Frankie!" Marco calls after me. "I thought our love was the always kind."

I freeze, tears streaming down my face. I want to tell him about the deal with Dad, and I almost turn around. Then the look on my father's face flashes through my mind—the one that said he would destroy Marco if I went back on my word.

A promise like that from my dad . . . it was the always kind, too.

"Frankie?" he calls out again.

297

I finally understand what Marco meant. . . . The sky *does* look different in the Downs. I want to tell him that we can still see the same stars if I tell him about the stars in my sky and he tells me about the ones in his. But I can't say that now. I swallow the thought along with all the other things I want to say.

Instead of answering him, I run.

After riding on a smelly bus with a bunch of strangers, I make it home and find Tyson's Crown Vic parked next to Dad's Tahoe.

I fumble with the house keys, exhausted and defeated.

Cujo's ears perk when I walk in, and Dad and Tyson look up from the papers spread across the coffee table.

"What happened?" Dad asks, without a hint of empathy.

"You lost the right to ask me questions like that when you destroyed my life. My note said it all."

"You didn't have to go see him." My father crosses his arms. "Your cell phone works."

It does. And I want hurl it at his head.

Tyson leans forward, resting his elbows on his knees, and scowls at Dad. "Take it easy, Jimmy."

"I held up my end of your warped little deal, and I have nothing else to say to you. So leave me alone."

Dad watches me from where he's sitting on the fake-leather sofa. "Don't try to turn this around. I told you to stay away from that boy. I'm sorry you're hurting, but you wouldn't be in this situation if you had listened to me."

"Is that what you believe?" I laugh, the sound bitter and razor-sharp. "I'm in this situation because you emotionally blackmailed me. If you're going to throw it in my face, at least be honest."

"Your dad is just looking out for you, Frankie." Tyson gives me a halfhearted smile. "We don't want to see you get hurt."

I march over to the sofa and stand across from my dad, the coffee table between us. "In case it's not perfectly clear, you failed. Because I *am* hurt, and it's *your* fault." Angry tears streak down my face. "You're supposed to be this badass undercover cop, but instead of looking for the guy who is blackmailing Marco into stealing cars, you went after the victim."

Tyson stares at the carpet like he wants to bolt.

"Marco was fifteen when his father went to prison, and some lowlife showed up and said he was responsible for his dad's debt." Thinking about the story makes me cry harder. "He had two options: pay the guy or watch his little sister get dragged away to foster care. I told you all this, and it didn't even matter to you."

Tyson's head snaps up, and he gives Dad an incredulous look. Did Tyson know the whole story? Or did Dad leave out some of the details?

"Because he could've gone to the police," Dad says.

Tyson looks over at Dad. "A fifteen-year-old living on his own in the Downs? If he narced to the cops, he would've ended up in the river, and you know it." He pulls up his sleeve, exposing the black burns branded into the brown skin on his forearm. "This is the kind of shit that happens when the wrong people see you talking to the cops. It doesn't matter if you were only giving them directions. You've worked in the Downs for a long time, man. But living there when you're a kid is different."

"We're talking about my daughter," Dad says through gritted teeth.

Tyson nods, but he doesn't back down. He's the only guy I know who isn't intimidated by Dad. "I was there when Frankie was born. You think I'd let anything happen to her?" Tyson lowers his voice. "Let's talk about this later."

"Are we done here?" I ask.

"I'm trying to protect you," Dad says. "One day you'll understand."

I laugh. "Protect me? You've hurt me more than anyone. You made me give up the guy I *love*—and I did it. And I'll stay away from him because you'll ruin his life unless I act like the daughter you want—instead of the person I really am. You want to control me and you succeeded. Congratulations, Dad. Now you're just like Mom."

Tyson shoves his hands in his pockets and examines the carpet. Dad's forehead furrows, as if I'm not making sense.

But for the first time, everything I'm doing makes perfect sense.

"I never asked you to pretend to be someone you're not," Dad says.

"You can tell yourself that, but we both know the truth.

You haven't trusted me since the DUI. I made a *mistake*. But mistakes aren't allowed in Jimmy Devereux's world, are they? You told me trust has to be earned, and maybe I haven't done enough to earn yours. But you broke my trust when you followed me around and took pictures of my friends. And you haven't earned mine back yet, either."

I stay buried under the covers for the rest of the weekend. Dad knocks on my door a few times, but I pretend I'm asleep. I e-mail Abel and Lex and tell them Dad confiscated my phone for the weekend because I came home late on Friday night. I'm not ready to talk about what happened yet.

Marco texts me nineteen times, and every single message breaks my heart open wider.

> i love you, frankie. the always kind.
>
> please don't walk away.
>
> frankie, are you there?
>
> i can't lose you.

I read the texts over and over, even though I'm torturing myself. Why does this hurt so much? I realize it's because Marco and I work, and my life was finally starting to work for the first time since Noah died.

Letting go of Marco isn't the same as losing Noah.

Noah is gone forever. When his head hit the ground the last

time, he never opened his eyes again. It wasn't my fault, but I feel guilty for being the one who is still here.

But Marco's pain is 100 percent my fault. I caused it.

I promised not to hurt him, and I did it anyway.

The reasons don't matter if I'm the only one of us who knows them.

CHAPTER 35

THE WRONG REASONS

On Monday morning, I slide a note under my door to tell Dad I am staying home sick. Then I text Lex to let her know I don't need a ride, and I turn off my phone. Reading Marco's texts hurt too much. When I make the mistake of turning it back on a few hours later, there are dozens of texts from Lex.

> cruz said u broke up with marco????
>
> what the hell is going on!?
>
> are u there?
>
> don't ignore me francesca devereux!!!
>
> marco looks like shit . . . he's
> following me around like a stalker
>
> plz text & tell me if ur ok

I sent one text before I turn off my phone again.

i'll explain when i see u.
promise.
just not ready to talk yet.

Dad resorts to leaving my meals in the hallway. Cujo has eaten most of them by the time I open my door, but he did leave the mac and cheese.

I leave Dad another note on Tuesday morning, identical to Monday's note. I can't play the sick card much longer, but I'm still not ready to see Marco. Because I have to do more than just face him. I have to lie to Marco about the reason I broke up with him.

On Wednesday morning, I finally drag myself out of bed, take a shower, and text Lex to let her know I need a ride. When I emerge from the hallway, Dad is camped out at the kitchen table with his eyes glued on the doorway, as if he was waiting for me to come out. The shower probably gave me away.

Dad sees me and his gaze drops to the sagging newspaper he's holding. "Are you feeling okay?"

I keep walking, without acknowledging my father or his pathetic attempt at making peace. I haven't spoken to him in four days, and I'm not breaking my streak now. I shut the apartment door behind me without saying a word.

Outside, Lex watches me from behind the wheel of the Fiat like she's driving a getaway car.

"Are you ready to tell me what happened?" she asks as I slip into the passenger seat. "You look like you haven't slept at all."

Lex pulls away from the curb, and I do a double take. She looks awful. Her choppy blond hair always has a sexy slept-in style, but today it literally looks slept in—like she hasn't brushed it in days. The shadows around her eyes rival mine.

"You look tired, too. Did you and Abel have another fight?"

She stops at a red light and takes a swig of the canned energy drink in her cup holder. "That would require knowing where he is."

"When was the last time you talked to him?" I'm not launching into the details about what happened with Marco until I find out what's going on with Abel.

"Monday." She sounds worried instead of annoyed. We both know Abel can't go more than twenty-four hours without talking to her. "I've called and texted him a dozen times. I told him that I was freaking out, and I asked him to text me back so I'd know he wasn't in a car accident or something. But he still hasn't called."

"Did you get in touch with his mom?" The odds of tracking down Abel's mother between parties, boyfriends, and her "Tommy Ryder's widow" appearances are worse than my odds when I raced Ortiz.

Lex's eyes well. She takes a deep breath and fights off the tears. "She hasn't seen him. Not like she was worried or anything. My parents might have to defend their title as the World Champions of Ignoring Your Kid."

"Maybe we should call hospitals."

Lex pulls into the Monroe parking lot. "I already did."

Only a handful of cars are parked in Lot B, and I don't

recognize any of them. Lot A is almost empty, too. Lex parks and checks her phone for messages.

"Do you think he's doing drugs?" I hate asking. Abel's dad overdosed, and his mom is a pill popper. As a result, Abel hates anything drug-related.

"I don't know. Maybe I'll ask Marco if he can ask around the Downs. He knows a lot of people."

I burst into tears when she mentions his name.

Lex hugs me. "I'm sorry, Frankie. I shouldn't have brought him up. I wasn't thinking."

"It's fine. I'm going to have to get used to it." I wipe my face on my sleeve.

"Want to tell me why you broke up with a guy you're in love with?" she asks. "Is it because he got arrested?"

"How did you know?"

"Cruz told me. It was all I could get out of her." Lex rubs her eyes. "She probably wouldn't have told me anything if Marco hadn't spent the last two days following me around. But she didn't give me details."

I take a deep breath. "On Friday night, Marco had to pick up a car for the asshole his father owes. When he left the Heights, my dad followed Marco and arrested him as soon as he got into the stolen car." I search through the glove compartment for a tissue and come up short. I settle for a crumpled napkin on the floor.

"How did your dad know Marco was in the Heights in the first place?" she asks.

I look right at Lex, waiting for her to put it together.

She shakes her head like she couldn't have heard me right. "Wait? Was he spying on you to see if you were sneaking out?"

"No. He was using me to find Marco." Saying it out loud makes me feel hollow inside.

Lex falls back against her seat. "You are shitting me."

"It gets worse. I told Dad about Marco's father and the debt, hoping he would understand and help him."

"Get to the part about why you broke up."

I take a trembling breath. "Dad offered me a deal. He'd let Marco walk if I promised to stop seeing him."

"Is that even legal?"

I nod. "Undercover cops do it all the time to build cases. If Dad or Tyson think they can get information that will benefit the case by letting someone go, or if they believe that following the person might lead them to a criminal who is higher up the ladder, they can let the person go without charging them."

"Even if they already arrested the guy?"

"In Maryland, a police officer has a year and a day to charge someone for a misdemeanor, and years for a felony. Some felonies don't even have a statute of limitations. I looked it up. As long as the person hasn't been charged, the cop can let them walk."

She narrows her eyes. "Screw your father. We'll figure out a way for you and Marco to see each other."

"I tried that already, remember? I can't risk it. If Dad catches us, he'll use what he already has on Marco and charge him."

Cars trickle into the parking lot—Mustangs and custom cars with street racing modifications in Lot B, and Land Cruisers and luxury cars in Lot A.

In the far corner of Lot A, only six spaces away, sunlight glints off the hood of a hunter-green Firebird. Deacon leans against the car, a black hood hiding his red baseball cap. He turns something between his fingers near his mouth—a toothpick, most likely. He's facing Lex's car and there's no sign of Marco.

Lex scrunches her nose. "Why is Marco's psycho friend watching us?"

Not us.

Me.

When Deacon realizes I see him, an unfriendly smile spreads slowly across his face.

"Does he go to school here?" Lex asks.

"No."

A flash of yellow whips by, and Cruz's GT-R pulls in next to Deacon's car. Ava gets out and Cruz shoos her away. Cruz points at Deacon with her good hand. She's not happy.

He alternates between grinning at Cruz like a mischievous kid and flashing me a wicked smile. The way his expression shifts in the space of a heartbeat gives me the creeps.

"Please tell me Cruz isn't getting back together with Future Inmate 666 over there," Lex says.

"That would be a *no*."

Mr. Santiago charges down the steps of the main building in his signature turtleneck and pressed jeans. He shouts at Deacon, then speaks into his walkie-talkie. Deacon hops into his car, flips a quick U-turn, and speeds past us.

Cruz rushes over to the Fiat.

"What did he want?" I ask, getting out.

"I don't know. But if Deacon finds out about your father . . ." Cruz looks around to make sure no one is nearby. "Just stay away from him. He usually only comes around if he's looking for Marco or me. Him showing up for no reason, it's—"

"Psychotic?" Lex closes her door and studies Cruz. "I can't really see you two together. You seem too . . . what's the word I'm looking for?"

"Stable?" Cruz offers.

"That's the one." Lex checks her phone for the tenth time and bites her lip. One look at her expression tells me Abel still hasn't texted.

"How are you holding up?" Cruz asks me.

I just shake my head. "Is Marco okay?"

Cruz stares at the ground.

"Tell me the truth." I hold my breath.

"He's having a rough time."

Lex loops her arm through mine and rests her head on my shoulder as we cross the street. "Today is going to suck."

It's still early and the halls are empty except for a few people sitting on the floor studying. I lean against my locker, wishing the day was already over.

"Shit." Cruz stares down the hall.

Marco heads in our direction. His beautiful tan skin has a pale cast, and dark smudges from oil streak his clothes, as if he raced last night and didn't bother to change.

I catch a glimpse of Chief standing at the vending machine not far behind Marco.

"Frankie? Are you okay? Lex said you were sick," Marco calls out.

"She's fine," Lex says. "I told you a hundred times that it was just a cold."

"Can we talk?" he pleads. "I tried to call you, but it kept going straight to voice mail."

No one moves.

I shake my head. "I don't think that's a good idea."

Chief heads in our direction. "Everything all right?"

Marco moves closer, and Cruz darts in front of him. She rests her hands on his chest. "You're only making it worse."

He jerks back. "How can it get any worse? She left me."

Cruz grabs his arm. "Have you been drinking?" she whispers.

Marco pulls away. "What difference does it make?"

"A big one to the people who care about you," Chief says. "And everyone else on the road."

I've never seen Marco drunk before. This is my fault.

I'm destroying him.

"Did you drive here like this?" Cruz yanks his keys out of his back pocket. "What the hell is wrong with you? Who is going to take care of Sofia if you get yourself killed?"

He rubs his forehead. "I need her."

I bite my lip, and Lex squeezes my hand.

"I know," Cruz says gently. "But showing up drunk and embarrassing Frankie at school isn't the way to get her back. And it will get you expelled."

Marco's head shoots up, and the brown eyes I love so much find mine. "Can I get you back? Just tell me if there's a chance,

Frankie. Give me something. . . ." He sounds desperate and angry, hurt and confused all at the same time—and I'm responsible.

Chief glances down the hall. "We need to get you home before anyone else figures out you've been drinking. When was the last time you slept, Marco?"

"I'm not leaving until I finish talking to Frankie." Marco makes eye contact with me again. "Is there a chance?"

How many times will I have to look him in the eye and lie? "It will never work. It's better this way." I barely get the words out.

"Better for who?"

"Come on, son." Chief motions for Marco to follow him. "What you're doing right now won't change anything. Just walk away."

Marco whips around. "Is that the brilliant advice you gave my dad before he blew his career out of the water?"

Cruz freezes next to Chief.

"Because if that's what you told him, I'm not surprised he threatened to screw up someone's car."

"Marco!" Cruz shoves him down the hall. "Shut up and come with me. Right now."

Chief's shoulders sag. "I tried to talk your father down. He couldn't see past his anger. But you're a better man than him."

Marco's jaw twitches, and he tips his chin in my direction. "Her dad doesn't think I'm a *better man*. Nobody does. Not even the girl I love."

Cruz pulls Marco aside. "You've got to stop."

Chief puts his hand on my shoulder. "He can't see those other doors."

I only have one thought. . . .

Neither can I.

Students filter into the hallway. I spot Abel dragging himself toward us, and I forget my own problems.

"Where were you?" I demand.

Lex crosses her arms, digging her nails into her skin. "Go ahead. Dodge the question like you always do."

He looks like crap.

"Are you hungover?" Not him, too.

"No." He rubs his bloodshot eyes and leans his head against a locker. "I just didn't get any sleep."

"Frankie?" Marco's voice makes my heart speed up.

Lex shakes her head. "He's never going to give up."

"What are you talking about?" Abel asks. He's out of the loop.

"Worry about yourself," she snaps.

I turn around and Marco is right behind me. Cruz looks at me and throws up her hands like she's out of ideas. Chief gives him space, but he doesn't leave. For a second, Marco just stares at me. I want to wrap my arms around him and confess everything.

"I'm sorry you were worried, Lex," Abel says, oblivious to what's going on between Marco and me. "Will you forgive me?"

"Not until you tell me where you were all weekend."

Abel sighs. "I lost my phone. That's all."

Marco glances over my shoulder in Abel's direction, distracted, before he turns his attention back to me. "I don't want to upset you," he says softly. "You and me are good together. Don't throw it away."

Lex steps between us. "You need to leave Frankie alone and give her some space."

"I know, but it's killing me." Marco gives her a weak smile and puts his hands on Lex's arms as if he's planning to step around her.

Abel looks over and sees Marco holding her arms, and his expression darkens. He pushes past me and moves in front of Lex. "Get your hands off her." Abel slams his palm against Marco's chest, shoving him back a few feet.

Lex pushes Abel away. "He wasn't doing anything."

People in the hallway slow down, bumping into one another as they stop to watch.

Chief rushes over. "Okay, that's enough."

Marco looks at the spot on his chest where Abel shoved him. His eyes flicker back to me, and he takes a deep breath. "I'll let that slide, Abel, because you're one of Frankie's friends. But if you're such a badass, why don't you tell your girl where you were all weekend?"

Lex's eyes dart between them, finally settling on Marco. "You know where he was?"

"Shit!" Abel punches the locker next to mine.

She turns to him. "How does he know, Abel?"

Abel stares at the floor.

Cruz tugs on Marco's arm, and he finally lets her lead him away. Chief sticks close to them. Marco stops when he reaches the end of the row of lockers and looks back at us. "Abel was betting on my races."

Lex doesn't bother to ask if it's true. The look on Abel's face says it all. She turns to walk away, and Abel catches her wrist.

"Don't touch me." She snatches it away. "I'm tired of worrying about you all the time."

Abel flinches as if she slapped him.

"I don't want a front-row seat when you self-destruct. The view already sucks from where I'm sitting now."

CHAPTER 36

BLACK DAYS

By the time Lex drops me off at the rec center that afternoon, my nerves are fried, and the pain tearing me apart has morphed into another emotion—anger.

Anger at my dad for manipulating me.

Anger at myself for letting him.

Anger at Abel for gambling and lying and hurting Lex.

Anger at Deacon for watching me in the parking lot like a stalker.

Anger at Marco for driving to school drunk.

The shirtless basketball players are hanging out against the wall as I walk up the sidewalk to the rec center.

One of them whistles, and another grabs his crotch and calls out, "I've got something for you over here, baby. And they don't have any of this in the Heights."

The tightrope I've been walking—between holding myself together and losing it—snaps.

I whip around and face the idiots. "Let's clear up a few things. First, I don't live in the Heights. Second, I'm sure they have plenty of *that* in the Heights." I point at his shorts. "Third, if I wanted any of *that*, I'd get it from someone else. By the way, do you guys even know how to play basketball?"

The three losers burst out laughing, but they don't say anything.

I'm almost at the glass doors when I hear barking and growling, followed by a piercing howl.

Cyclops.

I sprint toward the side of the building. A dog has Cyclops cornered, and the cat's fur is matted with blood. Not just any dog—the husky mix that chased Cyclops the first day I saw him. The dog advances, and the one-eyed cat turns, limping on an injured back leg.

Cyclops doesn't look like he'll survive another round. Without a hose and serious water pressure, there isn't much that will send a dog running once it's in attack mode.

Except . . .

I grab the biggest rock in sight. I'm not going to throw it, but the dog doesn't know that, and I need to establish the alpha position fast. With my arms raised to make myself look as big as possible, I shout, "Get away from him! Get away!"

The dog's head jerks in my direction, but I keep yelling. The husky has to think I'm not afraid. It growls, watching me.

It isn't working. What if the dog turns on me?

I'm seconds away from panicking when the husky backs away. In a last-ditch effort, I wave my arms and yell louder. "Get out of here!"

The dog turns and bolts down the hill toward the parking lot.

My knees buckle and I drop down on the grass, trying to catch my breath.

People shout behind me and a couple of guys wearing weightlifting belts tear after the husky and chase it down the street.

Miss Lorraine runs up beside me. "Are you all right?"

I nod and point at the cat. "Yeah. But he isn't."

Cyclops lies on his side, watching us from his eye. I crawl toward him, hoping he'll sense that I'm trying to help. The second I move, he hisses and lashes out with one of his paws.

"He won't let anyone near him except Marco." Sofia rushes over with Daniel.

I kneel in the dirt next to the cat. "We have to get him to a vet, or he might not make it."

Miss Lorraine studies Cyclops. "I'm not sure how to move him without getting our eyes scratched out."

The cat makes a low sound in his throat and rests his head in the dirt.

"We need a box to carry him in," I say.

The other kids from my group are outside now. Kumiko cranes her neck to get a better look at Cyclops. "What you need is a cage."

"Or a milk crate," Sofia says. "If we slide something under the crate, it will work like a cage."

"I'll find the stuff we need." Carlos runs back to the building.

"A milk crate has holes in it." I look over at Sofia and Daniel. "He'll claw us through them if we try to pick it up."

"I've got an idea," Daniel says.

The cat's legs twitch.

"Don't worry," I whisper to Cyclops. "We're going to take you to the hospital, and they'll patch you up."

Carlos and Kumiko return carrying a blue milk crate and a huge cookie sheet. Daniel follows, wearing boxing gloves and a thick canvas work jacket that's way too big. He punches the tops of the gloves together like a prizefighter. "Okay, I'm ready."

Sofia smiles at him.

"How are we getting Cyclops to the vet?" Kumiko asks.

"Will you take him?" I ask Miss Lorraine.

"Wish I could, but I can't leave the rec center until it closes."

If Miss Lorraine is out, I need someone else to drive. "Sofia, call Cruz and see how long it will take her to get here."

Sofia pulls her cell out of her back pocket. "I can try calling Mar—" She stares at the ground. "Sorry. It's hard to remember that you're not together anymore." My heart squeezes. He must have told her.

I touch her shoulder. "He's your brother. You can still say his name around me."

It takes three of us to hold the milk crate in place and slide the gigantic cookie sheet under Cyclops—plus two extra pairs of boxing gloves. I end up wearing the gloves and the work jacket Daniel borrowed, because our makeshift cage requires someone to hold it together. Cyclops thrashes at first, until the pain wins out and he slumps against the side of the crate.

Ava and Cruz pull into the parking lot. Cruz takes one look at me wearing the red boxing gloves and carrying the crate, and shakes her head. "You can't bring that thing in my car. If it gets loose, it will tear us up—and my leather seats."

Daniel walks beside me holding the milk crate in place.

"Cyclops could die," I say. "We need to take him to an animal hospital now."

Cruz rolls her eyes and climbs in the backseat. "You're going to a lot of trouble for a one-eyed stray cat."

Cyclops is more than a stray cat. There's only one person who understands that, and I can't call him.

The waiting area in the animal hospital smells like antiseptic and wet dog. I'm alone, holding a pair of shredded boxing gloves in my lap.

"I don't do hospitals," Cruz announced as soon as we pulled up to the building. Ava helped me carry the milk-crate cage inside and then retreated to the car and her sister.

The vet took one look at Cyclops—a ball of matted hair and blood—and rushed him through a door marked MEADOW-BROOK DOWNS VETERINARY HOSPITAL STAFF ONLY.

That was eighteen minutes ago.

I called Lex and told her Cruz was driving me home. I

didn't tell her about Cyclops. If he doesn't make it, I want to be alone when the vet tells me. It feels like Cyclops is Marco's cat and, in a weird way, like he's mine, too.

Outside the window a skyful of stars blink above me, and it's easy to forget I'm in the Downs. Marco doesn't have the luxury of forgetting. I realize that's what he meant when he said the stars look different from the Downs.

My cell rings, and I make the mistake of answering without checking the display.

"Frankie? Where are you, and why aren't you home yet?" Dad. Perfect.

"I'm at an animal hospital. A cat from the rec center got mauled by a dog."

Silence.

"If you don't believe me, feel free to come down here and check out the cat blood all over my clothes. Or call Miss Lorraine."

"When are you coming home?" he asks.

So much compassion. "When I find out if the cat is okay."

"I'm calling you in forty-five minutes."

"Fine." I hit end without saying good-bye. Tense doesn't begin to describe our relationship.

My cell rings again and I ignore it. Dad can text whatever he forgot to say. I'm sure he'll call back in two minutes anyway. I pull my knees up tight against my chest and rest my forehead against them.

The knotted rope of bells on the hospital door jingle and Marco walks in. He stops, and the door hits his back. He has fresh bruises on his face. A cut runs down the center of his bottom lip, and a ripped T-shirt is tied around the knuckles on his right hand.

My first day at Monroe was the only time I've ever seen a mark on him.

I point at his lip. "What happened?"

Marco shrugs and leans against the wall beside the door. "Ran into a guy's elbow." He keeps his eyes fixed on the floor.

"And your hand?"

He frowns and turns his wrist, as if he forgot about the injury. "A guy ran into my fist. Do you care?"

I rest my chin on my knees. "Of course I do." I shouldn't say more, but I can't stop myself. "I've never *not* cared about you."

"Sofia called and told me what you did for Cyclops." He glances at the door designated for employees only. "You could've gotten hurt. Why would you do something crazy like that for a stupid cat that doesn't belong to you?"

"Maybe for the same reason you feed him."

Marco rubs the cut on his lip with the side of his hand, and my heart skips. "How long have you known?"

"Since before . . ." *I kissed you.* "The night of the party."

He sits in the chair next to mine. "Throwaways like me and Cyclops have to stick together."

Hearing him talk about himself that way makes me want to kill his father . . . and mine. "Don't call yourself that. Please."

Muffled voices drift into the waiting area from the other side of the door. A moment later, a vet comes out.

"Is he going to be okay?" Marco asks.

The vet tucks her hands in the pockets of her white coat and gives us a sympathetic smile. "It's hard to say. Your cat lost a lot of blood, and he's in shock."

Marco reaches over and takes my hand. The familiar buzz starts in my fingertips.

"If he makes it through the night, I'll be more optimistic." She holds out a bill.

Marco takes it and follows her to the counter. He opens his wallet and pays in cash. I bet all the money I had left racing Ortiz.

"Leave a number and we'll call you if anything changes," she says.

"Thanks." Marco scribbles down a number.

She slips through the door and we're alone again.

"I left your number." Marco drops down into the seat next to me and takes my hand, intertwining his fingers with mine. He stares straight ahead. "Cyclops can't die."

"He won't."

He nods, and his gaze falls on our hands. "I miss you."

My heart aches. "Me too. But that doesn't change anything."

"It should."

"We've been through this. I'm the daughter—"

"Of a cop, and I'm a car thief," he says softly. "But if I wasn't?" Marco watches me. He's playing *what if*, and I already know how the game ends.

"Are you saying you stopped stealing cars?" I already know the answer.

He frowns and bites his cracked lip.

"You have to stop acting crazy and take care of yourself." I can't stand the thought of what else he might be doing—and if any of it involves other girls. "Sofia needs you."

I need you—that's what I want to say.

"I know." Marco's hand tightens around mine. He closes his eyes. "But when I'm racing or fighting, it's the only time I don't . . ." He pulls our hands against his chest, and his heart beats against my fingers. "Hurt."

"Marco—" My voice shakes along with the rest of my body. I'm not strong enough to protect us both. I pull away from him and rock forward, holding myself together.

"I understand why you left, Frankie. You deserve someone who can pick you up at your house for a real date. Not a guy your dad is trying to lock up." Marco gathers me in his arms and kisses the top of my head. "I wouldn't want my little sister to date a guy like me. I wish I'd met you earlier—before I made all the wrong choices. I love you." He's out of his chair and through the door before I have a chance to say a word.

CHAPTER 37

COLLATERAL DAMAGE

My cell rings right after first period the next morning. "Hello?

"I'm calling from the Meadowbrook Downs Veterinary Hospital for Frankie Devereux," the woman says.

Knots tangle in my stomach. "This is Frankie. Is Cyclops all right?"

Say yes. Please say yes.

"He isn't doing well. He developed a staph infection after surgery. You might want to come see him tonight." *Because he's dying.*

"Is it okay if I come late tonight?"

"We're open twenty-four hours. You can visit your cat whenever you want."

My cat.

I end the call without saying good-bye. After the milk crate and the boxing gloves, the one-eyed cat is still going to die. I

324

can't save him—just like I couldn't save Noah from getting beaten to death in a parking lot. I can't save Marco and Sofia from losing each other. Or Cruz from her father or Abel from gambling or Lex from her fears.

I can't even save myself.

Things can't get any worse. It's a stupid expression.

Things can always get worse. And in my experience, they usually do. So when I get a 911 text from Lex at the end of Shop, I'm not surprised.

"What's the deal?" Cruz asks, reading over my shoulder.

"I don't know."

The bell rings and I head for the hall to speed-dial Lex.

She picks up on the first ring. "You have to get over to Abel's house now." I hear knocking in the background. "Open the door, Abel!"

"What's wrong?"

"I don't know. I came to talk to him this morning, and he wouldn't answer the door. I knew he was home because I saw him in the window. His mom is out of town, but I still have a key from this summer, so I let myself in. He's locked in his room, and there's all this banging."

"What kind of banging?"

"How am I supposed to know if I can't get in there?" She's borderline hysterical. "Can you just take a cab and get over here?"

"Okay. I'll be there soon."

I hang up and Cruz holds out her hand. "Well, what's the deal?"

"Something is wrong with Abel, and I have to get to his house."

"Ava can drive us." Cruz pulls out her cell and starts texting. "You already tempted fate once."

"There's no time." I hold out my hand and Cruz gives me the keys.

It takes us fifteen minutes to get to Abel's house.

Lex meets us at the door and she gives me a strange look when she sees Cruz. "He's still upstairs. Come on."

The second-floor hallway usually looks like a gigantic issue of *Rolling Stone* magazine—complete with framed gold records and photographs of Abel's dad with other rock legends. Today there is nothing on the walls except nails.

"Do you think we need to take the door off the hinges?" I ask.

Cruz bends down in front of the door. "Or we can use a credit card, but I can't do it with one hand."

Lex hands me her platinum card.

"Now what?" I ask Cruz.

"Run the card down between the door and the jamb. When you feel the card hit something solid, jiggle the knob until you can slide the card in front of it. Then open the door."

"Okay." It's a lot easier than it sounds. On the second try, I feel a piece of metal inside the door move. I turn the knob, and the door swings open.

Lex gasps.

"Holy shit." Cruz stares, wide-eyed.

I've probably been in Abel's room fifty times, and it never looked like a self-storage unit before. Boxes are stacked against the walls, from floor to ceiling—some labeled with a year or the name of an album. Other boxes overflow with clothes and leather jackets, concert photos and memorabilia. Framed albums, most likely the ones that used to be in the hallway, are stacked against the wall. But the guitars are the craziest part. Guitar hooks cover an entire wall, and more than a dozen acoustic and electric guitars hang from the hooks by the necks.

"It looks like we're in the basement of the Tommy Ryder Museum," Cruz whispers.

Abel is sitting in the middle of his bed, surrounded by stacks of paper and photos.

Lex runs over and wraps her arms around him. "You scared the shit out of me. Why did you lock yourself in here? And what is all this stuff?"

"I'm trying to keep my mom out." His green eyes dart to the door, and Cruz closes it.

"Your mom is out of town," Lex reminds him.

"She's probably auctioning more of my dad's stuff. I had to buy most of this back." He waves his arm around the room.

Used scratch-off lottery tickets litter the floor. I pick up a long strip. "Is that why you were buying these?"

"My mom was selling everything—photos and tour jackets, the notebooks he wrote his songs in. Most of the time I had to pay twice as much to buy them back." Abel looks lost. "That's

327

why I was gambling. I needed more money. I still remember the morning I found out he OD'd. My mom didn't even tell me herself. Dad's manager did the honors. For weeks I saw photos of my father in newspapers and tabloids—lying on the bed in a fancy hotel, with pill bottles scattered around him." Abel closes his eyes. "His guitars and notebooks, his songs . . . That's all I have left of him."

Lex presses her forehead against his. "Why didn't you tell us?"

He rubs the back of his neck. "That my mom was selling everything my dad ever touched, like a pill-popping pawnbroker? I'm not all that proud. She even tried to sell this." Abel holds up a framed sheet of paper, his hand shaking. "It's the first song my dad ever wrote. It's never been recorded. And she was going to sell it."

Abel holds out the frame like he wants me to take it. I do. On the sheet of loose-leaf paper, song lyrics are written down the center in black ink.

"The Lovely Reckless"
Sleepwalking through life, damaged and scarred
Wishing and searching for the one thing I can't name
Ugly and destructive, a vessel for the pain
Punishing myself for things I can't remember
Paying for ones I can't forget
They find you in the darkness
And lead you back to the light
The lovely reckless souls that hear your battle cry
So beautiful and broken

Making wrong turn back to right
The world stops trying to destroy you
With weapons forged from tears gathered
from your mistakes
Mending, stitching, sparing a heart that always aches
Forgiving myself for things I can't remember
Owning the ones I can't forget
They find you in the darkness
And lead you back to the light
The lovely reckless souls that hear your battle cry
So beautiful and broken
Making wrong turn back to right

I wrap my arms around my friend. "It's going to be okay, Abel." I'm not sure how many times I repeat the words, but I don't stop until I start to believe them.

CHAPTER 38

SILENT ECHOES

Marco doesn't show up at school the next day, and I can't stop worrying. Even Cruz doesn't know where to find him.

Halfway through English, I get a text from him.

> call me. i need to talk to u.

I can't call him back without making things harder for both of us. At least I know he's okay.

Abel and Lex are both out today, too. He stayed home to sort things out, and Lex is helping him until she has to get ready for the gala at the country club tonight. Unfortunately, I promised to go, too. Then I made the mistake of mentioning it to Miss Lorraine. She insisted on giving me the afternoon off so I won't be late.

Without Lex around to pick me up, I'm stuck taking the

bus. Last night I couldn't sleep, and I'm feeling it today. My backpack feels like it weighs fifty pounds as I lug it across the rec center parking lot. I yawn.

"Long night?" The voice comes from behind me, and I yelp.

Deacon stops in front of me and twists the toothpick in the corner of his mouth as he watches me from underneath his hoodie.

Where did he come from?

"I'm worn out, too. I've been trying to figure out how I'm gonna find a driver to replace Marco tonight. We've got a big job, and he backed out at the last minute. He wants to 'be a better man' or some bullshit like that."

I stop paying attention after he says Marco backed out of a job. Hope swells inside me. Is that the reason Marco texted earlier?

"So thanks to you, I'm a man down." Deacon snaps his fingers. "Then it came to me. I was thinking about this shit all wrong. I've got the perfect driver standing right in front of me."

"What?" Now I'm listening again. "I'm not helping you steal a car or anything else." I cross my arms and jut out one hip, channeling Cruz.

The corner of Deacon's mouth tips up and forms a dangerous half smile. "You've got balls for a rich girl, I'll give you that much." He narrows his eyes, and the smile vanishes. "This isn't a game. My boss has orders to fill, and if he can't deliver the merchandise, it looks bad and costs him money. Two hundred grand is a lot of fucking money. He's killed people over less. And I'm not putting my life on the line for anyone. You got me?"

Stillness spreads through me, as if I'm inches away from a viper and a single breath could mean the difference between walking away or getting bitten.

"Seems like this is a tough decision for you, so let me make it easy. You're gonna take Marco's place, or I'm gonna have a chat with the cops."

When I don't respond, Deacon pretends he's shocked. "What? You don't believe me? That hurts, Frankie. I've worked hard to cover my tracks . . . and make new ones. Guess whose footprint I used?"

My stomach bottoms out.

"I can tell from the look on your face that I've got your attention now, so let me break it down for you. I've kept track of all the illegal shit Marco has done in the last two years— every car he stole, every part he stripped. And I have plenty of evidence to prove it. Taped phone calls of Marco talking about jobs, lists of dates, pickup locations, and serial numbers of the cars he stole. I've even got pictures." He holds up his phone. "You can pretend you're texting and take a picture of just about anything these days. Marco is into some other bad shit, too."

This is the power move in the game Deacon has been playing all along.

He reaches toward me in a lightning-fast movement and raises my chin with his finger. "Actually, that's me. But the cops won't know that. People believe what they see, and Marco's dad *is* a car thief."

"You would ruin Marco's life over a *car*?"

"Better his life than mine." Deacon turns his cap around. "And it's a pretty sweet-ass car." He glances from his cell to the street as if he knows he's running out of time. "So here's how this is gonna go down. There's a party at the country club in the Heights tonight."

The charity gala.

"Be out front near the valet at eleven. I'll meet you there." He hands me his cell. It's open to a new contact page. "Add your number. I'll text you with the details later. Just be ready to drive. If you follow instructions, nobody gets hurt . . . or goes to prison."

"That's it?" I don't believe him. It sounds too easy.

"Yep. Nobody is gonna question a rich girl driving an expensive car in the Heights. It would've been a lot harder for me and Marco to pull off. Do what you're told and there won't be any problems."

Deacon's cell phone rings. "What?" he barks at the caller. There's silence as he listens to the person on the other end. "Bullshit. We already discussed terms. Tell that bitch we can do this the easy way, the hard way, or *my* way."

My blood turns to ice in my veins.

Deacon's conversation fades into the background. Doors open in my mind—one by one like dominoes, triggering a chain reaction. Memories collide and overlap as I struggle to process them.

The stench of puke and stale beer. Water glimmering on the asphalt. Noah's baby-blue polo shirt . . .

I hear voices.

No.

I hear one voice. "We can do this the easy way, the hard way, or my way."

The hard way, or my way.

The words echo through my head, and the memory comes into tight focus.

A guy standing in front of Noah—a guy wearing a blue baseball cap. "Give me your fucking keys."

"The car has a built-in GPS chip, man," Noah says calmly. "You won't get very far. If you take off now, I'll pretend this never happened."

"You think I'm stupid?" The guy's voice drops. "We can do this the easy way, the hard way, or my way."

Deacon was *there.* I watch the scene replay in excruciating detail.

Deacon holds out his hand, but instead of handing him the keys, Noah tosses them toward the curb, and they fall into the sewage drain. "Screw you."

Deacon turns his hat around, and his ice-blue eyes settle on Noah. "That was a mistake."

Fists fly, blood spatters.

I want to scream at Noah and tell him to run, but I can't find my voice.

Deacon throws a punch. Noah falls and his head cracks against the asphalt. But Deacon keeps hitting him over and over and over.

It's all coming back now. Deacon standing in front of Noah, wearing a black ribbed tank and baggy jeans. The sleeve of tattoos on his arm that I hadn't remembered before—the withered hand on his forearm reaching for a girl trapped in a birdcage.

"Are you paying attention, Frankie? Because I don't like to repeat myself."

It takes a minute for my vision to clear.

Deacon is off the phone, watching me.

I force myself to nod.

He killed Noah. He killed Noah. He killed Noah.

"Good. Then I'll be in touch." Deacon walks to his car. Before he gets in, he stops and looks back at me. "This conversation stays between us, or Marco ends up in handcuffs—and that's the best-case scenario. You already have one dead boyfriend. I'd hate to see you end up with another one."

A shiver runs up my spine.

He just admitted to killing Noah. He didn't come right out and say the words, but we both know what he meant. I watch Deacon climb into the Firebird.

For months all I wanted to do was remember.

Now I wish I could forget.

CHAPTER 39

OFFENSIVE MANEUVERS

"Come on . . . pick up." It's the third time I've tried to call Marco since I realized the truth about Deacon. But my calls keep going to voice mail.

Where is he?

Cruz doesn't know, either, which only makes me worry more. I need to tell Marco the truth about his best friend—a guy who saved his sister's life and Marco thinks of as a brother—is a murderer. How do I tell Marco one of the people he trusts most has been setting him up? It will crush him.

But I don't have a choice.

If Deacon lies to the police, Marco could end up in prison.

I can't shake the image of Deacon punching Noah over and over in the parking lot. Even after Noah stopped moving, he kept swinging. I have to tell Marco about all of it—every hit and every threat.

Deacon Kelley is a monster.

What if Marco already knows?

My worst fear keeps rearing its ugly head. I close my eyes. Marco would never keep that kind of secret.

You know him. You held him when he cried, and he held you.

My head hasn't left the parking lot at the Sugar Factory. All the things I couldn't remember flooded back at once. But the initial fear I felt when the memory returned has transformed into something more powerful.

Rage.

Tonight I'm supposed to steal a car for the monster who killed Noah—a monster who is controlling me. I'm sick of being manipulated, feeling like someone is always pulling my invisible strings.

The only way to make it stop is to cut the strings myself.

I burst through the apartment door, and it bangs against the wall. I open the fridge, prepared to drink a Diet Pepsi even though I hate the stuff, and see a six-pack of Diet Coke.

I consider telling Dad everything . . . for about ten seconds. He would lock Deacon up, but the likelihood of Marco ending up in jail along with him is too high.

My father made it clear that he doesn't trust me, so I can't count on him. With Marco's future on the line and the possibility of Noah's death going unpunished, I have to rely on myself.

In my room, I stand in front of the dresser with the stupid flowers painted all over it—and six silver frames sitting on top. My hand hovers over the one that's facedown, third from the left. I flip it over, my hand shaking.

Noah grins back at me. It's the same grin he gave me when we rode down the big hill on his Mongoose when he was twelve years old. The same one he gave me when he beat up Bobby McIntyre.

"I'm sorry I couldn't save you, Noah. But I'm going to make him pay." I run my fingers over the glass.

Tonight Deacon Kelley is going to jail. Dad won't believe his lies about Marco or anything else when Deacon shows up at the dockyard in a stolen car he forced me to drive. And Dad will finally catch the guy Deacon and Marco have been working for—the one who is blackmailing Marco. Telling Dad that Deacon killed Noah is the part I'm looking forward to most— that, and seeing that asshole in handcuffs.

Everybody wins.

Like any great plan, this one sounds crazy. It's the kind of plan Noah would've come up with if he were still alive. I slide the back off of the frame, fold his picture into a small square, and tuck it in my bra.

Now I just need a dress. I rifle through my closet, hoping I packed at least one. A flash of satin catches my eye, and I smile. The dress my mother hates more than any other article of clothing I own hangs on the center of the rod. I bought it on a whim and never wore it.

Red satin.

Too short to wear at a formal party and too red to wear in front of my mom. It's trashy and obvious—a sad cry for attention. Girls in the Heights don't wear this type of dress.

But I'm not a girl in the Heights anymore.

"I still don't understand why I have to come." Cruz lounges across the backseat of the Fiat with her arms crossed.

"I'm not ready to face all those Woodley girls alone."

"You've got Lex," Cruz says.

"At least someone notices," Lex says from behind the wheel. "Unfortunately, I can't play bodyguard all night. My mom is hosting the gala, which means she'll remember I exist. She's already angry because I refused to ride in the limo."

"Yeah. That would've been rough." Cruz stares out the window at the mansions with sprawling gardens and circular driveways.

"Money doesn't solve all your problems. Trust me," Lex says.

"It would solve a ton of mine," Cruz mumbles.

Lex glances at Cruz in the rearview mirror. "It didn't solve Abel's."

"Is he going to be okay?" Cruz asks.

"Yeah. We called his dad's manager, and Abel told him everything. He flew out yesterday and checked Abel's mom into rehab."

"She went?" I'm surprised.

"I'm not sure he gave her a choice." Lex speeds past my mom's house. "He's going to help Abel, and that's all I care about."

Cruz sees the country club gate and sits straighter.

Lex stops at the guard station. "Hi. Lex Rivera, Francesca Devereux, and guest."

The guard checks our names off a list and waves us through. White lights hang in the oaks that line the road to the main clubhouse. Cruz leans forward and pokes her head between the front seats, transfixed by a scene Lex and I have seen dozens of times.

"Look at that shit," Cruz says quietly.

Lex glances out the window. "They really are pretty."

Cruz snorts and falls back against her seat, hugging her waist with her free arm. "It's a waste of electricity. I would probably pay six months' worth of electric bills for what it costs to keep those stupid things on tonight."

Everything in the Heights must look that way to her—wasteful, excessive, proof of how much we take for granted. I'm not that kind of person anymore, but I'm still ashamed. When Lex doesn't make a sarcastic comment, I wonder if she's feeling the same way.

She pulls up to the valet, and a guy a little older than us rushes to open Lex's door. Her floor-length black gown fits her perfectly, and her choppy blond bob looks more elegant than usual with the sides slicked neatly behind her ears.

The valet notices Cruz's sling and tries to help her out of the car, but she gives him a death glare and he backs off. "I can't believe I'm wearing this," she mutters, pulling at the bottom of the silver strapless dress she borrowed from Lex. "I look like a Disney princess."

"You look amazing. Don't be a brat." I shake out the back of the skirt as she follows Lex up the sidewalk. "And stop bunching up the bottom."

Cruz tugs on the front of the strapless dress. "The girls are gonna fall out."

Lex rolls her eyes. "Stop messing with your boobs. We're going in."

Cruz looks up at the main clubhouse and stops. "Wow."

"Wow, like they're wasting electricity?" Lex fidgets with one of her diamond studs.

"No. Just the regular kind."

I never thought of this place as *wow*. It always reminded me of a smaller version of the White House. But witnessing Cruz's reaction makes it feel like more.

The ballroom is already crowded. Enormous crystal chandeliers hang from the ceiling, scattering rainbows of light across the ivory tablecloths. The circular tables border the dance floor, and men in black tuxes and women wearing floor-length ball gowns weave between them.

Cruz takes a deep breath, her expression guarded. "I don't know why rich kids hang out in the Downs getting high and partying when they have lives like this."

"There are lots of nice *things* in this room," Lex says. "But there aren't many nice people here."

"If you want to leave, I'll understand," I say.

I would if I had a choice.

Cruz eyes a waitress in a white tuxedo, offering guests sushi from a silver tray. As the waitress passes, Cruz nabs a California roll and pops it into her mouth. "I'm good. It's like being at the zoo, and there's free food."

"Speaking of people who aren't very nice," Lex says to Cruz, "you're about to meet one of them."

Lex's mom walks toward us.

"Hello, darling. You look gorgeous." She air-kisses Lex's

341

cheek. "And, Frankie, it's wonderful to see you here again. Everyone has missed you."

Yeah. I'm sure. "Thanks, Mrs. Rivera."

Mrs. Rivera eyes Cruz. "I haven't met your *friend*, Lex. Isn't that your dress?"

Lex nudges Cruz's back and pushes her forward an inch. "This is Cruz. She's a friend from school."

Her mom flashes Cruz a fake campaign smile. "I see. It's nice to meet you, *Cruz*."

"Nice to meet you, too." Cruz chokes out the words. But her expression says *Screw you*—something I've wanted to say to Lex's mom, and mine, a hundred times.

"There are several important donors I want you to meet." Mrs. Rivera loops her arm through Lex's and leads her away.

Cruz exhales. "What a bitch."

"Wait until you meet my mother and King Richard."

She drags her attention away from an ice sculpture of a ballerina in mid-twirl. "If your mom is married to a king, I'm out of here."

"He just thinks he's a king."

"So what kind of charity gets the money from this snob fest?" she asks.

"It's for scholarships—"

"To college? That's cool." A waitress walks by with a tray of crostini, and Cruz takes one.

"Not exactly." I don't want to tell her the truth, but she'll figure it out if she stays at the gala long enough. "The scholarships are for kids to attend the spring and summer programs at the National School of Ballet."

Cruz drops her crostini on the table next to her. "You're shitting me. They're raising money for kids to go to *ballet* class? Why don't they give out real scholarships?"

"I don't know."

A chorus of giggles erupts near the bar. A group of girls from Woodley loiter at one end, flirting with the bartender and downing champagne whenever they think no one is watching. Katherine Calder—shit poet, student body president, and reigning gossip queen—notices us, and the whispering starts.

"Let me guess. Those are your friends." Cruz gives them the once-over. Even in a borrowed Cinderella dress and her sling, she still looks intimidating.

"That would be a *no*."

Cruz scrunches up her nose and rubs her forehead. "Remind me why we came to this party again?"

"Facing my demons seemed like a good idea."

She tips her chin toward the bar. "Then you're in luck. The demons are coming over here."

Katherine leads the charge, fluttering her fingertips at me. "Frankie. I can't believe you're here. We've all been worried about you." Caroline, Hope, and Avery chatter away next to her, ignoring Cruz, who looks like she wishes she could strangle them.

"It's sooo good to see you." Katherine smiles, her professionally whitened teeth blinding me.

The old Frankie would be polite. But she's long gone. "Wish I could say the same, Katherine."

Caroline, Hope, and Avery stop talking. Cruz looks at me, and breaks into a slow smile.

Katherine's cheeks flush and she crosses her arms. "If that's a joke, it's not funny."

I put one hand on my hip and tilt my head. "Then I'm lucky it wasn't a joke."

Cruz covers her mouth and laughs.

Katherine presses her lips together in a tight line. "If this is about the poem . . ." She lowers her voice. "Someone had to step up and pay a tribute to Noah. You obviously weren't going to do it."

Cruz gathers up her dress, but I hold up my hand, sending her a silent message: *I've got this.* I take a step closer to Katherine. "Noah couldn't stand you, Katherine. He was tired of catching you in the locker room hooking up with his teammates."

Caroline and Hope gasp, and Avery's eyes widen.

The color drains from Katherine's face, but I'm not finished. "And if you're planning to major in creative writing next year, you might want to rethink it. Because your poem sucked."

"You classless bitch," she hisses. "I bet you fit right in at Monroe."

Cruz stops smiling and turns on Katherine. "What the hell is that supposed to mean?"

"I—I didn't mean you . . ." Katherine stammers.

Caroline, Hope, and Avery back away so fast they almost trip over one another. So much for loyalty.

I shoulder my way in front of Cruz and face Katherine. "If your definition of classy is being an epic bitch and hooking up with random guys in the boys' locker room, I'll pass."

Katherine's chin trembles, and I wave at her. "See you around. It was fun catching up."

As we walk away, Cruz flashes me a conspiratorial smile. "Careful. If you keep scaring stuck-up rich girls, people will think you're from the Downs."

"Would that be so bad?"

She shrugs. "I don't know. You tell me."

My cell vibrates and I slip it out of my clutch. "Sorry. I have to take this."

It's 10:21—thirty-nine minutes until my debut as a car thief. The call shows up as an unknown number. Deacon.

"Hello?"

"Are you at the country club?" he asks. The sound of his voice makes my skin crawl.

"Yes."

"I'll call you back at eleven. Be ready. This isn't a practice run." He hangs up without waiting for a response. He doesn't need one. We both know he has me backed into a corner.

For now.

"Frankie?"

I turn around slowly, dreading the conversation ahead of me.

Mom looks gorgeous in a black strapless Valentino gown. Her hair is arranged in an artfully messy bun that makes her appear even younger.

"Hi, Mom."

Cruz inches behind her and mouths the word *Mom?* She points to the nearest empty table and tiptoes toward it.

"It's so wonderful to see you, sweetheart." She takes a slow and careful inventory of my ensemble. The red "mall prom dress," as she called it the first time she saw it, is an affront to my mother's impeccable taste and completely inappropriate for the occasion. "You look . . ." She searches for the right word: *tacky, vulgar, unsophisticated, tasteless.* Which one will she choose?

Mom traps me in a hug. Not the kind that accompanies her air kisses, but an actual, wrinkle-your-dress hug. "You look beautiful."

When Mom releases me, I'm speechless. My mother doesn't offer compliments. She provides constructive criticism. She doesn't like this dress or the color red. And she doesn't hug.

"How many glasses of champagne have you had, Mom?"

She fidgets with her diamond necklace. "I suppose I deserved that."

Who kidnapped my mother?

"No, seriously? How many?"

"One." She sighs and opens her YSL clutch. "I brought you something. I wanted to give it to you in person." She hands me a folded sheet of heavy card stock.

I unfold it and immediately recognize the Stanford University seal. I hold the letter out to her without reading it. "I'm not interested."

Mom raises an eyebrow. "Don't be so quick to judge."

Okay, I'm curious.

I open it and scan the type. "What is this?" Because it can't be what it looks like.

"I withdrew your interview request, which had been

346

granted, by the way." She taps on the letter. "Third paragraph if you need confirmation."

Richard must have promised to build a new wing on the library to make that interview happen. "Why? I don't get it."

Mom brings her hand up to her collarbone and feigns shock. "My daughter made it very clear that she was *not* interested in attending Stanford or even interviewing there. Do you think I misunderstood her?"

A smile tugs at my lips. "No. I'm pretty sure you got it right."

She sighs dramatically. "That's a relief. I really am trying, but I'm not sure if my daughter will give me a chance to prove it to her."

I can't remember the last time Mom joked around with me or treated me like anything other than her protégée. Tonight my mother feels like my *mom*.

"What about Ki—I mean, Richard?" I ask. "Won't he be upset, since he set up the interview?"

Mom raises her chin. "I'll deal with Richard."

"Thanks." I hug her for real because I love her and she tried, and I'm scared out of my mind. And because she's my mom.

She kisses the top of my head. "Go have fun. I noticed you brought a new friend."

"Her name is Cruz. She goes to Monroe with me."

Mom sends me off toward Cruz like a kid heading off to cotillion.

I check my cell.

10:40.

Cruz is eating maraschino cherries out of a bar glass. "Have you seen Lex?" I ask her.

"Someone else is looking for her, too." Cruz points a cherry stem at the ballroom entrance.

Abel walks in wearing a tux without a tie or cummerbund, and with the first two buttons of his shirt open. He looks amazing.

Cruz cracks a smile. "Go say hi. I'll be here until all this netting cuts off my circulation."

As I walk toward Abel, I catch a glimpse of Lex's blond hair. She's on the other side of the dance floor, trapped between two guys jockeying for her attention.

"Hey." I nudge him. "Are you okay?"

Abel shrugs. "Getting there. I met with a therapist this morning, and my father's manager rented a storage unit for Dad's stuff."

"It's hard to lose someone you love."

He glances at Lex. "I almost lost her, too."

"Lucky for you she doesn't want to be lost." I remember telling Marco I didn't want to get lost. I still don't.

Abel grins and crosses the dance floor.

When we make it over to Lex and her admirers, he pushes his way past them. "Excuse me, gentlemen." He hooks his arms around Lex's waist and pulls her close. Abel winks at the guys. "Thanks for keeping her company."

She smiles at him and rests her head on his shoulder. "Thanks for the rescue—I almost died of boredom."

He kisses her on the cheek. "I owed you a rescue."

I check the time.

10:51.

Cruz walks up beside me and I jump. "Your mother just asked me how you're doing in an urban school setting. Is she for real?"

"Unfortunately."

Cruz nods at Abel. "How's it going?"

He looks at Lex and smiles. "Pretty great."

My cell vibrates again.

> go to valet station & ask for Brian
>
> say u lost ur ticket

I stare at the words in the message field.

I'm about to steal a car, and I'm taking orders from a violent criminal who already killed one person I love and has threatened two others.

Things just got real.

CHAPTER 40

HIGH OCTANE

I tell my friends I'm going to the restroom and leave through the back entrance. I can't risk anyone following me. I circle around to the front and find the valet station.

The guy who parked Lex's car notices me and quickly stubs out his cigarette. "Can I help you with something?"

"Is Brian around?"

"You're looking at him." With his brown hair brushed to the side and his whitened teeth, preppy Brian doesn't look like someone involved in a car-theft ring. But I guess that's the point. Neither do I.

"I lost my ticket."

"Give me a minute." He jogs away and returns moments later with a silver Mercedes. It's a sleek two-door that looks vintage. Brian gets out and my jaw drops. The door opens straight up, like the doors on a Lamborghini.

"Most people never see a Mercedes Gullwing, let alone get to drive one." He helps me into the car and pushes the door closed.

Before I can ask him if he knows where to find Deacon, the passenger-side door opens and Deacon gets in. He's wearing a tux jacket and a white dress shirt that hides his scars, with a black bow tie hanging loose around his collar. I want to strangle him with it.

"Have fun at the party?"

I'll have more fun when we get to the dockyard and the cops drag your ass to jail.

"I just want this over with." I hate sitting so close to him. "Where are we going?"

"Let me worry about that. Your job is to get us out of the Heights."

"Fine." I act annoyed.

"Just remember, Marco's ass is on the line."

As if I could forget.

Deacon taps on the dash. "Let's go. We're on the clock."

I drive out of the lot. I'm officially a car thief.

A light glows in the guard station up ahead. I take a deep breath. The guard leans out of the open window, looks at me, and waves us through.

"Nice job." Deacon relaxes. "I knew you were a smart girl. Keep doing what you're told and we'll get along just fine."

I'm done taking orders. Tonight I'm calling the shots, even if he doesn't know it yet.

I'm going to do the wrong thing for the right reason.

I follow one of the main roads out of the Heights and keep heading east toward the docks while Deacon texts. Anything is better than talking to him.

We're only a few miles away.

At the intersection, Deacon looks up. "Turn right."

"You mean left, don't you?" The dockyards are east. If I turn right, we'll be headed west.

Deacon narrows his eyes. "I mean take a right."

"Marco mentioned he takes the cars to the docks."

"Oh, he did?" Deacon tucks a toothpick in the corner of his mouth. "Well, Marco is being tailed by the cops. Plans have changed."

Including mine.

I am trapped in a stolen car with a murderer, and I'm not delivering him to the police anymore, like I thought. Instead, I have no idea where we're going. My pulse races, and I flash on an image. Deacon pounding on Noah. Bones cracking and blood everywhere.

Don't panic.

I fight to stay calm. "Do you want me to get on the beltway?"

Maybe we'll pass a police station or state police barracks.

"No. We're gonna take Old Bering Highway." He pauses, giving me time to absorb what he's saying. "Fly under the radar. You know what I mean."

If Old Bering was ever a highway, it must've been a hundred years ago. The curvy two-lane road runs through the woods—no streetlights or traffic signals. At night, the road is so dark people rarely use it unless they live nearby.

So I know exactly what he means. He wants me to drive out to the middle of nowhere and leave me there or kill me.

The exit is a mile away, maybe less. That's all the time I have to get out of this situation. I can't open the door and throw myself out of the car—not when the door opens *up* instead of *out*.

I hear Dad's voice in the back of my mind. *Critical life skill: If someone tries to move you from one location to another, odds are they're planning to kill you or do something a lot worse. Do whatever you can to get away.*

The street narrows, and construction signs and sawhorses line the shoulder on the right side.

Do whatever you can to get away.

My only option is a dangerous one, and it involves precision timing, expert driving, and serious guts—which, given my lack of stunt-driving experience, means it's crazy.

But it's the only shot I have at getting away from Deacon.

I think about the photo of Noah and me.

Noah, if you're a guardian angel or something now, I could use some help. Let's take one more big hill together.

The street inclines, and when I reach the top, a row of orange-and-white construction barrels stretches below me.

The Gullwing crests the hill.

Am I really going to do this?

I jerk the steering wheel to the right.

"What the fuck?" Deacon grabs for the wheel, and I slam my foot down on the gas pedal.

"Bitch!"

He grabs at me, but there's no time.

The Gullwing crashes into the barrels. I hear the sound of metal scraping, then crunching, and Deacon yelling. . . .

My body slams against the driver's-side door.

The back corner of the car hits another barrel, throwing the Gullwing into a tailspin. I try to turn into the spin, but I can't hang on.

Rubber squeals.

Lights blur and stretch into colored ribbons. The glove box pops open, and a pack of gum whips by me. It's like I'm trapped on a Tilt-A-Whirl at the fair, seconds away from puking. I squeeze my eyes closed and press my palm against the steering wheel to brace myself.

The car whacks against something hard and flings my body sideways again. The shoulder strap slices into my neck. I brace myself for another impact. It never comes.

The Gullwing is facing the wrong direction on the street.

Clutching the steering wheel with both hands, I struggle to catch my breath.

I'm not dead.

Deacon's head leans against his chest. He isn't moving.

Get out. Fast. Call 911.

My ribs and right shoulder ache, and pain shoots up my neck when I lean over to grope for my purse. My hand catches the strap and I drag the bag into my lap. Dumping out the contents, I feel around for my phone while I try to figure out how to open the door at the same time.

Come on. Where's the handle?

A rush of dizziness hits.

What if I pass out?

I run my hand across the door panel until I find the handle and yank hard. The door opens and I manage to get my legs out of the car.

Leather squeaks and I see a flash in my peripheral vision.

"Where do you think you're going, bitch?" Deacon grabs for me. His nails rake across my skin. My hand closes around something in my lap, one of the items from my purse. I throw my body forward and hit the ground hard. I tighten my grip on the metal cylinder in my hand.

Get up!

I scramble across the asphalt, pushing myself upright as I gain momentum.

Cars slow on the opposite side of the road, and I run toward them.

Is Deacon still behind me?

I look back.

Deacon's ice-blue eyes lock on mine from only a few feet away. The Deacon Kelley with rage and hate in his eyes. The Deacon Kelley who murdered Noah the parking lot of the Sugar Factory.

This time his rage is focused on me. Deacon swings his arms over his head, and that's when I see the metal and realize what he's holding.

A tire iron.

"You little bitch! I'm going to bury you in that car!"

My heartbeat pounds in my ears.

The sound of Deacon's boots hitting the pavement gets louder.

He's going to kill me, too.

I have to get away from him.

Sirens pierce the silence. Red and blue flashing lights turn at the end of the street behind me.

Fingers dig into my wrist and I wheel around, holding the

pink cylinder. I aim it at Deacon and press down. A stream of pepper gel shoots out.

"Shit!" He drops the tire iron and tries to shield his eyes, but they are already swelling shut.

The flashing lights grow brighter and brighter as a police car pulls up beside me. A door slams, and a cop with a handle-bar mustache rushes toward me.

"Get down on the ground and put your hands behind your head," a younger-looking cop calls out.

I start to get down when the cop with the handlebar mus-tache takes me by the arms. "Are you hurt?"

"I'm—I'm fine," I stammer.

I need Dad.

"Why don't you give me that?" He takes the pepper gel out of my hand. "Can you tell me what happened?"

"We hit the barrels." I point behind me. "He attacked me."

"An ambulance is on its way."

"I don't need to go to the hospital."

"Is that your car?" Handlebar Mustache asks. "Were you driving?"

"No . . . and yes."

"It's not your car?" he asks.

I shake my head. "I need to call my father."

"We're going to take a ride," I hear the other cop say to Deacon.

Translation: *You're under arrest.*

"You have the right to remain silent. Anything you say can and will be used against you in a court of law. You have the right to an attorney. If you cannot afford an attorney, one will be appointed to you. Do you understand these rights as I have read them to you?"

"Fuck you," Deacon snarls.

"I'll take that as a yes." The cop opens the back door of the squad car and shoves Deacon inside.

Handlebar Mustache leads me to a second squad car and opens the back door. I sit down with my legs hanging outside the car and my red satin prom dress puffed up around me.

"Can you tell me what happened?" Handlebar Mustache bends down to my level.

The other cop walks over, and Deacon leers at me from the backseat of the other squad car. "I ran the plates. The car is registered to a William Lords the Third. We're trying to track him down now."

"He's at the country club. The car is stolen."

"How do you know that?" the younger cop asks.

"I stole it." I look at them. "My name is Frankie Devereux, and my dad's name is James Devereux. He's a state trooper. Badge number 14755."

"Shit," the older cop says under his breath. "I don't need a badge number to recognize that name." He turns to his partner. "Do you know Jimmy Devereux? He's a state trooper on RATTF."

"Not personally, but I hear he's a tough son of a bitch."

"He is." Handlebar Mustache points at me. "And that's his daughter."

It only takes the officers two calls to get my father on the phone.

The paramedics arrive and check me out while Handlebar Mustache talks to Dad. "Yeah. She seems okay. We'll bring her in."

I hold out my hand. "I want to talk to him."

The cop gives me his phone. "Dad?"

"Are you all right?" He sounds rattled.

"Yeah."

"What the hell happened? Why were you in a stolen car with Deacon Kelley? One of the officers said you told him that *you* stole it."

"I did. I'll explain when I see you, Dad. But for once, I need you to trust me."

He's silent for too long.

I imagine the best version of this moment. Dad taking me at my word, because he knows I'm not capable of stealing a car.

But my father doesn't know me.

"You just told me that you stole a car, Frankie. Why should I trust you?"

"Because I'm telling the truth. Because I'm your daughter, and I deserve the benefit of the doubt." I take a deep breath and speak the words that I've longed to say for months. "And because I know who killed Noah."

CHAPTER 41

THE RIGHT REASON

Sometimes you have to do the wrong thing for the right reason.

The trick is knowing when the reason is right.

It's a lot like the bite point. You know it when you feel it.

At the barracks, I watch every door, hoping Dad will come out of one of them. An officer leads me to the door of an interrogation room. I lean against the wall while he unlocks it. Another door opens at the end of the hallway.

Tyson walks out and I stand straighter, expecting Dad to follow.

"You can go in," the cop tells me.

But I can't move.

The walls close in, pulling into razor-sharp focus the one thing I see at the end of the hallway.

No, the one *person*.

Marco emerges and stands next to Tyson, his shoulders rounded and head hanging. Tyson unlocks the door to another interrogation room, and ushers Marco inside.

They arrested him.

That's why Marco wasn't answering the phone.

I did it all for nothing.

My knees buckle and I stumble.

"Are you okay?" The cop catches my elbow.

Do I need a glass of water? Or something to eat? When I don't respond he gives up and leads me into the room. He pulls out a chair for me, but I sit on the floor instead, with my knees pulled up against my chest.

I did everything right . . . and Marco still ended up here.

Was there another job I didn't know about? Or did my father decide to charge Marco?

It all hits me at once, and my eyes well up.

Handlebar Mustache comes in. "Your dad is tied up, but he should be finished soon."

Tied up? Is that code for ruining my life?

It feels like forever before Dad walks in, his shoulders slumped and the scruff along his jaw unshaven. I don't look at him. He broke our deal, and I'll never forgive him.

Dad stands across from me and leans against the wall.

"Why is Marco here?" My voice sounds like ice.

"I'll answer your questions about Marco after you tell me what happened tonight."

He's probably lying, but I need to tell him about Deacon.

"Deacon Kelley killed Noah." It's the first time I've actually said it out loud.

"How do you know?"

I dig my nails into my palms and keep going. "The flashbacks were happening more often, and every time I remembered a little more about that night. The other day I heard Deacon say something—exactly the same way he said it the night he killed Noah. I guess it triggered my memory. It all came back to me, every detail—what Deacon was wearing, the things he said, even the look on his face. He was trying to steal Noah's dad's car. That's how it started."

"Why didn't you tell me?" Dad walks over and bends down next to me.

Because I can't trust you.

He won't like my answer, but I'm not worried about his feelings. "Deacon threatened Marco. He wanted Marco to steal a car from the country club tonight and deliver it to the dock, but Marco backed out of the job. Deacon blamed me. He said if I didn't drive the car, he would pin everything on Marco—including things Marco didn't do. After what Deacon did to Noah, I believed him. And I knew what you thought of Marco, so I had to do something. I couldn't let him go to jail." I look at my father. "But Marco still ended up here."

"How did you know where to pick up the Gullwing?"

"Deacon didn't tell me anything about the car ahead of time. A valet at the country club named Brian gave me the keys. I drove it out of the Heights with Deacon, and he told me where to go. I thought we were going to the docks, but he said the cops were tailing Marco and the plan had changed. I don't know where he was trying to take me. That's why I crashed the car."

"You crashed the car on purpose?" The color drains from his face.

I describe the details and Dad cringes. When I get to the part about Deacon chasing me, he goes ballistic.

"Do you have any idea how lucky you are? He could've killed you. And if you had hit those barrels too fast or from the wrong angle . . . " My father shakes his head and scrubs his hands over his face. "You risked all this because you thought I would believe Deacon Kelley?"

I sit up straight and look my father in the eye. "Are you saying you *wouldn't* have believed him?"

"I'm a cop, Frankie. I don't take the word of a convicted felon without investigating."

"After the *deal* you offered me, I wasn't willing to take that chance. You're wrong about Marco. You can't see it, but that doesn't make it any less true. Sometimes people do the wrong thing for the right reason."

"Come with me." Dad stands and motions toward the door.

Is he taking me to see Marco?

I follow, but when Dad starts to open the door, I block his path. "I'm not going anywhere until you tell me why you arrested Marco."

"Why don't you ask him yourself?" Dad opens the door, and I step into the hallway. Tyson is standing at the other end with Marco.

Marco freezes as if he can't believe I'm real.

I forget about Dad and the deal, and the fact that we're in the middle of a police station, and I run straight into his arms. Marco catches me around the waist and buries his face in my neck. "You're here because of me, aren't you?" I ask.

Marco pulls back and looks at me. "Yes."

CHAPTER 42

THE HARDEST THING

"You said a cop's daughter and a car thief can't be together." Marco wipes away the tears under my eyes. "That's why I'm not a car thief anymore."

"I don't understand." He's not making sense.

"I turned myself in this morning. I tried to text you."

That's why his phone kept going straight to voice mail—he was here.

I look at Dad for confirmation, and he nods. "It's true. Marco gave us all the information we needed on the guy he works for and his operation. I guess sometimes people do the right thing for the right reason, too."

"But you could go to jail." I can barely say the words.

Marco nods. "It's a chance I'm willing to take. Miss Lorraine is going to take care of Sofia."

"Why?"

"Because I love you, and I don't want to be that guy anymore."

I turn to my father. "Can I talk to Marco alone?"

He holds open the door to the closest interrogation room. "Ten minutes."

When the door closes, I bury my face in Marco's chest, and the familiar scent of leather and citrus calms me. The story about Deacon tumbles out in bits and pieces, between tears and kisses.

Marco's arms tighten around me. "I'm so sorry, Frankie. What he did to Noah . . ." He tenses. "Deacon could've *killed* you."

"It's not your fault."

"We were like brothers. There must have been signs. I should've seen them." Marco's voice drops. "I never thought Deacon was capable of killing an innocent person. An abusive bastard like Cruz's dad? Maybe. But Deacon isn't the same guy I grew up with anymore—the one who risked his life for my sister. How do you go from crawling through broken glass to save a kid to beating someone to death three years later?"

"You're asking the wrong person."

Marco lifts my chin, and his eyes search mine. "I didn't know about what happened to Noah. I would've turned Deacon in myself. You know that, right?"

"Yes."

"Why didn't you tell me?" Marco traces the outline of my jaw.

"I couldn't. You would've done something stupid."

He nods. "You're right. I would never let anyone hurt you."

"Then you understand how I feel? And why I did it?"

Marco stares at the floor. "Everything except the part about you breaking up with me."

"I made a deal with my dad." The words come out as a whisper. But I know he heard them, because his body goes completely still.

Marco closes his eyes. "What kind of deal?"

"The night you got arrested—" I take a shuddering breath. "My dad told me he'd let you go if I promised to stop seeing you."

Marco's eyes fly open. His hands tunnel through the back of my hair and slide around to cup my face. "Does that mean you still love me?"

I look into his beautiful brown eyes. "I never stopped." I touch Marco's arm below the sleeve of his T-shirt and trace the black rose. "I don't know if you can forgive me—"

"For what? Nobody has ever done anything like that for me before." Marco brings my hand to his lips and kisses my palm. His hand curls around mine, and he holds it against his chest.

I slip my hand out of his and loop my arms around his neck. "I missed you every second, and I wanted to tell you."

He pulls me closer and my body melts into his. "My life doesn't make sense without you, Frankie. And I don't want it to."

Marco presses his lips against mine and the world slides

back into place. I abandon every fear that kept me from giving myself to him, and I let go.

A lot can happen in two weeks.

Dad agreed to let me see Marco—not that he's running out to buy the two of them matching sweaters. Marco and I don't have much free time anyway, now that we both have probation officers and community service.

Richard, my not-so-terrible stepfather, paid for the damage to the Gullwing, and I'm working off the debt at charities of his choice—probably until I'm thirty. When I'm not doing that or going to school, I'm still fulfilling my community service at the rec center.

The district attorney didn't bring charges against me for stealing the car, since it led to Deacon's and Brian's arrests. Tyson said Brian confessed so fast that he barely had enough time to find a pen. Deacon is currently residing at Jessup until his trial. Maybe they will let him share a cell with Marco's father. I'll have to testify against Deacon, but I'm looking forward to it.

Marco cut a deal for three years of probation and community service in exchange for giving the police the name of the guy he and Deacon were working for and information related to his auto theft operation. The guy is in jail, where he'll stay until he goes to trial. Marco will have to testify, but Dad and Tyson busted some of the longshoremen who were involved, so Marco won't be the only witness.

I stand in front of Dad's building, waiting for Marco to pick me up.

When he finally pulls up, I hop in the Fastback. "You're late."

"Sorry. I was with Chief. He was working on something for me." A smile tugs at the corner of his mouth.

"What?"

"He talked to my old teachers, and I might be able to get back on the AP track for some of my classes."

I grab his shirt and pull him toward me. "I'm not surprised."

My lips find his, and the sweet tension I missed so much rolls through me. I lean back to catch my breath. "I sort of have some news, too."

He tilts his head to the side. "Give it up."

"I decided to apply to American University in DC. They have lots of creative writing and journalism classes."

"You'll kick ass wherever you go." He starts the car and drives out of the complex.

My admissions essay is almost done. After some prodding from Mrs. Hellstrom—who isn't as crazy as I thought—I'm basing it on my journal.

It turns out that it isn't just Noah's story.

It's mine, too.

When we reach our destination, Marco hands me the black mesh bag from the backseat.

"Ready?" he asks.

"I think so. Are you sure this isn't a crazy idea?" I ask as we get out.

Marco takes my hand and we walk toward the building. "I never said it wasn't crazy, but Sofia couldn't talk Miss Lorraine into taking Cyclops."

Miss Lorraine is applying to foster Sofia, and Child Protective Services granted her temporary guardianship. Marco is old enough to live on his own, but Chief insisted that Marco move in with him. Chief claims he's going to teach Marco how to race *for real*, as he calls it. Marco said he's going to teach Chief how to dress cooler.

I take a deep breath and open the glass door. The nurse looks up from the counter and smiles at me. "Someone has been waiting for you."

Doubtful.

Marco squeezes my hand and I give her the bag. I'm starting to wish Dad hadn't said yes.

The nurse returns with the one-eyed cat in the carrier. "He's a little grouchy today, but he'll let you hold him if you give him tuna and scratch behind his ears."

I study Cyclops—the cat who never should've survived that first night at the animal hospital.

"Thanks." I take the carrier, hoping he won't claw me through the mesh. Cyclops watches me with his good eye and purrs when he sees Marco.

"He likes you better than me."

Marco grins. "I'm pretty irresistible, and I feed him."

"I guess."

"Are you sure about this?" he asks. "I think Chief will take Cyclops if it's either his place or the shelter."

"I want to keep him, but Dad says we'll have to see if he and Cujo get along." I peer through the zippered panel. The cat is a fighter, like me. "And I saved Cyclops, so that makes me responsible for him."

"Does that mean I can move in with you?" Marco takes my elbow and steers me toward him. "You saved me, too."

I push up onto my toes and press my lips against his. The kiss burns through me, like it's the first time.

A few months ago, I thought remembering was the hardest thing in the world. I was wrong. Forgetting is harder than remembering, but forgiving is the hardest. I'm working on that with Dad.

I was wrong about something else, too.

Before I crashed the stolen car, I thought saving Marco was the most important thing I would ever have to do.

One thing was even more important. . . .

Saving myself.

ACKNOWLEDGMENTS

This book would not exist without the support and hard work of these Lovely people.

Jodi Reamer, my amazing agent—for listening to my crazy ideas and encouraging me to see where they lead, and shepherding my books into the world as if they were your own. Your insight, passion, and faith in this story allowed me to take a risk and tackle a new genre. I'm so lucky you took a chance on me.

Erin Stein, my publisher and editor at Imprint—for your creativity, insight, and never-ending patience. Writing this book was a challenge, but you never doubted the story or my ability to tell it, even when I did. Collaborating with you has made me a better writer.

The "Lovely" Team at Imprint and Macmillan: Natalie Sousa, creative director at Imprint, for her work on the breathtaking cover; John Nora, senior production manager, and Christine Ma, senior production editor, for their attention to detail and diligence; Allison Verost, vice president, marketing and publicity, and Brittany Pearlman, associate publicist, for your excitement about *The Lovely Reckless* and for creating PR opportunities to spread that excitement; Lucy Del Priore, director school and library marketing, Kathryn Little, associate director marketing, Ashley Woodfolk, marketing manager, and Mariel Dawson, director of advertising and promotion, for thinking outside the box and telling the world about *The Lovely Reckless*; Caitlin Sweeny, digital marketing manager, for the gorgeous digital content; Jennifer Gonzalez and her incredible sales team, for convincing booksellers and retailers to take a chance on the book; and Nicole Otto, editorial assistant, for all her help.

Angus Killick, vice president and associate publisher at Macmillan—for your enthusiasm for *The Lovely Reckless* and your innovative ideas. Thank you for making me feel welcome at my new publishing house. I'll hang out with you at Comic-Con anytime.

Jon Yaged, president of Macmillan—for inviting me to join Imprint/Macmillan, assembling and leading such a gifted group of people, and for sharing your creative vision.

Artist Loui Jover—for creating the gorgeous illustration for the cover.

Elizabeth Casal—for capturing the essence of *The Lovely Reckless* in a book cover that takes my breath away every time I look at it.

Barbara Bakowski, my copyeditor—for catching all of my mistakes and fixing them.

Writers House, my literary agency—for representing me and *The Lovely Reckless*. Special thanks to: Cecilia de la Campa, my foreign rights agent, for sharing her excitement about this book with sub-agents and publishers all over the world; and Alec Shane, for answering the same questions over and over and pretending I didn't ask them before.

Kassie Evashevski, my rock star film agent at UTA—for your intelligence, passion, and innovative thinking. But most of all, for championing this book and everything I write.

My foreign publishers—for sharing *The Lovely Reckless* with readers in other countries. *Merci. Grazie. Danke. Obrigado . . .*

Margaret Stohl and Holly Black, my friends and extraordinary YA authors—for talking me into taking a leap of faith to write the contemporary book I kept telling you about. Margie, thanks for always knowing when to push and for believing I could do this before I believed it myself. Holly, thank you for sitting in my living room late one night and making me write down my ideas for this book, and for reading the draft and giving me notes after I did.

Carrie Ryan and Rachel Caine, my friends, writing gurus, and two of the most talented authors writing today—for reading and re-reading my draft and giving me revision notes that made a huge difference. Thanks for always taking my calls.

Lauren Billings and Christina Hobbs, my friends and superstar romance writers—for the constant encouragement and the early read to make sure there was enough kissing.

Erin Gross and Yvette Vasquez, my "think tank"—for always having the answers, cheering me on, and yelling at me when cheering doesn't work. You are two of my best friends.

Chloe Palka, my social media assistant—for your social media expertise and creativity and for typing my messy handwritten chapters. You are the Mother of Dragons (and books).

Vilma Gonzalez, my friend, for your advice and enthusiasm. You rock.

Jennifer L. Armentrout, Holly Black, Cora Carmack, Kresley Cole, Abbi Glines, Colleen Hoover, Marie Lu, Tahereh Mafi, Richelle Mead, Katie McGarry, Jamie McGuire, Alyson Noël, Carrie Ryan, Anna Todd, my friends and a group of authors whose novels I adore—for offering quotes for *The Lovely Reckless*. I cannot thank you enough.

John Racca, my stepfather and a retired police officer from the Washington, DC, Metropolitan Police Department—for teaching me "critical life skills" that I ended up needing, and for the years you spent as a plainclothes police officer chasing down real car thieves in Auto Squad.

David Stein, automotive aficionado—for sharing your knowledge of auto mechanics, muscle cars, and fast driving to correct my mistakes. You are the real "Chief."

Bobby Duncan—for answering my questions about street racing and RPMs.

Vania Stoyanova, my friend and photographer—for making me look cool in all my author photos, especially the one for this book.

Lorissa Shepstone of Being Wicked, my graphic designer—for designing my amazing new author website, along with postcards, bookmarks, business cards, and swag.

Eric Harbert and Nick Montano, my attorney and brand manager—for being the guys who watch my back and protect me. You are brilliant and badass, my favorite combination.

Alan Weinberger, my rheumatologist—for making sure that my knees survive tours and events.

Librarians, teachers, booksellers, bloggers, bookstgrammers, booktubers, and everyone who helped spread the word—your passion for reading and love of books is an inspiration. You work, often for little or no money, to inspire a love of reading in others and you have been so kind to me over the years. Thank you for reading my books and sharing this ride with me.

My readers—for supporting me, following me when I write a new book or series, encouraging me on social media, forcing your friends to read my books, sending me letters and fan art, and sharing your stories with me. You bring my books to life.

Mom, Dad, Celeste, John, Derek, Hannah, Alex, Hans, Sara, and Erin, my parents, step-parents, siblings, and sister-in-laws—for your love, encouragement, and excitement. Thank you for always being there.

Alex, Nick, and Stella—for giving me stories to tell and the time it takes to write them. You give up so much for me to do this. I hope you know how much I love you.

KAMI GARCIA TALKS TO DANIELLE PAIGE,

NEW YORK TIMES BESTSELLING AUTHOR OF DOROTHY MUST DIE AND STEALING SNOW

This is an edited version of an interview that appeared on BookTrib (booktrib.com).

Danielle Paige: I can't wait for everyone to read *The Lovely Reckless*. It's a departure for you. You are such a master of paranormal. Where did this book originate? I think of it as *The Fast and the Furious* meets *Romeo and Juliet*.

Kami Garcia: The story was floating around in my head for a long time, and it has a lot of my life in it. In *The Lovely Reckless*, Frankie's boyfriend dies and she makes some bad decisions that result in her getting kicked out of her elite private school. Frankie's mom sends her to live with her father—an undercover cop who works with stolen cars. This was one of the places where my personal experiences provided inspiration. So Frankie moves in with her dad and she has to attend public school for the first time in her life. That's where she meets Marco Leone—a bad boy and an illegal street racer. Frankie thinks they have nothing in common, but she's wrong. I drew a lot of inspiration from my friends in high school and the guys I dated.

Danielle: I know you have a personal connection to *The Lovely Reckless*. Can you tell us a little about that?

Kami: My stepfather was an undercover cop, who worked with stolen cars, like Frankie's father in the novel. I grew up right outside of Washington, DC, where the novel takes place, and I'm very familiar with how lines were often drawn between the haves and the have-nots.

Danielle: I remember distinctly slipping into my mom's room and lifting her copy of Anne Rice's *Lestat*. What was the first romance novel that you remember loving?

Kami: That's so funny. I had the same experience with Anne Rice's *The Witching Hour*, except I checked it out from the library. But I think my first real introduction to romance was either Judy Blume's *Forever...* or V.C. Andrews's *Flowers in the Attic*. My friends and I would debrief everyday after school to discuss the scenes we considered scandalous.

Danielle: You could give a master class in romance. Ethan and Link in *Beautiful Creatures* are both swoony, but Marco is all kinds of steamy. How do you build a book boyfriend?

Kami: You think about all the guys you dated in high school and compare them to the kind of guy you *dreamed* about dating.

Danielle: The love scenes are things of beauty. Hot and real at the same time. How do you know how far is too far? Do you take the YA audience into account? Tell me your secrets, Kami.

Kami: I wrote the kind of love scene I would've wanted to read when I was seventeen (which is not that different from what I like reading now). For me, the most powerful love scenes focus on the connection and intimacy between the characters rather than the way the physical elements play out. If you set up the right level of chemistry and sexual tension, what readers imagine is often sexier than what's actually on the page.

Danielle: How close to the world of street racing did you get? How far did you go to research this book?

Kami: I didn't need to do that much research. But I don't want my stepfather to know exactly *how much* I know about street racing. So let's just say that as a teen I had a few friends with the inside scoop.

Danielle: I can't wait for everyone to read and fall in love with *The Lovely Reckless* the way I did. But you also wrote an *X-Files* novel about Fox Mulder as a teen. Can you share any secrets?

Kami: *The X-Files Origins: Agent of Chaos* is an origin story. It explains how Fox Mulder became a believer. Jonathan Maberry is writing the story of how Dana Scully became a skeptic in his novel *The X-Files Origins: Devil's Advocate*. Both novels released on the same day—January 3, 2017. In terms of secrets, the Cigarette Smoking Man is a character in *Agent of Chaos*, as well as another member of the Syndicate.

Originally published on BookTrib (booktrib.com). Reprinted with permission.

COMING IN 2018

BROKEN
BATTERED
HEARTS

Keep reading for an excerpt of Kami Garcia's
next contemporary romance, full of Southern charm,
underground fights, and red-hot chemistry.

I lose my train of thought the moment I see Owen. He's sitting on the floor propped up against the lockers behind him. His hands are still wrapped and he's wearing the same black and green shorts from the fight.

Why hasn't he showered or changed?

Owen tilts his head and looks at me, his lids heavy. Even in the dim light of the locker room, he looks pale.

"I told you not to come in—" He gasps and sucks in a sharp breath.

His breathing . . . it sounds wrong.

My heart drops.

"I'm okay," Owen mumbles, struggling to keep his eyes open. I rush over to him, just as he loses the battle and they flutter shut.

My stupid leg brace makes it impossible to get down to Owen's level. I unstrap it and lower myself to the floor beside him—carefully. I'm not worried about hurting my knee. Owen is the one in pain, and I don't want to do anything that might make it worse. I sit facing him, with my legs tucked to the side, my thigh pressed against his.

"Is it your ribs? Are they broken?" That would explain his labored breathing. How could Cutter and Lazarus leave him alone in this condition?

"My bag." Owen tries to point, but it seems like too much effort and his hand drops to his arm.

I scoot backward and reach the gym bag easily, which terrifies me. It's only a few feet away from Owen, and he couldn't get to it himself.

I unzip it for him. "What do you need?"

Owen's chest heaves with every breath as he gropes through the bag. Whatever he's looking for, he's not finding it. I reach across his lap, grab the bag, and dump out the contents. Rolls of white cloth he uses to wrap his hands unfurl and land in our laps, as energy bars and bottles of pain reliever clatter against the floor.

"Tell me what I'm looking for," I plead.

"Medicine."

I pick up a bottle of Advil, as if that will do him any good. "This?"

"No."

Another white bottle lies on the floor, next to me. It has a prescription label.

"This one?" I hold up the bottle and he nods. I wrestle with the child safety cap, my hands shaking. I finally get it open. "How many do you need?"

"Two."

I hand Owen the pills and he shoves them in his mouth and swallows.

"Should I call 911?"

He clutches my arm. "No!"

"Relax." I raise my hands so he can see them. "I'm not calling."

Unless he gets worse.

"Thanks."

When Owen closes his eyes again, I grab a T-shirt from the bag and wipe the sweat off his face. My hand lingers on his jaw, my thumb only inches from his lips. I listen to his breathing until it evens out, our faces so close they're almost touching.

"I'm okay," he says, as if he senses me watching him. Owen's breathing is returning to normal and he sounds like himself again. But without knowing exactly what's wrong with him—and why he's taking medication—I have no idea if I should be worried about anything else, like his pulse rate or blood pressure.

"No, you're not." Tears prick my eyes. I feel helpless. "I think we should go to the hospital and get you checked out."

The color still hasn't returned to Owen's cheeks, and his expressive brown eyes, which usually give away his feelings, look dull and glazed over.

Owen's back stiffens and he shakes off the fog. "No hospitals."

I bite my lip, unsure of how to persuade him, and he adds, "I just don't like hospitals. My medicine is kicking in. I'll be fine in a couple minutes."

"Why don't I believe you?" I pick up the prescription bottle on the floor and flip it over to read the label. "What kind of medication is this? Why are you taking it?"

Owen swipes the bottle out of my hand and shoves it back in his gym bag. "I don't like talking about it."

I pull back and stare at him. "Then you'll have to get over it, because I just found you sitting on the floor of an empty locker room, gasping for air. You don't know how bad you looked. I thought . . ." My voice wavers. I can't say it.

Owen reaches up and drags a calloused thumb over my cheek. "I'm glad you didn't listen to me."

"About which thing?"

The corner of his mouth turns up. "Coming in here."

His eyes drift past my face to the narrow space between his chest and mine. The way I'm leaning over him makes it look like I'm about to jump into his lap.

I pull back, suddenly self-conscious. "Tell me what happened. Did you take a bad hit? If you were having trouble breathing, you could've broken a rib. Tell me if this hurts." Without thinking, I gently run my fingers over Owen's rib cage. The moment my fingertips touch his bare skin my nerve endings buzz.

"I took a few hits. But nothing's broken," Owen says, staring at my hand. I yank it away, drawing even more attention to the fact that I was touching him.

The disadvantage of putting more space between us is that now I have a better view of Owen's chest—and the rest of his gorgeous body.

"Are you going to tell me what kind of medicine you're taking?" I ask, circling back to my original question.

Owen rubs the back of his neck and frowns. He glances at his wrapped hand and brings his wrist to his mouth, tugging on the end of the cloth strip with his teeth.

"Stop." Taking his wrist, I quickly unwind the wrap—following it around his wrist three times and threading the cloth out from between his fingers and then back down to his wrist, before moving on to the next finger. After that, it's easy. Around the knuckles several times then back down to his wrist and up to the thumb loop.

I free one of his hands and drop the wrap on the floor and begin on his other hand.

My thumb grazes the soft skin under his wrist. Owen's pulse drums against the pad of my thumb, and a tingling sensation travels all the way up my arm to the back of my neck.

"Have you done this before?" Owen asks as I slip his thumb out of the loop and toss the other wrap aside. "You're better at that than I am."

"No," I say automatically, realizing my mistake. It takes practice to unwrap someone's hands. "You don't have to be a genius to figure it out," I add. "The . . . cloth stuff only unwinds in one direction."

Owen rubs his wrists. "Most people still need to practice before they can do it that fast."

"I'm super coordinated, and don't try to change the subject to get out of answering my question." Which is exactly what I'm doing.

He takes a deep breath. "Is there any chance you'd be willing to put that question on hold?"

"That's a *no*." I cross my arms and introduce him to my stubborn side.

Without a word, Owen stands and extends his hand to help me up. As soon as I'm back on my feet, he picks up my leg brace and gives it to me. I put it on, watching him from the corner of my eye. Owen's hands are on his hips and he's staring at the floor, the contents of his gym bag scattered around his feet.

But he won't look at me.

As much as I want to know what happened, Owen doesn't want to talk about it even more.

"You win. You don't have to tell me." I sigh. "I'll wait in the hall while you change, in case you need me . . . I mean, need help."

As I turn to walk away, Owen touches my elbow and lets his fingers slide down my arm until he's holding my hand. "Don't leave." He takes a deep breath and raises his eyes to meet mine. "I've got . . ."

Whatever he's about to tell me is difficult for him. Instead of pushing him, I wait until he's ready to talk. I understand how it feels to need time. I rarely tell people that my dad is dead, but when I do it takes me a minute to collect my thoughts.

Owen leans his shoulder against the locker and faces me. "I have asthma. It gets bad sometimes."

"A black eye is *bad*. You could hardly breathe when I got here." The image of Owen sitting on the floor, pale and gasping for air, flashes through my mind. "What would've happened if I hadn't come looking for you?"

The moment I ask the question, the truth hits me.

I care about what happens to Owen.

"Eventually, it would've let up enough for me to grab my medicine. You walked in during the worst of it." He sounds so calm. Too calm.

"What if your bag wasn't nearby?"

"It would've been okay, Peyton."

"You don't know that for sure." Before Dad left for a mission, he'd give me a bear hug and tell me that he would "be okay." Even though high-risk ops were the norm for him, Dad believed he would always come home to us. Then one day he didn't.

Thinking about my dad sets off my internal panic button. "Don't dodge the question. What happens if you have an asthma attack and you don't have your medicine?"

"Peyton—"

I'm not giving up that easily. "What would happen?"

"I wouldn't be able to breathe."

Something else occurs to me. "Does fighting increase your chances of having an attack?"

Owen sighs. "Yeah. But so does running across the street. Should I stop doing that, too?"

"If it keeps you alive," I fire back.

"I don't want to live that way—avoiding anything that *might* hurt me." He looks directly at me.

"Normal people don't want to get hurt, Owen."

"Being normal is overrated." He takes a step toward me. "I can't let this . . . condition control my life. I don't want to play it safe all the time. I don't want to be afraid to go after the things I want and take risks . . . like this."

Owen wraps his arm around my waist and pulls me against him. He never takes his eyes off mine, and when I don't protest, he slides his other hand up my back and into my hair. I bite my bottom lip to keep from gasping, as he brushes his lip against mine. The contact sends shockwaves through my body. He continues to tease me, tracing the seam of my lips with his tongue.

I part my lips and Owen accepts the invitation. He pulls me against him and kisses me for real. My hands touch the bare skin on his chest and he moans—low and sexy. He tastes sweet, with a hint of copper from the cut on his lip. I loop my hands around Owen's neck and he tightens his hold around my waist, carefully turning us until I'm leaning against the lockers.

The combination of the cold metal against my back and the heat of Owen's skin against my chest creates a delicious burn inside me. Part of me knows I should stop kissing him, but the other part of me that wants this wins out.

Owen lets his hands trail up my sides and he reaches over my shoulders and plants his palms on the lockers, boxing me in. His bottom lip is swollen from the fight and I brush my lips across it. Owen's breathing speeds up and he deepens the kiss. I'm breathing just as hard, and our chests press together whenever one of us exhales.

When Owen finally pulls back and looks at me, his eyes are glassy and his cheeks flushed. "I knew that's how it would feel to kiss you."

"How?"

He leans over and whispers the answer in my ear. "Like it was worth the risk of getting decked if you didn't feel the same way."

I do. That's the problem.

"We can't do this, Owen." I turn my head away and try pull myself together. "We're just friends."

Owen uses one finger to turn my face back toward him until his mouth hovers in front of mine, so close that his breath teases my lips. It takes every ounce of self-control I have left not to kiss him again. "If that's what you want . . ."

It *is* and it *isn't*, but I can't say that without giving him an explanation.

When it's clear I'm not going to respond, Owen leans over to my ear and whispers, "We can be *just friends*. For now. As long as you aren't *just friends* with anyone else."

How did Fox Mulder become a believer?
The X-Files Origins: Agent of Chaos
has the answers.

By Kami Garcia,
the #1 *New York Times* Bestselling Coauthor
of *Beautiful Creatures*